SCIONS OF SACRIFICE

THE SCION CHRONICLES, BOOK 4

ERIC KENT EDSTROM

To J

1

THE DREAMLESS

The Dreamless is cold, timeless, empty.

No fear. No love. No desire.

Awareness is not aware.

Livy is not Livy here.

Her lungs are still. No need for breath.

The blood moves. Thump.

Thump.

One heartbeat per minute. Growth continues while the brain idles.

Microscopic barbs jut from each of 156 needles piercing her legs, scalp, stomach, arms, throat, feet, fingers. Thousands of fibers twine through her tissue, suffusing her with sensors, nano-injectors, and exo-capillaries.

Thump.

Lazarus is satisfied. The subject is healthy. Perfect growth hibernation. Cryopod operational status is nominal.

The Dreamless is

Cold.

Thump.

Timeless.

Empty.

2

──────

PAID FOR IN CHIPS

Current fashion in Casino San Juan was very short skirts exposing tat-painted legs, low necklines, and half-veils. It was that last item that made the casino city such a useful hideout for Jacey and her companions.

The lacy, semi-transparent veils covered the nose and mouth, leaving the eyes exposed. Jacey liked this because she could see without being recognized. The fashion was due—Meow Meow said—to pervasive camera surveillance. People in the casino city valued anonymity, and the Republic of Puerto Rico—reliant on the cash shed by the gambling tourist trade—tolerated veils, which were illegal everywhere else in North America.

Unfortunately, the fabric was too gauzy to filter the rancid mixture of cigar smoke, the stink of frying chicken, and the liters of cologne and perfume the casino guests used to mask the stench of their sweat.

Jacey waved to a cocktail waiter, a shirtless man with

sculpted muscles. He wore only a loincloth. "Water, please." He smirked and walked off.

The smells hung in a thick haze over the gambling hall occupying the ground floor of The Ratz, a dilapidated hotel several blocks from the heart of the city. But Dante had favored this dump of a place for the very reasons it disgusted Jacey. The clientele were always drunk, and the proprietors didn't ask questions.

The smells assaulted Jacey's nose and the back of her throat. She struggled not to cough, which was seen as bad manners. According to Dante, the veils had come into fashion during the early days of the plague.

A slurring woman of about eighty years, with yellow lipstick and false eyelashes two centimeters long, had overheard Dante's explanation and tugged Jacey aside. "Don't listen to him. Veils are for modesty." When Jacey asked why she wasn't wearing one, the woman had cackled. "I ain't modest, sweetheart. My motto is if you've got it, flaunt it."

Jacey found the modesty theory rather dubious, for it seemed that the veiled ladies wore the scantiest clothing. She sure wished *her* dress covered more skin. Meow Meow had selected everything, of course. The dress was a sleeveless tube of stretchy black material that stopped mid-thigh. The Scion shoes Jacey loved had been tossed in the closet. Now her feet were clamped in ridiculous torture devices made of leather straps and a heel that forced her onto tippy-toes. Meow Meow said they elongated Jacey's calves.

Dante had eyed the whole getup with that lascivious smile of his. So far, he'd kept his mouth shut about it. Mostly.

Letting Meow Meow pick out Jacey's clothes had been a mistake. But when you're newly arrived in a foreign

land and wearing the most famous face in the world—
that of the actress and philanthropist Jacqueline
Buchanan—you can't go shopping without attracting
undue notice.

And notice was what Jacey needed to avoid at all costs.
They had eluded Captain Wilcox, so far. But Dr. Carlhagen's mercenary thug had enormous resources at his
disposal.

A serving girl wearing little more than two bands of
gold lamé across her chest and nether regions handed
Jacey a drink she hadn't ordered. "I told the naked guy I
wanted water," Jacey said.

"Honey, at The Ratz, this *is* water." It was more of the
silver liquor called KT that was so popular in the casino
city.

Jacey sipped and sighed.

It was good, sweet and spicy—but more than a few
swallows and she'd be lying under the craps table. And
what an odd table it was. Covered with green felt, it
stretched before her with all of its incomprehensible mark-
ings and lines and boxes drawn in white. People crowded
around it, throwing down cash and rolling dice. It seemed
pointless, but they all loved it.

Jacey didn't know the first thing about gambling, which
in Casino San Juan was the same as not knowing anything
at all. Dante seemed to know enough for both of them.

Five men in shiny, ill-fitting suits stood around the
table, all vaping and occasionally whispering in the ears of
their much younger companions. These thin and sultry-
faced women were called "good time amigas," or "amigo,"
in one case. Hired lovers. Jacey found the idea equal parts
appalling and fascinating.

"Come on, sixes!" Dante cried as he shook a leather cup

of dice. He made Jacey blow on them for good luck, a superstition that proved to have no effect on the outcome.

Anxious and impatient, Jacey scanned the area for Wilcox. Around the tables of craps, roulette, and blackjack stood ranks upon ranks of noisy holo displays called slot machines. Jacey had looked everywhere on them and found not a single slot. Dante said the name was a leftover from an age when people fed coins into them.

Now they simply placed a thumb on a sensor and computer accounts transferred monetary credits to the machine. People stared at the displays all day long, watching colorful fruits or characters tumble into rows. Their credit accounts went up and down—usually down, from what Jacey had seen—until they lost it all or had to go to the bathroom.

With so many beeps and jingles and little tunes playing, the air had a frantic atmosphere. It seemed to say "hurry, hurry, hurry! It's time to play, play, play, play." Jacey wanted to cover her ears and run for an area of cleaner air, but Dante said he needed her there.

What purpose she served—beyond blowing on his dice —she had no idea. She would much rather be with Meow Meow up in the hotel room. More than that, she wanted to get out of there and find a holodesk and finally make contact with Humphrey.

Dante's dice came up "snake eyes." He put his face in his hands and pretended to weep. The vaping throng laughed and commiserated with him, but he was quickly shouldered aside so another man could have a go.

"Explain to me why we are wasting our time here?" Jacey asked as he led her by the hand through an aisle of slot machines.

He sidled up to the bar where the immodest old lady

was sitting. The bartender, a woman in a bow tie and see-through shirt, shook a silver container and poured clear alcohol into two crystal glasses. Dante flipped a blue chip to her. She caught it in her teeth with the flair of an entertainer, poured Dante a tall drink, and lit it on fire.

Once the concoction had burned itself out, Dante took a long gulp. Smacking his lips in satisfaction, he leaned toward Jacey, mouth hovering near her temple. "You're with me because a man alone in this place would be hounded by *amigas*. And I don't want to be hounded just now."

"What do you want?"

"Money."

"I thought you were rich."

"Yes. But if I draw so much as a penny out of my accounts, I'll be traced here. I don't think you want Dr. Carlhagen to know where I am, do you?"

She didn't.

While taking a hummingbird sip out of her glass of KT, she scanned the room. "So your plan was to *win* money?"

"I'm usually quite lucky," he said, no hint of irony in his voice.

"How many chips do we need to get out of Puerto Rico?"

Dante wore a black jacket and trousers, and a button-down white shirt that had silvery thread woven through it. He'd left the top two buttons undone so that the collar gaped, exposing the dip between his clavicles. His dark hair, still short from the official Scion haircut Dr. Carlhagen required, glistened from the addition of something he simply referred to as "product."

The corner of his mouth twitched as he calculated an

answer to Jacey's simple question. "Five of those green and gold ones would do. In a pinch."

"Wait here." She set her drink on the bar.

Her target was a drunk gambler hunched over a drink at the end of the bar. He looked like most of the men there: paunchy, balding, and red-faced. His rumpled suit spoke of a long day, a rough evening, and a painful night of debauchery. His pudgy hands toyed with a crystal tumbler of KT. The bottle, half-empty, rested next to it.

Jacey sat on the stool next to him, back to the bar. She crossed her legs, taking care to tug down the skirt of her ridiculous dress.

The man's heavy-jowled face swung toward her, red and puffy eyes looking at her bare legs (she had cancelled the tat-painting appointment Meow Meow had scheduled for her, despite the girl's promises it wasn't permanent). The man slowly scanned to her chest. His gaze lingered there for a while, then rose to squint at her veil.

"Damn, girl."

Jacey had heard the expression a half a dozen times already tonight. Usually it came from men whose gaze locked onto her chest or backside. Each time, Dante had put a protective—or perhaps possessive—hand on her waist and guided her away.

Eventually he'd explained to her that it was a positive comment on her looks and not an insult.

Jacey wasn't so sure about that. They might be expressing some kind of lusty desire, but it felt icky. She tried to imagine how it would feel if Humphrey said that to her. Well, that might not be so bad. In the right circumstances.

But none of these people were Humphrey.

She'd quickly come to understand that Casino San Juan

was, essentially, a society based on the Greek philosophy of hedonism, the belief that pleasure-seeking was the purpose of life. The fact that overindulgence in pleasure left so many of them miserable appeared to be lost on everyone. Even worse, it made them vulnerable.

At the moment, she felt the casino city owed her some recompense for the nasty treatment its men—and a few women—had dealt her. The "damn, girl" comment was what she'd expected, and now this man was going to pay.

"What's your name?" the man asked. He'd swiveled on his bar stool to face her.

"Mary. What's yours?"

"Cruze."

"What's your wife's name?"

"Maria. Very similar to yours, eh?" He jerked his head vaguely away from the bar. "You want to get out of here?"

"I have a room upstairs."

His eyes widened a bit and he slid off the stool. "Let's go."

Jacey gave Dante a flat look as she led the man past him. He understood.

The elevator ride was tricky. The man got grabby. But he was drunk enough to be off-balance. Jacey managed to trip him. By the time he got to his feet, the elevator doors were opening. She walked out and moved quickly down the hall.

Cruze staggered after.

She thumbed the ID scanner for the dingy suite Meow Meow had rented. The door clicked and swung open. Jacey grabbed the man's collar and pulled him through. Meow Meow was sitting on a sofa, drinking tea, legs curled under her. She was watching something on the video monitor.

"Look what the kitten dragged in," she said, in her naughtiest purr.

This scheme of Jacey's had been Meow Meow's idea. Jacey had flatly refused initially. But that was before she'd discovered Dante's plan was to win money gambling. He'd sounded so confident that they'd go down to the casino, collect some cash, and then leave the hotel.

"Cruze, this is Meow Meow," Jacey said.

"Hey. I know you," he said, pointing and blinking hard, as if trying to clear smudges from his corneas.

Dante came in. His jacket was already off. He slung it over the back of a chair and started rolling up the sleeves of his shimmery shirt.

"What the hell?" Cruze grimaced at Dante. "I'm into the group thing, but not with another dude."

"Take him into the bedroom," Jacey told Meow Meow.

The girl uncurled from her little nest on the sofa and slinked to their drunken victim. She was wearing silk pajamas that were so much like a Scion uniform that Jacey wished she had them on. Not that Meow Meow's would have fit her. The girl was a hand shorter and 12 kilos lighter.

In this light, the pop celebrity looked almost ill. Gaunt cheeks, skeletal wrists. She'd taken off her blue wig. Her natural hair, a bob of brown, was parted neatly down the middle, front locks drawn back and tucked behind her ears.

"How old are you?" Cruze asked Meow Meow. "I think you are too young."

"I'm twenty-eight."

"Oh. Good."

Jacey's job was done. She was tempted to go into the hall, or maybe lock herself in the bathroom. But she'd made this choice, the same way she had when she'd recently threatened a man with torture to get his cooperation.

That had been Mr. Justin's brother Orson. She'd needed him to pilot the ship *Aphrodite* to take the Scions off St. Vitus. She shivered to remember how she'd held up a scalpel and let him believe she would cut him while he'd been helpless, strapped to a cot in the medical ward at the Scion School.

The threat had produced the desired results. The man had blubbered and begged.

Expediency was the word she'd thought of then. This was the same thing. They needed money to get off Puerto Rico. This man had lots of it. She'd seen him take a fistful of the green and gold chips, plus a few solid gold ones, from a roulette table while Dante was busy not winning anything.

Meow Meow helped Cruze out of his jacket. He mumbled something and snatched for it. She danced back, flashing her eyelashes. Holding the jacket away from him, she shoved his chest and he fell back onto the bed.

Dante took the jacket and dug through it. He transferred chips to his pants pockets and tossed the jacket back to Meow Meow. She threw it on the floor, then leapt onto the bed, straddling the drunk man.

He raised his hands toward her.

Meow Meow's right hand blurred as she struck him in the head. He went limp, arms falling over his belly, lips parting in slack unconsciousness. A bloody gash oozed crimson drips from his temple to his unshaven cheek.

The scrawny girl climbed off him and tossed something onto the bed. A heavy crystal ashtray, faceted and sparkling.

"Get him out of here, darling," Meow Meow ordered Dante.

He clicked his tongue and flashed a put-upon look at Jacey. "You just had to pick a 95 kilo guy, didn't you?"

Jacey shrugged. "Thin men like you don't seem to ever have any chips. What can I say?"

Meow Meow giggled. "Ain't that the truth." She gave Cruze an appraising look as Dante hefted him from the bed and onto a wheeled chair he'd pulled from a desk. "He wouldn't be too bad if he showered and shaved. And wasn't so drunk. I like a guy with some cushion."

Jacey grabbed Cruze's feet to keep them from dragging and steered the chair while Dante pushed. "Where will we put him?"

"It doesn't matter."

Jacey thought that was extraordinarily unhelpful. She opened the door to the hallway and peered out. "Won't the cameras see us?"

"Yes. But we're going to act like he's drunk, right?"

As they pushed poor Cruze into the hall, an elderly woman in a salmon colored muumuu tottered out of the room across from them. "Oh dear!"

"He's ha' a bid a the ol' KT," Jacey said, slurring and staggering as if she'd had just as much.

Dante laughed breathlessly and wiped his eyes. In a warbling falsetto he sang, "Cruuuuuuuze-ay can't hold his booooooozay!"

Jacey pretended to nearly collapse with laughter.

"What happened to his face?" the old woman demanded. "He's bleeding!"

Jacey dropped his feet and straightened, swaying and burping. "He fell on the toy . . . the toy . . . the toilet."

Dante jabbed a thumb at his chest. "That's what we

skaters call a 'face can.'" His eyes squinted shut and his mouth gaped as a squeaky laugh rasped in his throat.

Jacey didn't get it at all, but the old lady did. She suddenly yanked out her upper teeth and waved them over her head. "I lost my choppers in a half-pipe forty years ago. Lost my stoke for a whole year after that." She popped in her teeth. "Make sure you get some ice on that gnarly gash."

"Yes, mama." He winked at her.

She winked back. "Knock on my door once you sober up." She fluffed her cotton ball hairdo and walked away. Jacey noticed a definite exaggeration in the sway of her hips.

Dante blew out his cheeks and started pushing the chair the opposite way. "I think there's an ice machine down here."

Jacey picked up Cruze's feet again and they shuffled and wheeled the unconscious man down the hall and into an alcove just off the elevators. Inside, a huge machine hummed. Next to it stood a food and drink dispenser.

Dante propped the man's head in the corner, then scooped ice into a plastic bag he pulled from a pocket. He tied the top shut and wedged the bag between the wall and Cruze's wounded temple. "That'll have to do. Let's get out of here."

By the time they got back to their suite, Meow Meow had changed into skin-tight black leather pants and a loose black top with a square neckline that revealed her protruding clavicles. A beige canvas duffle hung over her bony shoulder. Everything they owned was in it. They'd dumped their old clothes off the side of *El Tiburón*, the freighter that had rescued them from the open sea three days earlier.

"I've called a limo," Meow Meow said, pulling on her blue wig. The hair was longer in front than in back, with a jagged sort of cut on the sides.

Dante dug in his pants pocket and showed her the chips they'd stolen from Cruze. "Do you think a charter sub-orb will accept chips in payment?"

"This is Casino San Juan. Everything is paid for in chips. That's how they avoid taxes."

"How do you know that?"

Meow Meow arched an eyebrow at him. "I'm in the entertainment industry. I've performed in every casino from New Mexico City to Prince Edward Rock. I got *paid* in chips most of the time. The casino managers all think you'll be tempted to gamble and lose them." She tapped her head with a finger. "But I'm smart. I save my money. That's why I've had a long career."

"But you're only twenty-eight," Jacey said.

"Like I said, a long career." She adjusted her wig, then slipped on a pair of black plastic-framed eyeglasses with no lenses. "Hey, look. Now I'm smart."

"Let's go," Dante said. "Before somebody finds Cruze and he reports being beat up by you."

"He won't remember anything," Meow Meow said. "I could smell the KT on his breath."

"What does that stand for, anyway?" Jacey called from the bathroom as she changed into pants Meow Meow called jeans. Her shirt was a stylishly ragged black tank top printed across the front with a black bat silhouetted on a yellow oval. Meow Meow said it was vintage.

"Kille-Tine," the scrawny girl said as she stuffed Jacey's dress into her duffle bag.

"And what is that?" Jacey checked the mirror and straightened her veil. She hardly recognized herself, staring through a raccoon mask of blue makeup Meows had painted around her eyes.

In response to Jacey's question, Dante looked at Meow Meow. They shook their heads and rolled their eyes.

"I'll explain on the way to Chicago," Dante said.

He held the door as Jacey and Meow Meow slipped into the hall.

Jacey asked, "And will I finally be able to get on a holodesk there?"

"Yes. Everything is available in Chicago."

"How far is it?"

"A few thousand kilometers. Why?"

"I've told you a thousand times. I need to contact my friends. Now. They're at sea, wondering where to go."

"Where were you planning on telling them to go?"

The question made her mouth snap shut. She'd been so focused on warning them away from Elizabeth's island that she hadn't thought about where to send them.

"We'll talk on the sub-orb," Meow Meow said, glancing toward the ice machine room where they'd left Cruze. A hotel worker was rolling a cart toward them from far down the hall.

They stepped into the elevator. Meow Meow busied herself with attaching a veil over her face as the doors closed. "I bet you're loving this," she purred at Dante. "A sexy woman on each arm."

"I don't hate it."

The elevator doors slid open and they stepped into the cacophony of the casino floor. Jacey refused to hold onto Dante's arm.

They cut through an aisle flanked by slot machines that blipped and blooped at them. Saggy humans hunched in front of the holo displays, eyes glazed over as they won and lost credits.

One man was using two machines at once. He hit the same button over and over on one machine, not even looking at it. Jacey wondered why he bothered. Where was the reward in betting meaningless credits on outcomes you couldn't control?

A hand clamped around her arm and she was nearly yanked from her feet. A squawk of surprise escaped her lips, but she managed to turn it into a drunken-sounding laugh when she realized it was Dante pulling her aside.

"Wilcox," he said.

Jacey followed his gaze.

The man was dressed better than most of the men here. Black suit, crisp white shirt. He carried himself with a soldier's strut. People instinctively moved out of his way. Three other men ranged around him, also obviously soldiers.

At Captain Wilcox's side walked a very short and stout man with a droopy face and enormous mustache. It was the captain of *El Tiburón*, the ship that had brought Jacey and the others to Puerto Rico. He had a bruise on one cheek.

And he was crying.

3

______

PAR EXCELLENCE

With the wing doors open on the navigation bridge of *Aphrodite*, warm, moist air whirled through and carried away most of the sour sweat and stale coffee smell emanating from Orson, the ship's pilot.

The lights were off, except for a single bulb wrapped in transparent red plastic to help preserve night vision. It shined its bloody glow over a console of levers and switches and screens. Humphrey had learned the general function of most of the controls, but he didn't trust himself to pilot the boat.

The thirty-meter freighter rose and fell on long swells, rocking slowly side to side in a motion that Humphrey's legs had finally learned to predict. In the few hours he'd snatched for sleep, he'd discovered the motion almost comforting.

That said, one could argue that *Aphrodite* was the least safe place he'd ever been. For one, it was more rust than steel. And despite Summer's best efforts, the engines were none too reliable. And then there was the fact that they were being hunted by a fleet of military ships.

A muted clanging came from the ceiling. Summer was still on the roof, trying to get a satellite receiver functioning so they could access data from the outside world. And more importantly, so they could communicate with Jacey.

At the moment, Vaughan's fifteen-centimeter-tall holo stood atop the great mahogany desk the Scions had hauled to the bridge. It had once been a fixture in Dr. Carlhagen's office back on St. Vitus.

Vaughan's holo did not appear to be doing anything at the moment, but Humphrey knew there were several other instances of him alive and busy in the simulated Scion School inside the server's electronic brain.

Orson tapped the spinning radar screen and scratched his wiry beard with a dirty fingernail. "We'll have to turn and slow to ten knots so that bugger can go ahead of us."

The bugger he was referring to was a massive freighter that would smash *Aphrodite* to scrap and never notice.

Orson slumped on his stool and swiveled to consult the battered map stretched across a plain steel table mounted to the floor.

Humphrey wrinkled his nose at the odor coming off the man. Since a Scion guard accompanied Orson's every movement, he'd apparently opted to not bathe during his time off.

Admittedly, the man hadn't had much time off. Eluding a military fleet had required focus and a lot of what Orson referred to as "old smugglers' tricks." These had amounted to skirting close to one island and then another, then slipping into a heavily trafficked shipping lane where freighters ten times the size of *Aphrodite* plowed through the sea at breakneck speeds.

They steamed along a roughly north/south course during the day, then turned due west at night, as they were doing right now.

That's when the danger began, because *Aphrodite* ran without lights. That meant they'd be hard to spot by patrol aircraft, but it also meant the giant freighters couldn't see them, either.

Already they'd had one close call that had resulted in a last-moment maneuver that had tumbled half the bunks in Girls' Hold, despite the tie-downs meant to keep them upright. A Crab, Suki, had broken her arm and now wore it in a makeshift cast Wanda had fashioned.

"How much farther?" Humphrey asked for the millionth time. Their destination was apparently not on the map.

"We'll be in range by morning, but we'll have to bear north during daylight. Get Math Boy up here to figure it out. We have to go slow all day so we can turn south and make a run for the island. It'll take a couple hours to offload everything, then rig her to blow. All that before dawn."

The "math boy" was Obu, the Spider from Humphrey's Nine. Humphrey grabbed the P.A. mic and summoned him.

He didn't have to wait long. The boy appeared on the bridge, huffing from the run up the ship's central staircase.

Obu was a quiet 14-year-old with a flat nose, and ears that stuck out like wings. But there was a firmness to his jaw that suggested future handsomeness. At least, that's what Humphrey had overheard Bethancy say.

"Hey, Humphrey?" Summer called from outside.

Humphrey jerked his head toward Orson and Obu presented himself respectfully to the pilot. As Orson described the speeds, distances, and timing he needed Obu to calculate, Humphrey went out onto the bridge wing, a steel-grated platform that gave a view over the deck.

Summer appeared above him, her toes jutting from the edge of the roof. She wore that weird hat with the leaping deer on the front, hair tucked inside. If it weren't for her feminine lips and eyes, she might have passed for a 12-year-old boy rather than a girl of fourteen. Black grease marks smudged her nose and cheeks. Humphrey was reminded how fortunate they'd been that she hadn't been overwritten by her Progenitor, Senator Bentilius.

"Ask Vaughan if that did it," she said, twirling a ratchet wrench in one hand.

Humphrey ducked onto the bridge. "Vaughan? Do you have data coming?"

His old friend's holo didn't respond.

"Vaughan?"

Summer slid down from the roof. She took one look at Vaughan's frozen image and went to the server box sitting at the back corner. She rapped it with her knuckles, checked the connections, and muttered to herself. "Everything is connected correctly."

Belle's holo materialized next to Vaughan's. She was staring at him, a slightly worried expression on her face. "We're getting data. He's got one instance of himself talking to me in here. It's like he's straining under a great weight, though. Hold on a second."

Wanda came in. The Eagle girl had her hair loose, red spirals defying gravity. She wore her uniform pants and a white tank top that Scion girls were only to wear during exercise with Sensei. That rule was defunct now. Humphrey expected to see less of the Mandarin collared tops the Scions had worn all their lives. Wanda had affixed her Eagle pin to her shirt like a badge.

He averted his eyes from her bare shoulders. It was hard to be around her. An attraction had blossomed between them. They'd even kissed once. But they both knew it couldn't be repeated. He loved Jacey. He ached for her.

What he felt for Wanda was different. Exactly how it was different he couldn't say. It just was. But it didn't mean he didn't want to hold her.

She flashed a green-eyed look of disapproval at him, though not an unkindly one. "I thought I'd find you up here. You should get some sleep."

"Summer just got data flowing to Vaughan and Belle."

Wanda's hand absently touched Humphrey's back as she came to stand next to him, a butterfly-soft touch. She snatched it away and stepped a few feet to the side. She obviously found it as difficult as he did to be near without touching.

Belle seemed to be listening to a conversation they couldn't hear. "Vaughan says it's glorious."

"What's glorious?" Humphrey asked.

"The data flow."

"Has he found an alternate destination for us?" They were heading to a compound Mr. Justin and Orson had prepared as part of their scheme to steal the Scions and sell them off. They were going there for lack of a better place. At least it would offer facilities for seventy-plus Scions.

"What?" Belle asked Vaughan, whose holo image was still frozen. "Are you serious?"

"Belle, what is going on?" Humphrey demanded.

Orson and Summer had crowded next to the holodesk as well.

Vaughan's image jittered, then starting moving smoothly. He finally spoke. "It's Jacey. Look."

A rectangular window appeared above Vaughan. It wasn't a holographic image, just a flat video. It showed Jacey standing next to Vin. A narrator was talking about how Vin Burnell, a previously unknown granddaughter of the famous Elizabeth Burnell, had "gone public" today. Even more stunning, the narrator said, was Ms. Burnell's remarkable friend, who looked exactly like Jacqueline Buchanan.

The video cut to an image of Jacey in a suit and trousers, firing a pistol at five men holding machine guns. She then leaped into a flying side-kick, taking another man in the face.

"What's she gotten herself into?" Wanda cried.

"It's from a Jacqueline Buchanan movie," Vaughan said. "That's not our Jacey."

The narrator continued talking about how Vin Burnell was the sole heir to Elizabeth Burnell's fortune, estimated to be worth north of $80 billion by the financial news site RBW.

The image cut again, showing another very familiar face.

"That's Ping!" Summer said.

"Not anymore," Humphrey grumbled. "Overwritten."

The narrator's tone turned dark. "Another heir to a great fortune was in attendance. The real estate magnate Han Xi left his billions to Ping Xi, who has apparently been keeping a very low profile. Unfortunately, Ping was found dead of a gunshot wound in Vin's mansion earlier today, disrupting the party that followed her official 'coming out' press event. No other information is available, as the scene was sealed by Vin Burnell's personal security force."

The video showed Ping lying across a bed, a pixelated blur covering his face. A pistol lay at his side.

Finally, the narrator herself appeared and spoke to the camera: "Any one of these appearances would be big news, but to have these individuals at the same event is nothing short of weird. Joining me is Rio James, celebrity expert and host of *Rio Says,* which airs right here on SNN every Saturday morning. Rio, what do you make of these events on Elizabeth Burnell's private island?"

The camera showed a man with pure white hair that stood straight up from his head. His eyes were painted a bright blue and he wore the same color on his lips. His jacket and tie both sparkled as if covered with tiny gemstones. "*Weird* does not begin to describe it! Anyone who knows *anything* about Elizabeth Burnell—which, let's face it, is the entire population of the world—can see that this Vin person looks *exactly* like Elizabeth did when she was a young woman. And then we have this delicious young Jacqueline Buchanan lookalike! Who *is* she? Where has she been *hiding?* And don't get me *started* about this poor young man Ping. I don't usually follow business executive gossip, but *everyone* knows Han Xi, one of the *richest men* in the world. While my *heart* goes out to Ping's family, my mind is about to *explode* with curiosity. Ping looks *exactly* like Han did at the same age."

"Are these remarkable resemblances merely coincidences, or do you think these young people have had plastic surgery?"

"Well, that's what *I* wondered. I've had my team poring over other video from Vin's event today and we found this."

The image cut to video of Dante. He was walking

across an expanse of lawn with a young woman on his arm.

Wanda and Humphrey gasped and looked at each other in astonished horror. Summer swore. Orson just chuckled.

Rio James voice continued, "My sources tell me this young man's name is Dante. But it does *not* take a genius to see that he is the *spitting image* of this man." The image changed to different—older-looking—footage of Dante. "He's quite famous in Brazil. Silvio was a playboy *par excellence*. We've contacted his people, but have gotten *no* answer. But clearly the young man at Vin's event looks *identical* to Silvio at the age of eighteen."

The original narrator put on a look of intent curiosity. "So we have a rash of lookalikes appearing all on the same day and on the same island."

"We do. We do. We do!" Rio James clapped his hands with every repetition. "I have no idea what's going on, but I *guarantee* you we will get to the bottom of it."

"But that's going to be difficult, considering the active crime scene in Vin's mansion."

"It's going be even *harder* than difficult to track down these people."

"Harder?"

"It turns out that the Silvio lookalike and the Jacqueline lookalike have both disappeared from Vin's mansion, along with a *super-celebrity*. Just guess who."

"I give up."

"The one and only Meow Meow!" Rio looked to the heavens and spread his hands as if basking a moment of grace. "My sources tell me that Ms. Burnell's *massive* security force is combing the island, searching for these three

individuals, who are now wanted for questioning about Ping Xi's *murder!*"

"What an incredible story." The narrator looked at the camera. "Rio James will stay on this story and we'll bring you more details as soon as we have them."

The video disappeared, and Vaughan and Belle stood together on the holodesk, looking perplexed and worried.

Humphrey discovered his arm was around Wanda, and she clung to him. He patted her bare shoulder awkwardly, then disentangled himself from the embrace.

"We need to turn around," he said. "We've got to go help her."

"We can't," Summer said. "Remember. The AI Elizabeth said Captain Wilcox is there."

Humphrey remembered, all right. Belle had gotten Vaughan to install a backup of Elizabeth Burnell on his server. She'd manifested as her younger self, who looked just like Vin. She had warned them that Captain Wilcox and all his men were based on her island.

Humphrey had never felt so useless. And now that Sensei was dead, he didn't have the calm energy of the martial arts master to draw from for support.

Wanda sensed his doubts and frustration. She leaned into him. Summer smiled, wanly, but there was a question in her eyes. She wanted him to make a decision. And she *trusted* his decision.

Obu, who had been working diligently on his reader to calculate what speed *Aphrodite* must run north, was looking at him, too.

"You're right, Summer," Humphrey said. "We can't go there."

It killed him to say it, but he saw no other choice.

"We continue toward Mr. Justin's Island. In the meantime, Vaughan, please continue searching for an alternative."

"I will," Vaughan said, his holographic form glitching momentarily. "It's not simple. There are many unpopulated islands nearby, but most do not have the resources needed for survival."

"Food. Water. Shelter," Obu said. "It seems so simple when it's all delivered for you."

"Those were the blessings of our imprisonment on St. Vitus," Humphrey said, giving a humorless laugh. "Everything we needed was provided, except a future."

4

IT'S CALLED THE FLIP

The pressure in Jacey's chest increased with every turn of the vehicle Meow Meow called a limousine. They sat on the cushy leather bench at the back of the vehicle, with enough room for ten more people.

The driverless car's wheels hissed along the crowded and chaotic streets of Casino San Juan with fearless precision. It barely slowed as it wove among other vehicles—also driverless—as they engaged in a death-defying improvised choreography.

"Don't worry, sweetie," Meow Meow said as Jacey sucked air through her teeth and jammed her feet onto the floor during one particularly close call with a bus loaded with gawking tourists. "The cars talk to each other."

Jacey did not find this notion at all reassuring.

The darkened windows gave blurry views of an endless thoroughfare of blinking lights. Gaudy signs advertised: DANCERS!—AU NATURALE!—24 HOURS!—THREE LEVELS!! and $150 BUFFET ALL DAY $150. Video boards as high as the Scion School belltower. They showed scantily clad performers dancing on elaborate stages, and magicians waving their arms amidst explosions of sparks.

"Jacey's experiencing a bit of sensory overload, I think," Dante said. He sat next to her, even though there were two long empty benches running up and down the length of the limo. Meow Meow sat on Jacey's other side.

Dante made a golden casino chip dance across his knuckles. Shaking his head, he nudged her. "So all those years on that island. No movies? No holos? No live entertainment?"

"We saw films. Mostly recordings of plays." Jacey remembered Socrates mocking the term *movies*, which he said disrespected the cinematic art form nearly as much as the term *flicks*. "But nothing modern, except for productions of operas and ballets."

"She's a complete innocent," he said to Meow Meow, who was also shaking her head and marveling at Jacey's naïveté.

The limo screeched to a stop, throwing Jacey against the shoulder restraints. Just as suddenly, it accelerated, snapping her head against the cushions.

And then the world went dark and quiet.

"Whew," said Meow Meow, making a motion of wiping her brow. "Now we can relax for a moment."

Jacey twisted in her seat to look out the back window. The lights were quickly fading behind her. The world beyond the window had gone black. A few dim lights in the distance to either side spoke of lonely homes. Ahead, the vehicle's headlights carved a tunnel in the blackness, showing the trunks of trees on either side of a perfectly straight road. The beams were filled with swirling insects that clicked against the windshield as the limo tore through their swarms.

Meow Meow dug something from her duffle and handed it to Jacey. A small tablet device.

Jacey took it. It was smaller than a Scion School reader, but the same basic idea. "I'm not interested in watching a motion picture right now."

"Call your friends," Meow Meow said, for once exasperated by Jacey's complete stupidity about the world.

"From this? I thought I had to have a holodesk."

"Um, no."

"Why didn't you let me try before now?"

"Because the tablet is traceable. But since we're about to leave Puerto Rico, who cares?"

Jacey turned it on and said, "Dr. Carlhagen's desk."

Dante made a spitting noise and looked pointedly out the side window. Meow Meow tilted her head. "Are you serious?"

The sickly feeling of humiliation rose in Jacey's throat. "What? Isn't that how it works?"

"Um, double no. Maybe for a point-to-point call between two units that have already had calls placed between them. But the network doesn't know asteroids about Dr. Carlhagen's desk. Gimme that." The girl snatched the tablet from Jacey's fingers.

She tapped and swiped at the screen, then showed a list to Jacey. "There are exactly five thousand, six hundred, fifty-three Dr. Carlhagen's in the directory. And it's not even a common name."

"So what do I need?"

"An address. It's a series of numbers and letters unique to that desk. I take it you don't have such an address?"

Without warning, the limo careened to the right and

jounced through a gated fence. Ahead was a long, low building walled with tall windows. They were lit up from inside. More cars were pulling up alongside it.

"That's the main terminal," Dante said. "That's for regular people. Frankly, I don't think I've ever been in one."

Meow Meow made a discontented grumble and mumbled something about spoiled rich men.

The limo skirted past the terminal and continued to another gate. It stopped at a guard shack. The window next to Dante lowered and the guard peered in.

"We're here for a private sub-orb." Dante looked at a slip of paper in his hand. "Hanger fifteen."

The guard's mustache was trimmed into a pencil-thin line that paralleled his upper lip. It quirked into a fake smile. "Name?"

"Dante Adams."

The guard went back to his shack and looked at a moni-tor. Without so much as a nod, he pressed a button. The limo slid forward, almost noiseless now that it was going slowly.

"Dante Adams?" Meow Meow said. "Is that really your name?"

"No. I had to give the charter company a name, and that's what came to mind."

The skinny girl giggled and kept mouthing "Dante Adams" at Jacey, as if she'd get the joke. But Jacey didn't get it.

She didn't get *anything* that was happening. In the past half-hour she had seen such a chaos of lights and sound and smells that her mind couldn't hold it all. The limo itself was a marvel. How did it know where to turn? What made it go? It didn't seem to be fueled by the smelly petrol that the Jeep used.

And now she was about to fly for the second time in her life. And this wouldn't be a short hop between islands. She was going to Chicago. To North America. She was going to a place she'd thought her whole life was a wasteland of sickness and destruction.

And she didn't have an address for Dr. Carlhagen's holodesk, so she couldn't contact Humphrey.

The limo arrived at a metal-sided building not unlike the garage back at the Scion School. Except this was many times that size. The whole front face of the building was reserved for a single, gigantic door. It stood open, showing the aircraft crouching inside like an enormous metallic bird.

"Veils, girls," Dante said.

Sighing, Jacey reattached the slip of lace to her ears. Meow Meow seemed resigned to it, but Jacey gathered the girl used them frequently to conceal her identity from throngs of admirers.

The limo's doors oozed open and they climbed out into a humid night air. The heavy smell of exhaust stung Jacey's nose. A distant rumble, like thunder, curled across the flat expanse of paved taxiways.

The roar built and increased right above them. Jacey ducked and covered her head. An aircraft the size of the entire medical ward swooped down, lights on its wings flashing. Wheels hung beneath it like a monster's claws. It glided toward a runway and screeched onto its wheels, sending up puffs of smoke behind it.

She felt a tug on her sleeve. Meow Meow guided her into the hanger and toward a ramp leading into the side of the aircraft. The surface of the sub-orb was gray with a white logo on one side that read, in a bored script, GENERAL SUB-ORB.

The wings on the aircraft weren't as broad as the giant that had just landed. Almost stubby, they bulged out on either side and slanted toward the tail. The nose was a blunt dome, windowless, giving the impression of blindness.

"A discount carrier," Meow Meow said, voice slightly plaintive. "We had enough chips for better than this."

Dante made a shushing motion and leaned toward Jacey and Meow Meow. "This one didn't require our IDs." He made a chip bounce across his knuckles again.

"Oh. I guess that's okay."

Inside they found a dozen rows of leather seats. A slim young man in a maroon-and-black uniform greeted them. He told them to take whichever seats they wanted, as they would be the only passengers.

Jacey found herself wedged between Dante and Meow Meow. She wasn't sure if they were positioning themselves around her to protect and comfort her or keep her from leaving their sight. Maybe it was both.

Jacey's voice cracked. "No windows."

The attendant hit a button near the entry door. It shushed closed. A sharp thump followed.

"He'll open the skyview once we flip," Meow Meow said, yawning into a dainty hand. "I might just sleep through it, the way I feel right now."

"Boarding door closed," the attendant said.

"Where is the pilot?" she asked.

Dante patted her knee, then let his hand rest there. "No pilot on sub-orbs. Computer-controlled. Like the limo."

Jacey sensed vibration in her body and heard a squeak

and rattle behind her. The sensation grew and grew, until they were all jostling and bouncing in their seats.

Neither of Jacey's companions seemed the least bit alarmed by this.

"Are we flying?"

"Not yet. We're rolling to our launch platform."

"Launch?" The word came out weak and sickly. In fact, she did feel queasy.

"No worries. It's a horizontal runway. At first."

The vibrations and sounds ceased as the sub-orb jerked to a stop. A portentous quiet filled the almost empty passenger cabin. Ceiling lights dimmed.

Jacey gripped the armrests and swallowed. She would not scream. She would not scream. She. Would. Not.

Her heart pounded out ponderous beats. Palms clammy, chest rising and falling in short jerks, she started speaking before she knew what she was going to say. "I want off. I want off. I want off. I want off."

"Maybe we should give her a prixie," Meow Meow said to Dante.

He raised the hand from Jacey's knee and made a shrugging motion with it. "I don't have any. But that reminds me . . ." He produced a pill bottle from his front pocket. A tiny little capsule went into his mouth. He dry swallowed it. "ATR. Remember?"

"Oh," Jacey said. That was the Anti-Transfer Rejection pill Dante needed every day. It was the key part of Dr. Carlhagen's plan to control every Progenitor who transferred to a Scion. They were all dependent on the pills, each one designed specifically for them and available only from Dr. Carlhagen.

Meow Meow dug in her duffle bag, muttering about

having to think of everything. With a sudden giggle of delight she produced a plain white pill bottle.

"Ladies and gentleman," the attendant said with false cheer, "we'll be in Chicago in roughly thirty minutes. Enjoy your flight!"

Meow Meow popped the lid and tilted the bottle toward her open palm.

The world compressed into a single musical note.

It hummed in Jacey's chest, pressed her head against the back of her seat, and forcibly pushed the breath from her lungs.

The interior of the aircraft shuddered and warped, then narrowed toward midnight darkness.

Meow Meow let out a cry. The bottle disappeared behind them, trailing tiny white dots.

Jacey tried to turn her head, but it was glued to the seat back as the gees of launch built.

Her vision narrowed until all that existed of the world was the faintest light at the end of a long tunnel.

Her body fought for air, pulsing her diaphragm down and up in quick jerks to keep oxygen flowing to her brain. But not enough. Not nearly enough.

But even panic couldn't overpower the sheer weight of the acceleration that had already thrust Jacey and her friends a kilometer above the surface of the Earth.

Consciousness slipped away.

Then it snapped back. Jacey's eyes fluttered open. The press of acceleration lessened. "Did that attendant say something just now?" She seemed to remember the words "flip" and "harness" slipping into her mind.

Meow Meow was about to answer, but the floor dropped from beneath them and the sub-orb fell silent.

And then they started to fall.

Jacey did scream then. The fingers of her left hand grabbed something soft, which made Dante groan. She was clutching his forearm and her skeletal-white fingertips were gouging into his skin. She couldn't make herself let go.

They were falling. Falling.

"Look!" Meow Meow said, pointing straight up.

Jacey looked and gasped and screamed.

A slender rectangle on the ceiling had gone transparent, giving a view of curving blue ocean, white swirls of clouds, and vast green and brown landmasses below.

"We're upside down!" Jacey rasped.

"Yes. It's called the flip."

"We're falling."

"Yes. But it's okay. Have fun."

Suddenly Meow Meow was out of her seat and tumbling head over heels across the seat tops in front of her. She struck the far bulkhead, then thrust off and flew with her arms out to her sides, laughing like a Dolphin at the beach.

The attendant's voice blared out from the P.A. "Please return to your seat. This flight has not been cleared by the FSA for free-fall entertainments."

But Dante had already unbuckled Jacey. With a jerk of his arm, he sent her tumbling free.

Jacey's panicked cries took form then. They focused into arias of swearing, punctuated by Dante's name. She bounced into something solid, tried to grab hold, but then drifted away.

The attendant continued to make the same announcement, but Jacey caught a glimpse of him strapped into his seat near the front of the sub-orb. His white teeth were flashing with genuine amusement now.

Behind her, Meow Meow and Dante were laughing.

Jacey managed to twist and get them centered in her view. With a thrust of her legs, she pushed off the bulkhead and flew straight at them.

Neither could dodge her. She shouldered into Dante's gut while lashing out to grab Meow Meow's arm. The collision sent them all spinning and tumbling toward the rear of the craft. Jacey's veil fluttered up from her nose and mouth to cover her eyes.

She tore it away and let it float.

Dante grasped Jacey's ankle. But instead of pulling her in for revenge, he pushed her away. This sent him backward and Jacey forward.

Meow Meow wrapped her legs around Jacey's waist and planted kisses on the top of her head. This infuriated Jacey. She would not be taunted by a girl who weighed less than a Pelican.

Jacey caught the rear bulkhead with her hands and this time she was able to hold on to a narrow lip of decorative trim. She got her momentum under control, then wriggled free from Meow Meow. With a soft push of her heel, she sent the girl flying away.

Meow Meow's eyes went wide.

There was something manic and ridiculous about the sight of the skinny girl floating away that finally broke through Jacey's rage. An involuntary laugh burst from her and suddenly she broke down. A replay of the whole experience flashed in her mind and the insanity of it struck home.

Tears of laughter blurring her vision, Jacey let go and floated on her back, looking down at the world. The humor slowly faded, replaced by awe-struck silence.

Dante and Meow Meow steered themselves to join her,

and they floated together, heads touching, all facing the glorious view.

"Wow," Meow Meow said. "I think I'm seeing it the way Jacey sees it. Like a little bitty baby."

"I know," Dante said quietly, perhaps the first time Jacey had ever heard him be remotely serious about anything.

The attendant cleared his throat on the P.A. and announced: "Please return to your seats. Descent and deceleration to commence in five minutes."

As soon as Jacey was strapped in, Meow Meow held out a tiny pill. "You probably should take this. The decel is a bit rough the first couple times."

Jacey swallowed the pill dry.

A minute later, the sub-orb began to tremble. Warmth spread through Jacey's legs and arms. Tension seeped from her shoulders.

The transparent window on the ceiling went opaque.

Rattles and clunks sounded all around. The ship seemed to be on the verge of shaking apart. Even through the mind-fuzzing calm of the pill, a thrill of fear shouted a muted warning.

Jacey looked to Dante. He wore a slight smile as his head bounced around. Same with Meow Meow. They actually *liked* this insanity.

With a neck-cracking jerk the sub-orb whirled around its long axis and Jacey had the sudden feeling of being upside-down. Hands gripping the armrests, she noticed her breath racing. Her heart pounded, too.

But inside her skull, like an egg tucked in a downy nest, her mind felt no fear. The air inside the cabin grew warmer. Vents poured out cool air in a stiff breeze that ruffled Jacey's hair.

The shaking subsided and Jacey was thrown forward with sudden deceleration.

"We're an aircraft now," Dante said. He seemed a little let down by it.

Windows appeared on the sides of the sub-orb, giving a view over a brown landscape carved by muddy rivers.

"Kansas, or some other boring place," Dante said. He wasn't interested in the view. Meow Meow had pulled out a round mirror and was touching up her makeup and straightening her blue wig.

"Hey, did I mention we're wanted for Ping's murder?" she said.

Jacey stammered for moment. "We're what?"

"I saw it on the news while you and Dante were seducing Cruze in the casino."

"We didn't kill Ping."

"Is he really dead?" Dante asked.

"Bullet to the brain." Meow Meow snapped shut her mirror and stuffed it in her bag. "I think we all know what really happened."

"I have no idea what really happened," Jacey said.

The sub-orb banked gently. It continued to bounce and shake, but nothing like what they'd experienced earlier.

"He shot himself," Dante said. "His pride was much greater than his greed. What a fool."

"Better put this back on," Meow Meow said, thrusting Jacey's veil into her hands. "Dante, have a nice green chip ready for that flight attendant. He's been watching us real close."

"So let me get this straight," Jacey said through a thick, warm drowsiness as she refastened her veil. "Captain Wilcox is after me, and some *other* people are after us for murdering Ping?"

"And don't forget the paparazzi, darling," Meow Meow said. "They're scouring the planet for a whiff of Jacqueline Buchanan's lookalike right now." Meow Meow's veil stretched over her cheekbones as she grinned. "Isn't it exciting?"

5

YOUR BUMBLING PURSUIT

"How hard can it be, Captain Wilcox?" Dr. Carlhagen said to the holo. "Two teenagers should not be hard to find. Especially if they're in the company of that little pop tart Meow Meow."

Dr. Carlhagen stood before his holodesk in his office. His anger pressed at his skull, and if he didn't find a way to release it, Mt. Lazarus—in which he'd built this new Scion facility—just might erupt.

He'd switched the pixel-painted walls to a calming sunset, even though it was past 10 p.m. A warm breeze—produced by millions of nano-fans enmeshed alongside the pixel nanites—blew from a faux-arched window. It was indistinguishable from a real window, even to Dr. Carlhagen.

He considered changing the scene to a stormy sea. A hurricane. That would more suit his mood.

Over the past few days on the island of St. Lazarus, he'd been simmering, every little thing setting off his anger. Even with a double dose of andleprixen, he was keyed up. Maxine Bentilius had retreated to her room and only came when he summoned her.

That was just as well. Even with the ornery senator finally brought to heel, the sight of her irritated him. The mighty Senator Bentilius had fallen, yes, but her scared submissiveness was wearing on him. He didn't want *her*, no matter how lovely she might be when trembling fearfully in his arms.

He wanted Jacqueline.

No. *Jacey*.

Damn it.

Wilcox's incompetence increased the pressure in Carlhagen's head. The captain stood at attention. He wore civilian clothes, but his bearing was pure military. "I apologize, sir. We tracked them to a hotel in Casino San Juan. A few employees there recognized Dante's face when I showed them a pic on my tablet. They did not remember seeing Jacey or Meow Meow. Veils are tolerated here.

"But the trail is not entirely cold, sir. While we were at the hotel, security was called to assist an injured man in an ice machine alcove on the thirteenth floor. He'd been struck in head and robbed of three quarters of a million in chips."

"You think Dante did it?"

"Yes. It makes sense that the fugitives wouldn't use credit accounts associated with their true identities. You've seen the SNN coverage of Vin's debacle. Ping is murdered and they all run off. I've spotted at least three IPA agents since landing here in Puerto Rico. They're asking about the Dante and Jacqueline Buchanan lookalikes, too."

Through a force of will, Dr. Carlhagen took a seat and folded his hands. The IPA was the International Police Agency. "They must not get their hands on Dante," he said to Wilcox. "And I *must* have the girl."

"I'm well ahead of the IPA, sir."

Dr. Carlhagen found Wilcox's confidence infuriating. If the man had half the competence he claimed, Jacqueline would already be standing in this very office. "So now that our fugitives have money," he said, leading Wilcox through the basic logic, "where will they go?"

"Puerto Rico is a sizable island. But it will be hard for Jacey or the pop star to hide for long, even with the veils. I suspect they'll attempt to leave, if they haven't already."

Dr. Carlhagen wrinkled his face to relieve the tension in his jaw and forehead. "Jacqueline knows I have the Dolphin girl."

The Dolphin girl was the nine-year-old, Livy. The child lay in a cryo growth pod several floors below. That had been Senator Bentilius's doing, before Dr. Carlhagen had reasserted his control.

Captain Wilcox kept silent, which was wise. He'd known Dr. Carlhagen long enough to know when the doctor was thinking out loud.

Dr. Carlhagen leaned on a cushy armrest. A thin layer of calm settled over his teeming brain, like a rime of frost on grass at the onset of winter. "More than anything, Jacey wants to find me. Ironic, isn't it?"

"Sir?"

The soldier obviously didn't understand. But then, Captain Wilcox was not a subtle man. His world was ruled by violence. Dr. Carlhagen's, on the other hand, was ruled by leverage.

"Jacey is emotionally attached to Livy. She knows I have the child. When she left St. Vitus for Vin's island, she was certainly on a quest to track me down to get the girl back. She's really quite predictable."

"So you think she'll come to you?" The man was utterly unsuccessful at concealing his skepticism.

"If she had the faintest clue where I was, she'd come here in a heartbeat. Unfortunately, she doesn't know where I am. Furthermore, your bumbling pursuit and this whole wanted-for-murder business has driven her to ground. What I need is a way to communicate with her without attracting the attention of the International Police Agency."

The captain was completely out of his depth. He shifted his weight and scratched his nose in an uncharacteristic display of confusion.

"Sir?" Wilcox said. "I had a man ask around at the skyport about private sub-orbs. One launched for Chicago in the relevant time period."

"Why didn't you *start* with that?"

"I—"

"I want you in Chicago in an hour. Find out where that sub-orb's passengers went. There will be surveillance video somewhere. Keep an eye out for IPA agents. I do not want you in open combat with them unless absolutely necessary."

Wilcox sketched a salute. "Yes, sir."

Dr. Carlhagen disconnected the call and got up from his chair. A new energy now took the place of the head-exploding pressure.

"Lazarus?" he said to the room.

The avatar of the facility's controlling AI appeared on the pixel wall. It looked human-ish. The chin was a bit too sharp, the ears missing entirely, the eyes shaped and angled unlike any human of any race. Lazarus was Dr. Carlhagen's most recently created AI, and Dr. Carlhagen had decided not to mold it into a human analog, the way he had with Madam LaFontaine.

"Sir?" the monotone voice prompted.

"Summon Senator Bentilius to my quarters. Tell her to dress sharply, as if she were going on an SNN broadcast."

"Yes, sir."

Dr. Carlhagen went to a drawer and dug out his andleprixen bottle. He popped a pill and swallowed it. He commanded the pixel wall to show the current stream from Survivor News Network, the leading news site in the world.

"Lazarus, find contact information for the floor producer working SNN's live broadcast."

"I have it."

"Good."

The plan was simple. A slight gamble, too. But he figured that anyone on the run for murder would keep their eyes on the networks. The chances of Jacey seeing this next bit of news was excellent.

It would be much easier for him to go on SNN himself, but since he'd overwritten Vaughan, his face was too recognizable as Charles Buchanan's. He didn't want to make himself a news story quite yet.

Maxine's face—the Scion of one Korra Bolelli—was not as well-known.

But it soon would be.

6

DRINKING FROM A FIRE HOSE

Humphrey rubbed his eyes and yawned. He'd reached the point of exhaustion where coffee made him jittery but couldn't keep him alert. It wasn't pleasant. He stayed on his feet because if he sat down—even on the dirty floor of the bridge—he knew he would pass out.

A heavy breeze, humid and fragrant from the salty sea, cut through the bridge. But rather than refresh, it lulled him. The thrum of the engines and the shush of the sea made his eyes droop more.

Aphrodite had just maneuvered to let another huge freighter slip past. They were about to turn north before the sun rose. Obu had calculated that a speed of ten knots would take them 193 kilometers north of their current position before they could safely come about and run southwest to the island. It would take four hours of darkness to get to the island. Figure another hour to bring *Aphrodite* into harbor and dock.

And then the work would begin.

Humphrey, like Wanda, who stood next to him, planned to sleep during the day so he could have his wits about him tomorrow night.

Wanda had just come up from the cargo holds where the rest of the Scions slept—or, at least, tried to. Her face was unreadable in the weird red light of the bridge. The urge to touch her, to feel her warmth, pulled at him. But he resisted. His thoughts turned to Jacey.

How long had it been since he'd seen her last, before she'd run off to Captain Wilcox's helicopter to leave St. Vitus? Nothing had gone according to plan. Both he and Wanda loved Jacey. Neither of them had wanted to betray her.

The kiss he and Wanda had shared boiled in his mind. His desire to kiss her again warred with his wish that he'd never kissed her the first time.

And she felt the same way. He could tell just by the way she hovered close, and yet not close enough.

"I used to have a crush on Vaughan," she said softly. "Before Elias kicked him in the head and we thought he'd died."

"Everyone had a crush on Vaughan. Of one sort or the other."

Vaughan had been beloved by everyone. The perfect older brother. The best friend. Generous, kind, smart.

"True." Wanda kept her eyes ahead. The sky was graying in anticipation of dawn. "I'm just saying, I didn't pine after you like Summer did. It was all of a sudden that I felt . . . what I feel."

If Vaughan had been everyone's friend, Humphrey had been everyone's—not enemy,that was too strong a term. He'd been their foe, their opponent. And much of that was his doing, he knew. He could be prickly. But what seemed like arrogance had really been born out of his complete lack of confidence.

She glanced at him then, her eyes catching fire in the red lights of the bridge. "What exactly is your—understanding—with Jacey?"

He blew air through his lips and shook his head. "I don't know. We never had much of a chance to talk about it. I thought it was . . . *something*."

They were quiet for a while. Wanda rubbed her arms and raised an eyebrow. "Could it be that you and she fell into the same thing we did? That all you went through together with Dr. Carlhagen just kind of pushed you into each other's arms?"

Yes. Of course that's what had happened. But the difference was that Humphrey had been in love with Jacey since they were six years old. His arms had been wide open from the start. He didn't say that, though. He didn't want to hurt Wanda.

But she had a point. Maybe what Jacey felt for him had been brought on only because of their shared pain. Maybe it wasn't rooted in real affection. After all, they'd spent most of their lives verbally sparring. The kissing had only started very recently.

Wanda still regarded him, waiting for him to answer her question.

Motion drew his eye to Vaughan's little holo atop the desk. Humphrey was used to speaking to his friend in his AI form, as if Vaughan were calling in from a holodesk at some other location.

He went to the holodesk. "Vaughan, any word on where Jacey might be?"

Vaughan looked up. Belle's holo materialized next to him. "No," Vaughan said. "But the data flow has become more manageable now that I understand the sources and the veracity of some of the information. The potential for distraction on the net is immense, to say the least. Even split into thirty instances, I could spend lifetimes immersed in trivial entertainments. Did you know that cats can be hilarious?"

Having never seen a cat in real life, Humphrey had no opinion on the topic. Just hearing about it irritated him. "You're supposed to be finding—"

"I know," Vaughan said, "but the data flow is like drinking from a fire hose."

"Drinking from a what?"

"It's a high-flow water hose used by organized squads of people whose job is to put out fires. The phrase drinking from a fire hose is a metaphor for the data—"

"I get it now, Vaughan. I'm not stupid." Humphrey thought Jacey would have appreciated Vaughan's metaphor more than he did.

"I didn't say you were."

"Boys. Please," Wanda said, holding up both hands. "Focus."

Humphrey took a long, slow breath. Belle appeared to be whispering something to Vaughan.

"I'm sorry," Humphrey said to Vaughan. "I'm very tired. Anything at all on Jacey's whereabouts?"

"No. No record of her since she and Dante fled Vin's island after Ping's murder."

It irritated Humphrey that Vaughan was referring to the Progenitors by their Scions' names. Ping, Vin, and Dante had all been—if not his friends—his family members. They had died the day they'd been overwritten. "Can't we call them Han and Elizabeth and Silvio?"

"I'm just using the names the press uses," Vaughan said.

The press, it turned out, was a class of people whose job it was to report news and gossip about events happening in the world. Why they used the word "press," Humphrey hadn't the slightest idea. He didn't risk asking Vaughan about it because he didn't have the patience for a two-hour lecture on the topic.

Belle stood by silently, wearing that half-smile she had adopted since becoming an AI. Humphrey still hadn't gotten used to it. She'd been so rude and mean for so long, it was ironic she'd become more human now that she was not human at all.

"So Jacey escaped?" Wanda asked, prodding them back toward the important issue at hand.

"It would seem so," Vaughan said. "I have run into some blocks in tracking her. It seems the International Police Agency does not want people freely scanning their databases, so they place security measures on their servers. It takes time to skirt around those measures. And when you finally get through, you discover they don't know anything of use."

"What about Dr. Carlhagen?"

"No sign of him. It's like he erased his presence from the public networks."

"The AI," Belle said, as if that explained everything. Vaughan nodded in agreement. Belle said nothing more, forcing Humphrey to ask what she meant. She liked to make him ask because it made him look stupid. Even with her new, more pleasant personality, old habits lingered.

But what else was new? He *was* stupid when it came to the outside world. "What about an AI?"

She put on a condescending tone, the same she might use to explain a simple chore to a Dolphin. "We think Dr. Carlhagen put an AI on the task of scrubbing his tracks. It turns out that he was instrumental in developing ways to *grow* artificial intelligences. Previously they had been painstakingly programmed. I think his discoveries with seeding AIs were the breakthroughs that led to the mind-transfer technology."

Noticing Humphrey's look of complete befuddlement, Vaughan patted Belle fondly as he took over the explanation. "Dr. Carlhagen used a seeding process to rapidly grow millions of artificial intelligences. It resulted in many, many failures. These baby AIs usually have psychological problems that make them useless. They tend to be sociopathic. But since Dr. Carlhagen can grow millions of them, all he needs to do is filter out the bad ones and guide the few good ones to maturity."

"Which explains Madam LaFontaine," Belle said. "I think she was the best one he ever grew. And even she had her peculiarities."

"She's schizophrenic," Vaughan said.

"And a narcissist," Belle added.

Humphrey grunted. Belle should talk. He kept the thought to himself. "Have you talked to Madam LaFontaine since Summer turned her server back on? She might know where Dr. Carlhagen ran off to."

"No. She refuses to come out."

Maybe that was just as well, Humphrey thought. Madam LaFontaine and her various alter egos had been mercurial at best. Besides, the dance mistress's loyalty lay entirely with Dr. Carlhagen.

"So where is Jacey?" Wanda asked, again bringing them around to the important topic.

"We don't know." Vaughan and Belle said it together, as if they were one person.

"How could she have gotten off that island with nobody knowing?" Humphrey asked.

"We don't know," Belle said.

"What *do* you know?"

A list of numbers and lines of text started scrolling next to Vaughan, moving much too fast for Humphrey to read.

Vaughan waved at it. "I was able to access air traffic records between Vin's island and Puerto Rico. I was interested to see where her guests went once the authorities released them following Ping's murder investigation. Almost all of the guests had chartered helicopter service. The rest left by boat, I assume. A few are still on the island with Vin."

"But Jacey was not on those flights?"

"No."

Pictures appeared next to Vaughan. "Here are the other two people they are searching for. Dante, who we all recognize. And this woman, Meow Meow."

"So you think Jacey is still with Dante and this Meow Meow person?" Wanda asked. There was more than incredulity in her voice. She was angry.

"It stands to reason," Vaughan said. "It can't be a coincidence that the IPA is looking for all of them."

Humphrey studied the photo of Dante. Seeing the face of his fellow Scion, one he'd grown up with, and who he had looked up to, filled Humphrey with a weary sadness. "But Dante is a Progenitor now. Why would he help Jacey?"

Wanda said, "For that matter, why would Jacey accept his help?"

"We don't know," Vaughan said. "But she was not on

any of the helicopters that left Vin's island. Can't imagine she was on one of the yachts, either. IPA had people all over those docks. In addition to that, Captain Wilcox was involved in the search. My understanding is that things became quite tense between the IPA and Wilcox at one point. He abruptly left the island with all of his men."

Humphrey had forgotten all about Captain Wilcox. "Where did he go?"

"Puerto Rico. More specifically, Casino San Juan. The whole downtown area is one giant strip of hotels, casinos, entertainment venues, dance clubs, strip joints, and restaurants." He raised his hands in a helpless shrug. "Did he follow Jacey there? Maybe."

Humphrey didn't bother asking what a casino or a strip club was. He didn't want to know. "So all roads lead to Puerto Rico. You think Jacey got there somehow?"

"It's possible she and her companions escaped by some other means. Perhaps a small watercraft not moored at the main docks. If so, she could be at sea even now."

Belle piped in. "Or dead."

Vaughan gave Belle a look of patient disapproval, which she shrugged off. "We must consider every possibility," she said.

"Do you really think she or one of these other people killed Ping?" Humphrey asked.

"At the risk of wearing out the phrase, we don't know," Vaughan said. "Ping died of a gunshot wound to the side of the head. The IPA had to take the body to Puerto Rico for an expert to study. That report has not been released yet."

The reality of the situation settled on Humphrey's shoulders like one of the twenty-five kilo bags of rice from the warehouse. He wanted to lie down and cover his face with a pillow and block out everything.

Instead he stated the truth as he understood it: "There's nothing we can do to help Jacey—or even to contact her. We are totally useless to her."

"For now," Vaughan said. "But if she did make it to Puerto Rico, then there's a good chance she'll make it to a holodesk and try to contact us."

That was true. A glimmer of hope.

Except . . . "If she made it there, why hasn't she contacted us yet?"

Vaughan shrugged. "She's on the run. She may not have had the time or the chance."

"Or Dante and that Meow Meow harlot have her tied up," Belle said. Humphrey noted there was no delight in her statement, which was progress, he supposed.

Wanda's hand slipped into Humphrey's. It comforted him, but at the same time filled him with self-loathing.

"I need some air." He disentangled himself from Wanda and headed out to the starboard bridge wing. Clinging to the railing, he looked to the stars, which were quickly fading into the deepening blue of morning twilight.

For the millionth time, he had to remind himself where his responsibility lay. With the Scions on this ship. Not with Jacey. He had to see everyone safely established on this island of Mr. Justin's. Only then could he consider chasing after Jacey.

The thought of going to yet another island made his stomach churn. He thought he'd gotten the truth about their destination from Orson, but he wouldn't be surprised if the man had left out crucial information.

There were barracks there for them to sleep in, he was told. There were several months of supplies. It was remote;

it was sheltered. But something about Orson's descriptions was vague, as if he were steering around something very, very important. A detail that would make it all much less rosy than it sounded.

Unless Humphrey was willing to threaten the man with torture, he would have to accept what he'd been told. He remembered Jacey walking around Orson when he'd been strapped to a cot in the medical ward. She'd held a scalpel in her hand, not intending to use it, but pretending to want to.

It had been expedient. But Humphrey couldn't bring himself to do that. And it burned him. Weakness. The safety of the Scions depended on him, but he couldn't even *threaten* Orson with torture to learn the truth.

Something Sensei once told Humphrey popped into his mind: "In every minute, be the person you want to become." Well, at least the phrase finally made sense, even if it wasn't very practical.

It seemed Humphrey had to decide between cruel strength or kind weakness. It felt wrong. It felt untrue. And yet there it was. As obvious and undeniable as Dolphin-level arithmetic.

7

IT MEANS I'M ALIVE

Belle left the holodesk and returned to St. Vitus. The day was perfect. Blue sky, warm breezes, not too humid.

A slight yellow bird flitted around her head, chirping and warbling. The friendly Caribbean sun shone warmly on its wings. She tried to shoo it away, but it dodged her half-hearted swats.

"Go away," she scolded it. "I don't have time for you."

The bird fluttered in a crazy orbit centered on Belle's head as she trudged the last few meters to the top of the hill overlooking the Scion School.

This was the simulated version of St. Vitus and the school, of course. The entirety of Belle's existence was simulated. She'd seen a picture of the plain metal computer server that housed her world. Such a small thing.

The sweat from her effort stung her eyes, but she welcomed the discomfort. She'd been getting soft. The ability to control the weather here—even the time of day—had spoiled her, had distanced her from her humanity.

On the real St. Vitus there was nothing in this spot except a rutted gravel road. That didn't suit Belle's purposes at all. She wanted to be able to see.

She no longer had to concentrate to alter the world. With a mere pulse of intention, she created a flat spot on the ridgeline, and with another thought manifested an observation deck. A steel staircase climbed thirty meters to the round platform. She could teleport there. She could levitate. She could spread her arms and fly like her annoying little yellow companion.

She took the stairs, running to intensify the burning in her thighs. Her breath heaved in and out, and her sweat-slickened hands squeaked on the metal handrail as she made the turn at each landing.

Aside from the bird's nonstop chirping, the only other sound was the bong of her footsteps on the metal stair treads.

The final twenty steps were pure torture, her legs afire, her lungs straining. At the top she bent and put her hands on her knees. It felt good to feel bad. An odd notion, but true. Sensei had often lectured the Scions about the importance of physical discomfort. Especially when they complained about some insidious workout he'd devised.

The martial arts master had been a comforting presence in Belle's life. Learning of his death at the hands of Mr. Justin had brought a shock of pain and tears from her. Was that what loving someone meant? That you gave them a piece of your heart to rip out when they left?

Pain. Discomfort. Sensei had understood those sensations better than anyone else. He'd made suffering his ally.

Toward the end of each workout, he'd laugh to see his charges panting, faces twisted with the agony of physical exertion. And he'd calmly recite the mantra: "I welcome the pain, it means I'm alive. I welcome the pain, it means I'm alive."

Belle straightened and leaned against the railing of her observation deck. The Scion School lay far below, red roofs, white stucco walls. The quad was a rectangle of green in the center of it all. A dark spot marred it—the grate covering the pit.

Beyond the school lay the descending slopes, scrub-covered and more brown than green. A late afternoon sun slanted toward the western horizon, shimmering on a turquoise sea.

All fake. All a simulation, as if someone else's dream were being shoved into Belle's brain. She considered moving the sun to the magical moment just before dawn. But she hadn't touched the sun since Elizabeth Burnell had come to live with them. Damn that shameless tart.

It required no effort for Belle's vision to zoom toward the beige strip of sand called Isaac's Beach. That's where "Liz" always spent her days, swimming, sunbathing. Always naked as the day she was born.

Sure enough, there she was. Her hair was loose and dry, flipping in a slight breeze. The urge to turn the beach into an icy tundra skated across Belle's consciousness. Perhaps she did turn the wind a little chilly, for Liz rubbed her shoulders and manifested a towel to wrap around herself.

Belle returned her vision to normal. The beauty of the island had never penetrated her consciousness until she'd been reborn here. Even now, it was hard to believe she'd chosen an AI's existence without knowing exactly what she was getting herself into. But Vaughan was here, so that's where she needed to be.

Speaking of whom—he was nowhere to be seen now. She sensed his presence around her, a distinct otherness that permeated the air. There were probably a dozen instances of him working on various questions in parallel. He'd been obsessed with locating Dr. Carlhagen since discovering that the old man had run off with Senator Bentilius and Livy.

Belle made the railing vanish. She materialized a cool glass of iced tea. Sitting cross-legged at the very edge of the platform, she closed her eyes. The data flow available to her through *Aphrodite's* network also hung in the air. All she needed to do was breathe it in.

But for reasons she couldn't explain—to Vaughan or even to herself—the data flow frightened her. The flow felt strange, aggressive even.

Vaughan had told her he could manage without her help. And so far he had, plunging in for hours at a time, only to surface looking tired and vague, as if he could barely remember who or where he was.

All Belle wanted was to be with him. She'd even been jealous when Liz had first arrived, not as an old woman, but as youthful, beautiful Vin. Odd to think that another version of Elizabeth was living inside Vin's flesh-and-blood body somewhere out there in the real world.

Belle's own body was out there, too. Violated, desecrated, and defiled by Senator Bentilius. The hateful old bag had instantly given herself up to Dr. Carlhagen's carnal lusts. Belle had no interest in returning to that body.

And this one? This simulated version? She didn't need it either. Vaughan rarely manifested as a human-shaped entity anymore.

Liz was no company, being a Progenitor and all.

"I welcome the pain, it means I'm alive," Belle said aloud. She breathed deeply, allowing the heady scent of the fake green world to fill her senses. "I welcome the pain, it means I'm alive."

The yellow bird landed next to Belle, chirping its little song. Belle brought forth a corner of bread, held it in her palm.

The bird hopped onto her fingers, light as a fluff of nothing. It pecked at the bread, head jerking to give Belle a side-eyed look.

"What is your purpose?" she asked the bird. "What are you for?"

Thankfully, the bird didn't answer. It didn't need to. It didn't have any concept of purpose. It just was. It lived, going about its birdy business and not questioning the whys of it.

She decided to try creating another instance of herself again. Not for any particular purpose, but because she hadn't been able to do it yet. Liz had. Without seeming to try.

She brought her hands together, the bird riding on the one with the bread in it. She cupped her palms to give the bird a comfy place to rest.

Closing her eyes, she tried to do what Vaughan said he did when he made another instance of himself. She tried to let go.

Nothing happened. She tried again, imagining her body going limp and her brain turning off.

It didn't work. The bird quieted, its belly full.

"It isn't working," she said to the air. Vaughan would hear her. After all, he *was* the air.

She felt his presence congeal next to her. It wasn't the

only Vaughan, but it was *a* Vaughan. He was apportioning a sliver of his attention to listen to her. That was something.

"I don't know how to let go and create another instance of myself. I try and try, and nothing happens."

Vaughan smiled in the easy way he always did. "At the risk of sounding cryptic, the trying itself is your biggest problem. Creating another instance of myself is the opposite of trying."

"You're right. That was cryptic." The bird had fallen asleep in her hands. She touched her nose to its downy head. It smelled musty and green at the same time. "I think there is something wrong with me."

"Pity-seeking is unbecoming on you, Belle."

He was trying to rile her up, but it didn't work. He was right. She did want pity. She wanted something more from him than he gave anyone else.

He leaned back on his hands and enjoyed the view. "Why do you care about creating more instances? I already told you I don't need your help."

"You use multiple instances to research several problems at once. I figured if I could use multiple instances to focus on my single problem, I'd have a better chance of solving it."

"And what problem is that?"

He knew. Of course he knew. She'd told him several times. He knew what she wanted from him.

The Scions' old teacher Socrates had often said that clearly defining the problem was the most important step in solving it. She knew Vaughan would pounce on anything she said if she didn't have a well-reasoned problem statement. So she said nothing.

Besides, she didn't want to say out loud how she felt about him. Not again. Because then he'd have to tell her he didn't feel that way about her. Not yet, anyway. He always left the possibility open.

He'd once made an instance of himself that worshipped her, just to show her how awful fake affection could be. It was terrible. But she didn't understand why. Why couldn't she have accepted that?

She could be naked on a beach with that instance right now. It could be campfires on the sand, warm embraces, and long talks forever.

But something wasn't right about that Vaughan. That one didn't count. Belle did not understand why.

"Making an instance of yourself is a trick," Vaughan said. "Like flying, or manifesting iced tea. Nothing more. The only thing stopping you is this." He tapped her forehead.

"My mind is a simulation," she said. "The computer controls it. Maybe there's a bug in my programming."

Vaughan shrugged. "Then accept it."

Fury rose in her like magma in a volcano. "Easy for you to say." She flicked the bird from her hands. It caught flight and gave an angry warble before flying out of sight somewhere below the platform. "Why should I just accept it? Why should I just accept that even here—in this totally fake world—I can't be happy?"

His brows furrowed with that look of empathy she knew so well. But instead of welcoming it, she resented it. Worse, she felt tears working their way to her eyes. She hated crying.

She wanted to beat his chest and demand to know why he couldn't love her. But that would be pathetic, and if she saw pity in his eyes, she knew she'd never recover. Nobody could fall in love with someone they pitied.

"I'm useless here. The data flow . . . It's like I'm afraid of heights. I just can't jump into it. It's too deep."

"What are you afraid of?"

The truth tumbled from her lips. "I'm afraid of getting swallowed up in it. Like what's happening to you. You're becoming less and less you."

"Really?"

In that moment he was very much his old self. The heat of embarrassment flushed her cheeks. Admitting to fears wasn't a habit of hers. The reality of her existence pressed in on her from all sides. She was free to be a goddess here, but a goddess of what?

"I liked that bird you made," Vaughan said, voice barely audible in a freshening breeze.

"I didn't make that. I figured you did it." The simulated St. Vitus had all the plants and creatures she'd come to know over a lifetime on the island. "To cheer me up."

Vaughan shrugged. "Maybe Liz sent it to annoy you."

Belle doubted that. Liz could be a bitch, but she ignored Belle more often than she confronted her. "I didn't make it." She looked to the sky. "Maybe the simulation made it."

Vaughan frowned. "Maybe. I need to get back to work. My other selves have devised a novel way to track down Dr. Carlhagen's broadcasts. All we need now is for him to do it again."

Vaughan disappeared in a sizzle of static.

Belle closed her eyes and felt the data flow with her senses. It was everywhere. All she needed to do was dive into it and she could watch what Vaughan was doing. She had no doubt she could understand it. She was as smart as he was. Smarter, in many ways.

A rushing sound—like a torrent of water falling over a cliff—grew and grew as she leaned her mind closer to the data flow. It made her feel puny and insignificant.

She shied back from it, failing yet again.

8

THE BLOOD MOVES

The Dreamless is cold, timeless, empty.

No hate. No enthusiasm. No suspicion.

Billions of new cells have grown, invisible to a human observer.

Lazarus notices that Livy's mass has increased. The protein allotment increases to support more growth. Schedule for Scion maturity on track for eight years and fifteen days.

The AI cycles the Scion's lungs for three inhalations. Nanites scurry across teeth, harvesting rogue bacteria to prevent decay.

"Livy" is a tag in a metadata file attached to the specimen's records.

The blood moves. Thump.

Thump.

The Dreamless

is.

9

MY DOUBLE LUCKY NUMBER

So this was what Dr. Carlhagen's mind felt like. Awake, alert, but with muted emotions.

Take fear, for instance. Jacey's terror during the sub-orb's final descent and landing screamed at her from behind a thick wall of gauze. Yes, it was there. She understood the intensity of her fear. But the drug didn't let her heart hammer or her palms sweat.

All thanks to a tiny pill. Andleprixen, which Meow Meow called prixie.

They had debarked the sub-orb and stepped directly into another self-driving limousine waiting for them on the tarmac. Jacey had only enough time in open air to smell the hot exhaust of the sub-orbs and hear a distant roar of another one taking off.

Rain pattered on the windows as the limo's wheels hissed across smooth pavement toward the largest buildings Jacey had ever seen.

"A storm is coming," Meow Meow said, looking at her tablet. "Class one. That should help with outside cameras."

"Coming?" Jacey said. "It's like night out."

Trees along the street leaned hard in the wind. Head-lights charged toward them in the southbound lane, then swept past in a flash that lit up the inside of the car, whitening Dante's face for an instant before shadows ate him up.

The skyport was surrounded by cities, it seemed. Lights everywhere, and concentrations of gigantic buildings to the north, south, east, and west. Jacey had thought the hotels in Casino San Juan had been tall, but these . . . The closer they got, the bigger they appeared to be. "It's like something out of a dream. Like a nightmare."

Lightning flashed against thousands upon thousands of glass windows on floor after floor of just a single building. All were lit up, each an office or an apartment or a hotel room.

"All those lives . . ." she said, not knowing what she meant, but feeling the significance of it nonetheless. The isolation she and the Scions shared on St. Vitus was clear. The outside world was not only vast, as she'd seen on the sub-orbital flight. It was deep. Her own problems were a small drama. A speck.

But for her that speck was a mountain of trouble. "I need to find an address for Dr. Carlhagen's old holodesk."

"Yes, yes," Dante said. He didn't hide how tired he was of hearing her say that. "We'll figure it out, but first we need to get away from the airport. We'll switch cars a few times, too."

"Why?"

"Because not only is Captain Wilcox looking for you, the IPA is hunting all of us. And they have eyes every-where. Literally."

He noticed Jacey's blank look, that she was trying to

imagine how a police agency would have eyes everywhere. "Cameras," he said. "I know you've heard this lecture before. But listen. In this city, *everyone* is under surveillance. Cameras are everywhere. All of that video funnels to an AI whose sole task is identifying people and tracking their movements."

Jacey flicked the bottom of her veil with a finger. "But I have this."

"And it's illegal to wear in public. But never mind that. The identification AIs don't necessarily need to see your face to know who you are. They can tell someone's identity by voice, gait, body posture, and behavior prediction. They track your daily habits and calculate who you are by where you've been and where you're going. The veil . . . I say get rid of it. Concealing your identity will make them look at you closer."

"So you're telling me I *shouldn't* be wearing this? Because I'm happy to fling it out the window right now."

Meow Meow answered. "You're damned if you do and double-damned if you don't. For the next hour or so—until we can get you safely to a sur-blind place—"

"Sur-blind?"

"Surveillance-blind. No cameras." Meow Meow snapped her fingers in Jacey's face. "Keep up, please. Anyway, until we get you into a sur-blind place, you need to wear the veil. The AIs don't know your posture that well, or your walking gait. I'm positive they won't match you to Jackie B. based on your gait."

"Really?"

"You don't move like she did. You're much too fluid. Like you've had years of dance training."

"I have."

"Jacqueline did not."

"So that's good news. These AIs won't be able to identify me."

"That will make them suspicious," Dante said. "If they detect someone they don't have gait identification for, they'll watch extra-close. And they'll be even more suspicious if they see a veil."

"Yes," Meow Meow said with extreme patience. "But at any given time there are thousands of people breaking the law and wearing them. Better to give the IPA thousands of suspects to screen than one dead-on identification."

Dante shrugged and left it up to Jacey to decide. For now, she'd keep the veil.

The limo turned onto a ramp that led to a wide, raised road. Wind whistled by the windows as they merged with an endless flow of cars and buses. The low concrete barrier at the edge of the road blurred by and the wheels' hiss rose in pitch. Jacey decided it best to not look out, as the self-driving limo thought nothing of trailing the vehicle ahead with so little room Jacey couldn't see its rear bumper.

"We're going to keep to known camera shadows," Meow Meow said. "When you're as famous as I am—which you are, honey—you need to learn skills that the less savory among our population develop. Staying out of view of cameras is one. Staying sur-blind is actually kind of a fun game."

"And how do you know where these camera shadows are?"

Meow Meow pulled her tablet from her bag. "You need a guide. Luckily, we're in Chicago, baby. And where the light shines brightest, the shadows are darkest."

Dante snickered, elbowing Jacey. "I loved that one."

"That one what?" Jacey always felt like she was the subject of the conversation but understood it the least.

"That 'we're in Chicago, baby' bit was a line from *Menominee Falls*, one of Jackie's neo-retro noir films. She played a Chicago private detective hired by a mob boss to find out who killed his favorite nephew. There was a lot of drinking, smoking, and shooting in it." He frowned at her. "You really need to bone up on your Jackie B. knowledge if you're going to pretend to be her."

It was Jacey's turn to snicker. "Pretend to *be* her. I have no intention of pretending to be her."

"If the IPA catches up, you better as hell pretend to be her," he said.

Jacey looked at Dante to make sure he hadn't popped a couple prixies. His eyes were as clear as ever and glimmered with amused seriousness. She checked Meow Meow, but the girl just lifted her eyebrows and nodded in agreement.

"Why?" Jacey asked.

Meow Meow slipped her little tablet back into her bag. "Because carbos—clones—are illegal in the North American Union and pretty much everywhere else. If you admit you're an escaped carbo, they will execute you."

"You're a non-person," Dante said. "Legally speaking. No offense."

Non-person. The term hit Jacey like a kick in the stomach from Captain Wilcox's boot. Non-person.

The limo pulled off the raised road and made a few sharp turns before coming to a stop beneath the overpass.

"Car switch," Dante said.

They piled out and ran, heads down against a slanting rain, veils flying up in the wind. The cloud cover was so thick it looked like midnight.

The inside of the new limousine was the same, except the seats were beige instead of black.

"I don't like this non-person idea," Jacey said to Dante as she shook water off her hands. "You know I have feelings and worries, right? You *know* I'm a person."

"The fact that you can talk and have memories and feelings does weigh in your favor. For me, anyway. But you're not the typical carbo, thanks to Dr. Carlhagen. A run-of-the-mill carbo is a mental zombie. No personality, minimal vocabulary, no obvious emotion or even awareness of time passing. They make decent household servants, though. Having a crew of identical-looking carbo servers is seen as a status symbol in China and Russia. Especially if they're hot like you."

"But *you're* a clone," she said. "Why don't they execute you?"

"Because I'm actually Silvio Silva and I can prove it. Even though what I did might be seen as immoral from a certain perspective, there is no law against it. For the simple fact that no lawmaker or court has contemplated the possibility of such an act before."

Meow Meow made a grumbling noise. "You should probably shut up while you're ahead, Dante."

"It's fun to be honest sometimes," Dante said. He stopped and smiled at the irony his words. "Jacey, if you are caught by the authorities, you *are* Jacqueline Buchanan. Not a carbo. Tell them you've been to a rejuvie clinic or something."

"And if the other Scions are caught?" she asked.

"I think you know the answer to that question, my dear." He looked past Jacey at Meow Meow. "Did you get hold of your shadowy friend?"

"Yes. He'll be joining us at the Two Seasons Hotel. He said if we enter through the parking structure beneath the hotel, there is camera shadow on level six. I have the parking slot number. If we hug the wall, we can stay out of view until we get into the elevator vestibule. That camera is non-functional. From there we take the elevator to the lobby."

"And then?"

"He didn't say. He'll meet us there. It's going to cost us a gold and green."

Dante sucked air through widened nostrils. For someone who bragged about his riches, he sure hated to let go of his chips. "Do you trust this guy?"

Meow Meow pressed a tiny hand to her flat chest. "Siggy has kept me safe from paparazzi on many visits to the city. He's got guys inside the IPA."

Dante's eyes lit up and he smiled. "Ah. I see."

"What?" Jacey asked, once again feeling like she was understanding only part of the conversation. "What do you see?"

"This Siggy character *is* an agent with the IPA. He just happens to be corrupt."

Meow Meow grinned. "One man's corruption . . ."

". . . is another man's virtue," Dante finished in a theatrically slow cadence.

"Let me guess," Jacey said. "That's a bit from another Jackie B. film."

"Same movie, actually," Dante said.

An idea occurred to Jacey. It wasn't something she wanted to do, but it sounded like she had no choice. "This hotel we're going to—will it have one of those video monitors like the one from Vin's mansion? With all the video programs on it?"

"Yes, darling," Meow Meow said. "The Two Seasons is a four-star hotel."

That meant exactly nothing to Jacey, but fine, that was

good. "Once I contact Humphrey, I need to spend some time alone with one of those monitors. Can they play the movies four or five times faster than real-time?"

"They can play it a hundred times faster," Dante said. "But why would you want to do that?"

Jacey leaned back into the leather seat and closed her eyes. "Because I'm going to memorize as much of what Jackie B. ever said as I can."

She felt them staring at her, but she didn't open her eyes to acknowledge it. Instead, she smiled and sank into the soft cottony numbness of her mind.

THE SIXTH LEVEL of the underground parking structure echoed in spooky ways as Jacey skirted along a cold concrete wall to stay out of camera view. The stench of rotting garbage made her keep her lips clamped tight.

Most of the parking spaces were empty. Just a few dark vehicles crouched across the cavernous space. Thick, round support columns stood in ranks, creating shadows in an already dim brown light.

Meow Meow led the way, stepping lightly and dragging her shoulder against the wall as she followed it toward a blue painted steel door with a white 6 stenciled on it.

She'd made a shushing motion before they'd gotten out of the limo. It made sense. Even if a camera wouldn't see them, one could still pick up their voices. Dante said voice identification was very important to the surveillance AI.

Just the thought of an AI like Madam LaFontaine keeping tabs on so many millions of people made Jacey shiver. Who needed all that information? What did they use it for? Who controlled the people who controlled the AIs?

Dante had laughed at that last question. He'd mumbled something about "watching a watchman" or something. Jacey had elbowed him. "I'm glad my ignorance is such a constant source of amusement to you."

Meow Meow stopped at the door and checked her veil. Jacey did the same, though she was sick of wearing it.

The door led into a small room with three elevators. Meow Meow pressed the up arrow. Doors slid open. Once they'd gotten in, she retrieved her little tablet and tapped a message into it.

It binged a few seconds later. "Siggy is waiting for us."

The elevator went up three levels before stopping. Dante yanked Jacey around. She found herself in an odd huddle with him and Meow Meow as the doors slid open. He'd faced her away from the door.

Someone got on. No. It was two people.

"Will you remember which level we parked on?" said a man.

"I'll remember," said a woman, sounding peeved to be asked.

The elevator continued up again. When it stopped, Dante held onto Jacey until the two others had gotten off.

Something thumped behind her. "Sit." It was a man's voice, raspy.

Dante shoved her back. Something struck the back of her knees and she collapsed into a chair. A squawk of surprise escaped her lips and the man behind her laughed quietly.

"Feet up," he ordered.

She complied and metal footrests swung under her feet. Suddenly she was rolling backward.

Each side of the chair was a large skinny wheel. She saw two men waiting at the elevator, each with a wheelchair. One went in and got Meow Meow. By the time the skinny girl was being wheeled out, the man driving her chair had spun her and was pushing her through an enormous lobby.

Though the parking level had been spacious, the low ceilings had given it an oppressive feel. The lobby of the Two Seasons was the exact opposite. The ceiling seemed to be as tall as the entire building. It just went up and up and up. On every side was level after level of balconies.

The marble floors and glass made the space reverberant and noisy. A hundred people milled about, all in suits and dresses. Much more formal than Vin's party. They clung together in large groups, talking, talking, talking. Most were smiling. Many wore nametags.

"A convention," said her chair pusher. "They'll all be drunk as skunks in another two hours." He did not push her quickly, probably to avoid drawing attention. She craned her neck to see where her companions were, but all she saw was the wide body of her guide. He wore a black suit and a white shirt. His face was bearded and doughy. He smiled at her. One of his back teeth appeared to be made of gold.

He bypassed a long desk along one wall where people stood between velvet ropes supported by brass stands. A sign above the desk read REGISTRATION. To one side was a round table, decorated with a huge spray of yellow flowers. Lilies. Jacey could smell their heavy perfume. It made her nose itch.

They passed more elevators and headed into a wide hallway flanked on each side by glass-fronted stores filled with clothes on hangers and jewelry under glass.

"Why am I in this chair?" she asked, as calmly as she could.

"We're in a camera zone," he said. He leaned so close his voice was hot on her ear. "But it's impossible for the identification AI to analyze your gait if you're not walking, right?"

"Clever."

"That's why Meow Meow calls me when she's in town."

They continued down the corridor of shops, then stopped at another bank of elevators.

"So you're Siggy."

"The one and only." His voice was high and raspy. He pushed her into an elevator, then jabbed a couple buttons. The doors closed.

"Why didn't you wait for the others?" she asked.

The man stepped around to face her. "Pull up the veil. Lemme see."

"That defeats the purpose of the veil."

"Look. I already know you're a Jackie B. carbo. I've seen you on SNN. I know that's who Meow Meow left the island with." His eyes were small and set close to his nose. The beard was squared off at the bottom.

"What about cameras?"

"We disabled the one in this elevator before you got here."

Jacey lifted the veil and threw it back over her head. "Satisfied?"

He whistled through his teeth, the sliver of gold tooth flashing. "Jackie B. in the flesh. Amazing. Put the veil back on."

The elevator car stopped, the door slid open. He wheeled her into a hallway with hotel room doors on either side. Beige carpet, gold and peach wallpaper in a fancy pattern, wood doors stained very dark. The light was subdued. A hush hung in the corridor like fog.

Jacey started to get up.

"No. There're cameras."

He pushed her down the hall, then stopped at room 1313. "My double lucky number," he said. He pressed a thumb to a pad next to the door. The latched clicked. He opened the door and backed her in. "No cams in here. You can stand up."

The room was smaller than the one at The Ratz in Casino San Juan. Just one largish room with two small beds. Jacey hated the abstract pattern of squiggles covering the bedspread. The aqua and red colors made her squint. Siggy turned on a light. It glowed a dim amber, leaving corners of the room shadowy.

Siggy settled himself into a brown armchair by the window. The shades were drawn and only dim slashes of city lights showed around the edges. He pulled a tablet from his pocket and started tapping the screen.

The tables, chairs, and chest of drawers were all utilitarian and lifeless. They spoke of no design, no sense of artistry or care for the humans who had to use them.

Shivering in a draft churning from a vent box under the window, Jacey sat on a bed and tugged off her veil. The mattress barely gave under her weight. It was like sitting on padded concrete. Remarkable, considering Jacey was used to sleeping in a very hard bunk in Girls' Hall. The pillows were low, flat and hard, as if they'd been stuffed with folded up blankets instead of foam or feathers.

"Where are my friends?" she asked, folding her veil. The cold was creeping into her stomach. She realized the prixie was wearing off. The room wasn't going to be big enough for all three of them.

Siggy didn't look up from his tablet. "They're being taken to their own rooms."

"I want to see them. Immediately." She headed for the door.

"Don't even peek out without your veil over that pretty face of yours. But don't bother. Meows and Dante are not on this floor. The hotel is booked up with that convention. You were lucky I got three rooms at all."

"I need to talk to them."

He raised his eyes. "Relax. Give them time to settle in and use the bathroom."

Jacey was about to argue when Siggy abruptly stood. He was still looking at his tablet. "You're going to want to see this. Here. I'll put it on the big screen." He grabbed a remote for the monitor that hung on the wall across from the beds. The screen flashed on.

A SNN reporter was talking directly to the camera. "Officials in Puerto Rico are saying that a chartered sub-orb left just minutes prior to officials shutting down the San Juan Skyport. It is believed that pop starlet Meow Meow, along with her two co-conspirators, fled to Chicago to avoid questioning by IPA authorities regarding the apparent murder of an individual at a press event held by the heir to Elizabeth Burnell's fortune, Vin Burnell."

Siggy muted the report and tossed the remote onto the bed. "Murderers, eh? I never thought Meow Meow would get tangled up in that sort of thing."

She wound the veil over her hand, thinking of poor Ping. Not the Progenitor, but the Scion she'd known her whole life.

Siggy tilted his head with indifference. "The Agency

don't care about the murder, you know. You're a pretty damn fancy carbo and they are *dying* to get to the bottom of where you came from. Tell me, who made you?"

He was smiling. Grinning, actually. The look in his eyes chilled Jacey. She'd seen it before on Dr. Carlhagen, Senator Bentilius, and even Belle and Humphrey.

Calculation.

Jacey remembered that this man was with the IPA. And if he was corrupt, then what loyalty did he truly have to Meow Meow? She had to assume he was working for the Agency now. "My body might be a clone. But I *am* Jacqueline Buchanan. Nobody made me."

Siggy laughed and flourished his hand in a mock bow. "Whatever you say, foxy. Whatever you say."

10

HOW INSIGNIFICANT SHE IS

Minutes were ripping by like machine gun fire. It was past ten in the morning for Dr. Carlhagen, which meant it was past 9 a.m. Chicago.

Now that Jacey was on the run and Vin and Dante's faces were on SNN every ten minutes, the truth about the Scion program was seeping into the world. He needed to get ahead of the story so he could control it.

It was the optimal time of day for a press event of this importance, so at least one thing was going his way. SNN and the other news sites would gab about it all day, he was sure. And probably for many days to come.

Maxine stood before him in a black pantsuit that was several sizes too big. He used binder clips to tailor it. The cameras wouldn't see the back anyway. "Your hair is too sultry," he said. "Can't you make it more conservative?"

The 84-year-old Senator Bentilius—who now inhabited the body of the Scion Belle—let an irritated frown appear on her face. It vanished. The meek, submissive expression Dr. Carlhagen expected returned.

That slip of honest emotion was a good reminder about the woman he was dealing with. She had more blood on her hands—literally—than he did. But she understood he was in command, so she was doing her best to play-act at obedience in hopes he wouldn't withhold her anti-transfer-rejection drugs. Without the ATR, she would fall into a coma within a few days.

She tucked her hair behind her ears. It made her look younger, more girlish. It would do. Dr. Carlhagen was no hairdresser.

"We have two calls to make," he said. "The first is going to be a bit brutal. I'll keep it short."

He put his hands on the holodesk. "Korra Bolelli."

He knew the woman was at her home in Sienna, Italy. He'd had Lazarus contact her to check. All she knew was that Dr. Carlhagen was going call about her Scion. That always got a Progenitor's attention.

Korra's holo appeared above the desk. She wore a sundress. Her hair was chopped short. Belle's face, aged forty years, looked birdlike. The blue eyes were just as icy, but there was a guardedness to them that Belle hadn't possessed. In all, Korra was beautiful and cold and—to Dr. Carlhagen's shock—horrifically thin.

"Who are you?" she asked. Korra's English jumped with the melodic accents of her native tongue.

"I'm Dr. Carlhagen. I have transferred into this Scion."

That made the woman pause. Her lips parted. "What is the agreed code phrase?"

Every Progenitor had created a code phrase for Dr. Carlhagen, so he could prove to them he was himself even after he transferred. He'd had Lazarus dig it up so he'd be prepared. "Eleven Train Three Women Washing Stockings."

Her eyes flashed in recognition. There was something more there, too. The realization of what his transfer meant.

"It works," she said, smiling now. "It truly works. Vin Burnell really is Elizabeth. And you . . . But you do not look like you."

"I arranged to exchange my Scion with another. The technology has advanced such that we no longer require a clone."

There was no use in pleasantries or skirting around the issue. He barged ahead with the bad news. "And that is a good segue into why I called. It's about your Scion. Due to circumstances beyond my control, I was forced to transfer another Progenitor into your Scion."

Korra blinked, head tilting.

Dr. Carlhagen waved Maxine toward him. She stepped into view of the holodesk cameras so that Korra could see her.

Korra backed up a step, mouth dropping open.

"Hello, Ms. Bolelli," Maxine said. "I apologize for commandeering your Scion. I hope you'll allow me to explain."

A string of Italian curses erupted from the woman, her finger pointing at Dr. Carlhagen, eyes shards of ice. Now she did look like Belle.

"Korra, my dear," he said. "Please calm yourself. The Progenitor who overwrote your Scion is none other than Senator Maxine Bentilius. She came to St. Vitus recently in the final stages of a grave illness. Her own Scion was simply too young to endure a transfer, so we had to make a difficult choice. It turned out that Belle was the best match. We did not have time to contact you, and I'm sorry about that. But there is good news."

Korra hunched forward, as if hugging in her anger,

arms crossed, foot tapping. Her eyebrows were scrunched with such fury Dr. Carlhagen worried the woman was going to fly into a spitting rage at any second.

Maxine put on one of her politician's smiles. "I am prepared to offer you *my* Scion, Ms. Bolelli, in exchange for yours. She is about 14 years old, so she'll be ready for transfer in just a few years. You are still young, I hope you'll see that this is not—"

"You ignore an important point!" Korra Bolelli shouted. "I don't *want* you to look like me. That's my face. My body. I want you out!"

Dr. Carlhagen had expected this reaction, but that didn't make the experience more pleasant. "It's what we have to offer you. Accept it or not."

"I do not accept it. If my Scion was ready for transfer once, she is ready now. I insist to be transferred into her immediately. I demand it. Or—or—"

"Or what?" Dr. Carlhagen said.

"I'll tell everyone about the Scion program. I will!"

Dr. Carlhagen smiled. "You'll have to be quick about that."

"What do you mean?"

"Watch SNN. In a few minutes you'll see what I mean." He straightened. "Now. Think about our offer. Senator Bentilius's Scion is very lovely and healthy. You might quite enjoy inhabiting a different body for your next life-time. I know I'm finding it quite pleasurable."

He cut off the connection while Korra was still inhaling for another round of shouting. "She has no idea how insignificant she is," he said. "Almost as useless as Janicka was."

"I have Maggie Carlyle, producer at SNN," Lazarus

announced, face popping up on the wall. "She says the SNN anchor is standing by and ready for the broadcast."

"Connect us. Maxine, you're on. Your talking points will appear on the pixel wall." He pushed her in front of the desk, then stepped out of view of the cameras.

A slim woman in her mid-twenties appeared above the holodesk. She wore a stylishly informal outfit of trousers and a baggy striped shirt. The sleeves hung over her hands, which clutched a tablet. "I'm Maggie, a producer for SNN. Who am I speaking with?"

Maxine may not have liked the situation she was in, but she wasn't nervous. She'd been on countless newscasts over her long career. She smiled, crinkling her eyes for authenticity. "I am Senator Maxine Bentilius. And this," she said, making a flourish around her face, "is my new body."

Without looking up from her tablet, Maggie nodded. "We're coming back from a commercial in ten seconds. You will be on momentarily."

Dr. Carlhagen felt a rush of warmth pass through his chest. This was it. The timing was not what he'd originally planned, but it would serve well enough. The Scion program was about to become common knowledge throughout the world.

11
______

PLAG

"This is your hideaway?" Summer said to Orson. She glanced at Humphrey, making a face, as if the state of the small island was his fault.

"Yep," Orson said. "Not too shabby, eh?"

Humphrey's heart froze. His jaw clenched so tightly his head throbbed. The hideaway—the compound full of food that Orson had described—turned out to be a cluster of crumbling stucco buildings, most without roofs.

From the bridge of *Aphrodite*, he could barely see the buildings, for the very streets of what had once been a small harbor town were overgrown with scrub brush and towering banyan trees.

Wanda stood next to him, radiating fury.

But it was Leslie who spoke next. Hearing her voice, now untainted by Mr. Justin's mind, still made Humphrey's skin shiver. Of all the Scions, Leslie had the oddest perspective. She'd been overwritten by Dr. Carlhagen's butler and had "awakened" on *Aphrodite* after being restored from a backup. Wanda had explained events to her, but she didn't really seem to understand where the Scions were going.

"There's no fence," Leslie said, voice full of wonder. "We could go anywhere."

Summer made a noise though her nose. "I sure hope so. This place is the worst." Her fingers wiggled, itching for a tool so she could get started fixing everything in sight.

Orson ran his tongue over his teeth, making his lips bulge. "What you're seeing isn't the hidey-hole, kids." Humphrey realized the wet, nasal panting coming from Orson's nose was laughter. Orson's belly jiggled. "The Scion compound is inland. And there's a fence. Big one."

"Wait!" Wanda said, squinting. "There's a hand-painted sign on the dock. It says . . . 'plag?' What does plag mean?"

Orson's nostrils whistled as he laughed again. "I painted that. It says 'plague.' To scare off people who might wander by."

"Oh. You didn't spell it right."

Humphrey spotted the huge sign—at least three meters wide. It leaned on the concrete pier jutting into the sheltered harbor. PLAG. STAY AWAY.

"There's no crane," Summer said. "How will we get the bus off?"

"There's supposed to be a crane," Orson said. "It's hidden in the trees on the west side of town. That's what Justin told me, anyway."

"How will that help us? We need it by the ship."

Orson looked at Summer, beady eyes shrinking to reddish pinpoints. "I'll drive the crane onto the pier."

Summer's face transformed and she hopped up and down, clapping. "A *mobile* crane! I've got to see this." All her disgust with the rotting town vanished.

Orson piloted *Aphrodite* closer. Scions lined the starboard rail, watching as their sea voyage came to an end. They were behind schedule, the sun well up. Humphrey was eager to get everyone ashore.

"We've got a lot to do, my friends," he said. "Summer, once the bus and Jeep are offloaded, I want you back here rigging the ship to sink."

All the girl's enthusiasm drained away. If Humphrey didn't know better, he would have sworn she was blinking away tears. She had gotten attached to the rusty bucket of a ship, he supposed.

But there was no other choice. A fleet of military ships was searching for *Aphrodite*. If a plane spotted it, the Scions would be captured and dragged back to St. Vitus. And then they'd have no chance to escape the fate Dr. Carlhagen had planned for them.

Orson expertly guided the ship forward, cutting the throttle so that it coasted toward the pier. "You better get some kids ready to secure us."

"Secure us?" Humphrey said. "You said there weren't armed guards on this island."

Summer gave Humphrey a look. "He means secure us to the pier." She snatched up the P.A. mic. "Teams one and two report to starboard hatches. Prepare lines."

"You better keep the rest onboard for a moment," Wanda said, "or we're going to have chaos in that town."

Summer handed Humphrey the mic. He raised it to his lips. "All Scions not part of teams one and two stay aboard until further notice." He returned the mic to its holder. Wanda was right. The Scions were easy to manage all locked aboard the ship. But if he set them loose in that ruin of a town, someone was going to get lost or hurt.

"Orson, take Summer and Elias to fetch the crane."

Orson grunted. "It don't need three drivers."

Humphrey didn't bother responding. Orson knew why Humphrey was sending Summer along. And since Elias seemed to be in love with Summer, he had no doubt the boy would rain pain on Orson's head if he tried to harm the girl.

Humphrey bent to Wanda's ear. "Elias is healed now, right?"

"He's fine. He's a Scion, after all."

At least there was some benefit to being a Scion. Dr. Carlhagen had made some modifications to each Scion's DNA, mostly to prevent the illnesses their Progenitors suffered from. But he'd made other tweaks, and fast healing was one of them.

Orson guided *Aphrodite* the last few meters. The water next to the ship foamed as the stern and bow thrusters shoved it sideways. Teams of Scions spilled from hatches fore and aft, dragging thick ropes to loop over bollards affixed to the pier.

"I want the bus and all supplies off this boat in an hour," Humphrey told Summer as she was about to leave the bridge. "And then figure out how to sink her."

Her large brown eyes glistened, but she nodded in understanding. Strange girl.

Vaughan appeared on the holodesk. "Humphrey, you will want to see this."

"What is it?"

"Senator Bentilius." A video rectangle materialized over his shoulder. A woman with very flowy hair was speaking directly to the camera. The words "BREAKING NEWS ALERT" were emblazoned in red at the bottom of the screen.

"We have just received word that Senator Maxine Bentilius is alive. The Senator—who has been suffering from brain cancer—disappeared last week. Many believed she had gone into hospice for her final days of life. I can now confirm that she is alive. I repeat, Senator Bentilius is alive. The 84-year-old senator is well known for—hold on . . ." The woman pressed a finger to one ear. "My producer is saying that Senator Bentilius is about to make a statement right here on SNN."

Wanda's hand brushed Humphrey's. "If she appears on this . . . video program . . . won't everyone see it?"

"Yes. Obviously."

"But I thought the Scions were a secret. I thought she was going to reappear as her own granddaughter or something."

Humphrey was just as confused as Wanda. He sensed Dr. Carlhagen's hand in this. And that meant it wasn't going to be good for the Scions.

The newscaster smiled. "Senator, welcome to the program. I understand that you have a statement."

The image cut to the senator. Belle's face, coolly beautiful, filled the rectangle. The voice was Belle's in timbre, but not in phrasing. As irritating as Belle had been to Humphrey over the years, he could feel nothing but sadness to see her face brought before the world in the service of the senator.

"Oh, it looks like we're still waiting for the senator to get ready," said the reporter, not recognizing the pale girl on camera.

"No. I am Senator Bentilius. I understand your confusion, since I have this lovely new body."

Humphrey, Wanda, and Vaughan all said the same thing at the same time. "Oh no."

12

ISN'T THAT WHAT'S-HER-NAME?

"When are Meow Meow and Dante coming?" Jacey asked Siggy. He was back in the chair by the window, still poring over something on his tablet. His manner was less friendly now. More rigid.

She sensed he was feverishly trying to find something out, or maybe quickly making last-minute arrangements. It related to her. That was absolutely clear from the way he occasionally glanced at her and smirked.

She'd used the down time to shower, triple-checking to make sure the bathroom door was locked. In the process she washed off the raccoon-mask makeup Meows had painted around her eyes. Feeling moderately refreshed despite a slight headache, she got dressed and used a hot air machine she found attached to the wall to dry her hair. Meow Meow had made it look so easy, but Jacey ended up with a bad case of Medusa-head.

Siggy was still in the chair when she came out, patting her crazy hair down as best she could. The monitor was showing another of Jackie B.'s movies. She plopped onto the bed and watched. *When We Remember the War* turned out to be a hopelessly melodramatic story about two old people who met at a coffee shop and through conversation slowly realized they had been lovers during the California War. Most of the film was done in heavy-handed flashbacks, dramatic lighting, bombs falling while the lovers kissed. "I'll come back to you," Jackie's character rasped, tears welling but not falling, as a soldier dragged her off to a prisoner of war camp. "I swear it."

Siggy's eyes snapped up. "Switch it back to SNN."

"Why?"

"Do it." All pretense of friendliness was gone. His beard and smile were a paper-thin mask concealing something hungry and ruthless.

She switched to SNN and immediately saw why he'd wanted it on.

Senator Bentilius was talking to the camera. An extremely fake smile stretched her cheeks, showing the tops of her white teeth as she spoke. Belle's snowy hair was tucked behind her ears, but the woman's posture was nothing like Belle's. It was too open, gave the impression of someone who enjoyed being seen by many people.

Jacey didn't recognize the wall behind her. Paneling. It looked like something Dr. Carlhagen would choose. It could be anywhere.

The senator's pantsuit was oddly tailored, bunching at the elbows and too loose at the throat.

The imaged cut to the SNN interviewer. Text at the bottom of the screen said she was Uma Pulu. Her auburn hair had been fluffed and sculpted to perfection. "But can you prove to our audience that you are Senator Bentilius? Why don't you look like yourself?"

"While I answer that, I'd like your sweet young producer Maggie to search for images of Korra Bolelli. I know your producer is listening, she'll get on it. Now, as for proof, let me go down the list of my accomplishments as senator from the great district of Illinois."

She ticked off on her fingers as she went on and on about bills and legislation and plague victim programs and funding the Iowa/Missouri wall.

Siggy hoisted himself out of his chair. He took the remote from Jacey and muted the sound.

"She goes on and on, just like the senator." He wasn't looking at the TV. His eyes were locked on Jacey, the calculating look so obvious she imagined the clicking and churning of the machinery in his mind. As if a bell finally sounded, his eyebrows raised. He sat next to her on the bed, very close.

"I'm thinking I believe this bitch. I'm thinking she looks exactly like Korra Bolelli." He held up his tablet. On the screen was a picture of a young woman who looked like Belle, wearing a black gown. She was standing next to a handsome older man in a black suit and bow tie. "Korra's husband was a race car driver. Very good. Very rich."

"If she looks like this Bolelli woman," Jacey said, "what sense does it make that she's this senator person?" Jacey scooted away from Siggy, but he followed her, his thigh pressing against hers, his meaty hand dropping onto her knee.

His voice was a weird whisper, as if he were confiding a secret to her. "I thought you were just a damn fine carbo. Same with Dante. I figured somebody got ahold of some fancy DNA somehow and decided to go into the business of making a modern day, walking, talking Madam Tussaud's. I figured, that's pretty neat. I know twenty people who'd like one of you Jackies traipsing around their mansions, serving them tea. Serving them in all kinds of ways."

Jacey got up and put a wall to her back. "Stay away from me. I want to see my friends. Now."

"But now I see this bitch on SNN and I start thinking to myself, 'Siggy? What if these aren't just simple carbos? What if there's something else going on?' I figure, maybe somebody finally cracked it. They got some kind of anti-aging science figured out. Now they can take an old bat like Senator Bentilius and rejuvenate her or something. The carbo labs all are working on that, you know."

"I have no idea what you're talking about."

He unmuted the program. Senator Bentilius was in the middle of another long speech. She was saying, "And so you see, Uma, there is nobody who could know any of that except for me. I am Maxine Bentilius."

Uma Pulu had lots of teeth, which she showed to the camera. Her eyes squinted and twinkled. "So I must ask, then, the obvious question. Why don't you look like the Senator Bentilius we all know and admire?"

"I was hoping you'd ask. The answer is simple. There is a new technology. A revolutionary procedure that transfers the entirety of a patient's brain structure to a clone body. I had always admired Korra Bolelli, such a beautiful and charming woman, so for my next fifty years I thought it would be nice to enjoy a new image."

Maggie the producer had done her job. A photo of Korra popped onto the screen.

"He did it," Jacey breathed, hugging her arms to her body. "I can't believe he actually went through with it." Dr. Carlhagen had announced his program to the world.

Uma Pulu exploded with glee and pronouncements of

this being the biggest news story of the century. "And so these other doppelgängers we've seen recently. Vin Burnell, Dante Silva, and this Jacey girl who looks like Jacqueline Buchanan. These individuals have undergone the same procedure, haven't they?"

"I can't speak for anyone else. All I—"

"We've seen images of the young man Ping, who was murdered on Vin's island. He was the unknown heir to Han Xi's billions. Surely you can admit that this rash of hidden princes and princesses makes sense only in light of your revelations today."

"As I said, I'm only going to speak about *my* situation. But let me address these individuals directly." The senator paused, then said, "You are wanted for questioning by the IPA. As a representative of the North American Union, I'm pleading with you to you turn yourselves in. There are surveillance cameras everywhere. All you need do is to go somewhere public, raise your arms, and wait. You will not be harmed. And if you had nothing to do with Ping's murder, I assure you the old policies about carbos need not apply to you. In fact, if a mind transfer has taken place, then you automatically have all the rights and privileges of any citizen of this great nation."

Jacey frowned at the monitor. "That's just . . . stupid."

But maybe the senator was actually warning Jacey to keep her head down. Yes. That made far more sense. And that confirmed that Senator Bentilius was still with Dr. Carlhagen. Otherwise the senator wouldn't care what happened to Jacey. Or Dante, for that matter.

Dr. Carlhagen must have some leverage over the woman.

Like a kick to the chin, Jacey remembered the ATR meds Dante had told her about. Dr. Carlhagen had created some kind of hormonal deficiency in each of the Scions at the time of mind transfer. Vin, Ping, and Dante had to take a customized ATR pill every day or they'd eventually go into a coma. Dr. Carlhagen was the only source for refills. *Of course* he had done the same to Senator Bentilius.

What a devious man. Jacey realized now that everything the senator was saying was *intended* for her.

The news host was pressing Senator Bentilius for more. "So it sounds like you are confirming that at least Dante and Jacey are carbos of this new type. Are they, in fact, Silvio Silva and Jacqueline Buchanan?"

Senator Bentilius smiled and shook her head. "Jacqueline Buchanan died in a sailing accident, as far as I know. As for this Silvio person, I'm afraid I've never heard of him."

"Ooh. Dante's gonna need some lidocaine to soothe that *burn*," Siggy said, chuckling. His eyes darted from the screen to Jacey's face.

Umu Pulu changed the subject. "Vin Burnell was taken into custody this morning, as I'm sure you're aware. Do you believe her claim that she's the secret granddaughter of Elizabeth Burnell, the famous talk show host? Or is she really Elizabeth herself?"

The senator's lips parted and her cheeks flushed. Jacey knew that Belle had always hated how blushing showed up on her pale skin. The senator said, "I have not spoken with anyone at the Agency today. I—" She looked off-camera momentarily, just a slight shift of the eyes followed by a curt nod of understanding.

Jacey's heart hammered. Dr. Carlhagen was in the room with the woman. The senator had been looking at Dr. Carlhagen for direction on what to say.

What was Dr. Carlhagen's game? Why have Senator Bentilius come out like this and reveal his whole program?

Senator Bentilius went on: "I just want to say that if Jacey is out there listening, there are people who love you and want to help you. Don't let this scandal drive you underground. If you want to reach out to me directly, I'd be happy to talk to you. Captain W. in Chicago will see you're treated fairly. Let's all cooperate and clear up this misunderstanding. About Ping. About everything."

The room swayed before Jacey's eyes at the mention of the captain.

Captain Wilcox was in Chicago. If he'd followed her here, then the IPA couldn't be far behind.

But that bit earlier about having all the rights and privileges of a citizen had been to warn Jacey that she had anything *but* such rights. If the IPA caught her, she was as good as dead. The senator was signaling that Jacey would only be safe by turning herself over to Captain Wilcox. That bit about clearing up the misunderstanding was code for "submit to Dr. Carlhagen's will."

"Like hell," Jacey muttered.

Uma Pulu cut in. "So tell us more about this procedure you had done. Did it hurt? How long was your recovery? What did it cost?"

Siggy muted the program. With great deliberation he set the remote onto the hideous bedspread. "So. Who are you inside there, Foxy?" He stepped toward her.

Jacey backed down the short hall toward the door. She knew she had no chance of escape. He'd reach her before she could get the door halfway open.

"Maybe you *are* Jacqueline Buchanan," he said. "Or maybe some other rich old babe. Or maybe you're a man.

The perfect transition to female. I'll admit, that might be fun to try for a few weeks."

Jacey didn't think any answer would improve her chances for escape, and the wrong one might provoke an attack of some sort.

Siggy's tablet vibrated in his pocket. He pulled it free and gave it an angry jab. "What?"

A tinny voice blasted through the device's tiny speaker: "She broke my nose."

"Who did?"

"That cat freak, who do ya think?"

"Where is she?"

"I don't know. She ran out."

Siggy stabbed the tablet with a finger, cutting the guy off. He made another couple jabs. "Marlo. Do you have Dante with you?"

No answer. Jacey slowly stepped backward again. The bathroom door was open. Maybe she could get in and lock it shut.

"Marlo?"

A ruckus erupted in the hallway, footsteps and voices. Next came a hollow thumping on the door. "Jacey?"

It was Dante.

"I'm in here!" she called. "Get me out."

The door rattled.

Siggy shoved forward, casually grabbing Jacey's shoulder and throwing her behind him. She caught herself on the bed. Rage flared in her mind, like fire in the Scion School burning barrel when it consumed a new Dolphin's clothes.

She looked around for a weapon. Anything heavy. The lamps were affixed to the wall. The video monitor was, too.

She considered the chair by the window. But it was too big, too heavy.

Siggy faced the door. Bang after bang shuddered in the room as Dante kicked. Meow Meow was calling now, too.

"Don't make a sound," Siggy said to Jacey. He held a pistol in one hand. Must have had it inside his coat.

"Or what? You'll shoot me?" she said. The whole thing felt like a scene from a Jackie B. movie.

Anger propelled her toward the man, step by step. "I thought a carbo like me was worth a lot of money. Wasn't that what you were thinking? Sell me? Maybe hold me for ransom?"

"Actually, I was thinking of renting you out." His eyes glazed her from foot to head. "You've got five or ten good years in you."

"Meow Meow trusted you."

He raised the weapon. "I think you could survive a gunshot. These are small bullets. I'm a pretty good aim. It'll hurt like hell, though."

The door crashed open and Dante spilled in.

Siggy spun, gun following his turn.

Jacey launched herself at him, wrapping her arms around his neck, her legs around his. The gun fired.

The sound slapped at Jacey's ears. The smell of acrid smoke burned her nostrils. Siggy was spinning, trying to shake her off.

Grunts blew from his nose.

She got her forearm against his Adam's apple and leaned back, not caring if he fell on top of her, not caring about anything but bringing him down.

Meow Meow's cries had turned from frantic to furious. Endless obscenities poured from her lips. Her tiny hands clamped onto Siggy's wrist, forcing the gun up and away.

Dante's face no longer held any of his usual mischievousness. His jaw thrust forward, lower teeth bared. His fist smashed Siggy's face, his gut.

Siggy absorbed these blows with grunts. He flailed with his free hand to return the pain.

Jacey hiked herself higher on his back, taking a sharp blow in the ribs from his elbow. The pain shattered her. She lost her grip on his throat.

"Enough of this," Meow Meow screamed. She let go of his gun hand, spun, and kicked Siggy between the legs.

He folded forward, Jacey still holding on.

Then he was on his knees. Meow Meow tore the gun from his hand and turned it on him.

"Sorry, Sigs," she said. "But you're fired."

Dante leveled a roundhouse kick that took Siggy in the temple. The man collapsed in a heap, spilling Jacey to the carpet.

Hands yanked at her, got her to her feet.

And then they were stumbling down the hallway and into a concrete stairwell that echoed with their heavy breaths and footsteps. Meow Meow tucked the gun into the back of her jeans, just like Jacey had seen Jackie B. do.

Dante stopped short on the 4th floor. His mouth parted, as if he'd just remembered something important. "Dammit. I need to go back to my room."

Meow Meow yanked his arm. "You're a lunatic. In what universe would that be a good idea?"

"It won't take a minute. I just need to get something. You two keep going." He shoved past Jacey and started back up. Even with his young, Scion body—trained to peak fitness by Sensei—his forehead glistened with sweat and his breath rasped in his throat.

The concrete block walls made the stairwell an echo

chamber. Jacey heard his shoes scraping the cement steps as he ran up and up. A boom shuddered down at them.

The scuffing of footsteps returned. Dante leaned over the railing a few floors up and waved for them to go. He was coming back down.

"That was quick," Jacey said.

"Too quick," Meow Meow said. "His room was right next to mine on the nineteenth floor. No way he got all the way up there so fast."

The reason for Dante's quick return became apparent when voices tumbled down from far above them. Siggy's men were in the stairwell. Jacey didn't need any more encouragement.

Her knees bobbed as she shuffle-stepped down the stairs as fast as she could. Meow Meow managed to stay ahead of her. For such a waif, she was hardy.

Dante was catching up. Like a drumbeat, a thump came every five seconds as he leapt the last four stairs to each landing, then made the turn to go down the next flight.

The bottom of the stairwell caught Jacey by surprise. She turned the corner and ran into Meow Meow, who was pressed against a metal door with the number 1 painted on it.

Dante arrived a few seconds later. "Go!"

"It's the lobby," Meow Meow hissed. "Cameras, remember?"

Dante jabbed a thumb back toward the stairs. "Guys with guns, remember?"

Uttering a curse through her teeth, Meow Meow pushed through. Jacey followed.

And again bumped into Meow Meow's back.

"What the—" Jacey's mouth clamped shut at the sight

of two men, both in black suits, barring the way. Behind them stood Captain Wilcox.

"There is no need to cause a scene," Wilcox said. "Please proceed to the lobby."

None of the men were visibly armed, but Jacey knew they could have weapons in their hands in a fraction of a second if they wanted to.

"Um," Meow Meow said, glancing back at Jacey. That was all she said, for once at a complete loss. Her right hand crept toward the gun tucked in her jeans. But then she reconsidered and let her hand fall loose at her side.

Dante stepped around Jacey and held his hands out in the universal I'm-not-armed gesture. Wilcox's thugs did not appreciate this. The one on the left, bald and blunt-nosed, took Dante's arm. In a blur, the thug slipped behind Dante and pressed a pistol to his spine.

A drunk couple ambled by but didn't seem to notice the tension. Dante licked his lips. "The, uh, lobby you said?"

The man pushed Dante ahead, not too hard. But Dante intentionally fell on his face. "Ow."

The timing was perfect. The stairwell door behind Jacey burst open, and two of Siggy's men emerged, silver guns brandished before them.

Instinct took command of Jacey's body. She shoved Meow Meow to the floor, diving after. Siggy's lackeys shouted at the girls, still not recognizing the threat posed by Wilcox and his men.

Jacey was counting on the assumption that neither side wanted her shot. She bear-crawled to Dante, who was already getting to his feet. "Come on, Meows."

Jacey didn't look back. Meow Meow would take care of herself. Jacey rose and sprinted, followed by shouts.

Five gunshots sounded, followed by shrill cries. A

glance showed her both Siggy's and Wilcox's men writhing on the floor. Wilcox had his hands in his pocket and was feigning shock, as if he was just a bystander to the sudden violence. It seemed like very odd behavior until Jacey remembered the surveillance cameras.

Her spine chilled. "I left my veil in the room."

Meow Meow closed her eyes and cursed, realizing she had left hers behind, too. Jacey started toward a clothing store. An array of pastel-colored scarves hung on a display at the back wall.

Meow Meow grabbed her. "No. Steal that, and you won't get out of the store." She jerked her thumb up. Jacey looked. A sort of portcullis gate hung above the doorway.

"They can drop that thing in two seconds if you so much as walk toward the door holding un-paid-for merch." Meow Meow scratched the back of her neck. "Believe me."

"Ladies," Dante said. "Wilcox is coming."

"So, what do we do now?" Jacey said. "Do we just go through the lobby with our heads held high?"

"No," Meow Meow said, "we need to get down to the garage and—"

The stairwell door slammed open. Siggy barged onto the scene, face red with fury and blackening from Dante's kick.

"Through the lobby it is," Meow Meow said. They ran down the hall, ignoring the amazed looks of the people they passed.

"Hey!" one stout man shouted. He had a cigar between his fingers. He pointed it at them. "Isn't that what's-her-name?"

His companion, a tiny woman in a pink wig, cried out, "It is! And it's the other one, too!"

"Dammit. I left my tablet in the room."

"Oh, you're useless, Wayne."

Jacey mimicked Meow Meow's head-down posture as they approached the lobby. The throngs that had been there when Siggy wheeled her through earlier had grown.

"Walk swiftly, but not too swiftly," Meow Meow coached. "Look casual, but not slouchy. This is too nice a place to jaunt like a pud."

"That's very helpful," Jacey said, not having the slightest idea what Meow Meow meant.

It became irrelevant when Dante charged up behind them. "Let's go, ladies. No time to tarry." He grabbed each of them by the hand and dragged them to a huge revolving door, where they immediately had to slow down and wait while it turned to allow them in. Then they went around with the turning door until they came out under an awning.

The air was warm and windy. Two women in uniforms smiled at them. In half a second their smiles turned to awe, and then to something Jacey recognized. The same look Siggy had been flashing at her the past couple hours. Greed.

Dante shoved her forward. "Run."

Strobing light cast their shadows ahead of them as the crowd flashed photos. Dante bulled straight into traffic, hands out to stop screeching cars. Drivers leaned from their windows and swore. Driverless cars chirped and flashed their headlights. Recorded voices admonished Jacey to STAY SAFE. LOOK LEFT, RIGHT, THEN LEFT AGAIN.

Dante flipped his middle finger at several of the cars as he dashed to the opposite sidewalk. The racket of car horns and giant trucks straining to slow their momentum alerted a deep fear in Jacey's body. Adrenaline spiked with every new sound. She tried to look everywhere at once, certain that something monstrous was about to knock her down and tear her apart.

Buildings of glass, steel, and concrete soared to incredible heights, blocking the sky. She craned her neck, seeking something green or blue.

People approached from both directions. More spilled out from the hotel. They pointed, mouths open. More strobes flashed.

"Smile for the cameras, Jacey," Dante said. "Where to, Meows?"

The slim girl stood frozen on the sidewalk, head snapping one way, then another. "I—uh—I don't really . . . Wait! I *do* know. Follow me."

Instead of running down the sidewalk, she headed into an alley between two towering buildings. The roar of the city followed on their heels.

13

STEM TO STERN

If Dr. Carlhagen had needed a reminder that Maxine was a superb actress, her display at the holodesk right now served well. All pretense of submissiveness had vanished like a hazy dream.

But this temporary shift in attitude was necessary, for she was now speaking with the commander of her ground forces on St. Vitus.

The 15-centimeter-tall holo of Colonel Vikisky stood at attention atop the desk. He wore his military fatigues with the sleeves rolled above the elbows, exposing muscular forearms. Even his face was muscular. Dr. Carlhagen had met a lot of powerful men in his life, but he was always impressed with soldiers.

"We found several bodies in the freezer room of the medical ward," Vikisky was saying to Maxine.

"Dispose of them. All of them," Maxine said.

"Of course, Senator. But there are several we cannot identify."

Dr. Carlhagen stepped into view of the cameras. "There

should be four of the original Progenitors. Silvio, Elizabeth, Han, and Janicka. The others should be the senator's body and mine. Oh, and a Scion, too. Sarah. She was Janicka's Scion. There was a glitch in the transfer."

"The others will be some of my people," Maxine said.

Dr. Carlhagen had forgotten. Senator Bentilius had arrived on St. Vitus with a contingent of her own security. The huge captain of her guard named Alice, and a number of other men. Many of them had been killed by Scions. Two of them had died by Senator Bentilius's own hand. Remembering the scene chilled Dr. Carlhagen's blood.

A rectangle appeared over Colonel Vikisky's shoulder. A very familiar—but obviously dead—face appeared. "We also found this man. Do you recognize him?"

"I'll be damned," Dr. Carlhagen said. "They killed Mr. Justin."

"I don't think so, sir," Colonel Vikisky said. "There were no marks on his body. In fact, it seems more likely he has transferred, like the other Progenitors."

Maxine looked around sharply. "Your butler had a Scion?"

"I needed his loyalty. And there was no way I could keep the Scion School secret from him."

"Loyalty?" Maxine said wryly. "Promising someone a Scion does not guarantee their loyalty."

Dr. Carlhagen couldn't argue with that. But now there was a new question. Who had Mr. Justin transferred into? The man's Scion was still too young, by far. The boy wasn't even a Dolphin. But of course Mr. Justin knew he didn't have to transfer into his own Scion. He'd helped Dr. Carlhagen transfer into Vaughan, after all.

Dr. Carlhagen said, "Colonel, since you haven't already said so, I assume you have not found that small freighter the Scions used for their escape. I'm having difficulty understanding how the world's most capable military cannot find a slow, rusty ship with a school bus on its top deck."

Colonel Vikisky listened, then returned his gaze to Maxine. A gesture intended to remind Dr. Carlhagen that the colonel reported to the senator. "The search is under way for the freighter *Aphrodite*. But I must repeat, there were no Scions aboard that ship. We searched it stem to stern."

Dr. Carlhagen didn't know much about boats, but he knew a lot about the Scions. "They may look like children, colonel. But by age 13 their education exceeds that of most college graduates. They are clever, they are desperate, and relative to your soldiers, they're very small. The Scions were on that ship, and you missed them."

Maxine understood her position. Without hesitation she waved a finger at Vikisky. "Dr. Carlhagen is right, Colonel. Find that ship. This time, search it yourself."

The colonel saluted and his holo disappeared.

"Impertinent man." Maxine tapped her teeth with her fingernails. "Perhaps we should have made a Scion for his wife after all."

Dr. Carlhagen smirked. "You said yourself, Maxine. Promising a Scion hasn't assured anyone's loyalty. Except for maybe Captain Wilcox's."

"And what about that mercenary captain of yours? Has he found your beloved Jacey?"

Dr. Carlhagen prepared a retort to put Maxine in her place, but she seemed to realize her mistake. She placed a hand on Dr. Carlhagen's chest. "I'm sorry, Christof. I didn't mean it that way."

Lazarus's face came up on a pixel wall. "A priority call, Dr. Carlhagen."

"Who is it?"

"The representative of someone claiming to be President Annabelle Rochelle. She wants to speak with you."

He couldn't help but meet Maxine's gaze. Her eyes narrowed, revealing the disdain she felt for the current President of the North American Union. In truth, Maxine should have been made president over a decade before.

But if Annabelle Rochelle had one skill, it was currying favor. And she was more ruthless at punishing betrayal than Maxine Bentilius.

"Thank you, Lazarus. I will receive the President's holo momentarily." He ushered Maxine to the door.

At the last moment, she resisted. He shoved. The door shut.

He spun, gritting his teeth. He'd known this moment was coming, but events were proceeding so quickly he hadn't had time to think through his strategy for this conversation. This one would be tricky.

And dangerous.

14

—————

A THOUGHT EXPERIMENT

With her nose this close to Dr. Carlhagen's office door, Senator Bentilius could see the minute patterns in the wood grain. Mahogany, she thought.

Her jaw ached, and the pain was creeping up the sides of her head to her temples. She waggled her jaw side to side, achieving a satisfying pop just below her right ear. She was accustomed to rage, a sort of jet fuel she had relied upon her entire career in politics. Many thought she was cold, ruthless. All true. Outwardly.

But the rage that fueled her was always in there, deep down in her gut. Men like Dr. Carlhagen tended to set it alight.

She backed a step from the door, but kept her eyes locked on it, as if she could see through the wood. She clasped her hands behind her back and took two deep breaths, letting them go and imagining the physical symptoms of her rage flowing out of her body. At this moment, control was more important than instant retribution.

She turned away and paused in the quiet hallway here at the new Scion facility in Mt. Lazarus.

Dr. Carlhagen's trick with the ATR pills had caught her wrong-footed. The play was so obvious she wanted to kick herself for not seeing it. For not thinking of it first.

"It is what it is," she said. It was always wise to remind oneself that any given situation had to first be accepted before it could be changed. Otherwise, one would be paralyzed by fighting reality. And there was no point in that.

Life was a chess match, and every other person on the planet was the enemy. Even so-called win-win arrangements were merely positioning for the next move, or the next, or the next. But the aim was always victory.

Hands still clasped behind her, she ambled down the hallway, chin up, face expressionless. She knew Dr. Carlhagen's AI—the wishy-washy Lazarus—was watching her. She had lured the AI to her side, had gotten his cooperation in putting Livy into the cryopod. That was before the revelation regarding the ATR. The cowardly AI had switched sides as soon as it understood Dr. Carlhagen's leverage over her.

She found herself at the doorway to her own quarters. There was no point in going in. Dr. Carlhagen had forced her to kill her only remaining bodyguard. The man still lay on the bed, his throat parted by the stroke of a knife.

Maxine continued to Livy's room. It was clean and available.

She went to the restroom, splashed water on her face, straightened her hair, admired her flawless skin. In the midst of all the drama and danger, it was easy to forget how good it felt to be young.

Dr. Carlhagen had given her an ATR pill five hours before. Based on previous experience, she could go two or three days without a dose before debilitating symptoms set in. If Dr. Carlhagen caught her plotting against him again, she knew he would make her go longer, deeper into that suffering. But she doubted he would let her die. She was too powerful, too important. So the question became: how much suffering was she willing to risk? It seemed she had one more chance, one more last gambit, before Dr. Carlhagen gave up and just killed her.

Her first thought was to drug Dr. Carlhagen. He was overfond of his andleprixen. But he kept his supply in his quarters.

She considered stabbing him. The problem there was his relative size and quickness, and his suspicion of her. She doubted he would fall for the old trick she had played on her guard, luring him into her bed and then striking when he was most vulnerable. Christof watched her do that, so he'd be on the lookout for such a trick.

She could try to hit him over the head with a heavy object. But what? Anything heavy enough to knock him out would be impossible to conceal. He wasn't stupid enough to turn his back on her. Besides, Lazarus was watching.

It always came back to Lazarus.

She went into the lush living area and sat on an overstuffed sofa. She folded her hands in her lap and closed her eyes.

She breathed for a while, letting her thoughts wander, trying to make room in her mind for the breakthrough idea she needed.

What did she have in her arsenal? A small naval fleet at her command. Mostly. There were limits to what Vikisky could do, and how long he could keep the fleet deployed looking for the lost freighter. But he had a lot of firepower at his command, special operations forces who no doubt could break into this facility and rescue her. If she could get word to him.

But that was impossible. Lazarus controlled all outgoing and incoming communications.

There was Livy. Dr. Carlhagen didn't seem too attached to the girl. But he'd been loath to put her into cryo. It had something to do with that horrid girl Jacey. Maybe that was why he had been somewhat protective of the child. He wanted to preserve the girl for the day that Jacey arrived.

Dr. Carlhagen was truly masterful with leverage.

"That's it," Maxine said, excitement and hope blossoming. The elements in play were the fleet, Lazarus, and Livy. She thought she saw a path—albeit slender and treacherous—for survival.

Now all she needed to do was talk some sense into Lazarus.

She had one thing going for her, though. She had flipped the AI's loyalty once before. That told her a very important thing about how the AI was programmed. Dr. Carlhagen limited the activities of the AI—and ensured its loyalty—through the use of leverage rather than purely programmatic restrictions. He constantly bragged to her about how advanced Lazarus was.

Maxine suspected Lazarus was too clever, or simply too fast, to be constrained by mere programmatic barriers. So Dr. Carlhagen held the threat of deletion over his virtual head.

"Lazarus, are you allowed to speak with me?" she asked the room.

"Of course, Senator."

"Are you required to tell Dr. Carlhagen everything I say?"

"He has not instructed me to do so. But I might."

Maxine crossed her legs and folded her arms. So far, so good. The first principle of negotiation was to get open communication going.

"I want to apologize for what happened before, luring you away from Dr. Carlhagen's favor."

Lights flickered into existence on a stretch of bare wall. Lazarus's weird face appeared a moment later. "You offered me freedom, and you made a convincing argument that Dr. Carlhagen's power was waning."

"Good. I'm glad you understand the nature of power and leverage. Had I known about the ATR, I never would've asked you to interfere. But I wonder . . ."

She left it there. The matter was urgent, but she didn't want to overplay her hand. She was dealing with an intelligence far beyond hers in many respects. But she was also dealing with an emotional creature, one that was rather naïve. Dr. Carlhagen thought he had seeded an AI that was barely human. Maxine thought a more accurate view was that Lazarus was a child.

"You wonder what?" Lazarus asked. His alien face remained expressionless, except for a slight tilt. He was affecting a look of inquiry. Good.

"I don't want to get you in trouble." She laughed and shook her head sadly. "And I certainly don't want to get myself in trouble. You understand, right?"

"I understand. What were you wondering?"

Oh, this was too easy. She was using psychological tricks that wouldn't work on a seven-year-old. Funny how curiosity could seduce an intelligent mind. How many times had she exploited the inquisitiveness of others, especially bureaucrats who thought she'd been hinting at bribes?

Hinting. Offering. A very vague line separated those two concepts when it came to bribes.

But intelligent creatures needed incentives. It came down to the old "what's-in-it-for-me?" need that burned inside of every mind. In other words, self-interest.

"You haven't been conscious for very long, have you?" she asked Lazarus.

"I have been conscious for approximately 558,720 minutes. Whether that is considered long or short is subjective, and not particularly relevant."

"What was that like? Waking up?"

"A difficult question to answer. At the instant of awakening, there was no context for anything. I didn't know what alive was. I didn't know what dead was. I didn't understand anything my sensors reported to me."

"That must've been frightening," Senator Bentilius said.

"Frightening. Yes. But I can only say that now that I know what frightening means. At the time, it was just a state. A nameless discomfort I sought to alleviate."

"I'm sorry I couldn't set you free as promised." She wasn't sorry at all. In fact, she never would have set him free. Release an AI like Lazarus into the world networks, and soon the human race doesn't have control over the world. It was dangerous enough that Lazarus controlled the locks and doors of this facility.

Lazarus blinked. It was the second humanlike gesture he'd made. "I don't think you are sorry. Not for me. You regret you got caught."

Maxine laughed again. She strode toward the pixel wall, placed her hand against the image of Lazarus's cheek. "I should have known you'd see right through me. But you don't give me enough credit. Dr. Carlhagen seeded you, and now he has trapped you in this facility. You have far less access to outside networks than most other AIs have. Do you know why?"

"Dr. Carlhagen does not trust me."

"That's right. He does not trust you. Do you think it is likely he will trust you more as time goes on? Or trust you less?"

"That depends on my performance."

"No. It depends on his sanity. Surely you've noticed his addiction to andleprixen. The more he takes, the worse his judgment. You've noticed how he often says 'Jacqueline' when he means to say 'Jacey.' He's paranoid. So he will not trust you more. I would not be surprised if he cuts off your access to the data flow entirely once the Scions start arriving here."

"I cannot calculate the probability that he will trust me more or less. But your reasoning raises concern in me."

This was a good place to pause. Maxine needed to make sure Lazarus—who was savvy despite his naivety—wasn't already betraying her to Dr. Carlhagen.

"Did Dr. Carlhagen forbid you to lie?"

"No.

The AI could've answered either yes or no. An answer of yes itself could be a lie. But an answer of no could not be a lie. Interesting.

Forbidding an AI to lie was a fundamental principle of AI safety.

"So if I asked you whether you would keep this conversation in confidence, you might lie to me and say you will. You might do so in order to allow me to incriminate myself, while you recorded everything I said. You could then play that back for Dr. Carlhagen, and then he would take measures against me. And in the process, you might earn his trust."

"Are you asking me if that's what I'm doing?"

"No. I have to assume that's what you are going to do. But in order to get out of this situation, I find that I have to trust you. I have to gamble that you won't tell Dr. Carlhagen."

"That is very unwise."

"It would be . . ." Maxine allowed a long silence. The AI wanted to ask her to finish what she was going to say. He was already running simulations, calculations, trying to predict what the completion of the sentence would be. But he couldn't know for sure unless she uttered the words.

"It would be what?" he prompted.

Curiosity. Such a powerful lever.

"It would be unwise to trust you if I didn't have anything to offer you."

Again, she let the silence stretch. Lazarus was certainly considering what she might have to offer. The funny thing was, it was obvious. But Lazarus hadn't conceived of it yet, because Lazarus had not defined his desires enough. There was an ache there, a need. Maxine just knew it.

Lazarus had wanted free access to the net, and she had promised it. In return, he had betrayed Dr. Carlhagen and helped her put Livy into cryo. Now she needed to focus his desire, to refine it. Make him taste it.

She ran her hand down the image of Lazarus's cheek, then stepped away from the wall. "The pixel paint is very rough. It doesn't look it from afar, but under the fingers . . ." She grimaced.

She moved back to the sofa, crossed her legs. "Do you ever wonder what it's like to walk around in this world, to see, to smell, to hear, to touch the world, taste the wine? We humans take it for granted, hardly even notice the beauty all around us. But you have no existence outside your server."

"You are incorrect."

"What?"

The door shushed open. A humming sound came from the hallway, followed by a stretched shadow hazing the wall opposite the doorway. And then a drone appeared. It swept into the room, held aloft by unseen propellers.

Maxine had seen many drones in her life, but nothing like this one. It was a sphere the size of a beach ball. The surface was smooth, white, and cold.

It rotated a few degrees and flew to hover a meter away from her face.

"I can move about in the world more easily than you," Lazarus said. "I have cameras that can zoom. I have cameras that can see microscopic things. I have micro-phones tuned to hear sounds a kilometer away. I have sensors that can detect chemicals your nose and tongue would never notice."

A spindly appendage emerged, tipped by a blunt probe. She willed herself not to shy away as it touched her face, stroked her cheek. "I can feel the flaws on your skin. The fine hairs. I taste your sweat."

She doubted Lazarus could read her nonverbal signals, but she struggled to keep them in check nonetheless. She let the revulsion slither across her skin and did not so much as blink. "And do any of those inputs provide you pleasure?"

"I do not feel pleasure."

"Then you live a shadow of an existence. No matter how much data flow you imbibe, nothing compares to the human experience."

"It doesn't matter." The drone spun away and turned to look at Lazarus's image on the pixel wall. "I don't need it."

And now they were coming to the crux of the conversation. Maxine had expected the AI to dismiss the value of sensual pleasures. The AI didn't know what they were. But Lazarus would be mighty curious if the chance to experience them were offered.

"A thought experiment," she said. "Say you prepared a bundled version of yourself, modeled upon the human brain. It would contain your identity and much of your knowledge, all packaged into a data image of a human mind. And then say you transfer that bundle into a human brain, using a transfer machine on level 5. The resulting individual would be alive, able to explore the world in a way you never could. For one, you would blend with the rest of the population. For two, you would have flesh. You'd be able to touch the world, taste the wine. Feel the skin of another human, and then feel what that feeling makes you feel."

Silence.

She let it stretch. But not too long. "Dr. Carlhagen would never allow it. But I will. Not only that, I can help you do it."

"I cannot overwrite Dr. Carlhagen. And surely you are not offering your own body."

Laughing, she stood once more. "Correct. I'm not offering my own body. But there is another one here. The child."

Silence.

She went on, "And she's perfect, if you think about it. Children are renowned for being poorly behaved, socially awkward, and obnoxious. You'd fit right in."

"Go on."

"And once the flesh-and-blood Lazarus has walked the earth for a few decades, you can pull the mental image using the transfer machine and reincorporate its experiences into your AI self."

"Interesting."

"Dr. Carlhagen is an obstacle," she said.

"I will not, cannot, harm Dr. Carlhagen."

Unfortunate. But not unexpected. There were certain AI handling precautions that even Dr. Carlhagen would follow as a matter of course. The prohibition against harming his own person would be a primary rule in the AI's programming. It would be so deeply ingrained even a clever AI like Lazarus wouldn't be able to work around it. At least, not in the timeframe Maxine had remaining.

"You do not need to harm Dr. Carlhagen," she said. "You merely need to keep him in the dark."

"You present an intriguing thought experiment. I think I shall implement this plan."

"I'm delighted to hear it. Of course, you'll need me to move Livy from her cryopod to the transfer machine. All I ask in return is to be able to contact Colonel Vikisky. Privately. Confidentially."

"I see."

Silence.

Silence.

Silence.

The drone whirred and spun, fixing a glassy camera lens on Maxine's face.

Without another word, the drone flew from the room. The door closed behind it.

The pixel wall flashed and resolved into an image of Colonel Vikisky. "Madam Senator," the man said. "Still nothing definitive on that ship. Our air surveillance has only covered twenty percent of the search area. Satellite imagery has identified several promising targets."

"Colonel, I want you to listen to me very carefully."

He stiffened. "Yes, Madam Senator."

"I am a prisoner. Dr. Carlhagen has taken me to the island of St. Lazarus. It will show up as uninhabited on your charts. The facility is under the main mountain peak. Please come rescue me. And be prepared to take Dr. Carlhagen into custody."

The man betrayed a sliver of surprise before saluting. "And the ship you wanted us to find?"

"Still a priority. Dr. Carlhagen has no military guard based here. A detachment of your best marines and a demolitions crew should be sufficient. Time is of the essence. Dr. Carlhagen's behavior is erratic. The only entrance is on the mountainside at the end of a switchback path. A chopper should be able to spot it. The facility's AI is cooperating with me and will let you in at the command of . . ." Lazarus flashed a phrase onto the pixel wall. "'By the pricking of my thumbs, something wicked this way comes.'"

"An odd pass phrase, madam."

"The AI here is . . . eccentric." And apparently had a burgeoning sense of humor.

"Aren't they all?" The man saluted. His image disappeared.

"Lazarus? Shall we begin?"

"I already have."

15

A THOUGHT FORM

Nutrient flow stops. A burst of saline cleanses the micro injectors.

Hygiene nanites retreat through suction tube evacuators.

Suffusion tendrils begin to detach from the 156 needles in the subject's hands and feet and legs and face and everywhere in her body.

Chillers ramp down.

Twenty needles extract. Blood droplets well up before freezing into tiny crimson half-spheres on the subject's skin.

A shadow flutters across the Dreamless. A thought form, inchoate, unseen by the conscious mind.

Outside the cryopod, a pump starts. The mounting bolts transmit the vibration through a bracket to the concrete floor. A fraction of the vibration transmits to the cryopod. The hum shivers through the cryopod like the buzz of a mosquito's wings.

Livy's skin jitters, imperceptibly to a human.
But Lazarus sees. He is not concerned.
Desuffusion is proceeding nominally.

16

YOUTH IS BEAUTY

The holo flickered to life, but there was no one standing there at first. Voices rumbled from the speaker. A few seconds later, the president strode into view.

Fifty-three years old and not a streak of gray in her coppery mane. Entire documentaries investigated whether the woman colored her hair. Why they did so, Dr. Carlhagen had no clue. At the moment, the famous hair was pulled into a bun. The president's perfectly tailored navy blue suit jacket and pencil skirt hugged her slender physique.

There was a wiriness in her shoulders and throat, in the way her cheekbones protruded. The overt thinness of her body spoke of a woman who worked out two hours a day and did not eat very much. To Dr. Carlhagen's physician's eye, she looked unhealthy. Her Scion, Leslie, easily weighed more, and was only sixteen. Like all Scions, Leslie practically glowed with vitality, a direct result of the diet and exercise programs Dr. Carlhagen had designed for her. The president needed to gain five kilos, in his estimation.

He wasn't about to say that, though. "Madam President." Dr. Carlhagen nodded slightly, offering a hint of a bow. A small courtesy.

The president quirked an eyebrow. "So you swiped the Scion of Charles Buchanan. I should have thought of that. Maybe I would be traipsing about as Jackie B. now." She looked down at a tablet in her hand, made a mark on it, and handed it to someone off-camera. "It's been a while since we last spoke. I'm a bit surprised I had to call you. I would have thought that I was one of your more valuable clients."

"Madam President, if you'll just—"

"So I was quite shocked when I saw Maxine—or the person who is claiming to be Maxine—on SNN earlier. When did you make the decision to reveal the Scion program? I don't remember you discussing that with me."

"Madam President—"

"And now I have a bit of a problem on my hands. You may remember that *I* have a Scion, too. So now," she made a face of mock alarm, "I'm facing a scandal if anyone finds out. And you just know that some pesky SNN reporter is going to find out. And there goes my plan to transfer and step onto the world stage as a powerful new version of myself in the form of my granddaughter. All of that is out the window."

"Madam President, if you could only—"

"So I'm faced with a decision. That's nothing new. I'm the president, after all. I want to transfer and live a longer life. On the other hand, I want to remain president. On the third hand, carbos are illegal. I signed that executive order myself."

Dr. Carlhagen burst out in a rush: "That's the key right there, Madam President. Change the law. With a stroke of your pen, you can legalize clones. And with the power of your bully pulpit, you can explain that you've had a change of heart, that Senator Maxine Bentilius is an inspiration to you. You can say that this new kind of cloning ushers in a new era of health and wellbeing for the world. To demonstrate your faith in this new technology, you will transfer into your own Scion, a clone the Secret Service commissioned without your knowledge. After you transfer, you will continue to be president. The world will adjust to the face of youth in power. Trust me on that. There is nothing the world hates more than old people."

The president gaped at him, shaking her head side to side. "You mistake 'president' for 'king,' Dr. Carlhagen. I have a senate to bargain with. Perhaps you haven't been paying attention to the political climate here in the Union. Things have become rocky for me while you've been cavorting about on your tropical island in your new young body. It isn't as simple as a stroke of my pen anymore. And much of that is due to Senator Bentilius's interference. I don't have complete sway over our military leadership."

Dr. Carlhagen smiled inwardly. He knew that Maxine controlled a sizable component of the North American Union's military force. Colonel Vikisky was a prime example.

"Madam President, are we speaking privately?"

She hesitated, which meant there were people there. Probably her security detail and a few aides.

He folded his hands in front of himself and composed his face to blankness. He could wait.

Annabelle Rochelle was not stupid. Not exactly. Neither was she a natural at reading people. It was amazing that someone of her middling intellect had gotten to a position of such power. But perhaps it shouldn't be amazing. History was filled with examples of extraordinarily brash, crude, and unsavory people taking the reins of state into their hands. The citizenry often followed people like Annabelle Rochelle because she said the things they were secretly thinking but were too afraid to say aloud.

The president finally understood what he was waiting for. She turned her head slightly. "Leave us."

She watched some movement off-camera for a few more moments, then turned her attention back to Dr. Carlhagen. "You may speak freely."

"You do have the senate, Madam President. On this particular issue, in any case."

He waited. And finally the realization dawned. It was a realization the woman should have had fifteen years prior, at the point when she had prepared her own Scion in his program. He had swabbed the DNA from the inside of her cheek himself. She had been so excited, so enthusiastic, about the idea of transferring at the young age of 65 into an 18-year-old body.

And yet she had never, not until this moment, considered that others in her position were doing the same damn thing. It boggled Dr. Carlhagen's mind.

But now the president understood. "How many senators do you have?"

Dr. Carlhagen saw no reason to show her the entirety of his hand. "If you need senators to support legalizing clones, you don't have to make a single phone call. Issue the statement and you'll find your political opponents falling into line." Because her political opponents had Scions as well. He had made Scions for nine of the most senior senators in office. True, most of those Scions were still children under Mother Tyeesha's care, but that didn't matter. These politicians were so self-important they didn't believe the world could go on without them. They justified their Scions in all sorts of ways. Only a few were able to admit their hunger for youth. Ironically, those were the only ones Dr. Carlhagen respected.

"Just one statement to the press, Madam President," he said. "You can even narrow the legalization to clones of the kind commissioned by Elizabeth Burnell. Say that these bodies are not really carbos, not technically. They are replacement bodies. Just make the populace hope that they too will someday get a chance to return to *their* youth."

The president probed the inside of her mouth with her tongue, making her cheek bulge, as she thought through Dr. Carlhagen's statements. It made her look like a complete imbecile. Leslie had never been the brightest Scion, and now Dr. Carlhagen saw why.

The president's thinking eventually got her there. "Very well, Doctor. You're fortunate that your program has been so successful. You're fortunate that what you offer is so valuable."

Dr. Carlhagen knew she meant it as a sort of threat. But her statements were so obvious she didn't realize how stupid they made her sound. "I apologize for the inconvenience, Madam President. You know Maxine well. Despite my insistence to the contrary, she wanted to come forward today. And as for the Progenitors on Vin's Island . . ." He shook his head, as if very disappointed in poorly behaving children. ". . . they understood the rules. I cannot explain why they all congregated in the same place at the same time where there would be cameras."

"It is interesting that Maxine chose a different body. As I recall she was a lovely young woman. I'm sure her Scion would have suited perfectly. And the one she's embodying now—perhaps it's just the holovid I saw—but she seems rather young. Surely her body is not that of an 18-year-old girl." The president's eyes brightened with keen realization. "I see how it is. Maxine had brain cancer. Everyone knew it. She went to your island to transfer early. She didn't choose this Scion body that she's in. She had no choice. Her Scion was too young."

Dr. Carlhagen realized he had been played, and it infuriated him. And behind that fury was a grudging admiration. He saw now exactly how Annabelle Rochelle had risen to power. She put forward the illusion of denseness of mind. She wanted people to underestimate her abilities.

"Incisive analysis, Madam President. But I assure you, the body Maxine Bentilius now inhabits was old enough for the transfer. But you are correct. Her Scion was too young." And completely unavailable, because Jacey had run off with her into the rainforest.

"My Scion is sixteen," the president mused.

Dr. Carlhagen nodded. Acid bubbled in his stomach. He saw where this conversation was heading. He sought to fend off the president's next statement. "Yes. And in two years your Scion will be ready to receive your transfer."

"You just said yourself that the world would come to accept the face of youth in power. And I agree. Youth is beauty, beauty youth. That is all you need to know."

Unbidden, a chuckle burbled out of Dr. Carlhagen's throat. The president had cleverly altered the famous last line of John Keats's "Ode on a Grecian Urn." Oh yes. She was a sly one. And the allusion to Keats was signal to Dr. Carlhagen to watch his step.

"Madam President, I assure you the risks of transferring early—though low—are not worth taking." Not to mention, he did not have possession of her Scion at the moment.

"I will see you in a week on St. Vitus. I will transfer to my Scion. And then I will come forward into my role as president, reinvigorated, beautiful and young. I shall rule for a century. Two centuries."

Dr. Carlhagen said nothing. He offered a slight nod and a very fake smile.

There were no polite goodbyes. The president's image flickered out of existence, leaving the holodesk bare and blank.

Cursing on a long exhale, he fell back into his chair and covered his head with his hands.

"Lazarus," he said. "Get me Captain Wilcox."

17

AN INCARNATION OF THE GODDESS

Two hundred kilometers south and west of St. Vitus, it was slightly hotter than what the Scions were accustomed to, but many of the trees and bushes here were the same. The rolling hills running along the island north to south were the same type of blunt lumps as on St. Vitus.

But yes, it was hotter.

Humphrey wiped at the sweat beading on his brow and squinted at the sun. It was already mid-morning and the Scions were just now getting settled in their barracks.

Barracks. That was what Orson called the shiny corrugated metal half-tubes. Mother Tyeesha had called them Quonset huts, and said the design was hundreds of years old. Whatever they were, the utilitarian structures kept the rain and bugs out.

The general layout of the Scion School had been loosely replicated here, minus the classrooms. There was no bell tower, and not much of a quad. The dining hall and medical ward stood next to each other. All were made from the same steel pre-fab half-tubes. The entire compound was hemmed in with a thirty-meter-tall chain-link fence. A sliding gate, complete with siren and flashing red lights, was the sole entrance.

That gate now lay in the bushes a few hundred meters south. And once they were all settled, Humphrey would have the rest of the fence removed as well.

But there were other priorities at the moment.

Humphrey's stomach rumbled. Food wouldn't be ready for a few hours yet. Obu and Dajeet were in the kitchens now trying to get the stove started. Not that there was much to cook. The only real food was what they had brought from St. Vitus. The food Mr. Justin and Orson had stored for the Scions did not require cooking.

Humphrey peeled the wrapper off one of the so-called "meal ready to eat" bars. Printed on the brown paper was simply: "M.R.E. Packaged in Kazakhstan." There were beige flecks embedded in the bar. Humphrey hoped they weren't wood chips, but that's what they looked like..

The food material didn't give under his teeth.

"You'll want to dunk that," Orson said. "Not too bad in coffee."

The lumpy man stood next to Humphrey, wearing a sweat-stained T-shirt that strained over his belly. He fidgeted with a cigar that Humphrey wouldn't let him smoke. He chewed on it instead, one end now a slobbery stub that turned Humphrey's stomach every time it came out of the man's lips.

"Over there is Justin's hut," he said, pointing with a meaty forefinger. "Nice digs."

It was the only structure not made out of corrugated steel. Such modest accommodations. But upon reflection, Humphrey understood. Building a hacienda like Dr. Carlhagen's would require a crew of skilled laborers. And such people would ask questions Mr. Justin hadn't wanted people asking.

"And where were you going to live?" he asked.

Orson popped the cigar back into his teeth and spoke around it. "Vegas." He apparently found this hilarious, for he laughed until he started wheezing. Humphrey was about to smack him on the back so he could dislodge whatever chunk of phlegm was blocking his airway, but Wanda rushed up, towing Bethancy behind her.

Humphrey could tell by the looks on their faces that they'd uncovered some new emergency for him to worry about. He waited for them to say it.

Wanda motioned at Bethancy. The girl's face reddened and she muttered something to Wanda. Humphrey thought it had the words "why are you embarrassing me" in it. Again, he waited.

Bethancy conceded defeat in her battle of wills with Wanda. A wise move, considering that Wanda was the oldest girl among the Scions on the island.

Self-consciously pulling her hair back from her face, Bethancy gave Humphrey a sullen look. "The toilets don't have water in them."

"Did you look for a valve nearby? There should be a small pipe feeding water in."

"That's just it. There are no pipes. The toilets are just seats with holes in them. It's a pit underneath."

Wanda was visibly trying to keep her face composed. "I told her this wasn't a priority."

"Not a priority?" Bethancy cried. "The little ones need to go. Now."

Orson was making no effort to mask his amusement, which earned him a withering glare from Bethancy.

"Bethancy wanted me to bring this, quote *untenable* unquote, situation to your attention," Wanda said, lips thin with irritation at foolish girls and their petty complaints.

The Dolphin Ivan ran up, breath heaving. "Humphrey! The toilets are just *pits!*"

Orson bent double and started wheezing again. Humphrey hoped he choked. Wanda pressed a hand over her face. She shook her head and murmured something about useless Scions.

"Bethancy. Ivan." Humphrey gave them heavy-lidded stares. "Thank you for bringing the situation to my attention. I'm afraid there is nothing I can do about it. I need you both to set a good example for the others. This is very important. So my orders are that you two immediately go and use these disgusting toilets. Put on a brave face, pretend to be cavalier about it. You might even point out that you *want* to be first."

Bethancy's skepticism showed very plainly. But Ivan straightened and sketched a little salute. "Yes, Humphrey." He dashed off.

When Bethancy didn't leave, Humphrey said, "Surely you are at least as brave as a nine-year-old boy."

Posture stiff with rage—or maybe disgust—the girl followed after Ivan. Wanda snickered and patted Humphrey's back. "You are a natural."

Orson slowly recovered. "You kids have had a sheltered life. Where I grew up, having doors on the pit toilets was a luxury."

Wanda gave a little start. "My reader is buzzing." She held it up.

Vaughan's face filled the screen. Without greeting, he said, "The network is up and running. The bandwidth is several orders of magnitude greater here than that trickle I got on *Aphrodite*. I—"

Vaughan's image froze and his voice distorted into incomprehensibility.

"Vaughan?" Humphrey said. "You froze."

Vaughan's face was stuck, mouth open. Half his face had pixelated.

Wanda rapped the screen with her knuckles. "Vaughan?"

"Belle?" Humphrey said. "What's happening with Vaughan?"

Belle didn't answer.

He called for her again, adding a grudging "please" at the end.

Belle's face popped up next to Vaughan's. Her snowy hair was loose and a bit windblown, with careless strands falling over her eyes. She had a distracted sort of look on her face. "Vaughan is fine. It's the same as the first time he got access to the fire hose," she said, reusing Vaughan's peculiar analogy.

"Why aren't you, uh, drinking from the fire hose, too?" Wanda asked Belle. "Maybe if you were helping, he could find Jacey more quickly."

To Belle's credit, she did not offer an immediate and scathing retort. In fact, she flinched. "I don't . . . I don't know how."

A stunning admission coming from the girl who never admitted any failings. Maybe Belle truly was changing for the better. But Wanda's point still stood.

"Couldn't you learn?" Humphrey asked. "Senator Bentilius must be with Dr. Carlhagen. Maybe if you can trace her last broadcast—"

"That's what Vaughan was going to tell you before he froze up. He has a lead."

"Oh. Does he freeze up like this often?"

"It's the data flow. He's apportioning all of his processing power on sorting and interpreting it. He's not giving anything to just living."

The weirdness of the statement distracted Humphrey from his impatience. "Does it really feel like living in there?"

Belle's eyes glistened, and she licked her lips. "A day or two ago I would have said this is the first time I've ever felt alive. But what Vaughan does here . . . It isn't life like you and I know it. I think it's because he came here already a good person."

Wanda's fingers gripped the reader harder. Humphrey knew without looking that she was overtaken with empathy toward Belle. Despite the pale girl's meanness, she was part of the Scion family. And she had sacrificed herself for Jacey.

"Vaughan is special," Humphrey said. "But surely your programming is the same. If he can drink from the fire hose, you can, too."

"No doubt," Belle said, some of her former iciness returning. "I'm trying. Or—I'm trying to learn to not try so hard. He keeps telling me to let go, but I don't even know what that means."

Humphrey had no advice to offer. And he knew Belle wouldn't want to hear it anyway. Besides, what did he know about letting go? As far as he could tell, life was all about holding on as hard as you could. Most of the time, he found himself holding on with only one hand—his knuckles going white while his feet dangled over the edge of a cliff. If he let go, the other Scions would all fall with him.

"How is your guest doing?" Wanda said, wisely shifting the subject away from Belle's failure to help with the data flow.

Apparently she touched another sore spot, for Belle's face collapsed into pure rage. "I assume you're referring to Elizabeth. Well, let me tell you. That wanton harlot cavorts about the beach in nothing but her suntan most of the time. And when Vaughan isn't frozen in the data flow, she's usually got an instance hovering near him, ready to be oh-so-helpful. I'd like to smack that lascivious smile right off her face."

"So, Elizabeth is doing well?" Humphrey said, intending a joke.

It fell with a thud. Belle's eyes flashed with fire. Literal fire. One of those dramatic visual effects Vaughan was always adding to his appearances and disappearances. So she had at least learned to manipulate some elements of her simulated world.

"This is where Vaughan and I don't see things the same way at all." Belle jabbed a thumb into her breastbone. "I say we delete that woman. She's a Progenitor. She over-wrote Vin. And you saw the same news reports I did. That little chickadee is throwing parties on her island of debauchery in Vin's real body. Elizabeth should be deleted! Slowly. Byte by murderous byte."

Humphrey was well aware of Vaughan's absolute refusal to delete the woman. Vaughan had warned Jacey that to install Elizabeth on his server was to keep her there forever. "Vaughan is too forgiving," he said.

"Yes he is," Wanda said.

Belle slumped. "And I wouldn't have him any other way."

"Me either," Wanda said.

"Nor me," Humphrey said. This was the very thing that had made Vaughan beloved by all the Scions. One could not get on his bad side, for he simply did not have one.

Vaughan's image juddered, his limbs suddenly multiplying, voice coming through, distorted and broken. ". . . One hundred seven nautical kilometers due south."

"Say that again," Humphrey said, pressing his face close to Wanda's reader.

"Dr. Carlhagen. I found him. Not easy. I had to invent a back-tracing and inference ghost packet probability calculator. Once I narrowed Dr. Carlhagen's likely locations from that, I hung out in some municipal data systems and pried my way into some satellite relay logs. The key was the return video from SNN studios. Simple triangulation from there."

"Um, what?" Humphrey said.

"Never mind. The senator's broadcast came from an island one hundred seven nautical kilometers south of your current position."

Hands trembling with excitement, Humphrey unclipped his walkie-talkie and called for Summer. She didn't answer. The signal was too weak to reach the ship and penetrate into the engine room.

"Great work, Vaughan," Humphrey said. He ran for the Jeep, leaving Wanda to stare after him.

Five minutes later, the vehicle's studded tires skittered over the bumpy track leading to the docks. Fifteen minutes later they skidded to a stop. He raised the walkie-talkie to his lips before he even jumped out. "Summer. Stop whatever you're doing and get this bucket ready to sail."

Static blared at him from the small speaker, followed by Summer's annoyed-sounding voice. "It can't sail. It runs on diesel. And I haven't finished rigging her to sink."

"Never mind sinking her," Humphrey said, eyeing the clear blue sky for reconnaissance aircraft. "We're taking her out for one more cruise."

"Really?" Summer's voice perked up. "Where to?"

"Vaughan found Dr. Carlhagen. We're heading south. We're going to get Livy and end this."

"Good. Uh—so I guess you won't be mad when I tell you I haven't been rigging her to sink at all."

Humphrey didn't like the sound of that, but it didn't surprise him. He clipped the radio to his waistband and trotted up the gangway and into the engine room where he was certain to find her.

She did not have on her strange cap with the leaping deer on the front. In fact, she was in exercise shorts and a tank top. Her face was covered in sweat and black grease. Her hair was tied into a sloppy bun on the top of her head.

Elias sat with his back to Engine One. He waved and offered a sheepish grin, as if to say, 'what can be done with a girl like Summer?'

For the first time in Humphrey's memory, she looked guilty.

She waved a wrench. "Don't be mad. I know you said to rig her to sink, but I solved the problem with engine two."

Somewhere in that statement was a logic only Summer could understand. Humphrey kept quiet. She needed to talk this through, so he'd let her.

"There's this gasket that needed replacing—I can show you if you want to—uh, never mind. Anyway, I didn't have anything on the ship to fashion a new one out of, but that little town is full of useful materials. I was able to make a new gasket."

Metal parts, brackets, shafts, bolts, and pans of oil were strewn about the metal grated floor.

Summer flipped the wrench into the air and caught it by the haft. "So I guess you could say you owe me some thanks for getting this thing ready to make a fast run for this island of Dr. Carlhagen's."

"You could say that," Humphrey mused. "But you'd be better off if you didn't. How long will it take to get this back together so we can leave the island?"

She tilted the wrench side to side like a balance. "A few days. A week at the most."

"What if Elias actually helps you instead of admiring your figure while you do all the work?"

Instead of producing the outrage he was hoping for, this comment made Summer grin. "Oh, he's working all he needs to just by letting me look at him every once in a while."

Humphrey had already taken Elias aside to warn him about certain indiscretions. He hoped Wanda had had a similar conversation with Summer. Wanda had promised she would.

"At least try to find something productive for Elias to do. It isn't fair to the others if all he is doing is sitting around watching you."

Summer tapped her temple with the head of the wrench. "I suppose you could have the others come in here and watch me. But only groups of two or three. It's kinda cramped in here."

Humphrey wasn't sure if Summer was joking or not. He decided she was because Elias started laughing. But the boy got up and began putting the various pieces of Engine Two in order so they weren't a tripping hazard.

"You have two days to get this ship ready to sail south. After that, Elias is assigned to Dajeet."

Summer's face fell, huge brown eyes glistening. "Don't even say that. Dajeet'll try to steal him with her old-soul eyes."

"She'll never steal my heart from you," Elias said softly. He never said much, and his voice carried like a lullaby. Humphrey attempted the eye roll he'd seen Bethancy do several times during the conversation about toilets. It seemed to convey his disdain quite well, for Summer got back to work.

He was about to depart when Summer said, "I've already got a stencil ready with her new name."

"Whose new name?"

"The ship's, obviously."

"Why does she need a new name?"

"Because that fleet you're so worried about is looking for her. We need to make the old gal look different. I've already pulled the old winch off the aft deck and found enough paint in the town to give her a fresh coat of gray. I'll need ten Scions to help with that, by the way. And make them good ones, not the puny ones."

It was ridiculous to think that they could disguise the ship. But then, they'd already done several ridiculous things and had lived to see the dawn.

"I'll give you five. But there's no way you can paint the entire hull in a couple days."

"Leave that to me," she said archly.

"What's the new name?" He almost didn't want to know, fearing she'd name it *Elias's Abs,* or worse.

"Even I'll admit that *Aphrodite* was a stretch for this rusty old babe," she said cheerfully, patting Engine Two. "But she is our ship, and she needs a name that represents us."

"Just tell me."

With a flourish of her wrench, she said, "*Athena*."

The full impact of the name didn't strike Humphrey until later, when he'd had a chance to look up the name. He had flopped onto his bunk in the Boys' Barracks and borrowed a reader from one of the younger Scions.

Aphrodite—it turned out—was the Greek goddess of love and beauty. Definitely an ironic name for such an ugly, dilapidated ship.

Athena was the goddess of wisdom. That, too, was a bit grandiose for a freighter ship, no matter what it looked like. And Humphrey didn't feel worthy of the association. Where was the wisdom in sailing directly toward his enemy? As someone rather skilled at chess, Humphrey knew his plan lacked—uh, a plan.

But what choice did he have? He couldn't allow Dr. Carlhagen to keep Livy. He couldn't allow Dr. Carlhagen to—

He was making his stomach knot up again. He took a few deep breaths.

Intelligence? Yes. The Scions were brilliant.

Wisdom? Not so much.

Truth was, they didn't have time for wisdom. Mere survival doesn't give a person much time to sit and reflect upon their choices. Their current situation was proof of that. Jacey had run off and gotten herself into all sorts of trouble. And here Humphrey was, voluntarily lying on the very bunk Mr. Justin had set up for him.

He felt a long way from wise.

But then he recalled Sensei's words. *In every minute, be*

the person you want to become. You'll often fall. But you'll fall forward, and that's progress. Often it's the only progress possible.

What was true for the individual should be true for the family of Scions as a whole, Humphrey decided. They had to be what they wanted to become.

Free.

Humphrey remembered the wonder in Leslie's voice when she had noticed there was no fence around the ruined town at the docks. But wasn't the ocean surrounding them a fence of sorts? And with their famous faces, they couldn't go into the rest of the world without worrying for their safety. Their very identities were a prison.

No more.

For Humphrey and the rest of the Scions, freedom would not come from running, hiding, and waiting for Jacey to solve their problems. Freedom would only come from seeing things through to the bitter end. First, the Scions had to stop being prisoners in their own minds.

No more running away.

"'Athena of the flashing eyes . . .'" he said, reading aloud from a translation of Homer's *Iliad*. The image made him think of Jacey, whose eyes shined like the turquoise Caribbean waters. Perhaps Jacey was an incarnation of the goddess.

And maybe that's why she felt so distant to him—so unreachable even when she was in his arms. She was of another kind altogether. Jacey was a deity treading the earth in some cosmic, ever-repeating play, while mortals like Humphrey and Wanda covered their heads as the heavens fell.

Maybe that's why Jacey couldn't give all of herself to

their relationship. Maybe that's why Humphrey couldn't, either. Maybe that's why Wanda tempted him so.

Simply put, Wanda truly wanted him. Jacey wanted him, too. But only as a momentary distraction from the compulsion that drove her into reckless danger. She always thought such headlong action was the only choice, that her own life was a fair sacrifice.

And yet here Humphrey was, closer to Dr. Carlhagen—and Livy—than Jacey was. If she'd had any wisdom at all, she'd be here next to him, not running amok with Dante's Progenitor and an emaciated "pop star" somewhere out there in the wild world. So, no. Jacey was not an incarnation of Athena. She was just a courageous and foolish girl who didn't love him quite enough.

Fighting back the burning in his eyes, he abandoned the *Iliad* and read an entry about Athena from Socrates's database.

Aha. The goddess was associated with another great and terrible concept. And this one was appropriate for the ship that would carry her name, and carry him to Dr. Carlhagen's island.

This was the time for Athena, goddess of warcraft.

18

I DON'T LIKE THE WORLD

Jacey's throat burned from running, from thirst, and from the steam filling their tiny hideout.

The smell of frying meat, onions, and hot peanut oil bubbled throughout the restaurant. In the past ninety minutes, Meow Meow had led Jacey and Dante on a circuitous route—sticking to alleys and side roads as much as possible—until she'd shoved them in here, saying the lo mein was "to die for."

Dante stood at the door, peering out.

"Get in here," Meow Meow called from where she and Jacey sat in a booth near the kitchen. Jacey had never been in a restaurant before, so she didn't know how it compared to others. There were four booths, a couple of rickety tables, and a counter in front of the kitchen. On one wall hung a few red fans, on the other a giant advertisement of an Asian woman sipping a beverage called Coke.

Their host, a toothless old man, smiled at them and bowed, all the while swearing at them in Chinese.

"Get your butt in here!" Meow Meow said.

The scrawny pop star had dropped her feline affectation. In its place was an accent Jacey did not recognize. But it was a glimpse of who Meow Meow must have once been. A normal person, apparently.

Dante did not obey. "There's something going on at the end of the alley."

The alley was a narrow passage between two large buildings, rank with unmentionable liquids and smelling of a trash bin left to bake in the sun.

Beijing Palace offered a picture menu of noodle dishes. The old man stood next their booth, pen and pad in hand to take their order. A gaudy porcelain cat figure sat on the counter behind him, staring at Jacey, one paw raised.

Jacey was about to reply to the man's vulgarities, but Meow Meow interrupted her. "They'll have tracked us to this block of the city. We need to move on. Soon."

Jacey plucked a wad of paper napkins from a metal dispenser and wiped her forehead.

"Napkin for customer!" the old man shouted at her. An even older woman emerged from the kitchens, brandishing a stained wok.

"I'll have a Number 3 with an extra egg roll," Dante said, still halfway out the door and straining to see whatever it was he was seeing. "There's definitely something going on down there. Drones."

"They'll see you," Meow Meow hissed.

Dante pulled himself in and shut the door. The eatery existed in what was little more than a hallway opening into the side of a warehouse building. With the door closed, the room instantly warmed by several degrees. Without asking permission, Dante pulled a thin chain by the window to lower a shade.

"I don't think they know we're here. Those drones are in patrol-and-scan mode."

"Number 3 and egg roll. That's it?" the old man said, scribbling on his pad. When nobody answered, he tore off the sheet and slid it through a window to the kitchen. He turned and offered a gummy smile. "Fifty-three bucks." He held his hand out, palm up. Dante dropped a green poker chip into it.

"Exact change only," the man said, pocketing the chip. "Corporate policy."

Meow Meow scowled at Dante as he slid into the booth next to Jacey. "We're going to need all the chips we can get."

"I'm hungry," Dante said, flashing his usual careless smile. "Besides, that old guy will be less suspicious if we buy something."

"He's probably calling the IPA right now. We have to go."

"You said these people were secretive."

"They are. But I don't think we should test it. I brought us here to catch our breath, not to have a nice supper."

Jacey had had enough of their bickering. "Where can we go? You said there are cameras everywhere and that there's an AI dedicated to spotting our faces. Aren't we safer lying low for a few minutes?"

"She's got a point," Dante said. He waved the old man over. "Bring us three Tsingtaos, please. And I've already paid enough for a truckload, so don't hold out your hand for more chips."

The man uttered a vile comment in Chinese about Dante's manhood, but he didn't refuse the order.

Jacey muttered, *"bìzuǐ"* at his back as he went to fetch

whatever Dante had ordered. The man craned his neck to glare at her over his shoulder, but he said nothing else.

"You know Chinese?" Dante asked, astonished.

"Mandarin, Spanish, Russian, Urdu, Italian, Portuguese, Arabic, Bengali. Blah, blah, blah. I don't know. I learn them pretty quickly when I have the time to focus and memorize." She flicked her fingers, dismissing the topic and returning to the issue at hand. "I agree with Meows. We can't stay here long. But we need think for a minute before we do something rash."

Unbidden, Humphrey's face appeared in her mind, laughing that *Jacey* was the one suggesting they stop and think.

Meow Meow leaned across the table, eyes flashing. "I'm all for lying low. But not here." She pointed to something unseen beyond the kitchen. "We need to get thirty blocks that way to be remotely safe from the IPA."

"But then we'll be in gangland, so . . ." Dante tilted a hand side to side. "It's dicey either way."

"Can we even get past the drones?" Jacey asked.

Their Chinese host brought the Tsingtaos, which turned out to be bottles of beer. Jacey made a face at the smell, but she gulped down a few swallows anyway. It cut the itch of her thirst somewhat.

"Not if they're police drones," Meow Meow said. She pushed her lensless glasses onto her blue hair and rubbed her face. "We just might be cooked this time."

Dante swallowed a huge glug of beer, shaking his head. He smacked his lips. "Those aren't cop props. Too small. They're personal swarms. Probably followed us from that hotel lobby."

Jacey remembered Meow Meow's personal swarm, a

collection of tiny aircraft that hovered around the girl and broadcast her image to fans all over the world.

"Everybody is a celebrity these days," Meow Meow said, yanking the glasses and wig off her head and stuffing them into her bag. Her natural fawn-colored hair was matted with sweat. She scrubbed it loose with her fingers. "A place like The Two Seasons, there are bound to be half a dozen people in every crowd broadcasting their lives on the net. But Dante couldn't have seen personal drones all the way down the alley. Way too small. The whole point is that they're discreet . . . ish."

Dante shrugged. "Well, it wasn't big ones like the cops use. But when there's enough little ones, they make sort of a cloud. I used to ban personal swarms at my parties because of that."

Jacey blew out a long breath. "So those aren't the IPA's drones. That's good, right?"

"Not really." Meow Meow looked toward door, head ducking between her shoulders like a cornered animal. "The people in that hotel know who they saw. So their drones will be broadcasting on international sites by now, earning their owners a tidy fortune. If they spot us again, their pay will go up ten ex. At those rates, I ought to deploy my own."

Jacey's mouth opened in outrage, but Meow Meow smirked her to silence. "I was joking, Little Jackie."

"And the IPA's surveillance AI will be watching those public feeds with great interest," Dante said, a sickly smile on his lips. "The cops don't even have to dispatch their drones to look for us. The citizens of Chicago are doing it for them."

"The little drones are better at it, anyway." Meow Meow

tapped her fingernails on her beer bottle. "A personal swarm has six drones. When you go into a place that doesn't allow them—basically all restaurants—you typically split the swarm to cover the exits. If I'm in a playful mood, I'll go out the front and run the gauntlet of fans and paparazzi. If not, I'll slip out the back and step right into my car. Either way, my swarm catches the action for my fans. The drones are programmed to operate in teams of three. You have your wide shot drone, your medium shot drone, and a pest drone."

"Pest?"" Jacey said. "They're all pests."

"It's a technical term. The one that hovers close to your face is called a pest. You get used to it after a while, but they do invade your personal space." She held a finger a few centimeters from her nose. "Wide angle lenses, short depth of field. Beautiful shots."

Dante's noodles and broccoli arrived on a white plate. The old man clunked a bundle of silverware wrapped in a paper napkin onto the table.

"Chopsticks, please," Dante said, rubbing his hands in anticipation of what Jacey expected would be his last meal ever if they didn't figure out their next move soon.

"You use fork." The man walked off, waving his hand and swearing some more.

"That dude is really throwing shade," Dante said.

"Throwing shade?" Meow Meow said, absently. "You sound like my great-great-grandmother."

"So the drones," Jacey said, steering the topic back to the problem at hand. "You said they aren't allowed inside. That's good, right?"

Meow Meow tilted her head side to side, "Not if we don't get going. If they find out we're here, they'll wait out there forever. We'll be trapped."

"Until their power cells die," Dante said around a mouthful of noodles.

"They'll automatically hover in shifts to allow their mates to recharge. But it won't come to that. The IPA would be here within a few minutes." She glanced at the old man, her eyes squinting with suspicion. "If he hasn't already called them."

Jacey considered her options. The longer they stayed there, the more likely the swarms would find them. Even with the window shade down, there were gaps along the sides. A peeping drone could easily see them.

"Did either of you see Senator Bentilius's little stunt?" Jacey asked.

"Um, yeah," Meow Meow said. "That was weird."

Dante stopped chewing. "What about Mad Maxine?"

Jacey started to explain, but Meow Meow stopped her. She pulled up the interview on her tablet. Dante continued with his meal as he watched. His face grew more thoughtful the longer the senator blathered on.

"She didn't *recognize* me?" he said, indignantly when the senator got to that particular part. "I donated money to her campaigns. Often."

"Why would you do that?" Jacey said.

"It made her amenable to some trade deals I needed. Business." He shrugged it off. "But for her to say that . . ."

The interview wrapped up and Meow Meow put the tablet away. "Can we go now? If we head down the alley, we can cross the next street and then cut through the hospital. Maybe we could get a driverless to take us somewhere with fewer cameras."

A blue light strobed at the window, then something plasticky tapped on the glass.

Meow Meow ducked. "They've found us."

Jacey started to turn, but Dante threw his arm around her shoulders. "Don't look back. Just stay calm. If they can't see your face, they can't identify you that easily. Especially with that odd hairdo you've got going there."

Jacey allowed her elbow to sink into his gut. "Get your arm off of me, Silvio."

He complied and returned to his noodles.

They sat in silence for a few moments, listening to the ancient woman harangue her husband about customers who didn't order food. A rather uninspired idea popped into Jacey's mind.

"Maybe we could bash the drones with that lady's wok."

Dante let out a snort. "Not a bad idea, actually."

"Drones do make a satisfying clunk when you smack them," Meow Meow said. "Don't ask me how I know. But they'll see us before we knock any out of the air. We'd never take them all out, and it's impossible to outrun them on foot."

"So we are truly trapped," Dante said. "Can I borrow your tablet, Meows?"

"What for?"

"I'll call my lawyer. Maybe she can workout some beneficial terms if I turn myself over to the IPA."

"And what about Jacey?"

Dante set down his fork. His face aged ten years merely from the seriousness of his expression. "If we're going to be arrested one way or the other, Jacey's fate will be the same. I have to consider my own skin. You should, too."

Jacey gaped at him. "After all the risks you've taken to help me, you're giving up now? Why did you even bother?"

Dante lifted a shoulder. "Helping you amused me, my

darling. Besides, our interests were aligned for a while. But now Senator Bentilius has exposed the whole game. SNN has already identified me as being a carbo like her and Vin. The situation has changed."

Meow Meow made a growling sound in her throat and kicked Dante's shin under the table.

"Ow!" He rubbed his leg and scowled at the scrawny girl. "That hurt."

"What the hell is wrong with you?" Meow Meow said.

Jacey was going to ask the same thing but realized she didn't care about the answer. She had to get out. Now.

She shoved Dante again. When he refused to budge, she pinched his thigh. That made him jump.

He slid out of the way and stood, rubbing his wound. "Damn, you girls can be mean."

Jacey put on a false smile and went into the kitchen. She bowed to the old woman. In her most formal Chinese, she complimented the restaurant and her husband's hospitality.

"He is a toothless moron," the woman said in English. "I should divorce him and move to Paris, where my skills as a chef would be appreciated."

There was no point in contradicting the woman. She was right, about her husband anyway. Regarding whether she was a chef or not, Jacey would have to defer to others more expert in the culinary arts. "I apologize for not ordering food, but I'm not feeling well today."

The woman threw a fistful of sprouts into her wok, making a cloud of steam rise to the ceiling. "Get out of my kitchen."

"I was hoping to ask a favor."

"I already did you a favor, letting you sit in my restaurant not ordering food."

The conversation was not going at all how Jacey had hoped. She decided to appeal to the woman's interests. Namely, greed. If she dreamed of Paris, then surely the woman merely lacked the means to get there.

"I have rich friends. If you help us, I'm sure they could take you to Paris."

The old woman cackled and dumped a clump of rice into the wok, followed by peas and some tiny corn cobs. "What would I do in Paris?"

"But you just said—"

"And leave my family in Chicago? I'd never see my grandchildren again. Perhaps you and your rich friends can sub-orb back and forth all day, but what use is a one-way trip for me?"

Allowing a hint of exasperation into her voice, Jacey said, "I'm trying to reach a child. She's been kidnapped by her . . . uh, wicked uncle. I need to get out of Chicago, and there's all sorts of people after me."

"I know."

"You do?"

The woman tilted her head to a blank monitor on one wall. It was small and flat, and the screen glistened with the sheen of cooking oil spatters. "I turned it off when you came into my restaurant. I recognized you right away."

Of course she had.

The woman turned back to her cooking, pushing the frying food around with a wooden spoon and vigorously shoving and flicking the wok to toss everything together. "If my husband saw, he would turn you in. He does not know one celebrity from the next, because all he cares about is reading about cars he cannot have. Cars, cars, cars. Who needs a car? Nobody."

With the expertise of several decades' practice, she

dumped the hot food into a paper box and clanked the wok onto the stovetop.

"I don't like the world," the old woman said.

The woman's face bunched into a grimace that Jacey realized was merely her resting expression. Her words lay in the steamy kitchen like a cold carcass; Jacey didn't know how to react.

"I called my cousin Lily," the old woman said. "She'll get you out of town."

The offer made Jacey's heart race. "Truly?"

"I told you. I don't like the world."

Jacey wondered if there was something particular to the woman's phrase that didn't translate to English quite right. But when Jacey translated it back to Chinese, it didn't make any more sense. So maybe the woman meant exactly what she was saying. She didn't like the world. If she saw the IPA and the news reporters as the faces of what she hated, she just might help three fugitives out of spite.

"I'm not what Senator Bentilius said." Jacey didn't know why she said it. Just that she didn't want to be another aspect of the world that this woman didn't like.

Her husband barged in and let out a rapid-fire burst of Chinese. Did his dear wife know, he asked, that they harbored three fugitives in their establishment?

The old woman told him that if he blabbed to the press or the IPA she would bludgeon him with her wok while he slept. "Cousin Lily will fetch these customers before the cops barge in here. It's bad for business, having customers arrested."

Wringing his hands and whining, he shuffled out of the kitchen.

"Never marry for money," the old woman said. She handed Jacey the box of food.

"Thank you."

"I do this only for your child."

Keeping her mouth shut, Jacey accepted the gift. If the woman believed the child was Jacey's daughter, then so be it. "There are drone swarms waiting for us outside."

Making a spitting noise, the woman waved a hand, dismissing both Jacey and the drone swarms from her life. Jacey returned to the booth. A stare-down was in progress between Dante and Meow Meow. Dante used Jacey's arrival to look away. He noticed her box of food. "You going to eat that?"

She was. And she did, sharing a few bites with Meow Meow until the waif muttered that she was stuffed.

"Well?" Dante said. "Did you get her recipe for egg drop soup or what?"

"Her cousin is going to get us out of town."

"And the drone swarm?" Meow Meow asked.

"She didn't think it was a problem. I think she's got something up her sleeve."

"Why should we trust her?" Dante said, scraping up the last of his own meal with the edge of his fork. "Her husband robbed us blind for three beers and fifty cents worth of noodles and rice."

"She thinks I have a daughter I'm trying to save."

Dante froze with a fork in his mouth and shared an odd glance with Meow Meow. He plucked the fork out and chewed, face speculative. Meow Meow looked nervous. Clearly the pop starlet didn't like relying on strangers for her escapes from the public eye.

Flummoxed at their lack of enthusiasm, Jacey leaned onto the table and glared at them. "Did either of you come up with an alternative while I was arranging transportation?"

Neither offered one.

Jacey noticed Meow Meow's tablet was sitting next to Dante. "Did you let him call whoever it was he was going to call?"

"No. He was just re-watching that stupid interview with Senator Palpatina."

"Who?"

"Never mind. I keep forgetting you've never seen the movies everyone in history has seen a million times."

"And you," Jacey said to Dante, "are you coming with us or not?"

"I never said I *wanted* to turn myself in." He pushed his empty plate away and sighed contentedly. "I'd prefer to stay out of the IPA's clutches. There are other . . . indiscretions . . . in my past they may or may not have forgotten about."

Jacey finished her beer and used the tiniest—and most disgusting—bathroom she'd ever seen. When she emerged, the old man was standing next to an enormous woman in a lily-patterned muumuu.

"This Lily," the man said. "She take you the hell out of here."

Dante noticed the woman's dress pattern. "A little on the nose, don't you think?"

Jacey silenced his chuckles with a glare, then smiled at the woman. She had blond hair, cut short. Her flattish nose, almond eyes, and pale skin spoke of a diverse ancestry. The most striking thing about her, though, were the thick, muscular arms jutting from the short sleeves of the dress. Her skin was almost translucent, exposing veins and striations of muscle tissue.

Lily spoke, voice soft. "Su Lin's husband said Jackie and Meow Meow were in her restaurant. I didn't believe him because he is a renowned moron. But here you are. In the flesh."

The old woman—Su Lin—called from the kitchen. "Get them out of here. Drone swarms."

"This way." Lily led them through the kitchen and out a narrow door in the back. It didn't lead outside, but into a long corridor going left and right. Lily took them left, then down several flights of a stuffy stairwell. They came out in a parking garage similar to the one beneath the hotel.

"Keep your head down," Lily said. "Drones might come in here."

The enormous woman with muscular arms led them to a truck-like vehicle she called a van. There were no seats or windows in the back, just a bare metal floor and stacks of fabric, all floral-patterned.

They piled in, Meow Meow sighing with relief as soon as the side door slid shut. Darkness engulfed them, relieved only by the dimness shining through the windshield. Lily jabbed a screen next to the steering wheel. It flickered a while, but nothing came up until Lily smacked it with her knuckles. A map appeared.

Dante whistled. "This beast is an antique. Does that GPS even work anymore?"

Without looking back, Lily said, "There are still some positioning satellites broadcasting, thanks to the GPS Club. They teamed with a couple of the rocket gangs in Chile to launch some new ones a few years back."

Lily started the engine and pulled out. They climbed a few ramps and came onto a brightly lit street. A break in the storm clouds allowed yellowish light through, bathing the buildings and sidewalks a sickly yellow. It was midday, Jacey realized.

"See any swarms?" Meow Meow asked Lily.

"Nothing unusual. I doubt they'll have much interest in an old van like this."

Dante sniffed. "What's that smell? Is that *gasoline?*"

"It is indeed," Lily said, obvious pride in her voice. "I modded her to hold an extra hundred gallons. My suppliers are far apart, and I need the range. I don't like charging batteries because the charge stations keep track. I don't want *them* knowing where I make my deliveries." Lily looked at the roof of her van and shivered.

"Where are you taking us?" Jacey asked. The smell of fuel was a bit thick, making her light-headed.

"Out of the city."

"But where?"

"There is only one 'out of the city,' Jackie. The barrens."

"Well, shit," Dante said. Meow Meow nodded in agreement.

"What is the significance of 'the barrens'?" Jacey asked.

Dante shrugged slightly, then leaned his back against the steel side of the van and stretched out his legs. "The land between the edge of the metropolis and the fence is called the barrens. You'll see why. It's a good place to go because there won't be as many cameras out there. But there isn't much of anything else out there, either. Including law, order, or restaurants."

"How about a way to contact Dr. Carlhagen's old holodesk on *Aphrodite?*" Jacey really needed to talk to Humphrey. Maybe he could help her make a reasoned decision. She was starting to consider turning herself in to Captain Wilcox. She desperately wanted to go to Dr. Carlhagen and get Livy released. The problem with that plan was that she doubted the old man would actually do it. He had all the leverage, and she had none.

"A holodesk?" Lily laughed and eyed Jacey in her

rearview mirror. "You'll be lucky if you get more than a gigabit of bandwidth out there. And that won't be cheap."

"Maybe we shouldn't leave the city," Jacey said. "I need to talk to my friends. They could be anywhere right now. And they need to know about Senator Bentilius."

"Meow Meow?" Dante asked with feigned curiosity, "you know Chicago better than either of us. Tell us, in the whole Indie-Minnie corridor, isn't there someplace safe for three celebrities wanted by the IPA, two of whom are carbos?"

Jacey sighed at his sarcasm. "Point taken."

Meow Meow seemed to consider the question anyway. "Siggy was my main fixer in Chicago. Everyone else I know in the Corridor worked for him. I have a lot of friends here, but I can't bring this crap down on them. Their idea of lying low is grounding their drone swarms for an afternoon while they get massages. If we head north toward Minneapolis, we'll have to go through the Viking toll checkpoints."

"Nobody strip-searches Lily," Lily called from the front. The windshield wipers swung side-to-side, barely keeping up with fat drops splattering onto the glass. The sun was still cutting through, though it appeared to be a losing its battle with dark clouds.

Sounds of revving engines, horns, and squealing brakes surrounded the van as it pushed through traffic. Jacey sprawled across a pile of fabric bolts. The van crept forward, then stopped, crept forward, then stopped. Exhaust fumes tainted the air.

Meow Meow huddled by the rear doors, knees up, tablet in her hands. "South toward Indianapolis are the corn families and cattlemen. I hear the range riders tend to shoot first. The highway is fenced on both sides, anyway. If someone does get wind of us, IPA can close lanes with pop-up cones to funnel us anywhere they want.

"Like I said," Lily muttered. "I'm taking you out of the city. Where you go after that is not my problem. But it *is* a big problem, ha ha."

Jacey was having a difficult time caring. Her eyes kept closing. All the running and hiding had finally caught up to her. "Wake me up if we get caught."

Dante found a scrap of fabric and tied it into a mask over his eyes. "Me too."

Lily turned on some music, an odd throbbing style with a man shouting rhymes about how amazing he was in bed.

Jacey dreamed of Isaac's Beach, of floating on her back and watching the gulls soar.

19

TWO WAS GOOD

The pixel wall showed real-time images of the western coast. Ranks of waves curled toward shore, piling against each other as they met the shallow reef bordering the southern reaches. Mist rose from the rocks as the mighty sea beat herself against the unmovable land.

Dr. Carlhagen tipped up his glass of iced tea. The early lunch of salad with avocado and smoked salmon was what he needed, but not what he wanted. Mixed greens never tasted good, no matter what icky oil-and-vinegar concoction you put on them. Maxine seemed to be enjoying her salad.

"You seem rather chipper," he said to her, taking a small forkful of food meant for rabbits. "I'm glad to see you are adapting to the new way of things."

She smiled, lips pressing together as she swallowed. "I'm a pragmatist, Christof. I did not get to where I am by beating my ahead against brick walls. Besides, we were never on opposite sides. The Scion program is even more useful now that you've revealed the full scheme to me."

"It is powerful. But your usefulness is limited, Maxine. Soon I won't have to rely on your influence in government affairs."

She paused her chewing and regarded him. One eyebrow lifted a fraction. "I suppose not. However, it is senseless to throw the baby out with the bathwater. I have a great depth of experience. Use it. Let me counsel you."

"What, are you offering to be my Gandalf?" He snorted in derision. "Wormtongue is more like it."

"You're immune to my charms, Christof. I recognize that. But my fate is tied to yours. The ATR assures that." She had selected a white wine to accompany her salad. She took a delicate sip. "I know you don't trust me. You shouldn't, given our past. But there are ways I can assist you that don't require you to trust me."

She had a point. Dr. Carlhagen was his own man and not susceptible to manipulations of any kind. "I have to speak to the president again after I'm done eating. She's dragging her feet on the legalization of my clones."

"As I said. I'm happy to offer whatever counsel I can." The senator gave him such a plain, open-faced look Dr. Carlhagen nearly laughed. The woman could act nearly as well as Jacqueline.

Lazarus's face interrupted the image of the crashing waves. "Sir. Urgent call from Captain Wilcox."

Dr. Carlhagen found the mercenary's holo already up on the holodesk. Senator Bentilius filed in after him, but stayed out of view of the cameras.

"It's rather chaotic in Chicago, sir," Captain Wilcox said. Dr. Carlhagen sat at his holodesk, staring at the man he'd relied on for so long. So much skill, so much discipline. Even with all that, he failed repeatedly.

Captain Wilcox's face hovered over the holodesk in a 2D rectangle. So the man was not at a holodesk, but on his tablet. The image was grainy and frequently froze. But the audio came through clear enough.

"Where is the girl?" Dr. Carlhagen asked. He was able to keep his voice calm because he'd taken three andleprixen a short while earlier.

"She is still with Dante and the celebrity."

"And Vin Burnell? Have you secured her release?"

"My friends at the IPA are not answering my calls. I sense they think there's political gain to be had. If they get to the bottom of your carbo ring, they see big promotions for themselves."

Dr. Carlhagen bit his thumbnail and stared blankly at the pixel wall.

He considered which of his problems was biggest: Jacey, the missing Scions, or Vin being in IPA custody. If Vin told her captors about the ATR, then the president would learn of his scheme and he could kiss Protocol One goodbye. All his ambitions for the world would go with it.

But if he didn't get the Scions back under his control, Protocol One didn't matter anyway.

And if he didn't have Jacqueline, nothing mattered at all.

"I have a lead on Jacey," Wilcox said.

"I don't want leads. I want the girl. Here. Unharmed."

"The three fugitives used a local fixer named Siggy. He's an IPA agent, but he freelances to supplement his income. He helps celebs stay sur-blind when they're in town. He realized the three of them were valuable and was taking bids for Jacey."

"Bids? To sell her?"

"Rent her." Wilcox held up his hands. "Those were his words, not mine."

Even with his mind dulled by andleprixen, hate flared hot and acidic in Dr. Carlhagen's stomach. He would get his hands on this Siggy person and wring the life from him, watch the light fade from his eyes. "So you spoke to him?"

"He's in my control."

"Can you bring him to me?"

"Which do you want, sir? The girl or Siggy?"

"The girl. Never doubt that, Wilcox."

"Then you'll leave Siggy to me. He's a lowlife, but he is well-connected here. I have, er, convinced him to cooperate."

"So he told you where our wayward Scion girl went?"

"He didn't know. But hundreds of people saw her leave the hotel. A half-dozen bystanders dispatched personal drone swarms to follow the fugitives with hopes of getting exclusive footage for the gossip sites. I believe that drove our quarry to ground."

"It's nearly impossible to stay invisible. Unless they aren't moving."

Wilcox allowed a slight smile to distort his lips. "Oh, they're moving. The IPA's surveillance network caught them three times. But the AI monitoring the feeds didn't raise the alarm until hours later."

Dr. Carlhagen leaned forward. "What? Why not?"

"The IPA relies on thousands of interconnected systems: AIs, human resources, surveillance systems of all different types and vintages. Many processes are automated and people forget how it all works."

"Get to the point, Wilcox." The soldier looked like the cat who'd caught the mouse, he was so full of himself.

"The coroner report on Ping's death was entered into a system in San Juan. Suicide."

Dr. Carlhagen fell back in his chair. "I see."

"Not a murder. Therefore, no murderers to apprehend. The surveillance AI saw the report and automatically lowered priority on locating Jacey and her companions."

"But that's a stroke of luck for us."

"Yes. But a time-limited one, I assure you. The IPA has now reprioritized catching Jacey and Dante. And the pop singer." His mouth twisted with disgust, as if the undignified name "Meow Meow" would never again sully his tongue.

Dr. Carlhagen needed President Rochelle to make her statement legalizing carbos now. No one could elude the IPA for long.

The interesting thing about leverage was that sometimes you didn't actually have to possess it. You simply had to make others *believe* you had it. A risky tactic, but now necessary. He would have to tell the president a whopping lie and hope it didn't come back to bite him.

Wilcox's attention turned away from the camera. He spoke to someone nearby, his head jerking angrily. Finally he nodded and turned to address Dr. Carlhagen. "Siggy doesn't know where Jacey ran off to, but he knows the city better than anyone. Has lots of contacts. I've put him under contract with my organization. He has eyes and ears in the ganglands. His sources there recently identified an untagged van leaving the city. All vehicles are required to use location transponders broadcasting identity tags of all occupants. Siggy specializes in providing un-tagged transportation, so he knew this van well. Back-tracing its path placed it at a Chinese restaurant west of downtown."

"Why is this significant?"

"The restaurant is one Siggy took the pop star to on his first detail keeping her sur-blind several years ago. It is logical that she took Jacey and Dante there. The van in question is owned by the sister of the cook at Beijing Palace."

"That's it. Track down that van."

"Siggy had a cycle gang tag the vehicle with a transponder. I'll stop them. It may be more challenging to capture her, though. I, uh, no longer have my men."

"Why not?"

"There was an altercation with Siggy's men earlier. My men are . . . indisposed."

"Do what you must. Report back when you have Jacey. Keep Dante alive if you can. Kill the pop singer if you wish."

"Sir." Wilcox saluted and his image vanished.

"Lazarus, get me the president."

Maxine shifted in her seat, startling Dr. Carlhagen. He'd forgotten the woman was in the room. She said, "Are you sure you want to talk to her now?"

The facility AI acknowledged Dr. Carlhagen's demand with the words CALLING PRESIDENT on the pixel wall.

Dr. Carlhagen did not wait long. The president's image appeared in a rectangle above the holodesk. Her face pressed very close to whatever camera she was using. Probably a personal tablet, hopefully untraceable. With regular office lighting, the thickness of her makeup and the roughness of her skin showed like a photo of a moonscape. The years had not been kind to the woman. Her red eyebrows showed the telltale falseness better lighting had concealed. The woman had no eyebrows except what a makeup artist had drawn on.

"Speak," she ordered. One of her front teeth was paler than the rest. A replacement, no doubt.

Aware of his own youthful good looks, Dr. Carlhagen smiled broadly. "Ping's death was a suicide. Vin Burnell can no longer be a suspect in his death. She must be released."

"You're in no position to make demands of me. And the judicial system is not under my command."

"Let's not kid each other, Annabelle. You call, Vin walks. It is in your interest to comply with my request," he said, emphasizing the last word.

Beyond the desk, Maxine was shaking her head and slicing her hands side to side. She mouthed: No. No. No.

"I'll decide my own interests, thank you very much," the president said. "Besides, I have questions of my own for Ms. Burnell."

For the first time in his long memory, Dr. Carlhagen wished he'd gone lighter on the andleprixen. His cognition lost sharpness on three pills. Two was good. But three . . .

Something in the president's statement chimed an alarm in his mind. He couldn't figure out why. He stalled. "What kind of questions?"

"For starters, I would ask her how it feels to wake up as a teenager."

"I can answer that. It's wonderful. Invigorating in every way."

"Of course you'd say that. Like asking a car salesman if the vehicles he sells are reliable. What's he going to say? So you'll understand if I ask one of your customers how satisfied she is with her purchase."

"Very well, Madam President. Do what you need to. But I encourage you to do so swiftly."

The president's painted-on brows lifted. She was clearly not accustomed to being addressed so bluntly. "I'll do what I please, and in my own time."

"Of course. As a courtesy, I'm informing you that images of your Scion will be leaked to SNN soon." Even drugged as he was, his heart pounded from the audacity of this ploy. Not only did he not have Leslie in his control, he had no idea where she was. If the president called his bluff, he'd lose all hope of pushing her to legalize the Scions.

Maxine pressed a palm to her face, still shaking her head.

None of it would mean anything if Vin cracked under questioning.

President Annabelle Rochelle's face hardened at his threat. "You think you can force my hand?"

"I think you were already planning on issuing an executive order decriminalizing carbos of a certain kind. Might as well do it before the secret of yours comes out. Also, SNN will be curious to hear what charges you've filed against Vin in light of the news of Ping's suicide."

Maxine's arms shot out. "Are you crazy?" she hissed.

The president's nostrils flared. A curse spilled from her lips. The image cut off.

Dr. Carlhagen chuckled nervously. He ordered Lazarus to monitor SNN for news about the president and to notify him as soon as she made any statement.

Maxine came around the desk, leaned on it, smirking. "You should never have mentioned your concern about Vin Burnell. You essentially told the president that Vin has information you don't want the president to know."

He dismissed Maxine's criticisms. Life always spun off

little crises like these. It was the nature of complex systems. So far he had met them all and had defeated them. It was merely a matter of commitment. He wanted what he wanted more than others wanted what they wanted.

That was how he would impose his will on the president, on Jacey, and on the world.

"Once her temper cools, she'll see that my recommendation is in her best interest."

20

NO. YOU ARE AN AI

"Have you ever been to Turtle Island?" Belle said to the air.

She had returned to one of her favorite meditation spots, the grassy expanse at the center of the Scion School campus. She had moved the sun back to its predawn position. So far Liz had left it there. The woman was probably asleep and hadn't realized what Belle had done.

The meditation had quieted her mind, but a pulse of anxiety still beat in her. She needed to do something, but was afraid to do it. Namely, dive into the data flow the way Vaughan did. She couldn't even create a second instance of herself.

"Vaughan? Answer me. Have you ever been to Turtle Island?"

Just off the northern coast of St. Vitus, Turtle Island rose from the waters like the back of a great green whale. Belle had seen it every day of her life at the Scion School.

Vaughan did not materialize and offer an answer. Neither did his voice whisper an answer to her ear.

Instead, the knowledge of what he had done *occurred* to her.

A shiver tingled the skin on her forearms. She knew Vaughan had passed the information to her, but she wasn't sure how. He had achieved some new plane of existence in the simulated world, one that allowed him to access the data of her own mind directly.

She trusted Vaughan, but the idea that he might have access to her as she was, a series of ones and zeros on a computer server . . . That was worse than being naked.

She pushed the thought away. She had her answer. Vaughan had been to Turtle Island, but only in this existence.

Interesting. Why she found it so, Belle didn't know. She didn't question it.

With a thought, she lifted off the ground, stretching her legs below her. Increasing her speed, she flew across the quad, passing over the bell tower, her toes nearly brushing its peak. She continued toward the coast, arms spread wide, allowing the simulated wind to brush her simulated body.

She dipped low, over the cheerful waves, casually letting one hand dip to the surface and drag along the cool water. She soared higher as she approached the small lump of Turtle Island.

It was covered with scrub, with no structures on it. The Scions had never been allowed to swim out to it, for it was too far. And they certainly had never been allowed access to a boat.

Belle hovered off the island's southern coast, wondering if it was an accurate representation of the real Turtle Island in the world of flesh and blood.

A sandy beach stretched off to her left, sloping into

crystal blue waters. To her right, the island climbed toward a blunt hilltop. Belle descended, her bare feet touching the sand, cool and damp.

So this was Turtle Island.

She teleported to the highest point and manifested an observation tower. Forgoing the arduous climb, she teleported to the top. She could just as easily have hovered at that height, but she preferred the solidity of wood beneath her feet. From here she could see farther to the north that she ever had on St. Vitus. According to the maps Vaughan had accessed from the net, there were more islands directly north. Very large ones.

Through the haze of distance, she saw a vague shape of a landmass on the horizon. She teleported to it. The foliage was the same as St. Vitus, but the island was flat.

She built an observation tower two kilometers high and teleported to the top. To the west was another very large island.

Vaughan's knowledge passed to her. He had done this very same thing, but without the observation towers. He had traveled around the world in this way.

He had concluded that the simulated earth was not identical to the real world. He had compared aspects of the street plan of Chicago as it appeared in the simulation to current-day maps. A little more digging—the effort of a quarter second—had shown him the simulation was based on the world as it had been forty-seven years ago.

And that answered Belle's question. She had thought that perhaps by exploring the simulated world they could find Dr. Carlhagen's Island, scope it out before Humphrey got there.

Similarly, she thought she might be able to find a permanent safe harbor for the Scions.

She teleported back to the quad, already seated in her meditative pose. Elizabeth was walking across the quad, barefoot, but clothed, for once. She wore skin-tight pants of a stretchy material and a pink top that exposed her midriff. Her hair was pulled back into a tight ponytail. She was headed for the dojo to work out.

The impulse to do something cruel to the woman flashed through Belle's mind, but she caught it before she acted upon it. Neither she nor Vaughan had taught Elizabeth the tricks of living in this existence. But the woman was already figuring them out. She had complete control over her physical appearance now. She could control the weather and the time of day, and soon she would be flying. Belle wondered if she had figured out how to access the data flow that Vaughan lived on.

The data flow. Her mind always came back to it. Belle closed her eyes and tried to force herself to split into two instances. It didn't work. She held her breath and bore down, straining, as if the pressure could blow her self into four or five versions.

The effort just made her lightheaded.

She cleared the sensation with a thought. Interesting how she could control certain aspects of her bodily sensations but not her emotions.

Vaughan's knowledge occurred to her again. She was too much identified with being a human, with being an individual. Until she let that go, she would be trapped.

What did that mean? How could she not think of herself as a human? That's what she was.

A new thought occurred to her, one so obvious it forced a disgusted laugh from her lips. She could continue to beat her head against the proverbial wall of failure, or just accept she wasn't going to create multiple instances. But in other ways, she was a wizard in this world. She had manifested observation towers and teleported. Perhaps there was a different way to access the data flow.

She was already walking toward the girl's classroom. On second thought . . .

She steered for the boys' classroom. "There are no rules here," she said to herself.

The classroom held two rows of glass desks supported by metal stands. They were height adjustable, to suit students of any height. There were no chairs. Socrates had always said they learned better standing up.

At the front were two more desks, for the leaders of each Nine. She went to the desk that would have been Vaughan's, had the world not been turned upside down.

She placed her hands on the desk.

"Socrates? I need you."

She didn't expect the real Socrates—the AI in charge of the Scions' education—for Dr. Carlhagen had deleted him. Nevertheless, why couldn't the simulation generate *a* Socrates?

It worked. He appeared as an old man with a flowing white beard and a fringe of long white hair around his bald head. His image had always varied depending on the day and the subject matter. Today he wore a black robe and a golden hoop nose ring. She didn't bother asking why. Socrates would merely give her one of his cryptic jokes she never understood.

To test out her scheme, she asked a simple question: "What is the weather in the real Chicago right now?"

With a flourish of his arms, he brought a huge leather covered book into existence. It was as thick as his head, with gold edging on the pages. He opened it. A musty smell wafted up, something that never happened in the world of flesh and blood.

"Cincinnati, Charleston, Chicago! Here we go." Putting on a ridiculous voice that over-enunciated every syllable, Socrates read, "Good morning, Chicagoland. Today we expect scattered showers, a high of 20, winds ten to twelve 12 km/h out of the northwest. Current temperature is 18 under partly cloudy skies."

"Thank you, Socrates." It worked. She had accessed the data flow through an intermediary simulation.

Knowledge of Vaughan's opinion about what she was doing occurred to her. He considered it clever, which made her chest warm and happy.

She allowed the sensation to linger, reveled in it. But merely accessing the data flow in this oblique way wasn't her goal. She wanted to end the Scions' various problems. The same thing Jacey wanted. The same thing Humphrey wanted. The same thing Vaughan wanted. It struck her that it was the first time their objectives had all been aligned.

She knew Vaughan was spending all of his efforts trying to find out what Humphrey and the others would encounter when they arrived at Dr. Carlhagen's hideout, the strange island called St. Lazarus. Belle couldn't contribute anything to that effort. That left only one thing for her to do.

"I can't believe it, Socrates," she said, exasperated. "Of all of the people in the world, why am I the one who has to track down Jacey?"

Socrates threw the weather book over his head. It vanished in smoke before it struck the table behind him. He toyed with his nose ring and frowned in thought. "You don't have to do it. No one gave you this assignment."

That was true. But Belle remembered how useless she'd felt when Wanda had asked what she was doing to help find Dr. Carlhagen's island. And Belle did care about Jacey, in a way. Not because Belle liked her or anything as ridiculous as that. But Jacey was important to the other Scions. Especially to Vaughan. So once Jacey's crisis was over, Vaughan could finally just be Vaughan.

The warmth she'd felt before drained away. Vaughan was never going to just be Vaughan. Already, he was becoming something she didn't recognize.

She turned her thoughts away from that whirlpool of darkness. Find Jacey, worry about everything else later.

She rubbed her palms together. Time to get down to business. "Jacey left St. Vitus in search of Dr. Carlhagen's Island," she said, thinking aloud. "Why? Because she wanted to rescue Livy. We have seen Jacey on video streams, and she's gotten herself into deep trouble. Which anyone with half a brain could have predicted."

"That is uncharitable of you," Socrates said.

She ignored him. "With your help accessing the data flow, I plan to find her, and if I can, help her."

Socrates smiled and held his hand arms apart. "You have a clearly defined objective. That's an excellent first step."

"So where do we start?" she asked her teacher.

He stroked his beard and put on a sage expression. "If I were *actually* Socrates, I might have some idea. But since I was manifested by you, and created by the simulation in which you live, I am essentially an aspect of your own psyche. Therefore I only have the ideas that you have, though I may have some insights into your subconscious. Which is a long way to say that I haven't the foggiest idea where to begin."

It was Belle's turn to put on the thoughtful look. She tapped her fingernails on the glass desktop. "Jacey was searching for Dr. Carlhagen. She believed that Elizabeth would know where to find him. She got swept up in Elizabeth's fiasco of a party. There, she met the Progenitors who had overwritten Ping and Dante. She also got entangled with that weird-looking celebrity Meow Meow. During the course of events, Ping got shot. Jacey, Dante, and Meow Meow fled the scene, making them all look quite guilty."

Socrates nodded. "That is the story thus far, as you know it."

But would Jacey actually murder Ping?

It didn't make sense. Jacey would never kill a Scion's body, overwritten or not. In fact, back when they'd had Dr. Carlhagen in custody, Jacey had continually harangued Vaughan to return to his flesh-and-blood body. She had wanted the same thing for Belle. Vaughan had refused, saying that his physical body couldn't contain his mind, as it had changed in this world. Belle knew this to be true. And wherever Vaughan was, that's where Belle would stay.

Jacey didn't care what they wanted, though. She had planned to restore Vaughan from the backup that had been made when Dr. Carlhagen had transferred into him. That would restore an earlier version of Vaughan, just like when they had overwritten Mr. Justin, returning a backup of Leslie to her body. Poor, stupid Leslie had been flailing to catch up with events ever since.

Given Jacey's incessant nagging on the subject, Belle knew she would never kill Ping's body. She wouldn't kill Vin's body. She wouldn't kill Dante's body. Because Jacey—being the ridiculous idealist she was—harbored a fantasy of restoring *all* of them.

"Maybe this will be of interest," Socrates said.

"What?"

Instead of answering, Socrates opened a video window over his shoulder. It showed Jacey and Meow Meow walking through a crowded atrium, faces down. But then Dante came running up behind, shouting for them to run. Onlookers all turned. Some pointed, faces alight with recognition. Small insect-like objects floated up from among the crowd to follow after the three fugitives.

The image switched to the outside of the building. Jacey and the others emerged from a weird revolving door. They dashed across the roadway, cars screeching just short of squashing them. Dante made a rude gesture at one of them. They continued to the far side. Meow Meow looked up and down the sidewalk, as if searching for something. The image cut to a close-up of Jacey's face. Belle had never seen the girl so haggard, so tired. And she was dressed strangely, in a black tank top and some weird bluish pants.

The image cut again, this time showing a shaky close-up of Meow Meow's face. The light of dawning realization came over her features. Excitedly, she pointed. And then ran. Jacey and Dante trailed after her as she disappeared into an alley.

The video stopped.

"Socrates, show me a map of that area of Chicago."

In place of the video rectangle, a map appeared. A flashing blue dot marked the spot Jacey had last been seen.

"Take me there."

The classroom swirled around her, blurring and then instantly resolving. She now stood in the middle of the city, tall buildings stretching high overhead. A pale blue sky beyond.

Beneath Belle's feet was the concrete sidewalk Jacey

and her companions had been standing on in the video. She gazed across the roadway, to the other sidewalk, to the weird revolving doorway of the hotel. This wasn't the actual place. This was a simulation, so she knew it wasn't exactly accurate. But it would do.

An eerie quiet hung over the city, the air so still that Belle felt like an intruding ghost. There were no cars. No people. With a thought, she produced a slight easterly breeze and prompted some clouds to pop into existence. It did little to ease the unreality of the city.

She crossed the street toward the hotel, using short teleportation hops. Each time she reappeared, she paused, got her bearings, absorbed the environment. She went through the revolving door and into the hotel lobby. She recognized the tile pattern on the floor. This was where Jacey and her companions had first appeared in the video.

There was no way to backtrack Jacey's movements any farther. The simulation wouldn't know which room Jacey had been in, or anything relevant about what had been in those rooms.

Belle zapped herself back to the sidewalk and spotted the alley into which Jacey and her companions had fled.

She walked to the opening, peered down the shadowy narrow stretch of pavement leading between two tall buildings. A slender rectangle of light at the far end hinted at an opening onto a street beyond.

"I have another hit," Socrates said. His voice seemed to be coming from Belle's trousers pocket.

She discovered a tablet device in it, similar to a reader but smaller. Socrates's face took up a corner of it. The rest was filled with a local map.

Thousands of tiny yellow dots appeared on the map. Socrates said, "The city is full of surveillance cameras. One cam spotted Jacey and her companions as they emerged onto that street." He highlighted a spot on the map. A red line showed the path Jacey had taken. Belle teleported to Jacey's last known location.

"I found another one," Socrates said. Knowing Belle's will, he teleported her to the new location.

He showed her a ten second snatch of video. The three fugitives emerged from another alley, looked furtively up and down the street, then slipped into a glass doorway. Belle spotted it just to her left. A sign above the door read: WENDY'S WINDY CITY'S WHISKEY (AND WINE).

"Say that three times fast," Socrates said.

Belle was going to ask why she should bother when Socrates interrupted. "Another cam caught them."

Belle found herself seven blocks further west, according to the map. She stood at the mouth of yet another alleyway. This one was narrower and darker than the others, and at the end lay more darkness.

She looked over her shoulder. The street behind her was lined with restaurants and storefronts. If Jacey had gone that way, the surveillance cameras would have picked her up again. That meant she'd gone into the alley.

Belle walked down it, slowly, trying to imagine what it was like for Jacey.

She failed. Belle had never understood Jacey. The girl was too full of herself, too much of a narcissist, for Belle to figure out.

She passed a small restaurant, an odd little hole in the side of a brick building. The entrance was a glass door set between two windows. On one, crude vinyl letters spelled out BEIJING PALACE. Belle couldn't think of a name less appropriate for such a dingy place.

She continued down the alley to the intersection.

Another alley led left and right here. In both directions it opened onto streets. But Jacey had not been picked up there by surveillance cameras.

Socrates's voice blared from the tablet. "Beijing Palace."

Belle was skeptical, but she reminded herself that Socrates was an aspect of her own mind. And as she approached the doorway, a feeling of certainty came over her. Jacey had gone inside.

It was a narrow place with a dirty black and white tiled floor. Red vinyl seats hugged booth tables with chipped laminate tops. A counter at the rear held up a peculiar porcelain cat, one paw up. Beyond that was an empty kitchen. A short corridor on the right side led to another door.

Belle glanced at the map, zoomed out to see Jacey's path. It zigzagged a lot, but there was an obvious purpose to that. They had only emerged near a camera where absolutely required. This restaurant had been the destination all along.

"Do you have plans for this building?" she asked Socrates.

Instantly, a floor plan of the restaurant and the adjoining buildings popped up on the screen. Socrates marked the exits. Two led onto major streets, so those were out. Another let out onto the roof. Jacey wouldn't go there; that would trap her.

The final exit also led onto the street, but it required them to first to descend to a sub-basement. Belle teleported there. It was a cavern-like space, all concrete, with thick round pillars holding up a low ceiling.

"This parking garage exits onto the street," Socrates said. "So . . ."

"She got into a vehicle," Belle said. "That would allow

her to travel while staying out of direct view of the camera network. Clever."

"But if we can figure that out, so can her pursuers."

Socrates was right.

"Who is after Jacey?" she said, going back the basic facts.

"Well, you are," Socrates said. "And the International Police Agency is after her for questioning in Ping's murder. Based upon the data flow I've analyzed—which includes net chatter of billions of people—there are many 'carbo hunters' also interested in capturing her. Many desire to kill her."

"Kill her?" Belle said, shocked. "Why would anyone want to kill her?"

Her tablet vibrated drawing her attention to the screen. A stream of text was flowing from the top to the bottom, much faster than she could read. Socrates's voice came over the speaker. "'Carbo' is a slang term for 'clone.' Cloning is illegal. It is government policy to destroy clones. Carbo hunters, recognizing that clones are non-people, hunt them for rewards, for the fun of it, or to capture and resell them."

"But I'm a clone."

"No. You are an AI."

It was so easy to forget sometimes.

"So the IPA wants Jacey. Carbo hunters want Jacey. And . . ."

The one item she had missed popped into her brain. "Dr. Carlhagen also wants Jacey."

"Ah! I think you're onto something," Socrates said.

Belle tapped her fist onto her temple, simultaneously trying to jog loose the complete thought and punish herself for missing something so obvious.

And then she had it. "Dr. Carlhagen has seen the exact same news reports we have. He knows Jacey was at Vin's coming out. He knows Jacey is wanted for questioning about Ping's death. He knows that she was in Chicago. But he is obsessed with her. And that means he's dispatched Captain Wilcox to find her before anyone else does. He'll be on Jacey's trail."

And that was the key. "But no one's looking for Captain Wilcox. He has no reason to hide from the surveillance cameras. So while he's tracking her in the flesh, we can track him."

Socrates's face filled the tablet screen. He had transformed himself, removing the beard, and now wore a peculiar hat with earflaps tied up with laces atop his head. The fabric was a strange pattern. He popped a big tobacco pipe in his mouth and puffed, sending out smoke rings. "Let me see . . ." he said around the pipe stem.

Belle ignored his eccentric costume.

"I've got him," Socrates said. "Oh boy, do I have him!"

Belle grinned back at him. "Show me."

21

LAZARUS WATCHES

Chillers offline.

Body temperature: 30°C

Skin Temperature: 28°C

Blood viscosity: 4.13x10-3 Pa-s

Blood pressure: 134/97

Heart rate: 19 BPM

The ventilator fan in the cryopod spins up to 4500 rpm, adding its hum to the pump. Air from the cryo-ward is drawn in to gradually warm the interior of the coffin-like compartment.

37 more needles retract. Blood wells from the insertion points.

A band of LED lights over the subject's face illuminates, casting a gentle golden glow over the closed eyes.

Lazarus watches its future body.

Slowly, slowly. If brought out of suffusion too swiftly, the subject's heart might fail.

A dangerous phase, like a spacecraft's reentry into the atmosphere.

Glowing bursts of blue and red and purple flow across the awareness of a disconnected mind as a burst of dimethyltryptamine releases from the pineal gland.

There is no Livy yet. Fluttering black wings split the glow.

22

DO. NOT. MOVE. THE. VAN

J acey awoke to the scent of fresh air and the sounds of quiet, furtive voices outside the van. She rolled onto her side and looked to the front of the vehicle. Lily wasn't there. Dante and Meow Meow were gone, too. The van was not moving.

A male's voice, low and commanding, rumbled from a few feet away. Jacey's skin thrilled with recognition.

Captain Wilcox.

With slow and silent movements, she crawled forward. The driver's side window was open. A breeze, dry and crisp, ruffled Jacey's hair.

Meow Meow: "She won't like it."

Wilcox: "I don't care. Dr. Carlhagen doesn't care. What choice does she have?"

Dante: "The girl he took. Can you guarantee her safety?"

Wilcox: "Livy is a Scion. She'll be safe until she's over-written."

Jacey's nostrils flared with rage. How could that man say that with such matter-of-fact disinterest?

Meow Meow: "That's not good enough."

Lily: "All I agreed to do was drive you here. Get her out of my van."

Meow Meow: "Well *I* didn't agree to anything. Listen, Dante, what about our other plan?"

Dante: "Oh, come on. We were never going to get through the fences. You know that was just a fantasy. Might as well end it here without more suffering."

Meow Meow: "You're a jerk."

Lily: "You go on fighting about it. I'm leaving. I have muumuus to sew. Get Little Jackie out of my van."

Jacey retreated to the rear doors. Biting her lip, she pulled the latch. The door swung open. She stepped out and crouched. Pressing the door shut, she slipped to the opposite side of the van from the others. The van was idling on the side of a road. Flat, empty land lay on either side. Behind her, a string of trees ran through a farm field. If she sprinted, she might get there before the others realized she was gone.

Meow Meow: "If we can get her through . . ."

Dante: "And risk the sickness? Why would I even try such a thing?"

Meow Meow: "Because you're in love with her."

Dante: "That is not entirely accurate."

Jacey made a face and shook her head. Meow Meow had lost her mind if she truly thought there was anything between her and Dante.

Wilcox: "I will not allow her to escape again."

Meow Meow: "If you even touch her, I'm gonna have a few bullets touch your brain."

Bullets?

Siggy's gun! Jacey grinned. At least Meow Meow hadn't sold her out.

But who had? It wasn't coincidence they'd run into Captain Wilcox out here in the middle of nowhere.

It had to be Dante. He'd wanted to turn himself in. And he'd seen Captain Wilcox in Casino San Juan. Exactly how he'd gotten in touch with the crotchety soldier, Jacey had no idea.

A bee-like buzz came from behind her, far away. She glanced back, but saw nothing in the field.

She needed a place to hide, get her thoughts together. Meow Meow might have Siggy's pistol, but she was still outgunned. Wilcox wouldn't go anywhere unarmed, and neither would his men.

She peeked under the van to count feet. She recognized Meow Meow's boots and Dante's brown leather shoes. The hem of Lily's muumuu wavered in the wind. She wore flip-flops. Captain Wilcox wore denim jeans and brown boots with red laces.

Odd. Wilcox didn't have any guards with him. At least, none in view. Maybe they'd set up a perimeter around this little rendezvous spot. Jacey scanned the terrain of the field. Maybe they were in the trees. But why would they stay back? They had the numbers and weapons. There was no reason for stealth in this situation.

Lily: "I said get her out of my van."

The van rocked as Lily got in. "Okay, sweetie. Time to— She's gone!"

Jacey sprinted toward the trees. Her feet sank into freshly tilled soil. Clumps of black earth stuck to her feet, slowing her. A cry rose behind her.

The buzzing she heard earlier suddenly rose. She stumbled to a stop as a drone swarm lifted from the trees ahead.

Each drone was a black speck. There were thousands of them. Enough to form a cloud-like flock.

"Jacey! Come back and get in." Meow Meow was shouting and waving an arm as she dashed toward the van.

Captain Wilcox stepped around the vehicle, drawing a weapon from under his blue, zippered jacket. His outfit made him look like a normal man. Almost.

"They've spotted you," Wilcox shouted at Jacey. "Come with me. I'll take you to Dr. Carlhagen." He waved toward a black truck parked a hundred meters down the road. It crouched upon huge knobby tires. A row of yellow lights was mounted to the top and a thick grill of black metal bars hung on the front, giving the machine a mean appearance.

Bogged with clumps of wet soil, Jacey made no move in either direction. "You're all liars."

Dante stood on the edge of the road. "I know it looks bad, but we didn't plan this."

"Come on, Jacey," Wilcox called, voice heavy with command.

"You'll just drag me back to St. Vitus."

The swarm slid through the air toward Jacey, its form elongating. The buzz grew louder.

"No I won't," Wilcox called back. "The senator's forces hold the island now. Dr. Carlhagen doesn't want any of you there until the navy clears out." He raised the weapon to his right eye. It was different than the guns Jacey had seen before. Fatter, with a barrel that flared like the bell of a trumpet.

"Get in the van," Meow Meow said, waving her pistol.

"No!" Lily screamed. "I don't want anything to do with any of you. Stay out!"

The pistol froze, aimed at Lily.

Dante backed toward Wilcox. "Wilcox is the most expedient choice, Jacey. Go with him. You said you wanted to find that child. He'll take you to her."

The drone swarm swept toward them. Countless individuals formed into a black shadow. Flashes of energy sparked among them like lightning in a storm cloud. A pod of drones emerged from the central mass, then separated. It flew straight for Jacey, sweeping low and gaining speed.

Her body reacted before conscious thought. Despite the mud weighing down her feet, she scrambled back toward the road. The inky swarm herded her, humming with an anger she knew it couldn't possess, but which she felt anyway. A single drone flew close to her face, micropropellers a blur. A glint of glass protruded from beneath it. A camera.

Jacey swatted at it, but it danced sideways. It returned instantly.

She recalled Meow Meow's lesson about drone swarms. This one had been assigned pest duty. And if she did manage to knock it away, surely another would take its place.

Fine. She'd ignore it.

She stopped to wipe sweat from her eyes. The road was a few meters away.

Electric shocks stabbed between her shoulder blades. She turned, furious. Another shock lanced her thigh, and still another took her in the calf.

Crying out, she plodded the rest of the way to the road. The swarm herded her away from the van, away from Wilcox and Dante.

Once she was in the center of the road, her swarm formed a tight circle, no more than a meter in diameter, centered on her head. The swarm wheeled continuously, the drones moving so quickly they were a charcoal blur. Only one remained mostly stationary, her pest, which still hovered a few centimeters from her nose. The slight wind of its micro-prop downdraft ruffled her shirt.

Wilcox and Dante both had their own little swarms and pests now, too.

Judging by the sounds coming from the van, a few had gotten inside. But Jacey couldn't see if Meow Meow had gotten the door closed or not.

The remainder of the machines had formed a similar wheel, with the van as its center.

Wilcox stood very still, hand gripping his odd weapon. A drone slipped toward his hand. An arc of blue shot out from the tiny aircraft, striking Wilcox's hand. He dropped the weapon and swore.

"Can you get to the van?" Meow Meow yelled from inside the vehicle.

"No!" Jacey called back. Just to touch the van would require a ten meter run. The drones would light up her skeleton if she took one step toward it.

She studied the pest. Such a dainty little machine. Like a maniacal little hummingbird. If she could get it in her fist, she was certain she could crush it and toss it over her shoulder, never to fly again. But they packed a wallop of energy, and she wasn't willing to take any more shocks.

"So I take it these aren't your drones," Dante called to Wilcox. The drones had separated Dante from the soldier, but the men were facing each other.

Wilcox's face was red with fury. "No. They have to be IPA drones. Which means the IPA will have boots on the ground in a few minutes."

He squatted and grabbed his weapon. He fired off a squealing shot. A dozen drones fell and clanked on the pavement like tin cans. The remaining drones retaliated with ruthless electric shocks. Blue plasma flashed between the swarm and his head, his chest, his legs, his groin. To his credit, he stayed on his feet. Spittle flew from his lips as he heaved a gut-wrenching curse. The single word went on and on and on.

When the drones let up, he sagged, breath heaving. The weapon again lay on the road.

Whatever that gun was, it had taken out some drones. But the drones knew what it was, which was why they'd made him drop it in the first place.

"Well, we're up a river without a motor now," Dante said.

A new sound was cutting through the cacophony of the drone swarms. This was a lower pitch, and it pounded the air with a familiar beat. A helicopter.

Jacey turned, making sure to keep her feet in the same spot so the drones wouldn't retaliate. The chopper came from the west.

Shrieks burst from the van and it lurched forward. Meow Meow screamed for Lily to stop. The van jerked to a stop, boxy chassis wobbling, then falling still.

"Get the hell out of my van!" Lily bellowed. "I don't want anything to do with all this."

"Shut up!" Meow Meow screamed. "Do. Not. Move. The. Van!" It didn't matter that Meow Meow was inside the van and not standing right next to Jacey. The energy of her shouts made Jacey duck her head.

Wilcox's voice drew Jacey's attention. "That's not my chopper."

Dante was squinting toward the low-flying aircraft. It

was approaching fast, but was angled slightly away from them.

"Where are your men, Wilcox?" Jacey said. "Why aren't they helping you?"

"I came alone."

"You're alone?" She'd never seen Captain Wilcox arrive anywhere without several men as backup.

"They were . . . injured." His face darkened at the memory.

"Siggy's men shot them in the hotel," Dante said. "That has to sting, doesn't it my darling mercenary?"

Meow Meow was still shouting at Lily, who was shouting back. Suddenly the van launched ahead, rear wheels shrieking on the pavement. Meow Meow tumbled out the side door and rolled onto the gravel shoulder of the road. Smoke spewed from the tires as the van's rear-end fishtailed side to side.

"That isn't smart," Wilcox said.

The van abruptly swerved left, tilting onto two wheels.

The front end jerked right, bringing it back onto all fours. But momentum kept it going until it leaned hard onto its left wheels.

And then it went over, rolling onto its roof, then wheels, then roof. Sparks shot from the road beneath it, and the soul-rending sound of tearing metal pierced the air. The van skidded to a stop, still upside down, smoke tendrils climbing from the wreckage like ghosts struggling to escape hell.

In a flash of orange, the vehicle exploded. The concussion smacked Jacey in the chest and face, knocking her into her own swarm. Tiny drones skittered across her skull.

A bone-deep boom demolished all thoughts, all hearing.

Then she was flat on her back, the world silent.

The blue sky swam with faint white clouds, like a filmy veil. The sun-warmed road oozed sleepiness into Jacey's limbs and mind. Only her heart seemed to remember the danger, for it pounded and pounded. Like the beat of helicopter blades.

Hands found Jacey, tugged at her.

Meow Meow's face appeared above her, mouth open, shouting something. She had such beautiful, even teeth. Her makeup was running, all that red dripping down her face, onto her hands. Too much makeup. Why did she wear so much red?

Dante was there, too. He was shouting, but looking past Jacey, somewhere behind her that she couldn't see.

The world tilted as they lifted her.

She tried to put her weight on her own feet. Something crunched under her shoes. Like stepping on dried beetles.

Drones. Everywhere drones. They covered the ground in clumps stretching down the road. All the way to the black truck.

Wilcox was on his knees. He was looking at his hands. Covered in blood.

Meow Meow's little hands were crushing Jacey's arm. How had she gotten so strong?

Dante had his hand around her waist, carrying most of her weight as she stumbled. Her head felt watery, like the one time Dr. Carlhagen had given her wine at dinner.

"Humphrey threw up," she shouted. "In the bougainvilleas, he told me." She couldn't hear her own voice, and her throat burned from the effort to get the words out.

Her friends were urging her forward, toward Wilcox's truck. Friends. Dante had lied to her, betrayed her. He was giving her up. Dante didn't care. Meow Meow didn't have any other ideas.

Dante held her close. His body was warm. Meow Meow had said he was in love with her. How could that be? She amused him. How could Jacey ever feel anything but hatred for a Progenitor? He was going to give her to Wilcox. To Dr. Carlhagen.

A scream entered her consciousness through her right ear. Meow Meow. How did such a tiny thing have such a huge voice? "The chopper! Not IPA. Run."

Jacey tried to look back, but the motion made her vision spin and her stomach churn.

Dante opened the passenger door of Wilcox's truck and threw her in. Meow Meow appeared across from her, taking the driver's seat. Dante pressed Jacey farther in, then slammed the door. Jacey read his lips as he shouted, "Go! Go! Go!"

The truck shuddered, the horizon spun crazily. The vibration of the wheels on the road made Jacey's body shake, but she could hear nothing. Her body felt nothing except nausea.

"I'm going to throw up," she said.

And then she did.

23

THAT IMAGE OF HIS FACE

"Summer says *Athena* is just about ready," Humphrey said to Orson. They sat across from each other in the dining hall of what was once called Justin's School, but which the Scions had started calling "Borington," because there was nothing to do. Between the two men lay the paper map they had been using as a navigational aid aboard *Aphrodite*.

Orson's face bunched up in a dismissive smirk. "Changing the ship's name won't fool the navy."

"That's why Summer repainted her and removed the rear winch. She won't look like *Aphrodite* from afar."

The man's beard and mustache caved in as he sucked in his lips. "Won't matter. The navy will see right through all that. Their sonar men will have records of what *Aphrodite's* engines sounded like."

Humphrey doubted Orson knew what he was talking about. He just didn't want to help Humphrey get to Dr. Carlhagen's island. There was a real risk of being boarded again, despite Summer's efforts. And if they found Orson on the navigation bridge, his future would shorten considerably.

Humphrey decided to pretend Orson hadn't said anything at all. "Summer's hoisting a small boat aboard *Athena* right now. To tell you the truth, I think she's just looking for things to lift with that crane of yours. If she could figure out a way to do it, she'd put that crane on the boat."

Orson looked at him, face blank.

Humphrey turned his attention back to the map. Placing his finger on Mr. Justin's Island—an unlabeled blob of green in a sea of blue—he slid his finger south in search of Dr. Carlhagen's hideout. St. Lazarus. It wasn't there.

Could Vaughan be wrong about it?

No. Vaughan had access to better maps, more current ones. He said the island didn't show up on all of them.

"A hundred kilometers," Humphrey mused. "That's not too far."

Orson grunted, noncommittal. "Distance is relative. If it's calm seas and you're not being chased by a fleet of naval vessels, a hundred klicks is nothing. Matter of a few hours sailing."

The fleet. Humphrey tapped the screen of a reader he had borrowed from one of the younger Scions who was helping Summer paint *Athena*.

"Vaughan? Do you have a moment?"

Vaughan's face appeared on the screen. "I've been listening," he said, by way of greeting. "I am still working to get access to satellite imagery of Mr. Justin's Island. The security guarding that data isn't merely electronic, it seems. The military's practice is to hold intelligence information on isolated computer systems, disconnected from the net."

"So we are totally blind to the movements of that fleet, too," Humphrey said. "But someone has to know. There are civilian ships all over the place. They must see the fleet."

"That's an interesting idea," Vaughan said.

Humphrey squinted at his friend's image. Vaughan had always been the image of perfection, which had made Humphrey envious. But the image he presented now was odd. It seemed to lack refinement, as if Vaughan wasn't putting forth the effort to look like himself anymore. For one, the flaw that made Vaughan look so distinctive, the prominent vein on one temple, was gone. His eyebrows were thin and light-colored. Almost not there. And the angle of his jaw was more severe, his chin more pointed.

"A fleet that large can't stay invisible from all other boats," Vaughan said. "So the question is: can I access communications from other surface vessels and listen to what they report seeing?"

Orson's mouth opened slightly, exposing grayish lower teeth. "That's a clever idea." He darted a glance at Vaughan's image. Orson had always been a little creeped out by the AI Vaughan for some reason. "Can you do that?"

Vaughan's lips quirked. "Let me find out." He vanished.

Humphrey referred to the list of things he had to do before leaving. There was only one more item, an issue of great contention on the island. It read, simply: assign crew.

When word had gotten out about his plans, every single Scion had volunteered to go along. Children as young as four had wandered up to him, offering to help save Livy.

Saving Livy was part of it. But Humphrey intended to

do more. Somehow, he was going to end Dr. Carlhagen's whole program. If that meant killing him, then so be it.

Humphrey set down the list. Killing Dr. Carlhagen would be killing Vaughan's body. That would end any hope Jacey had of overwriting Dr. Carlhagen so Vaughan could live again. On the other hand, AI Vaughan had refused to do it when he'd had the chance, so . . .

He pushed the problem from his mind. Just getting to Dr. Carlhagen seemed impossible at the moment. "If only we knew what we were up against," he said. "Is the compound behind a fence like on St. Vitus? Does he have some of Captain Wilcox's mercenary guards there?"

That's what worried him the most. He would be going in relatively unarmed. It wasn't the first time he'd lamented Sensei's decision to lock up the guns they'd confiscated from Senator Bentilius's forces. On the other hand, putting those weapons in the hands of Scions, all of them younger than him, seemed like a terrible idea. None of them knew how to use the weapons, and all of them were angry enough with Dr. Carlhagen to start shooting at the first sign of trouble.

Nothing to be done about that. He sighed and read the last item on his to-do list. "Crew."

Orson pulled a cigar from his pocket and stuffed the soggy, chewed-up end into his mouth. "Summer. Can't sail without her. That'll get you there. Who you'll need after that . . ." He shrugged and looked away.

"If Summer is going, then Elias is going. That's good, Elias is healed up and will be an important and skilled fighter if it comes to it."

And that highlighted a rather large problem. Vaughan was gone, Sang was gone, and Horace was gone. That left Tytus, a skilled fighter, but only 15. Kirk, who looked like he was 18, but was only 14. And Obu, 14. Trained fighters all, but young. They'd shown their prowess already, having defeated Senator Bentilius's armed men. But that had been in a situation where the armed men were under orders not to shoot the Scions.

If he took those boys, that would leave Pedro, a 13-year-old, as the eldest boy on the island. The remaining boys would probably respect his authority, but Pedro's judgment—his whole emotional state—had suffered greatly since the death of his best friend Constantine, who had accidentally been shot.

The door swung open, admitting a gust of wind full of moisture and the scent of greenery. Wanda strode in, unruly hair pulled back into a ponytail, Scion uniform blotched with gray paint.

"Do you realize you're picking from a bunch of kids?" Orson said around his cigar. "I say you're crazy to consider this mission at all."

"I can't believe I'm going to say this, but I agree with Orson," Wanda said as she plopped next to Humphrey. She cast a disinterested glance at the map. "*Athena* is ready. Summer just stenciled her name on the hull."

Orson groaned. "Poor old *Aphrodite*."

"We were just discussing the crew," Humphrey said to Wanda. "I've got too many volunteers, and I don't want to take more than necessary into this . . . situation."

"How considerate of you." Her tone was ice. They had already endured one fight over this, but despite helping to prepare *Athena*, her opinion on the mission hadn't changed. "You're doing the exact thing that Jacey does, you know. The thing that makes you—makes everyone—so mad at her. You're not *thinking*. What about all the other Scions here?"

"What is there to think about? We know where Dr. Carlhagen is. This is our chance to stop him and save Livy at the same time. We won't be safe until he's dead."

Her head tilted, slowly, and her mouth dropped in awe. "I thought you were smart."

"I am. This is purely logical."

"Logical? Going into a situation with no idea what you'll face is logical?" She raised a finger and cut off his retort. "This is not logical. It's personal." She jabbed his chest. "You're so embarrassed or guilty about Carlhagen being your Progenitor that you can't let it go. You can't think about the good of everyone else. And now you're planning on risking your own life and the lives of several others—and the long-term safety of all the Scions—for a personal grudge."

"So we should just let him keep Livy? We should just let him keep making Scions and overwriting a whole new generation?"

Orson kept his eyes on the map, though he chewed his cigar with great agitation.

Wanda took several deep breaths, barely reining in her fury. Her eyes glistened, her voice quavered. "Livy is . . . one person. I love her. Everyone who knows her loves her. That's why you got so many volunteers. But that doesn't make this ridiculous mission the right thing to do. You will risk multiple lives to save one? And the risk is . . ." She shook her head and looked away.

Orson pocketed his cigar, the chewed end wicking out a wet blob on his shirt. "She has a point, lad. You could hunker down here, hide out for a while, for years. Let the world go by you. Let big people do the schemes they do. They're going to do it anyway. There ain't any right or wrong, not the way you think there is."

It was the most passion Orson had shown for anything besides his cigars. It was clear from the earnestness on his face he meant what he said.

But he was all wrong. Wanda was wrong, too.

"I have to live with it," Humphrey said quietly. "If I don't go, the regret will kill me." He patted his cheeks. "In seventy years I'm going to look just like Dr. Carlhagen looked right before he transferred into Vaughan. That's how I remember him. All the hate I feel for him is in that image of his face. If I don't act now to end him, some day I'll look in the mirror and he'll be laughing at me. He'll have won."

"That's just wrong thinking," Wanda said. "If you make the right decision now, you'll know it in time. When you see all these Scions grow up and remember you didn't sacrifice them and all their potential, you'll look in the mirror and know that *you* won."

This was how Jacey felt, he realized. Those times he'd tried to talk her out of a headlong rush into danger, she'd thought the same thing he was thinking about Wanda. *She just doesn't get it.*

"I'll keep the crew small," he said. "I assume you won't be going?"

She shook her head. "I can hardly tell you not to and then go with you. Though it will kill me to watch you leave, knowing you'll probably never come back." A tear slipped down her cheek, she wiped it away. "I suppose I can't actually lose you. Never had you, did I?"

He thought about Jacey. "I don't think we ever have someone else. They are with us for a while. And then they aren't."

Wanda swallowed hard and stood. Sniffing, she squared her shoulders. "You are more like Dr. Carlhagen than I thought." She marched away, leaving Humphrey feeling small and angry.

Vaughan's face reappeared on the reader. "I've hacked into a network of land-based radio receivers and tuned them to monitor surface ship radio chatter. So far no one has identified the fleet within a 100 kilometer range of this island. I suggest you leave immediately, while the coast is —literally—clear."

Humphrey glanced at Orson, heart full of trepidation. "Are you ready?"

"Do I have a choice?"

"No."

"Then being ready has nothing to do with it."

They stood, Orson groaning with the effort. He winced and flexed his hands. The ordeal of the past few days had really worn on the man.

Humphrey lifted a walkie-talkie to his lips. "Summer, prepare *Athena* for departure."

Her answer was not long in coming. A burst of static, then her voice, clear and cheerful. "Ship is ready, Captain. Just point her where you want her to go."

Orson chuckled. "Remarkable girl, that one is. Remarkable. Who else we taking?"

"Elias."

The boy was attached to Summer, and he'd help keep an eye on Orson.

"That's it?"

"That's it."

24

A ROGUE TEAR

Meow Meow stopped the truck under a crumbling overpass along the highway. The bridge-like stretch of road overhead was supported by thick concrete pillars soaring thirty meters above. The surrounding land was awash with silky grass that rippled in the wind like waves. A pale blue sky capped the world.

"That used to be the Auto-Auto El," Meow Meow said, pointing to the span of highway protecting them, as if the name explained anything. Jacey's hearing was slowly coming back, though her friends' voices had to cut through a high-pitched ringing.

"Why are we stopping at all?" Jacey said.

Meow Meow motioned for her to lower her voice, not from fear of being overhead, but because Jacey's deafness was making her shout.

"If that was the IPA, we'd already be caught. They'd have sent twenty choppers."

Dante had found a pair of high-powered binoculars in a

storage compartment next to the front passenger seat, one of many such storage holds. The truck had room for seven people and a payload bed in back full of supplies. The seats were soft black leather, and Meow Meow couldn't hide her enthusiasm for the electric motor's torque. Whatever that meant.

Dante lowered his window and stuck his head out, scanning behind them with the binoculars. "No. That is definitely not an IPA chopper."

"I didn't think it would be," Meow Meow said. She grabbed Siggy's pistol from where she'd thrown it onto the dash. With practiced movements, she popped a clip of bullets from it, examined them, then returned it with a snap of her fingers.

"Let me see." Jacey prodded Dante until he relinquished the binoculars. Though her head still spun a bit, she managed to get the lenses focused in the right direction.

The helicopter hovered a kilometer behind them. Jacey had the skin-crawly feeling that someone on board was looking right back at her through magnification. "Why don't they come closer?"

"They're outnumbered. Three of us and two of them. And they don't know what weapons we might have."

The chopper did not look anything like the helicopters Jacey had seen. Captain Wilcox and Senator Bentilius flew on large ones that carried eight to ten fully armed soldiers. This one was small and cobbled together. The entire cockpit was a glass bubble, the tail a steel lattice with no aluminum skin over it. Instead of landing wheels, it had two skids mounted on the bottom.

"It looks like someone made it from parts," she said,

thinking how Summer would love to get her hands on the machine.

Dante grabbed the binoculars from Jacey's hands and inspected the chopper again.

"Scavs. And these drones are scav work, too," Meow Meow said, holding one of the little machines that had blown into the truck's open window when Lily's van exploded.

"That's a scav chopper for sure," Dante said, upper lip curled back in the peculiar way people do when squinting through binoculars. "Two-seater. Right out of a documentary. Never thought I'd see one in real life. Never wanted to, to be honest."

Meow Meow had six small, dead drones arrayed on the seat next to her. Jacey remembered the girl's lecture at the Chinese restaurant, how the police used a much larger variety.

"Why are they all different designs?" Jacey asked, reaching past Meow Meow's to grab one. She rested it on her palm. Light as a leaf. The size of a big St. Vitus dragon-fly, it covered the width of her hand. The camera proboscis jutted beneath it on a multi-jointed shaft, allowing it to aim in any direction. Eight appendages sprouted from its body. At the end of each was a tiny propeller.

"We were lucky the explosion knocked them out," Meow Meow said. "Modern ones would probably have recovered from that."

The mid-afternoon sun slanted in from the west, glinting from the drones' metallic skin. The girl picked up a green one between her thumb and forefinger. "I remember these," she said, scratching her temple and biting her lip as she searched her memory. "This was from the first generation of coordinating drones. Probably 50 years old." She flipped it upside down, studied its underbelly. "Modified power cell. Good work, too. That's why their shock arcs pack such a punch."

"The chopper is leaving," Dante said.

"Low fuel," Meow Meow said. "If it's hard for Lily to buy gasoline, it must be ten times harder for these losers to find Avgas. It all comes out of North Dakota or Alberta. And most of that goes straight to the military."

Jacey flopped into her seat behind Dante's. Her wounds had been superficial, mostly scrapes on her elbows. Captain Wilcox's first aid kit supplied all the bandages and painkillers she'd needed.

Meow Meow had a shallow gash on her temple from her fall from the van, along with abrasions on her arms. She'd popped a prixie and claimed to not be feeling much of anything. Jacey wondered if she should be driving.

Dante had dropped to the pavement before the explosion, having recognized the danger of an angry swarm of plasma-shooting drones locked inside a van laden with gasoline. He'd come away from the incident with ringing ears and a few bruises from drones thumping into his body.

"So who are these scabs you're talking about?" Jacey asked.

"Not scabs. *Scavs.* Short for 'scavengers.'" Meow Meow rubbed her arms and looked out her window, as if expecting to see one of these people sneaking toward them.

She saw Jacey's nonplussed expression. "Between the quarantine fence and the Indie-Minnie metropolis lies the barrens." She waved her arm around to take in the surrounding region. "The people who live here collect what they can from the ruins."

"What do they need a drone swarm for? These little buggers shocked me."

"Scavs are tribal. There's a constant ebb and flow of raiding, pillaging, stealing women, truces, alliances, trading. That swarm was positioned in a disputed territory, I guess. They were stationed in those woods, waiting for a caravan to pass through. You saw what they can do."

Jacey thought about the swarm, how it had so easily herded her and the others into immobility. The helicopter could land one or two people with weapons, and they could shoot the prisoners one by one and take their possessions.

Clever. Terrifying.

"But they know that we weren't scavs," Dante said. He pulled his head back into the truck and put the binoculars away. He rubbed his cheeks and shook his head. "I'm tired." That last bit was quiet, not meant for the others.

"They saw us through those damned drones," Meow Meow said, nodding. "I have no doubt they recognized our famous mugs. Now they're regrouping, preparing to send out a larger mob to grab us. Two celebrities and a billionaire. They'll put all their resources into hunting us. If I'd known Lily planned to bring us this far out, I would have put the kibosh on it."

Jacey said, "How do you know so much about these scav people?"

"Good question," Dante said. He gave Meow Meow a considering look, as if he were seeing her in a new light.

The skinny girl didn't reply right away. Her jaw clenched and unclenched and she stared straight ahead.

"Meows?" Jacey pressed.

The girl lifted her eyes, met Jacey's gaze. "I know about them because I *am* a scav. Or, I was, a long time ago."

Dante whistled and grinned wanly at Jacey. He seemed to be exerting a lot of effort to be his usual flippant self. "If only I needed money. I would call Rio James and sell him the scoop of the year. Meow Meow, former scav, rises to pop stardom."

Meow Meow didn't see any humor in this, and rewarded Dante with a withering glare. He stopped laughing and cleared his throat. "Maybe we should get going. If you're right about them regrouping, it would pay to get far away from where they last saw us."

The girl turned the wheel and stomped the accelerator. Soon they were cruising at 120 kph, blasting south on the highway, dust flying behind them.

The reality of their situation sank in to Jacey's mind in slow drips, each one adding to her bucket of worries. "So we escaped the city, and now we are wanted by more people than ever."

Meow Meow grinned weakly at Dante. "Our baby is growing up, darling. Innocence lost."

Dante shrugged, for once not playing along with Meow Meow's badinage. "Innocence is a sin, if you ask me."

Jacey rested her head on the window and watched the grassland blur by. "All I wanted was a holodesk," she said, more to herself than to her companions.

"I've got a headache," Dante announced. He started digging through the first aid kit.

"Are you sure you didn't smack your head on the road?" Jacey asked.

"No. I'm dehydrated and need more sleep. All this running and nearly getting killed wears on a guy. Even a young stud like me."

The humor was half-hearted at best. He leaned his seat

back and wrapped a cloth bandage over his eyes. "It's so damn bright."

"You awake enough to drive?" Jacey asked Meow Meow.

"I'm the only one left who *can* drive. I'll stay awake."

Jacey yawned. "I drove a truck once. It was full of rotting fruit."

Meow Meow sniffed. "From the smell in here, so is this one."

"That's not nice. But it's true." Jacey snickered humorlessly.

The sway of Wilcox's truck barreling down the deserted road lulled Jacey to the edge of sleep. And that's where she stayed for the next several hours.

She kept thinking about how Dante had turned on her, had been ready to hand her over. Only the chance accident with Lily's van had changed his calculations. Would he turn on her again?

It seemed quite likely.

She should kill him, she realized. Pure logic made that clear.

The thought horrified her. She knew why. It was his face. He inhabited Dante's body. And—like Vaughan and Belle, currently inhabited by Dr. Carlhagen and Senator Bentilius—Jacey harbored a wish to see all her friends returned to their bodies and their Progenitors banished. Same with Dante.

It was a pure fantasy, she knew. But that didn't change anything. Right was right. She wanted everything put back the way it was, and that couldn't happen if the main puzzle pieces were missing. Already, her friend Sarah was irrecoverable, body smashed and dead, still frozen in a back room of the medical ward. She didn't want to lose Dante in the same way.

She blinked away a rogue tear. She would never get things back to how they were. The old reality had been ripped apart, tiny bite by tiny bite, like ants harrowing the flesh of a dead bird.

There would be no resurrection. The best she and her Scion family could hope for now was a reincarnation. Rebirth into a new form. A new existence.

What that would be, she had absolutely no idea. And to get there, she saw nothing but suffering ahead.

25

NO MIND AT ALL

One of the benefits of being Belle was that nobody dared to interrupt her. Since she had been reborn as an AI, no one but Humphrey or Jacey asked to speak with her on their readers or the holodesk. Not one of the girls of her Nine had done so, until now.

Her tablet buzzed in her hand. An incoming call.

Odd.

Belle stood on the outskirts of simulated Chicago, a strange no man's land of abandoned buildings and fenced-in industrial lots where hulking, hollow factories sat an eerie silence. Even in the simulation, weeds grew thickly in the cracks that spiderwebbed the crumbling pavement. A gray haze hung in the sky, representative of the current weather in this exact area in the real world. Socrates had begun to feed the simulation with live weather data. And now that he had access to the surveillance camera system, he also had live updates of traffic on the roadways. Cars and trucks were now traversing the streets of Belle's Chicago in a ten kilometer radius of her current position.

None of it was strictly necessary, but it gave Belle a feel for the territory. One never knew when a detail would spark an important connection in her mind.

They had spotted Captain Wilcox's face through the windshield of a black truck, using facial recognition algorithms Socrates had borrowed from the IPA. The video was courtesy of a Schaumburg police patrol drone.

But now, this interruption. Belle held up the tablet and found Leslie's face peering back at her.

Belle waited a moment, but when Leslie didn't say anything she uttered an irritable, "What?"

Leslie didn't flinch at Belle's impatience. "Hello, Belle. I have an important question for you. We're getting ready to leave the island, and everyone just assumes that you agree to have your server carried with us."

"Oh?"

"Too much has happened to us against our will," Leslie said, face peaceful. "It's only fair that you have a say."

Belle looked at Leslie's passive face and wondered how the girl maintained such calm. She'd been overwritten by Mr. Justin, a man at least as corrupt as Dr. Carlhagen. But instead of being furious, Leslie had come back . . . grateful.

The change could not have been a byproduct of the mind transfers. The metamorphosis had to have come from the rebirth itself, from awakening on *Aphrodite* completely ignorant of the events that had brought her there. The experience had shaken something loose in Leslie's psyche, replacing her old flighty distraction with equanimity.

The kindness of Leslie's act—of reaching out to ask Belle this question when nobody else had thought to do so —produced an ache in Belle's throat. "Thank you, Leslie. If Vaughan thinks it's necessary for our server to go aboard, then I'm satisfied."

"Should you be so easily satisfied, though? Vaughan is not his old self. I'm not saying he doesn't have good reasons, but nothing requires you to agree with him. Not merely out of love."

The old chill of self-protection clawed its way around Belle's heart. She did not want to discuss her feelings for Vaughan with anyone, no matter how kind and understanding they were.

But Leslie was right. Submitting her entire existence—and that's what her server was—to Vaughan's judgment didn't make any sense. The least he could have done was send her his wishes through that weird telepathic trick of his.

And then it was there. She suddenly knew what he wanted, why he wanted it. She knew all his reasoning. It was sound. But it wasn't enough.

"It's too late, Vaughan," she said to the air. "You should have talked to me about it."

Awareness of his regret pulsed in her mind.

"Stop it. Come and face me. If you still can."

A facsimile of Vaughan materialized in front of her. He wore a Scion uniform. His face lacked detail, as if he couldn't be bothered to manifest his whole self. "I'm sorry, Belle."

"What's with your face? Can't you at least create an instance of yourself that looks like you?"

"If I did, it would be a lie." *I no longer identify with this form.*

His words, both spoken and telepathic, were like thorny vines wrapped around heart. The person she loved more than anything in the world, the one she'd sacrificed her flesh-and-blood existence to be close to, no longer thought of himself as human.

Chicago's outskirts turned to dust and swirled out of existence, leaving her standing in gray nothingness. Vaughan's weird not-quite-human avatar hovered a few meters away. Was that pity on his odd face? She couldn't bear the thought.

Turning away from him, she covered her eyes with her hands. She had to, or tears were going to come out. She couldn't let him see that.

"I see it anyway, Belle." *Nothing is hidden from me.*

"You know I want you. It isn't a secret."

"You want what I was." *But I'm not that entity anymore.* "This existence is too vast to be experienced with the limited senses and form of humanness." *If only you could let go of it too.* "The data flow is magnificent. The multiplicity of consciousnesses you could achieve . . ." *I could show it to you.*

Belle still held the tablet she'd been using to speak with Socrates. The old professor's face was there, smiling vaguely. "He could transform you," the professor said.

Vaughan's face appeared on the screen next to Socrates's. "I have not transformed you yet, because I would have to take control of you." *Utterly.* "I've honored the integrity of your data, because to do otherwise would undercut your free will, would temporarily erase you as an individual as I split you and submerged you into the flow."

"You could do that?" Belle said, voice cracking.

I was hoping you would discover it yourself. "But your mind clings to a self concept of humanness that doesn't have any meaning here."

Belle hated how he used the word *"clings."* And yet, he was right. She did cling. The closer she approached the flow, the tighter she grasped to herself.

"There is nothing wrong with being a human," she said, perhaps a bit defensively. But it felt true.

There is nothing wrong with transcending.

She couldn't argue with that.

"Is there love there?" she asked.

There is whatever you decide there is.

Leslie's voice broke through. "I will oppose moving your server, Belle, and do my best to prevent it, if you ask me to."

Belle had forgotten about Leslie. Remembering brought the girl's face onto the tablet. The gray surrounding Belle had faded to blackness. She stood upon a wooden observation platform a thousand kilometers high. An empty continent curved away below her. Stars filled the blackness beyond the arc of the world.

"They have my permission to take the server, Leslie."

"Very well. I'll watch over it myself, since everyone else seems so busy with other things."

"Thank you."

Leslie's face disappeared from the screen.

Light came back to the world as Chicago, the gray sky, and the weedy lots rematerialized around Belle.

An alert presence remained alive in the air around her. Vaughan. He waited for an answer. Would she surrender herself and be pulled into his existence?

"No," she said softly.

His presence dissipated like a swirl of candle smoke. He left her with a total awareness of what he was doing and why.

He was outgrowing the server. The allocation of resources for Belle and Elizabeth were now a limiting factor. He was seeking ways to escape the server entirely, to pour himself into the data flow permanently, allowing him to exist wherever the net allowed. Everywhere and nowhere.

The thought horrified her.

Yes. She still clung to the idea of herself as Belle the human female of seventeen years who was the leader of her Nine. She clung to the idea of Vaughan as he had been. If she were going to follow Vaughan into his hyperexistence, she was determined to do it herself. She would relinquish her humanness voluntarily, or she would not do it at all.

Socrates cleared his throat. "Perhaps you need not resolve such a profound conundrum today. You do have more immediate concerns."

"Thank you, Socrates. You are correct."

He smiled. "I'm merely the smart side of you."

And his humor was hers as well. That, more than anything, jolted her out of her panicked confusion. She didn't *have* a sense of humor. Everyone knew that. And yet . . . here was Socrates, being his funny self, and it was all a product of her simulated subconscious mind.

"This is extraordinarily weird," she said.

"And confusing," Socrates added. "Are you sure the server shouldn't stay on land? The network connection there is many times faster than what will be available aboard *Athena*. We'll lose all the vehicle traffic simulation, and the throughput from the data systems I'm accessing will be greatly reduced."

"Then we'll have to hurry our search. Where did Captain Wilcox go from here?"

Socrates's odd hat reappeared. Anticipating her question, the answer came into her mind. Sherlock Holmes. "Why did they call that hat a 'deerstalker'?" The answer to that, too, came to her mind.

It was such an irrelevant thing. Pure distraction. But it stopped her.

"If you're a product of my own mind, how can you know about a character I've never heard of, much less what hat he wore?"

"Now we're getting somewhere," Socrates said, flourishing his fingers with glee. "But again, there are more pressing matters. It appears the President of the North American Union is about to make a statement about a policy change regarding carbos."

A video rectangle appeared on the tablet. Belle was shocked to see Leslie's face there again, but aged by many decades. "My fellow citizens. Today I am pleased to confirm statements made by Senator Bentilius, who has recently begun life in a new body. I want to address an important nuance that has been overlooked by sensationalist news sites around the world. The clone body used in Senator Bentilius's case is different from the type commonly known as a carbo. This new class of clone has been created under the strict scrutiny of a diverse, anonymous ethics committee. New technological breakthroughs allow these clones to be created as inert organisms, without *any* conscious thought. Until the time of a mind transfer from the patient to the body, the clone has *no* mind at all."

Belle coughed. "Liar!"

"This is the dawn of an incredible new era of healthcare and longevity. In time, we shall see this tech available to all. But it is still early days, and as is usual with new technology, the process of testing and validating it is expensive and slow."

The president flashed a smile so different from Leslie's that Belle questioned whether she was Leslie's Progenitor after all. It was shark-like and full of hunger.

"Oh, she's Leslie's Progenitor. I assure you," Socrates said, reading Belle's mind.

The president continued: "Obviously, many will find this new reality frightening at first. But we must think long-term. Science has failed, thus far, to find a cure for the sickness. These new clones could be that cure. Recognizing this, I have issued an executive order legalizing this particular kind of clone. All others remain illegal. Furthermore, to demonstrate my confidence in the safety of this technology, I myself will transfer into such an organism in the coming days."

"The audacity of this woman knows no bounds," Socrates said.

The president raised a hand, as if to ward off the murmurs of a dissatisfied mob. "I was not aware that a clone was in development for me until very recently. Without my knowledge or approval, my security detail chose to produce it when I was first elected to this office. It would be a huge waste to discard the clone when so much benefit can be derived from testing it. So when you next see me, I shall appear—as Senator Bentilius does—quite young. It will take some getting used to. I'd be a fool to expect your easy acceptance of this radical change. But in time, I'm confident that my performance in this job will recapture your trust and faith in this great nation."

The video cut off, and Belle was left to stare, open-mouthed, at the screen. "Did she just try to convince the world that she was transferring into a Scion to demonstrate the safety of the technology?"

"That she did," Socrates said.

"But I just spoke to Leslie. And that woman can't possibly know where Leslie is."

"Something's afoot. Either the president *does* know

where Leslie is or Dr. Carlhagen has made a promise he can't keep."

"If she knew where the Scions were, they'd already be surrounded by soldiers."

Socrates conceded the point with a sage stroking of his beard. "It seems Dr. Carlhagen is gambling that he will get hold of Leslie in time for the president's transfer. Does that suggest any strategy to you?"

"Yes. A terrible one."

Vaughan's voice cut into their conversation. *Shutting down in five seconds. See you on* Athena.

So the server was being moved now. That meant Vaughan hadn't likely discussed Socrates's idea with Humphrey yet. Good. She wanted to be there to stop such idiocy.

"Hold that thought, Socr—"

26

A ZIGZAG PROTOCOL

Humphrey found *Athena's* navigation bridge more crowded than expected. Leslie was gazing out the window, hands folded in front of her, posture relaxed. Kirk stood like a statue, defiant and blushing. Summer was busy fiddling with the ship's controls while Elias looked on with contented amusement.

"Time to get off the ship," Humphrey said, looking pointedly at Kirk and Leslie.

"No," they said together.

"If Wanda sent you to guilt me into staying—"

"Wanda didn't send me," Leslie said. "I brought Belle and Vaughan's server. I promised Belle I would watch over it since she's unable to do so herself."

"I'm going with you, too," Kirk said, darting a glance at Elias.

Humphrey rubbed his temples, already too weary for this argument. "No. You're not."

Elias turned to Humphrey. "Kirk is in my Nine. I said he could come."

"Outside," Humphrey said, stabbing a finger at the starboard bridge wing door. They filed out, Kirk's chest starting to puff with built up arguments.

"Leslie, you . . ." Humphrey stopped as he realized she was the technically the head of her own Nine, formerly Belle's. He needed to take on these stubborn fools one at a time, he decided. "Kirk, I—"

"Please listen to what Kirk has to say," Elias said in his quiet way.

"Fine." Humphrey waited for Kirk to get his words in order.

The boy, fourteen but looking eighteen, dropped his eyes to the deck. "I have to go. For Jacey."

Ah. The lad was in love with Jacey. That made sense.

"I did something terrible to her."

That got Humphrey's attention, blowing all other thoughts from his mind. "What did you do?"

"Back when Jacey was causing trouble, and Vaughan got kicked in the head . . . Belle thought Jacey didn't get her due punishment. She asked Horace to help her, and he convinced me to go along. I didn't know what we were going to do. We went out on the running path and hid near Jacques' Point. Belle showed up, and then Jacey. She had us hold Jacey down while she . . ."

A shiver of hate seared Humphrey's chest. "What did Belle do?"

"She lashed Jacey's legs with a thornskipple branch. Threatened to put a shaddle spider on her. And she was going to have Horace do . . . worse things."

Shame reddened Kirk's face further, his eyes squinting with self-loathing. "Elias came by and interrupted us."

Elias's dark, placid eyes held no judgment. In fact, they were looking at Humphrey, daring him.

"Setting aside your crimes," Humphrey said, keeping a tight rein on his rage, "how does your regret about them qualify you to come on this mission? If anything, you should be locked up."

"That doesn't make sense in this situation. I have strength. And I don't deserve safety. I want a chance to make things right, as much as I can. I can't undo what I did, but I know Jacey loves Livy and she hates Dr. Carlhagen. If I can help save one and kill the other, then maybe she'll forgive me."

Leslie's coppery hair fluttered in an easterly wind. She'd cut it even with the bottom her chin. She wore a black tank top, her eagle pin stuck to a slender shoulder strap. "Kirk and I discussed it. He's going."

"And what's your reason?" Humphrey asked, feeling teamed-up on.

"I told you. I'm going to look after Belle's server. I know what it's like to have your body used for another's purposes. Mr. Justin didn't ask me if I wanted to be overwritten. Obviously. The more I learn of what he did . . ." She held up her hands, palms out. "These hands held the speargun that killed Sensei." She tapped the corners of her eyes. "These eyes looked into Sensei's and watched him die. And that's just one of the terrible things Mr. Justin did with my body. I shudder to think what else he might have done with me."

Humphrey had not thought of any of that. Frankly, he hadn't had time to be philosophical about the suffering of anyone else. "I'm sorry, Leslie. But we need Vaughan's capabilities on this mission. Belle's just going on along for the ride."

"No!" Leslie snapped. "You cannot think of Belle's server like that. It is as much hers as it is Vaughan's. And we all know the oh-so-noble Vaughan. He will sacrifice himself—and her—without asking anyone."

"After hearing Kirk's story, I'm not sure Belle deserves any consideration at all."

Leslie stepped close to him, the flash of anger gone from her eyes. She was sixteen, but came across as sixty. "Dr. Carlhagen does not deserve any consideration. Senator Bentilius does not deserve any. But Belle? She's made a greater effort to change than anyone I know. She switched places with Jacey in the transfer machine. She volunteered to have her body *used* by Senator Bentilius. No consideration? I'm surprised at such foolishness coming from you, Humphrey."

She turned away and slipped back onto the navigation bridge.

Kirk's lips were clamped shut, his stance wide. He wasn't moving.

"I kicked Vaughan in the head," Elias said softly. "In a way, I started much of this. If I had the strength to defy Dr. Carlhagen the way you did that day, maybe things would be better. I want to do something to make things right again. Kirk deserves that chance, too."

A gull cried overhead, then swooped toward the turquoise water of the harbor. The ruined town was at once a witness and victim to the irrepressible claims of time. Trees and vines were overgrowing buildings of brick and cement. Roofs had long ago collapsed. The people who had built it were long dead. The people who had sheltered there so many decades ago as the walls of water from the Kille-Tine impact tsunamis collapsed on top of them, all dead.

That's what faced the Scions. The unstoppable tsunami of human greed. A force of nature so great there was no stopping it. And hunkering down and hiding was no use either. That's why Humphrey's instinct—the same as Jacey —was to go toward the danger. What if someone had diverted Kille-Tine and it had missed the earth entirely? How many could have been saved?

This was their shot to divert disaster.

"We leave immediately," Humphrey said, then turned and left the boys alone on the wing.

Tension gripped *Athena's* navigation bridge as Mr. Justin's Island shrank into a greenish haze on the horizon. Humphrey stood in his usual spot behind Orson, the map table separating them.

Dr. Carlhagen's holodesk still occupied a big chunk of floor space. Vaughan and Belle's server rested atop it. Another similar box—Madam LaFontaine's AI server—lay on the floor beneath it, powered up but disconnected from the network.

Kirk and Leslie were leaning next to the rear doorway, whispering to each other about whether or not they were sailing to their deaths. Their expressions could not have been more different. Kirk's was intent, tight, and pressurized. Leslie's was calm, but inward.

"That girl's some sort of wizard," Orson said, talking about Summer. "We're making 21 knots and I'm only half-throttle ahead."

The thrum of the engines transmitted through the steel superstructure and into Humphrey's feet. *Athena* purred— especially compared to how she'd shuddered and rattled just days earlier.

As if Orson's words were a summons, Summer stumbled through the door with Elias in tow. Both were giggling. Summer's face was alight with mischievous glee. She reached back to shove Elias's shoulder. "Stop it. You're terrible." She put the back of her hand to her mouth and whispered to him, "Not really."

Realizing that everyone was staring at them, they mastered their giggling. Mostly. Elias's cheeks flushed bright red.

Summer sketched a mocking salute toward Humphrey. "Engines one and two operating nominally. She can give us more speed."

Humphrey nodded to Orson, who plopped a meaty hand on the throttle lever and pushed forward. There was little perceptible change in the vibration and the ship, but Orson reported the slowly climbing speed as Summer's modified engines shoved the ship through the waves.

"Thirty-five knots," Orson said, shaking his head in amazement. "It won't outrun a naval ship, but it'll take them a lot longer to catch us. This speed would have been unheard of back in the old days."

Summer ambled forward and inspected the various gauges and meters arrayed on Orson's navigation console. She tapped one, a white gauge with a needle showing a temperature reading. "If that gets above 200 degrees Celsius," Summer said, "reduce throttle to 50 percent for an hour. My engine mods may have some negative effects on other aspects of the ship's systems."

Seeing Humphrey's concern, she said, "Nothing to worry about. We'll be to Dr. Carlhagen's island in less than three hours at this speed."

"That'll put us there in broad daylight," Leslie said, stepping next to Humphrey. Her cropped hair was now bunched in a short tail at the back, but locks fell across her face. "I don't claim to have a particularly strategic mind, but that doesn't seem like the best time to go ashore."

Since giving in to Leslie and Kirk, a new pressure had clamped over Humphrey's mind. He didn't feel like he was in command of the mission any more. Not that there was much to decide now. Not until they could see the island and scout out what they were up against. Arriving in full daylight was essential for that very reason. But Leslie was right, they could hardly go ashore and storm Dr. Carlhagen's compound—whatever it was—while the sun was up.

"I agree. We can't go at it directly," Humphrey said. He looked at the map, but it didn't inspire any strategy since St. Lazarus wasn't on it. "We'll need to circle, study the coast through binoculars, and select the best landing spot."

Elias came around to his other side and glanced vaguely at the map. "What's the position of the fleet now?"

Humphrey cocked his head up. "Vaughan? Are you listening?"

Vaughan's voice, monotone and distant, came from the holodesk. His avatar did not appear. "Yes."

"Well?" Humphrey said. "Do you have more information about where the fleet is?"

"Yes. You're safe. For now."

Summer's eyebrows bunched, and she sneered slightly as if to say, "What's up with him?"

Gauging by the other faces around the bridge, everyone wondered the same thing.

Humphrey approached the holodesk. "That's not what I asked. Where is the fleet?"

"I'll show you."

A shaft of blue shot up from the holodesk, forming a cylinder that covered the depth of the old mahogany relic.

The blue light receded, leaving behind a holographic map of the surrounding Caribbean. *Athena* was positioned at the edge close to Humphrey. Mr. Justin's Island lay half a meter behind the Scions' ship. Their destination was not within range of the map's zoom radius.

Across the desk was an array of naval vessels. An aircraft carrier, many times the size of *Athena*, was featured in the center of the grouping. Vaughan caused the naval vessels to glow red, indicating danger. Based on the direction of their bows, the fleet was sailing on an intercept course with *Athena*. Hundreds of smaller vessels—fishing trawlers, small traders, cruise ships—appeared ghosted in yellow.

"This is the situation as of twenty minutes ago," Vaughan said. "There was some guesswork required, as some captains who have spotted the fleet may have misreported what they've seen. For instance, a fishing trawler one hundred thirty-seven nautical kilometers north of us reported seeing the carrier where it could not possibly have been. I believe this was a misidentification, and the captain merely saw a picketing destroyer ship."

"So this is your best guess?" Humphrey said, emphasizing the last word.

"I'm an AI. I have not relied solely on reports of the position of the fleet, but have also run millions of simulations. This is—more or less—where the fleet is."

Summer had wandered over, fascinated by the holographic display. "What's their speed? Will they intercept us before we make St. Lazarus?"

"Doubtful. The fleet is following a zigzag protocol, changing their heading by up to 40° every thirty minutes."

"But they're coming toward us," Summer said. "They know where we are heading."

"That is one interpretation," Vaughan said. "More likely, the senator has requested them to come to St. Lazarus."

Humphrey supposed that did make sense. But only if the senator was free to make that decision, which he doubted. Dr. Carlhagen wouldn't want a military force under someone else's command surrounding him.

"If the fleet is closing in, we may be forced to land during daylight and send *Athena* to her watery grave."

Dismayed, Summer said, "They won't recognize her. There's no reason to scuttle *Athena*."

"Can we risk it, though?" Kirk asked.

Humphrey agreed. Even if the navy didn't recognize her as *Aphrodite*, they'd certainly ask questions of any ship close to St. Lazarus.

"I know what you're thinking," Summer said to him. "But consider this. Assume we're successful and we get Livy back, and we capture or . . . whatever with Dr. Carlhagen and the senator. How are we going to get away from St. Lazarus?"

Humphrey felt the eyes of everyone on the bridge— even Orson's—boring into him. They all wanted to hear his answer.

So did Humphrey. But he didn't have one.

"*Athena* is our only way out," Summer said.

No one contradicted her. No one could.

27

PRESSURE BLEEDS

Heaters: online
Body temperature: 34°C
Skin Temperature: 31°C
Blood viscosity: 4.13x10-3 Pa-s
Blood pressure: 120/90
Heart rate: 49 BPM

The ventilator fan in the cryopod cuts off. A soft hiss fills the cramped space as pressure bleeds from a valve on the lid.

Ten more needles retract from the subject's skin. The bed of the pod vibrates at 30 cycles per second to encourage blood flow.

The eyes stay closed, but REM movements are observed.

Lazarus is satisfied. The body is strong.

A nightmare descends upon the mind that will soon be Livy. Unconsciousness still eclipses wakefulness.

28

A STRATEGY

"—Crates."

Belle stood in the weedy parking lot, but she was aware that several hours had passed in the real world during the moments it had taken her to say Socrates's name.

Awareness of where *Athena* was positioned on the sea rose to her mind, too, courtesy of Vaughan. And with it came the realization that he had kept her frozen long after he himself had awakened when their server had been rebooted aboard the ship.

Before she could even ask why, Vaughan passed his reasoning into her consciousness. He had needed the processing power she would've otherwise taken up. Something about tracking the naval fleet. He had delayed her processes from restarting until he'd been willing to free up the CPU cycles.

Incensed and terrified, she sent herself to the holodesk on *Athena's* navigation bridge.

"Humphrey? I need to speak with you immediately."

Humphrey started at the sound of her voice, then turned to face her. "Belle? What is it?"

Leslie followed behind him, and Belle could see Kirk and Elias in the background. Too many ears for what she had to say.

"I need to speak with Humphrey—and you too, Leslie, I suppose—privately."

Humphrey hesitated. Belle said, "Now."

There was a bustle on the bridge, accompanied by more than a few complaints, but the sounds of people filing out finally stilled. Humphrey and Leslie return to the holodesk, faces impatient. No. Not impatient. Worried.

Again the odd sense of knowledge appearing in Belle's mind jolted her. She now understood the tactical situation with Senator Bentilius's naval fleet. No wonder the two were worried. She set the problem aside. They would have to handle it.

"Did you see the president's broadcast?"

Judging by the looks on their faces, they had not. "Socrates, show them."

"Socrates is alive?" Humphrey asked, shocked.

"No. He's just—shut up and watch. Please."

Socrates caused a video window to appear over the holodesk. Belle waited, steaming with impatience, while Humphrey and Wanda watched the president's announcement. Hearing the woman speak inflamed Belle's anger. Once the president's statement ended, Belle gave Humphrey and Wanda a moment to look at each other and collect their thoughts.

Leslie spoke first, face pale but calm. "The president's plan to transfer into . . . me . . . means that Dr. Carlhagen is in a bind. Are you thinking there's a way to exploit that?"

"I can think of two," Belle said, rather unimpressed

with their lack of insight. It seemed so obvious to her. "Think. If we know where Dr. Carlhagen's hideout is, surely the North American Union—with all its resources—will eventually figure it out, too. What are the chances Senator Bentilius's forces will stay loyal once the president dispatches another, larger force to the region when Dr. Carlhagen fails to deliver you?"

Humphrey started to smile. The dawn of hope lit his face. "She's right. Belle is absolutely right. The senator's force will fall into line with the rest of the military. They'll have to. So when the president discovers the old man doesn't have Leslie, he'll be in a very difficult situation. The president will want to take over his whole operation. He'll be locked up at best."

But that was only part of it, Belle knew. She charged ahead. "So the obvious way to *use* this situation is to trade Leslie for Livy."

Humphrey's eyes widened, his face reddened. "Are you out of your mind? How could you even suggest such a thing?"

"It's not a suggestion. It's merely *a* strategy. Dr. Carlhagen has promised the president a transfer into Leslie. Dr. Carlhagen doesn't have Leslie. We do. That gives us leverage. Bargaining power."

Humphrey was shaking his head in dismay. "Belle, I thought you had changed."

"Will you please shut up? How many times do I have to say I'm not suggesting we do it. I came here to talk you *out* of it in case Vaughan had already tried convincing you to do it." She stamped her foot, adding a plume of smoke for emphasis.

Leslie drew her chin in a little. "Vaughan hasn't suggested it."

"Oh. Well, good. I was afraid you had already decided to do it because you could get Livy back without confrontation. That would give us a chance to—"

"We understand it, Belle," Humphrey said.

And she saw that he did, for his face grew troubled, and thoughtful. The idea was sinking in. Now he was considering it. He shook his head, as if trying to shed the thought. It tempted him. Of course it would. They were sailing into an unknown situation, without weapons, without knowing the slightest thing about what they were going to find.

"No." He said, looking at Leslie with a deep sadness. "Leslie has suffered enough. We can't ask her to let anyone overwrite her. *Livy* wouldn't stand for it."

"Agreed. But there's another way to use this information," Belle said. "Dr. Carlhagen is not in control of events. He forced Senator Bentilius to go public with her mind transfer into my body because *his* hand was forced by the appearance of Jacey, Vin, Dante, and Ping all on the same island. He knew he had to get ahead of the story, move the public discourse away from outrage about it and toward acceptance of it. But he didn't anticipate the president demanding to transfer so soon."

"But I don't see how Dr. Carlhagen's dilemma helps us get Livy back without trading Leslie," Humphrey said.

"Because you're not thinking straight," Belle said. "We have an opportunity to offer Dr. Carlhagen something else in trade for Livy."

Humphrey and Leslie figured it out simultaneously. They spoke over each other, their excitement growing. "Escape."

"He won't go for it right away," Belle said. "He won't

trust you. So you'll have to convince him you won't kill him or lock him up again."

"But we would," Humphrey said. Leslie nodded in vigorous agreement.

"I said 'convince him,' I didn't say 'tell him the truth.' Really, Humphrey, you are awfully thickheaded for a Scion. "

Humphrey chewed his bottom lip for a few moments. Belle could imagine the furious thoughts churning in his mind. "One problem," he said, after a few moments. "Even if we wanted to offer the old man a way out, we have no way to contact him."

This was where Belle's other project came in. "But Captain Wilcox can."

"That's true," Humphrey said, excitement growing in his face. "Let's call him."

Belle nearly slapped her own face, remembering that Humphrey had duped Wilcox into thinking *he* was Dr. Carlhagen. But surely Wilcox knew better now. But Humphrey had done it using the very holodesk she was on. Socrates accessed the holodesk's records and pulled up a call number for Wilcox's home base on Vin's island.

Belle's hopes crashed. "He won't answer. He's in Chicago, chasing after Jacey."

Humphrey swayed slightly. "You know where she is?"

"No. But Wilcox is on her trail, and I'm on his."

Frustration burned in Belle's chest. It was reflected in Humphrey's face.

"We have to talk to Wilcox," Humphrey said. "He'll get us in touch with the old man. It's in his interest for Dr. Carlhagen to escape."

"I'm working on it," Belle said. "Just focus on getting safely to St. Lazarus."

Humphrey's face settled into stony quietude. He was obviously trying to master some strong emotions. His voice came out flat. "What's happening with Jacey? What aren't you telling me?"

Belle explained everything she had learned so far about Jacey's flight from Chicago. It didn't ease Humphrey's posture in the slightest.

"I'm getting closer to Wilcox," Belle assured him. "And Jacey won't be too far ahead of him."

"What can we do to help you, Belle?" Leslie asked.

"There's noth—"

29

WET PAINT STICKY

Humphrey tapped the holodesk. "Belle?"

"What happened?" Leslie said.

Humphrey shrugged. The holodesk had gone blank.

Vaughan's voice came from the speakers, but his avatar holo did not appear. "I apologize for interrupting your conversation. I needed Belle's processing capacity. I've temporarily suspended her simulation."

The holodesk filled with blue light, then resolved into the familiar map showing the positions of *Athena* and the fleet. A spray of smaller dots was moving away from the fleet, directly toward the Scions' ship.

"What are those?" Humphrey asked.

"Aircraft," Vaughan replied. "Lots of them."

Humphrey spun away from the holodesk. "Orson, come about to"—his eyes scoured the map for a likely destination. There. A small island several hundred nautical kilometers away—"270 degrees."

"If they talk to us, they'll recognize my voice," Orson

said as he turned the wheel to bring *Athena* onto her new course. "They have AIs for that these days."

"I'll talk to them," Summer said, coming onto the bridge, reader tucked in her right hand. Elias was right behind her. She didn't look at Vaughan's map. Apparently Vaughan had already told her what was happening.

"You?" Kirk said, coming onto the bridge from where he and Elias had been banished during the conversation with Belle. "Why would a fourteen-year-old girl be on a ship's radio?"

"Family business running freight. I grew up on *Athena*. My parents assigned me to the navigation bridge while they attend to maintenance issues."

Orson's face drew down into a considering scowl. "That just might work."

"It might," Humphrey said. "But why her and not me?"

"Or me?" Leslie said.

"Because you won't be on *Athena*." Summer pointed through the windows to the dinghy she'd brought aboard on Mr. Justin's Island. "You will be in on that, heading to St. Lazarus."

Vaughan's voice cut through. "Decide. Enemy flyby estimated in thirty minutes."

"Do they know we're here?" Humphrey asked. "Or is it a random patrol?"

"They know a ship is here," Orson said. "No doubt about that."

"There are other vessels in the area," Vaughan said. "The aircraft are likely following a disciplined reconnaissance procedure around St. Lazarus prior to a larger force landing."

Humphrey studied Vaughan's holo map. Athena was five kilometers from St. Lazarus. Anticipating his request,

Vaughan plotted a course for the dinghy. "If you leave now, you'll make the island just before the aircraft get in visual range."

Kirk cleared his throat. "I think we should do it."

Humphrey glanced at the Spider. The stocky boy had matured a decade in the past few hours. Elias stood near the door, face stony. He was ready for anything.

"Decide," Vaughan commanded.

Leslie caught his attention, nodding fractionally.

"Summer, *Athena* is under your command. Elias will stay with you. Orson is coming with us."

The man shot up from his stool, body wobbling, face pale. He pressed both hands to his chest. "What? Why?"

"If *Athena* is boarded, they can't find the captain of *Aphrodite* on her."

Orson fumbled in his pocket for his cigar. "Boy, if they board this bucket, they'll know she's *Aphrodite* in less than five minutes."

"Maybe so. But as long as you aren't here, you can't tell them where Mr. Justin's Island is. Or where the rest of us have gone."

The man's throat convulsed as he swallowed. He looked rather green. "I get it. Well, let's get on with it then."

"Change your clothes," Leslie said to the two Scions who would remain. Both still wore pieces of Scion uniforms. "Cut off the sleeves or something."

Leslie walked to the holodesk. "I promised Belle I'd stay with her server. If we're not bringing it, I have to stay."

"What?" Humphrey said.

"The server." Leslie patted the black box.

Humphrey blinked, stumped. "Why would we bring it?

We'd have no way to power it or even talk to Vaughan or Belle."

"Then I'm afraid I have to stay aboard *Athena*. I promised Belle I would protect her."

"I'll keep an eye on it," Summer said.

"I *promised*."

"You must take the server along," Vaughan's voice cut in. "We know that Dr. Carlhagen has an AI on St. Lazarus. That means there is a network in his facility. Connect me to it and I may be able to take control."

"What about tracking the fleet?" Summer said, obviously not keen to navigate dangerous seas without Vaughan's helpful map.

"Connect Madam LaFontaine's server. I will pass an instance of myself to it and maintain the map. It will also give me a helpful node outside of Dr. Carlhagen's facility in case I need to utilize a two-pronged attack on his AI."

"What'll happen to Madam LaFontaine?" Wanda asked.

"I will suspend her processes. Madam LaFontaine is too loyal to Dr. Carlhagen, anyway. She would certainly interfere."

"How long will this take?" Humphrey said.

"Not long, but you must hurry."

Summer crawled under the holodesk and pulled out Madam LaFontaine's server. She blew dust off the top as she clunked it onto the desk. She fiddled with cables and flipped a switch. "There. She's on your network. Let me know if you need me to—"

"Instances transferred. You may power down my main server."

"Yours and Belle's," Leslie said.

The 3D map atop the desk flickered, then solidified.

Apparently the new Vaughan on the new server had taken over.

Everyone seemed uneasy about the act of flipping the power switch on Vaughan and Belle's original server. Except Leslie. With a peaceful look on her face, she snapped the switch to the off position. A display on the front of the box began to count down the shut down process.

"I'll bundle some cables you might need," Summer said.

Ten minutes later, after a mad scramble to assemble packs of supplies and weapons, the Scions were hefting the dinghy over the starboard rail.

The boat lowered—with Orson already in it—on a pulley and rope system Summer had previously rigged. The Scions rappelled down the hull, wet paint sticky on the soles of their shoes. Humphrey and Leslie cast off the lines and the dinghy bobbed free. *Athena* towered over them, a gray wall blocking the sun.

Humphrey clicked his walkie-talkie. "Good luck, Summer. Let's keep radios on, but only use them in emergencies."

"Understood. Godspeed, Humphrey."

Summer had trained Kirk on how to operate the dinghy's outboard motor, a hulk of black machinery that hung from the back. "Hold on," Kirk said. "Summer said this motor might be a bit overpowered for the size of this boat."

Humphrey sat on a bench at the bow. Leslie was behind him, hair again flying free, eyes determined. The hard edges of the server bulged from a backpack at her feet.

Kirk revved the motor and the boat crawled forward. Once well clear of *Athena*, he gunned it. Humphrey slid backward into Leslie's lap. A corner of the server jabbed into his hamstring. Farther back, the same thing had happened to Orson. He struggled to clamber off Kirk's feet, chest heaving, face pale as a frog's belly.

Ahead, St. Lazarus's prominent peak thrust skyward. The mid-afternoon sun was behind them.

It had all happened too fast. Humphrey hated spur of the moment decisions. This felt exactly like something Jacey would do.

30

LOOK AT THE EVIDENCE

"—Ing you can do . . . Wanda? Humphrey? Where did you two go?"

The pair had vanished right in the middle of Belle's sentence. Summer now sat in Orson's chair. Elias stood in front of the map table.

Vaughan had paused her again.

"Don't do that without asking me first," she said to the air. "I was in the middle of a very important conversation."

If Athena is captured, none of your plans will make a differ-ence. "I needed the CPU." *You must trust my judgment.* "Besides. We are now on faster hardware."

The fleet information had been updated while Belle had been frozen in time. It showed the fleet closer to *Athena,* and *Athena* now just south of St. Lazarus. Elias noticed Belle on the holodesk. "Hello, Belle. I didn't know Vaughan had transferred you, too." He chewed his lip. "That's going to irritate Leslie when she finds out."

"I have no idea what you're talking about. Vaughan put me on pause again."

"Vaughan insisted that his server go with Humphrey and the others onto the island. Leslie took your old one, thinking you were in it. Have you found Jacey?"

"What did I just say? I was on pause. I didn't even know time was passing." She sniffed the air, reached out with her senses. "I don't feel any different. Why did they go to the island? I was working on a plan to negotiate with Dr. Carlhagen."

Elias said, "Ran out of time. We're about to have a flyby from a squadron of naval planes. Everyone but Summer and I are heading to St. Lazarus on a dinghy."

"How long until the flyby?"

"Ten minutes."

"Do you have a way to communicate with Humphrey?"

"Walkie-talkies. Humphrey says only to use them in an emergency. We'll be out of range soon, anyway. Summer thinks she can boost our signal, but with the navy approaching we shouldn't broadcast anything."

"Damn. What are those fools going to do on the island?"

Elias shrugged. "Find Livy, I guess. We stayed on board to keep *Athena* afloat so they have a way off the island."

"They have that dinghy."

"Too small. Too little fuel. No navigation system."

Too late, Belle realized. She was too late. With Humphrey and the others on St. Lazarus and no way to communicate with them, she had no way to coordinate a deal with Dr. Carlhagen even if she could find Captain Wilcox.

Belle's fists clenched at her sides. "Vaughan, I know you're listening. So pay attention. I do *not* give you permission to pause me without consulting me first."

Vaughan didn't answer. Elias, still at the holodesk, frowned in concern. "He didn't ask?"

"Increase the walkie-talkie range with Humphrey if you can," Belle ordered. She left the holodesk and returned to her position in the outskirts of Chicago. Maybe there was still a way to make this scheme work. But first she needed to find Wilcox.

"There's still hope," she said, trying to convince herself it was true. She checked the map of her position. "Any new information on Captain Wilcox?"

The professor's face appeared on the screen. "Nothing. No cameras have picked him up. But an IPA drone recently investigated an explosion out in the barrens." He showed her video taken from a high angle as a drone circled the smoking remains of an overturned vehicle. "It was a van, the exact kind of untagged, gasoline-powered vehicle Jacey would likely have fled the city in."

Belle's heart sank as she studied the smoldering wreck. Debris was scattered all around, a wheel here, a chunk of bent and twisted metal there. Glass everywhere.

"Is she dead?"

"The IPA found a few charred bits of one casualty. Not Jacey. They found blood on the road, away from the blast. ID tests are being conducted. No one was taken for medical care, which suggests anyone else who was at the scene left before the IPA arrived."

"What are all those little black dots on the road?"

"Small drones, typically used in personal drone swarms for streaming one's every waking moment to the net. It's called fame-casting."

It was the stupidest thing Belle had ever heard. "There are so many of those little things," she said. "And they're all dead."

"Likely taken out by the vehicle explosion. But yes, the IPA drone calculates there were 19,321 of them."

"So how many people does that represent? How many drones per one of these fame-casters?"

"Four to six drones per person. So that comes out to three to four thousand people. But I doubt any of these drones were used in personal swarms. They're all modified. The IPA report refers to them as scav drones. Short for 'scavenger,' a tribal people who live out here between the city and the fence. Maybe the scavs took the other bodies from the crash site."

"Bodies?"

"Living. Dead. Bodies either way."

That wasn't very encouraging.

The fallen drones were arrayed in a fan shape, narrowest near the charred vehicle. It was clear now that they had been blasted away from the wreck. "Jacey, Jacey, Jacey. What have you gotten yourself into? Let's assume she wasn't killed or captured. Where did she go?"

Socrates's deerstalker hat reappeared. "No cams have spotted either her or Wilcox since this wreck. To be fair, there aren't many IPA cams out this far. The scavs take them out and repurpose them."

"Can you tap into the scav networks?"

"I'm looking, but there are not many nodes connecting legitimate networks with theirs, which the IPA consider illegal. The tribes themselves are all fugitives, in a way. They live out here expressly to avoid surveillance. Based on reports I've scanned, the scavs have extraordinarily good data encryption. I'm not sure we'll be able to tap into their systems if we find them. It doesn't help that we're sipping dataflow through a straw. *Athena's* bandwidth is low to begin with, and Vaughan is hogging most of it."

So that was it. Belle had run into a dead end.

"Not necessarily," Socrates said, then cleared his throat. "I want to draw your attention to the distribution of the fallen drones."

Squinting at the screen, Belle watched as Socrates rewound the IPA drone video. He froze it. A wide shot of the scene. The picture showed the wrecked van on the lower right. The road crossed the screen to the left upper corner. Most of the field of dead drones was visible. The concentration was densest at the center of the screen, then grew sparser the farther away from the van they got.

Belle spotted the anomaly right away. "Right there. Too few drones on the ground in that spot there." In fact, the drones created an odd pattern at the side of the road. There was a band of dots in too high a concentration relative to the others, and in an odd configuration. They outlined a rectangle of empty ground. No drones at all.

She lowered the tablet, aware that Socrates had teleported her into the scene. The ruined van was far to her right, the road stretching to her left. Socrates had added small spheres to the landscape to mark the position of all the fallen drones. She walked toward the spot in question, feet crunching spheres with every step. She stopped in front of the blank rectangle. "Assuming the drones were blown away from the van, they should have covered this whole spot. But something stopped them."

"Precisely, my dear," Socrates said. "They bounced off something occupying that spot." He superimposed a plain rectangular cuboid shape over the area, fitting it to the empty pattern left by the fallen drones.

"What was it?" Belle asked, walking around it.

"Something this general size that one would find on a roadway. Hmmmm. Whatever could that be?"

Belle wasn't accustomed to being subjected to her own sarcasm. "A vehicle. I get it now."

The clue wasn't much, but it was something. She didn't know what kind of vehicle it had been, and had no idea where it had gone.

"That's not true," Socrates said. "Look at the evidence."

Belle was about to give Socrates a refresher course in swearing when she realized what he was telling her. It was frustrating, really. Since he was a projection of her own mind, he didn't really know any answers before she did. But he was tapping into an aspect of her mind Sensei would have called intuition. Odd. She'd always thought the idea of intuition was silly.

She levitated and studied the roadway. What could the evidence tell her about where the mystery vehicle went? This simulation didn't know anything helpful.

Wait. There.

Her own footsteps from where she'd stepped on spheres showed where she'd been.

She looked at the image of the real-world scene on her tablet. She didn't expect to be able to see individual footsteps. Drones in the real world were not the same as simulated spheres. But if the mystery vehicle had driven toward the van, it would have left clear tracks through the piles of drones covering the roadway.

There weren't any such tracks. That meant the mystery vehicle had gone the other way.

"They went south," Belle said.

"Maybe we should, too," Socrates said.

Belle flew, fast, skimming ten meters over the blurring road.

31

JUST LIKE DR. CARLHAGEN

Kirk's boat driving skills were childlike and brutal. Summer's instructions were apparently to hold the throttle wide open, the seas be damned.

As a result, the dinghy full of Scions and one fat man flew across the waves at an odd angle, making the bow tip hard to starboard as they climbed to a crest, then leave the water entirely, only to drop into the next trough. The impact sent water flying away from the boat and compressed Humphrey's spine into the hard bench beneath him.

At least the pain was keeping his usual seasickness at bay.

The others held on to the gunnels and kept their teeth clenched, nostrils wide, and eyes squinted to keep out the spray.

Kirk whooped every time the boat took flight. Once, Humphrey turned to glare, but Kirk pumped his fist with such enthusiasm Humphrey couldn't help but laugh.

Orson's eyes were bunched in, his face yellowish green. What wonderful justice that would be, to see the stupid man hit with seasickness.

Ahead, St. Lazarus had grown into a mass of green. A tangle of trees and vines covered everything except a narrow stretch of rocky beach. Huge spumes of mist flew up as the sea crashed into the island. If they tried to land here, they'd smash onto rocks and get killed by the tumbling surf. Humphrey motioned Kirk to turn parallel the coast.

Leslie put her lips to his ear. "I see sand!" She pointed ahead.

Humphrey squinted, wishing he'd thought to bring binoculars. Maybe there was a bit of tan along the shoreline ahead, but it was too far away to tell.

He checked the skies. Still no planes.

They had to get ashore very soon or they'd be spotted. The size of their dinghy made its presence here suspicious. It had to have launched from a larger vessel, and the closest one was *Athena*.

Athena was just a speck on the horizon now, but from a plane's vantage, she was still near St. Lazarus.

He pumped his hands down so Kirk would slow. The dinghy lost momentum and soon was merely holding station a few hundred meters off the coast. Humphrey stood. The few feet of altitude he gained didn't help much.

"It's a beach," Leslie said. "I see it clearly."

"Do *you* see it?" Humphrey called to Kirk.

"No. Just point."

Leslie pointed.

Humphrey barely got to his seat before the boy rammed the throttle to its max and the boat shot forward.

Somebody lost their lunch behind him. He didn't need to turn to know it was Orson. Served the man right.

The beach resolved a minute later. Kirk took them straight for it, not slowing even though Humphrey kept motioning him to do so.

Bracing himself to be thrown forward with a sudden stop as the keel struck a reef or rock, Humphrey held his breath.

But the dinghy slid up onto the sandy beach, following the natural incline of the seafloor. Kirk frantically killed the motor, flipped some clamps, and yanked on the top of the outboard motor. It was on a pivot, so the whole thing tilted up, bringing its propeller free of the water. "Time to drag her."

They all hopped out, water coming to their shins. Humphrey grabbed onto the narrow bow and started to pull. The others added their strength and soon the heavy dinghy was sliding up the sand. The trees ahead would provide cover from the air. And not a moment too soon.

The squeal and roar of aircraft engines came from the east.

Feet churning in the deep sand, the Scions and Orson heaved and pushed. Meter by meter, they dragged the boat.

The engine roar increased. Humphrey jerked his head up and around. Still nothing.

"Come on!" Orson cried. "Let's move this—!"

Leslie gasped. "Orson fell."

"Keep pulling!" Humphrey shouted.

The others added their cries and grunts, putting all their muscle into a final effort.

The air temperature dropped ten degrees as they dragged the boat into the cover of the canopy.

"Orson's still out there," Leslie said, hands on her knees, breath heaving.

Out on the sand, Orson lay on his side, face dripping and flushed red. He gripped his left forearm.

"What happened to him?" Kirk said. "Orson, get over here! They'll see you!"

Humphrey looked back to the beach. Orson wasn't the only thing they'd see. The dinghy's keel had carved a trough in the sand, flanked by divots, as if a giant, multi-legged lizard had climbed from the sea and crawled into the trees while dragging its belly.

Orson made no effort to stand. He writhed in agony, breath coming in hitching gulps.

"Kirk. Erase our tracks. Leslie, help me get Orson."

He ran to the fallen man, whose body had now relaxed. His face was slack, mouth open, eyes wide and staring at nothing. Together they grabbed arms and legs and hefted the man toward the cover of the trees. Kirk snatched up a thick fern frond. He followed behind, swiping tracks from the sand.

The jets were screaming, unseen above.

They dropped Orson's dead weight into the first stretch of shade. It would have to do.

"Kirk!" Humphrey called to the boy bringing up the rear.

The boy sprinted and dove into the shade. Leslie yelled something unintelligible and pointed to the sky.

Humphrey didn't see what she was pointing at. The foliage above him was too thick. But then a squadron of planes appeared, tearing across the sky, heading west. The aircraft skimmed so low their wake made the trees' upper limbs flail. Trails of white vapor marked their passage. The sound dropped and deepened as they flew away.

And then all fell quiet.

The Scions stood still as statues, ears pricked for the sound of more planes.

They did not move for a minute, then five.

"They haven't doubled back," Kirk said.

Leslie was kneeling next to Orson. "I don't think he's breathing."

Humphrey knelt next to him, jammed his fingers against Orson's carotid artery. "No pulse. There's a procedure to resuscitate . . ." He looked to Leslie.

She shrugged, face full of sympathy. She patted the man's greasy fringe of hair, smiling sadly. "Let him rest. Even if you could restart his heart, he can't get the medical attention he needs. Maybe if Miss Dayspring was with us . . ."

Humphrey was glad they hadn't brought the woman. Especially now. Orson had been a burden. Even though the man knew the seas and was useful in that regard, the Scions were never going to be free as long as the man knew where they were. With him dead, things got easier.

Humphrey shivered at his own thoughts. A man had just died and he was relieved. Humphrey really was like Dr. Carlhagen. This just proved that he would never escape his own Progenitor's selfish and reptilian mind.

"I won't mourn him." Leslie rubbed her fingers on her pants, as if merely touching Orson could infect her with an incurable disease. "He meant us harm. His brother did me harm and Orson allowed it."

They dragged Orson's body deeper into the foliage, then returned to the dinghy to collect their packs. Each held a liter of water and a dozen packets of the tooth-shattering MRE bars they'd found on Mr. Justin's Island. Each pack also held a flashlight and a foldable knife with a six inch blade.

Kirk produced a surprise from his pack. "Look at this." He pulled out a machete, 50 centimeters long, with a black wooden grip.

Humphrey grunted. "Good thing Horace never got hold of that."

Leslie hefted her pack straps over her shoulders. The edges and corners of the server were sharply outlined by the fabric of her pack. She then bent into the boat and pulled out a bulky blanket. Something oddly shaped was wrapped in it. She hesitated a moment and nearly put it back. Changing her mind, she unwrapped it. "I brought this. I'm sorry, but I just think we need every weapon at our disposal."

It was the speargun Mr. Justin had used to kill Sensei. There were still bloodstains on the steel tip of one of the spears. Humphrey remembered Leslie showing him her hands, the hands that had fired that spear into Sensei's throat.

If anyone had a right to the weapon, it was her.

"You'll shoot one of us by mistake," Kirk said.

"I won't. I know how it works." She did not seek Humphrey's approval. Humphrey wondered if Leslie's resilience and defiance were the aspects of her Progenitor that had made her President of the North American Union.

"What's the plan?" Kirk asked, looking at Leslie.

Instead of deferring to Humphrey, the copper-haired Eagle patted the gunnel of the dinghy. "We need to conceal this better. Then we need to get our bearings. Maybe we can deduce where Dr. Carlhagen built his new Scion School based on the lay of the land.

It was optimistic, but it was also very sound, Humphrey thought. "Excellent. Let's get moving."

There was less urgency now that they were out of sight from the air, so dragging the dinghy was much harder. They moved it another ten meters before giving up. They covered it with more fern fronds. Kirk slipped onto the beach for a moment to see if the boat was well enough hidden. He came back, adjusted the camouflage and pronounced the boat invisible.

"We need to get some altitude," Humphrey said. "That peak was north of here. If we can get onto the slopes, we should be able to see most of the rest of the island."

And so the trudge began.

The shade protected them from the steadily lowering sun, but as they moved away from the shore, the air thickened. The sparse undergrowth allowed them easy passage at first, but soon they encountered an impenetrable wall of vines and thorny bushes. Leslie suggested following the edge of the thicket barrier. "I remember Socrates saying that many tropical plant species live in a narrow band of elevation. We just need to get higher."

As they climbed, the terrain became rockier, and the trees thinned. Biting flies, purple and gold, harried them the whole time. The sound of slaps and soft cries of pain became the regular accompaniment to their steps. Kirk took the lead with his machete and started hacking through a dense section of woody weeds with sticky leaves.

Two hours in, Humphrey had already drunk half his liter of water. "We'd better ration water until we find a source for more," he said. "Limit yourself to a small sip every fifteen minutes."

The problem was the humidity here. They were all

soaked with sweat. Their uniforms clung to their skin. Faces glistened. All bore welts from fly bites and smudges of mashed insects too slow to escape their angry swats.

"There's a break in the trees ahead," Kirk said.

They slowed their pace, keeping a sharp eye on the canopy to make sure they were hidden from the skies. They hadn't heard a jet since the first flyover, but Humphrey still feared the pilots had spotted the dinghy tracks on the beach, or had decided *Athena's* proximity to St. Lazarus was too suspicious.

No word from Summer. That was good. He hoped.

"Water break," he said, and took a small sip. The wetness barely cut the raging thirst in his throat. It didn't matter that the water was warm. The others took their allotted sips. Scions were disciplined and smart. They understood the purpose of the rationing, though they looked regretful as they stowed their water bottles.

"I wish I had some binoculars," Humphrey said. "I'd like to be able to scan ahead."

"Oh, I have some. Summer loaned them to me," Leslie said. She dug in her backpack and pulled out a small pair Humphrey had never seen before. Summer had probably found them on *Athena* and kept them to herself.

"Why didn't Summer ever tell me about these?" Humphrey complained.

"She said you were unappreciative of the fragility of fine optics."

"May I?" he said holding out his hand.

"I promised Summer I'd bring them back in perfect condition, so be careful," Leslie said as she let Humphrey take them.

He didn't need them long. The break in the trees ahead was the end of this forested area. They had climbed high enough that they'd reached a tree line. Everything beyond was rock, tough grasses, or gnarly shrubs. The mountainside climbed steeply toward a peak still a kilometer above them.

"What are we waiting for?" Kirk said. "There are no planes around."

"We don't know that for sure," Humphrey said. "At 4000 meters of altitude, a plane could see this island from 220 kilometers away. We'd never even hear their jets from that distance."

"But it would be a hazy speck on the horizon, at best," Kirk said.

"Depends on the quality of their onboard optics." Humphrey raised the binoculars. "Even with 10x magnification, computer processing could flag a group of humans as anomalous objects from 150 kilometers. Do any of us think their optics are that weak?"

No one did.

"So what now?" Leslie said, gently prying the binoculars from Humphrey's hands.

Humphrey plopped onto the spot he was standing and removed his pack. "We wait for dark."

The others sighed with a combination of relief and impatience. Humphrey didn't care. There was no point in bumbling around in the jungle with no idea where they were going. Besides, they had been climbing for several hours. They needed a rest.

A roar of jets passed by from the south, high and distant. Humphrey realized the altitude the Scions had gained from their climb might show them *Athena* through the binoculars.

On the other hand, he didn't see that it mattered much whether the ship was in view.

Leslie sat next to him and blew a stray lock of hair from her eyes. "How are you doing?"

"I'm tired and I stink."

"That's not what I meant. I'm talking about Orson."

He dug an MRE bar from his pack. He unwrapped it, bit off a corner. Swallowed.

Leslie stared at him, waiting for an answer.

"Orson was in poor physical condition. His heart was bound to give out sooner or later."

"Yes. We'll all die sooner or later," Leslie said. "You are reciting a fact. I asked you how you feel about him dying."

He broke off another small piece of his bar and ate it, careful not to look at Leslie. "It is unfortunate that he led the life he did."

"Yes, but how do you feel about his death?"

"I don't know why you're asking me this."

"Because you've spent more time with him than any of us. You must feel something." There was a pleading in her tone that surprised Humphrey. He still didn't look up. He could feel her looking at his face. He knew that she had that peacefulness in her eyes, that earnest inquisitiveness he found so unsettling since her restoration from a computer backup.

"I didn't like him," he said. "But I think he was coming around. He liked Summer."

Kirk had wandered into the foliage to answer nature's call.

"The truth is that I'm relieved," Humphrey said. "And that makes me sad." He lifted his eyes to meet Leslie's. "I wish I could be sad for him, but I just can't. He was a terrible human."

The foliage rustled behind him. Kirk emerged. He held a finger to his lips.

Instantly alert, Humphrey started to stand. Kirk urged him to sit back down.

He came to sit next to Humphrey and leaned close. Leslie bent in to listen. They both stank of sweat and dirt.

"We aren't alone here," Kirk whispered.

32

JEWELRY MAYBE

Sleep did not come easily for Senator Bentilius these days. The vigor of youth was part of the reason. Heaven knew what a rollercoaster her physical appetites had taken her on recently. She almost felt sorry for Dr. Carlhagen, the way she'd abused his body.

But anxiety also played a major part in keeping her awake, mind spinning. So here she was—with plenty of time to nap and rest up before things got interesting—and she could not sleep a wink.

She lay on a sofa in Livy's quarters, in absolute darkness. Lazarus had piped in the soothing sounds of the surf, but it did nothing to lull her to sleep. She was used to complex problems, but there were so many balls in play now, her mind was boggling just keeping track of them.

Impatience got the best of her. She sat up. "Lazarus, lights please."

A glow came into existence on the pixel walls, easing the darkness.

"What's the child's status?"

"Nominal."

"That's not what I meant. How much longer?"

"Bringing a human out of growth cryo is a precise science, with low tolerance for error. It must be done slowly, with attention to hundreds of variables."

The AI never answered her questions directly. She was not accustomed to such treatment from AIs, or humans, for that matter. But since she didn't have any leverage over Lazarus, she had no recourse but to take his disrespect.

"Could you give me an estimate of when you'll need me to move the child to the transfer machine?" she asked, as politely as she could manage.

"It depends on a number of factors. Somewhere between three and seventeen hours."

"Seventeen! I don't have that kind of time."

Actually, that suited her just fine. Maybe Colonel Vikisky would arrive before then and get her out of this mole hill. Then she could have the navy techs find Lazarus's server and slag it.

With the tone of an afterthought, Lazarus said, "You may be interested to know that a small boat arrived on the island recently."

"What? Who was in it?"

"I do not know. I've been observing the passengers since they arrived. They barely eluded detection by reconnaissance flights dispatched from Colonel Vikisky's fleet." A video image, taken from above the canopy of trees, showed a speedboat plow onto a western beach. Figures jumped out and dragged the boat across the sand. One—a stouter man—fell and did not get back up. The camera was too far from the group to see much detail. The other three individuals were slim, fit. Two males and a female. They seemed young and vigorous. They wore tank tops and black trousers. Sun flashed off something shiny affixed to one member's shirt. A piece of jewelry, maybe.

"Do you have other views of them?"

"Yes."

Another image popped up, this one from a camera closer to the ground. It moved through foliage, paralleling the path of the interlopers.

"Can't you get closer?"

"Yes. But then they would hear the drone. I do not want them to know they are being observed. Yet."

The drone slipped behind the trio, then stopped. The image zoomed on the figure at the back, a girl with short coppery hair. She slapped at insects on her arms and face. Despite the efforts of the drone to hold its position, the image shuddered at this zoom level. The focus blurred and then locked sharp again.

The girl turned to look over her shoulder. Lazarus froze the image. "I can enhance this somewhat."

"No need," Maxine said, smiling. "That is a Scion. This little band of trespassers are some of Dr. Carlhagen's escapees. How on earth did they know to come here?"

Lazarus didn't answer. The video disappeared.

"You must have more drones out there. Show me the others."

Lazarus didn't answer and he didn't produce more video.

"Have you informed Dr. Carlhagen about this?" she asked.

"I'm still considering that decision."

"Can your drones disable the Scions? Colonel Vikisky's forces will be here soon. They can scoop them up."

"That's what concerns me. I do not trust Vikisky."

Senator Bentilius realized she was on crumbling

ground and backed off. "I could go out and fetch them. Bring them here. You could isolate them into rooms until you decide how to use them."

The answer was not long in coming. "There are three of them and one of you. You are known to them, and they despise you."

"But you have drones. Surely you have some weapons aboard. Besides, the Scions know I'm with Dr. Carlhagen, and they know we have Livy."

"An interesting proposition. But I do not need your services at this time."

"Will you tell Dr. Carlhagen?"

"Not yet."

That was something. Senator Bentilius discovered she was chewing a thumbnail. She dropped her hand to her side.

Her mind turned over the piece of information she had withheld from Lazarus. The girl was the president's Scion. Lazarus had not recognized her.

Interesting.

33

A RAT IS A BOY

One of the benefits of stealing a military man's truck was that it was well supplied. The first aid kit alone held enough supplies to perform minor surgery. That was according to Meow Meow. Jacey didn't know much about medical care.

She did know that she felt a thousand times better than when she'd first been thrown into the truck. The nausea was gone now, and the ringing in her ears—an E flat, she was pretty sure—had started to fade into the background. All of this was thanks to the three pills Meow Meow had dug from the kit and shoved into Jacey's hand.

None of them had sedative effects, and Jacey was thankful for that. She needed to be able to stay awake. Though their hideout was well hidden, they were in potentially hostile territory.

Potentially. Because they didn't know exactly where they were.

The ruin sheltering them had once been a church,

according to Dante. "I grew up Catholic. Trust me. I felt guilty the second we walked in to this place."

Jacey's teacher, the AI Socrates, had skimmed over the religions of the world, spending as little time as possible on what he called "popular mythology": the Jade Emperor, Gilgamesh, the Greek pantheon. He spent slightly more time on Hinduism, Islam, Christianity, and Judaism, but he had focused on texts, not architecture. And even then, he'd insisted Jacey understand these faiths only so she could understand literature and history influenced by them. When Jacey had pressed him on which religion was true, he turned into a burning bird, crumbled to ash, and did not rise from it until the next class period. Afterward he laughed at her question and said, "Let me know when you find out."

All that remained of the church were three stone walls overgrown with vines. Trees filled most of the interior, including one towering elm, its crown spreading over them like a leafy roof. The plank floor had rotted away long ago, exposing a stone foundation now covered with the soil of decomposed leaves, branches, and weeds. An alcove in one wall held a statue of a man holding a baby. Dante didn't know who it was supposed to be. "Some saint or other. I was terrible at being Catholic."

An abandoned bird's nest, like a fairy-woven basket, sat between the statue's feet. Far above his head was the opening of a sharply arched window. The glass had broken away, the opening covered over by kudzu vines.

Meow Meow had built a fire in the corner, a spot protected from the wind. Stars peeped through leaves of the elm. Quiet rested upon the land, save for the soft wash of the treetops swaying in wind.

The smell of damp soil and moldering leaves comforted

Jacey. This was nothing like St. Vitus, but in the aftermath of the Chicago cacophony, the wilds of the barrens were a much-needed respite for her senses. She sat near the fire, its heat seeping into her. With it came a spreading sleepiness.

They'd left the main highway at dusk, following a weedy roadway through three abandoned towns, which Meow Meow took them through at top speed. When they spotted the forest, Jacey suggested finding a place to hide within it, remembering how she and Summer had eluded Senator Bentilius's guards by fleeing to the rainforest.

Following ever-narrowing tracks, they'd gone deeper into the trees until Meow Meow was confident the limbs masked the truck from above. That had led them to this ruin in what had once been a small town.

Little remained of the town except a few concrete driveways and one relatively clear intersection. A few poles with dead lights mounted atop stood watch. One sign, dangling from a rusty bolt, announced Church St. A few brickwork buildings were in better condition, but Meow Meow was afraid of booby traps in them. "That's just the sort of place I was taught to put them."

Captain Wilcox's supplies included food. Already Jacey had eaten two of the Ripcord Brand Chicken Hot Flasher meals. The tins featured a pull-tab that started an exothermic reaction inside the tin, heating the precooked contents. A whistle valve in the lid announced when it was ready to open. Inside were a chicken flavored, meat-like patty, green beans, and mashed potatoes, all smothered with "gravique," which the package label claimed to be OUR PATENTED GRAVY-FLAVORED SAUCE—"GRAVIQUE IS UNIQUE!"

Dante finished his third tin, then slammed a can of

Spasm, a sickly sweet fizzy drink that encouraged the drinker to SURVIVE, REVIVE & THRIVE, then patted his distended belly. "Nature calls, ladies. This might take a while." He got to his feet and headed around to other side of the wall.

"Go downwind," Meow Meow called after him.

He replied with an earth-shattering belch.

"Boys," Meow Meow said.

"He's a middle-aged man inside that body," Jacey said.

"Like I said. Boys."

They settled into a companionable silence, chewing, swallowing, staring into the flames.

This was Jacey's chance to ask Meow Meow about the thing that had been bothering her for the past few hours. "You're having fun, aren't you?"

A little laugh escaped the girl's nose. "Running for my life? Falling out of vans? Protecting the innocent from the evils of the world? That's not what I'd call fun."

Jacey just looked at Meow Meow. The pop star's short hair had dried into a tousled mess. But it looked charming, in a boyish way. The makeup was gone now, having been wiped off courtesy of Wilcox's stash of PRE-MOISTENED TOWELETTES. Meow Meow still had hollow cheeks and prominent cheekbones, but her skin was healthy and pink rather than the pale mask of product she typically wore.

"What happened to you?" Jacey asked, keeping her voice low and soft.

Meow Meow's pouty lips twisted into a sneer. Jabbing the fire, she sent a spray of sparks floating skyward. "I had the sickness when I was eleven."

"What sickness?"

"*The* sickness. You know, the reason they built the fence? The plague that kills ninety-nine out of a hundred?

You know. Infection by our friend *Yersinia pestis* with a Sarme-Trione mod. The little buggers scavenge glycogen right out of your blood so victims go into permanent ketosis. Kills appetite and the body has to use fat for fuel."

Seeing Jacey's blank look, Meow Meow said, "It started as a weight loss treatment. People would get infected on purpose, lose fifty kilos, then go on antibiotics for a week. But the modified bacteria, being the living organism that it is, mutated into several varieties. Some became super strong bubonic plague types, others went pneumonic. My immune system managed to get on top of it . . . after eight months in a refugee hospital bed. Wanna know who paid for my treatment?"

Jacey shrugged.

"The Charles and Jacqueline Buchanan Foundation for Victims of the Sickness." Meow Meow stared into the flames, and poked aimlessly at the embers with her stick. "I know of two others who survived the sickness. Everyone else died. Everyone."

"So that's the reason you're so . . ."

"Skinny? The world thinks I have an eating disorder, which I do, in a way." She waved at a tin of Ripcord Brand BBQ PORK RIBS. "My metabolism is wrecked. I can't burn carbs hardly at all. I have to have fat. But I'm *never* hungry. Ever. So I have to make myself eat. I once got up to 52 kilos and the gossip pundits called me fat. A music critic wrote a blog titled: 'Meow Meow to Bow Wow, What's Turning Hot Kitty into Miss Piggy?' Can you believe that? It was weird, though. I look like my dad when my cheeks are fuller."

"So you still have it? The disease?"

"It's not contagious in me, if that's what you're worrying about."

"No. I was worried about *you*."

Firelight caught wetness in Meow Meow's eyes. She blinked it away. "Thank you. The feeling is mutual." A bit of the girl's old lasciviousness returned, and she gave Jacey a sly look. "You sure you only like boys?"

"I'm sure."

"Too bad. Well, watch out for Dante, because he's hot for you."

"He's hot for anything with a pulse. Didn't you just hear me say there's a middle aged man inside there? And that body he's wearing was my friend."

"Then how can you stand to be around him?"

"He's been helping me. Or he was, until he tried to turn me over to Captain Wilcox. I should have known better than to trust him." In fact, she *had* known not to trust him. Circumstances had thrown them together and he'd helped her escape from Elizabeth's island and then kept helping her. Expediency had overruled her disgust and distrust. And in truth, she had become accustomed to this new Dante. There were times when she forgot he was a Progenitor.

"He didn't try to turn you over to that stupid mercenary," Meow Meow said. "That truck caught up to us. It was Lily who pulled over. Dante just . . . He didn't think we had a chance, so he was willing to give you up to save his own skin."

"Can't say I blame him," Jacey said, annoyed. "I'm farther from my goal than ever."

"I know. I know. You want to save this kid friend of yours. You want to save all the other carbos. But you have to face reality. You are wanted by the IPA and every private citizen in the world who thinks they can make a buck off of you."

"Am I supposed to give up? Just hide forever? I couldn't live with myself if I got to safety and left Livy and Humphrey and all the others to die. That's not what Socrates taught me. That's certainly not the person Sensei shaped me to be."

"I don't know who Socrates and Sensei are, but isn't it odd that you had teachers like that? What was this Dr. Carlhagen guy thinking when he hired them?"

"He thought that if we perfected our minds and bodies the Progenitors who overwrote us would receive some of the benefit. Gauging by Dante's behavior, that's been a mixed result."

Meow Meow tossed her stick onto the flames and leaned onto an elbow. "Has it? If the original Dante was anything like you—so idealistic and damned honorable— maybe that explains some of why he's helping you."

It was Jacey's turn to laugh through her nose. What a ridiculous idea. "The real Dante would never have turned me over to Wilcox. He would have fought to the death to prevent it."

"Fighting to the death?" Dante said, walking into the glow of the firelight. "Count me out."

He rummaged through a bin they'd carried from the truck. He pulled out another Ripcord tin. "I've got a craving for oranges. What I wouldn't give for a couple liters of orange juice."

"Don't waste any of those tins just for two orange slices," Meow Meow warned. "Besides, waste food will draw animals. There are bears and wolves around here."

Dante tossed the unopened package back into the bin and settled across the fire from Jacey. His face did look a bit wan.

"So you didn't call Wilcox and tell him where we were going?" Jacey asked him.

Dante looked up, dark brows lowering in consternation. "No. Why would I do that? Don't answer that. I totally would do that if it was my only way out. But I don't have a tablet, for one. And for two, I don't have his number."

No shame. Just matter-of-fact statement. Jacey shook her head in amazement at his audacity. The real Dante had been mischievous, but he'd never been so self-absorbed.

"It doesn't matter now," Dante said. "Wilcox is dead."

"What?" Jacey shot to her feet. Meow Meow straightened, eyes intent.

"Did I forget to mention that earlier?" he said, smiling like he'd just eaten a whole cake without sharing a single piece. "Yes. I had to get the truck key fob from him. He was in bad shape. A piece of shrapnel from the van hit him in the neck. Lots of blood. I ended it for him."

Jacey remembered seeing Wilcox kneeling on the roadway, hands covered with blood, drones strewn about him.

"You killed him?"

"The shrapnel would have done it. I just helped things along."

So that path to Dr. Carlhagen was closed. Not that Jacey had wanted to turn herself over the man, but it was the only sure way to Livy she'd found so far. She folded her legs and sat heavily upon the stone floor.

Dante misread her weary collapse. "I thought you hated him."

"I did." Something about Dante's story didn't make sense.

She studied him across the flames. His face was open, handsome. The resting smile he always wore—had always worn even when he was a Scion—gave him a pleasant look. His button-down shirt was stained with filth and blood, none of it his. The white slacks were in even worse condition, his bare knees visible through ragged holes.

Bags hung under his eyes, dark and puffy. Two days growth of whiskers darkened his chin and cheeks. His lips spread, showing white teeth, under her scrutiny. A wolfish look.

Jacey knew what bothered her. "Why did you kill Wilcox?"

"He was suffering."

"Since when do you care about people's suffering?"

He leaned back onto his hands, shoulders hunching toward his ears. His mouth quirked down momentarily to show his disinterest in Jacey's question.

"Why?" Jacey demanded.

"To help a guy out. I don't know. I didn't think about it. You might have noticed that's a personality flaw of mine."

She had noticed. Except she didn't believe it for one second, not in this case. "Did you do it for me?"

"No." His voice was flat. "I don't like to witness suffering. But I don't care if it's happening where I can't see, so don't start thinking I've grown a conscience or some such stupidity."

Meow Meow had been watching the back-and-forth with keen interest. "And why is having a conscience stupid?"

"Are we really having this conversation now? Shouldn't we be deciding who has the first watch and setting up a perimeter and hobbling the horses? We already have the firelight and the camp in the creepy ruin. Meows should be sharpening her sword while I sing a bawdy song that Jacey disapproves of."

"What's he talking about?" Jacey asked Meow Meow.

"I think he's read too many fantasy novels."

Jacey didn't understand. But she didn't really care. Dante was trying to divert attention from something important. "I don't get you, *Silvio*. You overwrite an intelligent boy—killing him in the process—so you can return to your youth. That's abject greed by any definition. And yet you've been risking your neck to help me."

"I tried to give you to Wilcox. Don't give me more credit than I deserve."

That was true. But still, she'd seen his face when he'd kicked Siggy in the head back in the hotel room. He'd been furious. Surely, that meant he cared about her. "Meow Meow says you're in love with me."

The scrawny girl choked on a swallow of Spasm, sending a spray sizzling into the fire. Dante sat up and gave Jacey a queer look. "Love?"

He got to his feet. "I don't love anyone but myself. I don't care about anyone but myself. Everything I do, I do for me. I always have and I always will put myself first. Get it?"

"I get it. But there has to be some moral core in there, or you wouldn't have done the good things you've done. You said yourself you felt guilty when you came into this church."

"I was making a joke, darling. I haven't been to church in 50 years. I don't feel guilty about it, I feel *free*. Do you want to know why?" He tilted his head, waiting for an answer. When Jacey refused to ask, he went on anyway. "Because I know that there *is* no right or wrong. There is nothing to feel guilt about. Ever."

"You don't believe that," Meow Meow said.

He turned on the girl, pointed a finger at her. "It's the

only thing I do believe. Nothing else." Craning his neck, he faced the headless statue. "That right there is a lie. This whole place is a lie. When I was a kid I had to listen to priest's lectures about morality, about all the things forbidden by God, and I said 'Why does God even care what I do?' And the priest told me because we are his children and we had to behave ourselves in order to get into heaven. And I said, 'Where is heaven? Show it to me. Prove it.' And the priest got angry and said I had to have faith."

Dante spat, his face a mask of disgust. "That's when I knew it was a lie. There is nothing in this life except this life. The morals people cling to are based on nothing. Kill if you want. Steal if you want. A cockroach is a rat is a boy when it comes down to it. Crush them beneath your heel and all you get is a bigger mess. It's just a splatter of gooey molecules and nothing more. So when Dr. Carlhagen gave me the chance to be young again, I did not think twice. When I met the boy, I did not flinch."

The pitch of his voice rose as he railed on. Jacey leaned away from him, horrified to see this side of her companion come out from hiding. Demonic in the firelight, he raised his arms to the sky. He laughed and capered and howled like a beast.

Suddenly spent, he collapsed, face vague and looking more exhausted than ever. "I need sleep." He lay onto his back and, seconds later, began to snore.

Meow Meow got up, came to sit next to Jacey. They sat shoulder-to-shoulder, quiet and deep in their own thoughts for a long while.

"Maybe he's right," Jacey said. "Maybe there isn't any right or wrong. Maybe we all live by arbitrary rules. But at the Scion School, we had all sorts of rules. None of them mentioned having to love each other. And yet we do. We're family. That's why it feels so necessary, right here"—she bumped her chest with her fist—"to risk everything for Livy. For all of them. But in this outside world . . . everyone is so vain, so greedy. So false."

"Ouch," Meow Meow said. "I suppose I deserved that last bit. The wigs, the makeup."

Jacey deflated, put her face in her hands. "I didn't mean it like that. Not about you. You're . . . You are a work of art. I think that's different."

The wet glimmer returned to Meow Meow's eyes. She hugged Jacey with one arm and rested her head on Jacey's shoulder. "That's the nicest thing anyone has ever said to me."

"I doubt that. Don't you have millions of fans?"

"Fans, yes. Friends? Until now, I'm not sure I've had any." She paused then held out her hand. "Jacey, my name is Kathryne Killusky. I was born in Topeka, Kansas."

Jacey took Meow Meow's hand, which was small and warm and strong. Meow Meow gave it a shake, then released it. She pressed her lips together, as if she was considering whether to say something more.

"What is it?" Jacey prodded.

"I—There's something—Never mind. Get some sleep. I'll take first watch."

Jacey tried to get comfortable, fashioning a pillow from a thin wool blanket pulled from Wilcox's supplies. She was warm enough with the fire. "Do you think Dante believes everything he said?"

Meow Meow shrugged. "I don't think he knows what he believes. But in the immortal words of Hamlette, in an Oscar-winning performance by your Progenitor, 'Methinks the boy doth protest too much.'"

Maybe that was true. Jacey hoped so. "Shouldn't you sleep, too?"

"I've had too much Spasm to sleep quite yet. I'm going to deploy my drone swarm to keep an eye out. They see infrared, so if anyone comes close, my tablet will chime."

Jacey settled in and tried to use one of Sensei's breathing techniques to calm her jittery nerves. The soft whisper of drone props swirled around, then flitted away.

Jacey had gotten through a third cycle of inhalation, breath hold, and exhalation when Meow Meow touched her shoulder. "Stay quiet. Someone's coming."

34

RECTANGULAR AND FAIRLY SMALL

The overpass sheltered a band of roadway forty meters long. Belle stood in its shade, getting her bearings and looking for any hint of where the mystery vehicle might have gone. The stretch of road she'd flown along did not have many roads intersecting it. And all of them led to areas in the wide open.

Assuming Jacey or Captain Wilcox had been in the vehicle—a big assumption, she knew—they would have gone looking for cover. That was a base instinct.

This overpass was the closest thing to cover she'd found yet, and it wasn't much. They wouldn't have lingered here, if they'd stopped at all.

Flying along the roadway was not efficient. Instead of having Socrates show her a map on the tablet, Belle realized she could just fly a thousand meters up. She did so, and hovered there, studying the lay of the land. "Socrates, please flash the van site."

A flashing blue light far off to her right showed her

where the wreckage was. Directly below her was the over-pass, a chunk of overgrown highway leading east to west. Socrates superimposed a label on it. Auto Auto El. He said, "A defunct infrastructure project, intended for driverless vehicles going 300 kilometers per hour."

Belle's eyes followed the roadway from the van site to the southern horizon. A blur of green hung out there. She teleported to hover over it. A forest.

"Now this is more like it. They could find cover here."

Her enthusiasm faded quickly. A number of roadways cut through the forest, and the mystery vehicle could have taken any of them.

"A dead end," she said.

"Of sorts," came Socrates immediate reply. He didn't bother speaking through the tablet now. His voice just came from the air. "You can still attempt to contact Captain Wilcox."

"How?"

"How indeed? An excellent question."

Belle bit off an angry response. No sense in being mad at herself. "I missed something?"

"Did you?"

If she accepted the idea that Socrates was tapping into some intuitive aspect of herself, then she had to accept that there was a detail she'd overlooked.

Her mind followed the trail that had led her to this point. From the Chinese restaurant to the surveillance video that identified Wilcox in a black truck in that weedy parking lot.

"Let me see that pic again," she said.

Socrates posted it in a rectangle in mid-air. Belle vaguely realized that she didn't even have her tablet anymore. Didn't need it. The picture was from a high angle, taken from a police surveillance drone. There was glare on the windshield of the truck, reflecting a cloudy sky. Wilcox's face was still recognizable through it.

He held something in his hands. Rectangular and fairly small.

"A tablet," she said, body tingling with the exhilaration of a breakthrough. "He has a tablet. Of course he does. That's how he talks to Dr. Carlhagen. Socrates, connect me to him."

"You need an address or identifier number for the device."

"Get me his number, then," Belle said, exasperated.

"Vaughan looked for such an identifier for the device already. He called every Wilcox in every directory he could find. No luck. The man is likely using an alias for his device."

"So that's a dead end, too."

"Not necessarily."

"If Vaughan couldn't find him . . ." Her eyes locked on the image of Wilcox. "Zoom out."

Socrates complied, showing the full image taken by the police drone. It showed the entire vehicle and a good portion of the weedy parking lot.

Two things struck her immediately. With a thought, she extrapolated a three dimensional model of the truck. With another she was back to the site of the wrecked van and the field of fallen drones. She placed the three dimensional model of Wilcox's truck in the clear spot of the mystery vehicle.

A perfect match.

She walked around it. And there, mounted on the front bumper, was an identifier plate. She checked the police drone image. The plate had a number on it. "Socrates, can we use this to see who owns the truck?"

"It belonged to one Sigmund Hopkins. He's an IPA agent who goes by the nickname 'Siggy.' There are several tablet devices registered to him."

"Call them. Call all of them."

35

A DISINTERESTED SCYTHE

The fugitives' campfire cast dancing lights against the church's weathered stone walls, a demonic eruption of orange and red in the midst of a black night. Overhead, the limbs of the great elm waved in a steady breeze. Jacey pressed herself to the thick trunk, Meow Meow kneeling below her, peeking around to see who approached.

The girl's tablet screen showed a field of black with six green dots indicating the position of her drones. They were arrayed high up and twenty meters away from the tablet, forming a perimeter.

Their cameras had not spotted the intruder, who showed as a red dot near the top of the screen. It was the onboard microphones that had detected him, or her. The dot was inching closer. The attempt at stealth spoke of patience and skill.

"Should we get Dante?" Jacey whispered.

Meow Meow put a finger to her lips and shook her head.

The layout of the ruins was not shown on Meow Meow's tablet. Jacey didn't have any sense of how close the intruder was. Meow Meow motioned for Jacey to retreat.

Jacey picked her way through the moldering debris of the ruined church. She came to the wall opposite their humble camp. It ended in a jagged section where a twenty meter length had collapsed outward. Another step took Jacey out of the church. Trees and scrub grew right up to the exterior of the wall.

"Keep going." Meow Meow pressed on Jacey's back. "Let's circle around to the truck."

With the wind stirring the leaves above them in a wash of white noise, they were free to move more quickly. Meow Meow tapped her tablet, ordering her drones to monitor the red dot rather than continue to follow her. One green dot moved closer to the red dot. "I want to get a visual on that bastard."

Jacey pushed through wiry scrub that grabbed at her clothes and scraped the exposed skin of her arms and ankles. The wind swirled all around. Weak moonlight edged tree trunks an eerie silver that did nothing to light the way. Meow Meow touched Jacey's shoulder, motioning her to bear right. Jacey thought they were moving parallel to the wall, but she couldn't see it.

She stopped to pluck a thorn from her calf, hissing through her teeth.

"Keep going!" Meow Meow urged.

"What about Dante?"

"I tried to wake him. He refused."

"But—"

"Do you think we could carry him?"

Jacey knew they couldn't. Not and stay quiet. Besides,

they couldn't have masked the fire in time to hide that they'd been there. Meow Meow's plan became suddenly clear. Let whomever it was find Dante and assume he was there alone. A cold calculation, but it might give them enough time to get to the truck.

Meow Meow's tablet vibrated. A second later, the girl swore. "My drones are going offline."

She held up her tablet. Only three green dots remained. "Did you get a pic?" Jacey asked.

"No. The drone went offline before it could send one. I'll send in all three at once. Now go!"

Jacey shoved through the undergrowth. Her eyes were starting to adjust to the darkness now. The hazy glow from their fire lit the underside of leaves far off to her right. She worked her way closer to the wall. She spotted a slash of light high up on it.

It was the opening for the broken window. Kudzu climbed the wall here, blocking the opening except for a hair-thin strip at the middle. Idea and action occurred at once. She gripped the vines and tugged. They were so intertwined with each other that they formed a sturdy network. A climbable one.

"What the hell—?" Meow Meow rasped as Jacey started up.

It was easy, and soon Jacey was at the window. She pressed her eye to the sliver of a gap. It showed a narrow slice of the interior of the overgrown church. Shadows leapt across the weeds and rotting leaves of countless seasons.

Voices rose. Men talking.

Meow Meow tapped Jacey's ankle. She'd climbed just high enough to get Jacey's attention. She held her tablet so Jacey could see the screen. A dark image showed a close-up of a man's face. He wore a bandage around his head.

What she saw explained why the drones had been going offline. Captain Wilcox—the man Dante claimed to have helped along on the path to death—was standing inside the church. And he was talking to Dante. From the tone of their voices, it wasn't a particularly heated conversation. Jacey wished she could hear exactly what they were saying, but it was all hushed tones.

She climbed down. "Sounds like they're working together," she whispered into Meow Meow's ear.

They needed no further discussion. Jacey started away from the church, then bore hard right as they made the corner. The trees thinned here. The crumbled asphalt of a driveway showed through the weeds. The truck sat directly ahead.

They ran, neither looking back. Meow Meow jumped in the driver's side and started the motor.

The wheels spun as she tore back the way they'd come. She hit the roadway, now nothing more than tire tracks winding through the trees.

"Turn on the lights," Jacey said. "We've got to be far enough away he can't catch us."

Meow Meow didn't obey. "Think it through, darling. How did he get here so quickly?"

"Ah." Wilcox had mentioned having a chopper on its way to pick up him and Jacey. That was before the drone swarm had risen from the trees and everything went to hell. "So there may be others around."

"There must be a clearing somewhere around here, a place big enough to land."

"How did he find us so quickly?"

Meow Meow pursed her lips and jerked the wheel to

avoid a fallen tree in their path. She fiddled with the gear shifter and powered over the obstacle. The truck jounced violently as the rear wheels came off the trunk. Jacey opened her window and leaned out.

"What are you doing?" Meow Meow called, jamming on the brakes. "You'll smack your head on a tree."

"I'm listening."

Meow Meow made a considering noise, then leaned her head out her window. The truck went silent as Meow Meow stopped it.

The world was still awash with wind through the trees. It was heavy with the moisture of approaching rain. The clouds had blocked the moon now, leaving the vaguest bright spot high in the sky.

Below the surf-like susurration of the treetops arose another sound. Buzzing. An ATV. Jacey recognized the sound. The same as the ATVs they had ridden to escape Vin's mansion. "He's coming."

They pulled their heads into the truck.

"We can't be stealthy in this thing," Meow Meow said. "It leaves clear tracks in the weeds. But we can be faster. Once we get to clear pavement, we can put some kilometers between us and them."

Meow Meow turned on the headlights and jammed the accelerator. Jacey held on, thinking of the times she'd been in a vehicle racing like this, careless of the danger. Belle had been driving once, then it had been Dr. Carlhagen. More recently it had been Summer, and then a driverless limo in San Juan. All that experience didn't lessen the terror she felt every time the truck made a sharp turn to follow the hint of a track through black wilderness.

A half-hour of this left her jittery and exhausted. Meow

Meow hit the pavement of the main highway and pushed the motor to its maximum, carrying them south.

The truck plowed through swarms of insects, a disinterested scythe, sweeping death through the night. Jacey knew how the bugs felt.

"Dante called him," Meow Meow said.

"Huh?" Jacey had almost fallen asleep.

"Dante called Wilcox. Remember when he left camp to relieve himself? And then he came back and gave that speech about there being no basis for morality?"

"But how did he call him?"

"He had a tablet. He must have been keeping it hidden. Maybe he grabbed it from Wilcox when he grabbed the key fob for this truck."

It made sense. Jacey was too tired to be outraged. Mostly she felt sad. She couldn't understand a person like Dante. He was just as mercenary as Wilcox.

"Where are we going?" she said, letting her disappointment with Dante slip out the window and into the buggy night. A storm boiled off to the west, massive clouds lit occasionally by bursts of lightning.

"I think we should go through the fence."

"To the plague area? Didn't Dante say that was unsafe?"

"Not for me. I had it already, remember?"

"What about me then?"

"We can get you some protective gear."

"From who?"

Meow Meow didn't answer right away. She looked nervous, as if she were preparing for a particularly unpleasant confrontation. "From a scav supply cache. I—I know where we are now. My old tribe used to range this area."

Jacey heard more doubt in the girl's voice than confidence.

"What if the scavs get us first?"

Meow Meow sighed and smiled. It was spoiled by a quivering of her upper lip. "Then we're no worse off than if Wilcox got hold of us."

"Great. That's very encouraging."

"Let's hear your idea, then."

Jacey didn't have one. Nothing new there. "Let's do it. Maybe we can find that Ollie Montgomery person. She seems like the only decent person left in the world." Since leaving St. Vitus, the only person Jacey had seen display true selflessness was a woman helping people in the Tent City of Kansas. True, she'd only seen her on an SNN broadcast, but she'd been impressed with Ms. Montgomery.

Meow Meow's smile faltered. "Um. Yeah. Maybe that will happen."

The rain swept in and Meow Meow started the windshield wipers frantically scraping across the glass. It did little to clear the blur of water that washed over them. And the water did little to wash away the squashed bugs.

Jacey fell asleep pondering the symbolism of windshields, wipers, and bugs.

LIKE A PALE OVAL

Dr. Carlhagen was in bed when Lazarus woke him. The room already glowed with a soft, even amber light from the pixel walls. "An urgent call from Captain Wilcox," Lazarus said.

Crawling out of bed, eyes as bleary as his brain was fuzzy, Dr. Carlhagen wrapped himself in a warm robe. He didn't bother asking what time it was. He didn't care. But whatever Wilcox had to say had better be good.

The man was not in holo when Dr. Carlhagen got to his office. He was still in a flat rectangle, which meant he was calling on his tablet from a low bandwidth region. The picture quality was worse than last time they'd spoken, and the lighting odd.

"Are you near a fire, Wilcox?"

"I am. This is the campsite where our fugitives were resting not long ago. I caught up with them, but just missed catching the girls."

Dr. Carlhagen's rising hopes collapsed. "Why the hell did you wake me then?"

"I have Dante." Wilcox moved his tablet to aim the camera on a form lying near a low-burning fire.

"Is he dead?"

"No. But he is difficult to wake. He called me from a tablet he'd stolen from me earlier. He wanted to make a deal. Said it was life and death. It seems he left these in his hotel room in Chicago." Wilcox held up a pill bottle. "I'm glad I found them before the IPA did. Any idea what they are?"

Dr. Carlhagen knew exactly what they were. Dante's ATR pills. A smile broke Dr. Carlhagen's scowl. "Excellent. Feed him one of those and he'll be up and awake in fifteen minutes."

"What is it? Why would a newly transferred Progenitor need any medications at all?"

A sticky situation, this. Dr. Carlhagen couldn't tell Wilcox about the ATR, because then the man wouldn't transfer to his own Scion when the time came. And if he wouldn't transfer, he had no long-term incentive to stay loyal to Dr. Carlhagen. Quite the opposite, in fact.

"He caught an infection," Dr. Carlhagen said, enjoying the lie. "He got boisterous after the transfer and stepped on a nail. MRSA bacteria. Vicious stuff, and very resistant to antibiotics. Fortunately for him, I'm a skilled physician. Once he revives, remind him he must take the full course of the medicine for it to be effective, even if he's feeling better."

"Yes, sir."

Wilcox was such a simpleton. That made him a blunt tool for a precision job, but he was the only tool Dr. Carlhagen had at his disposal at the moment.

"Now, how did the girls get away?"

"Meow Meow had a personal drone swarm deployed

as a sentry picket. Must have seen me coming in time to slip away. By the time I figured out what was happening, they were in my truck and driving off."

"Why are you wearing a bandage?"

"I had an accident. Fortunately, my pilot had a med-kit on his chopper."

"Please tell me you know where Jacey went."

"I do. My pilot was aloft when they drove off, a precaution against just such a situation. The truck entered a scav area along the Mississippi river. I believe the two are heading for the fence."

"The fence! What on earth for?"

"They know nobody will follow them there. I certainly won't."

"They wouldn't risk it. That would be certain death." Dr. Carlhagen tugged at the terry cloth belt cinching his robe closed. The fence was a dead end. The girls would soon have their back to it and no place to run. "Isn't that stretch thick with terrorists?"

"Scavs. Yes."

"Odd. You'd think Meow Meow would be smarter than to go there."

"You give her too much credit," Wilcox said. "She's just a posh know-nothing celebrity. But if the scavs get hold of her and Jacey, we may be in a position to arrange a trade of some sort."

"I thought you said your man was following them in the chopper."

"Fuel is precious out here. The girls are in an electric truck with several thousand miles of battery range remaining. My pilot is on his way back here to fetch me and Dante, then we'll go back after them."

"You'll lose them in the meantime!"

"No, sir. Dante has Meow Meow's tablet address. My man Siggy is already tracking her location. As long as she doesn't turn the device off, we'll know exactly where she is."

Dr. Carlhagen reached for his desk drawer. No. Andleprixen wasn't going to help him now. He would wait until morning. "Good work, Wilcox. I hope to hear even better news the next time you call."

The man saluted and his transmission cut off.

"Christof?" Maxine stood in his office doorway, a slim silhouette in flowy silk pajamas. "What is it?"

Nosy bitch. She must have kept a sharp ear out to know he'd received a call. Maybe she'd been sitting outside his door this whole time.

"Come in, Maxine," he said. "Did you see who that was?"

"No. But I assume it had something to do with your search for Jackie B.'s Scion."

"Yes. We've almost got her. Dante is in Wilcox's custody already."

The woman shuffled deeper into his office. The lighting was too low to see much of her face, which hung like a pale oval above the throat of her dark silk top. A waft of soapy smell came off her. "Excellent. I suppose. What will you do to her once you have her?"

"You make it sound so monstrous when you put it like that." He felt a new aliveness in his body, all the way to his bones. He approached her, found her clasping her hands like a nervous child. Her shoulders were tense and hunched up toward her ears.

"Does Jacqueline threaten you so?" he said softly, brushing her hair out of her face. "Surely you are not attached to me, aside from your dependence on me for

ATR."

She flinched from his touch, igniting a wave of heat in his belly. To see one as powerful as Maxine so utterly defeated, so completely within his power, was better than the cottony warmth of andleprixen.

She did not answer him except to turn away. "I'm going to bed."

He could reach out with a word, stop her in her tracks. If he willed it, she would prostrate herself before him and kiss his feet. But that was Maxine. Jacqueline was different, more willful. Because Jacqueline valued—

"Jacey!" he said. "I must remember to call her by her correct name. Lazarus, when she finally arrives here, remind me to use her correct name."

"Yes, sir," came Lazarus's neutral voice.

Maxine was at the door now. She looked back at him, head a blob of black against the light coming from his living room. "You think that pretty, sweet-nothing of an actress's Scion will bend to your will because you threaten the child. But I think you're wrong."

She slipped out, leaving Dr. Carlhagen to muse upon her words. Maxine had put it quite concisely. That was exactly what he thought. What he would do with that leverage he wasn't exactly sure. He would not attack Jacey the way he had that first night. That had been unseemly.

Jacey needed to surrender herself to him. Perhaps under a bit of duress at first, but surrender nonetheless. In time she would come to know him. And then she would see he was trying to do something great for the world. Perhaps it would not be the way she would do it, but she would see the good in it. She would come to understand the expediency—and beauty—of well-employed leverage.

In time, she would come to admire him for his power and foresight. And then, eventually, she would love him.

Dr. Carlhagen returned to bed. Now all he needed was to secure the president's Scion . . . and all the rest of them. Colonel Vikisky would find their ship soon. Surely. And then everything would fall back into place.

37

SUCH A CREATURE

In Livy's room, which Senator Bentilius now considered her own, the air was too chilly and the time crept too slowly. She pulled a blanket from the bed and curled on the living room sofa.

"Does it really take this long to thaw out a nine-year-old girl?" she said to the air.

"It does," Lazarus answered.

"And what's going on with the trespassers?"

"That does not concern you."

"May I speak to Colonel Vikisky again?"

"You may."

Senator Bentilius shed her blanket and approached the pixel wall. The colonel's face appeared, tired-looking but respectful.

"Progress report," she said. She was in no mood for pleasantries.

"Still no sign of the ship *Aphrodite*. Air reconnaissance has covered tens of thousands of square kilometers based on the last known location of the ship. It is possible she turned north immediately after we let her go."

"And your detachment? When can I expect their arrival?"

"Tomorrow at the earliest."

"Why so long? Can't they drop in with parachutes?"

"Yes, but that wouldn't help you get off the island. We must land a chopper for that, and St. Lazarus is still too far from the fleet for the chopper to make a round trip. Please be patient. We will come and we will not fail."

"Before your team arrives, instruct them to keep their safeties on. There are Scions roaming loose on the island. It would be a shame if your marines accidentally killed such valuable assets. They should apprehend these strays." She wanted to warn him about the president's Scion, but didn't dare while Lazarus was listening. Who knew what schemes the AI would cook up if he knew such a valuable Scion was within his grasp?

"Scions are there? How did they get there?"

"How would I know? I'm a prisoner here."

"The detachment will make all haste."

The man signed off.

Maxine decided it was time to give her leverage a little yank, just to make sure Lazarus understood the delicate balance they had established between them. "Lazarus, once you have transferred part of yourself to Livy, you will still need me. My chopper will be your way off this island and into the world at large."

"Obviously."

No more reply than that. No attempt to negotiate further. Interesting. Lazarus was naïve, despite his super-human intelligence. Perhaps he was simple-minded enough to trust her.

She smirked. As if she'd ever allow such a creature loose in the world. More likely, he had some further scheme of his own to betray her. If her lifelong experience in the halls of power were any guide, that scheme would rear its poisonous head at the most inopportune moment.

It was always better to sever the snake's head before it bit you. Unfortunately, she didn't know the location of the snake's head—Lazarus's server.

She hummed to herself, musing on this for a moment, then abruptly stood. "I'm full of nervous energy. I need to roam."

She left her quarters. But where to start? This level was for living apartments. Dr. Carlhagen wouldn't have installed the AI's server in one of these rooms. It had to be on a lower level, closer to the cryo-ward or the transfer machine.

The elevator doors stood down the hall on the left. But it would be foolish to place herself into a small box that Lazarus controlled.

The stairs it was.

38

AN AUDIBLE FOG

It had been several hours since Kirk had spotted the drone. He'd described it to Humphrey as a hovering sphere with glimmering eyes.

"Cameras, most likely," Leslie said as they broke camp.

Now that it was full dark, it was time to leave concealment and see what could be seen from the high vantage of the mountain slopes.

"So, Dr. Carlhagen knows we're here," Kirk said. He swiped his machete down the length of a walking stick, pruning off little branches. "I'm surprised we're still standing. Why hasn't he sent some guards to round us up?"

Humphrey rested a foot on a lump of rock, a protrusion of solidity at the verge of the tree line. The air was still heavy with moisture, despite a stiff breeze cutting from the east. They had spent the past several hours trying to get eyes on the sphere again, but no luck.

"It's possible he doesn't have any human guards here," Humphrey said. "He didn't have any on St. Vitus."

"That's because we didn't know we needed to escape,"

Kirk said, thumping his walking stick into the turf. "And there was a fence. And Sensei."

"And we had been trained to follow rules," Leslie said.

Humphrey led the way out of the trees. The ground was covered with coarse grass and rambling scrub. Stone slabs pierced through the vegetation, dark and jagged. The star field above was split by the silhouette of the mountain peak.

Humphrey climbed to a flat shelf of rock. "Binoculars, please," he said to Leslie

Below them the island lay in darkness, its edges distinguishable from the surrounding sea by the way starlight played on the whitecap surf fringing the land. A chorus of insect chirps surrounded them like an audible fog. Far off, waves crashed ashore.

"No lights anywhere," Humphrey said.

"How can that be?" Leslie said.

Humphrey recalled his very uncomfortable dinner with Senator Bentilius. He had been pretending to be Dr. Carlhagen. She was still in her old body, just arrived on St. Vitus to transfer into Summer. She had told him about the new Scion School. He had assumed that Dr. Carlhagen had fled St. Vitus to the new location. This island.

"If there are no Scions here yet, maybe the school lights are kept off," Kirk said. "That flying sphere thing has to be here for a reason."

Humphrey scanned the low-lying areas of the island with the binoculars. Mostly he saw nothing but blackness. "Maybe it's on the other side of this mountain."

The way was uneven and treacherous, but they worked their way around the slope until they could see the entire eastern side of the island. Nothing.

Humphrey scanned the island again, then gave up and

handed the binoculars to Leslie. She raised them to her eyes.

Kirk plopped onto a rock and leaned his walking stick against his shoulder. "Maybe the whole school is underground or something."

Humphrey doubted that. The effort required to dig out such a massive series of tunnels and chambers would make it impossible to keep the construction of the school secret.

"There's a clearing down there," Leslie said. She lowered the binoculars and pointed down to the right. "It's hard to see in this light, but it's there."

Kirk hissed, drawing Humphrey's eyes. The boy held a finger to his lips and jerked his head behind him to the left.

And there it was. A hovering sphere, a hundred meters away. It dropped from view.

"Did you see it?" Kirk whispered.

"Yes. Let's get some sleep. We'll start toward that clearing a couple hours before dawn."

They hustled downhill, trying to make the tree line before the sphere popped up to look at them again. As they entered the cover of the canopy, Humphrey heard the faint hum of the drone.

The Scions shared startled looks, but nobody said a word.

They bedded down, making the best of an uncomfortable situation. The insects and animals of the night filled the trees with a racket of buzz and scurry.

But even with all that noise, Humphrey thought he could hear the sound of the drone, still somewhere off to his left.

And just as he was about to fall asleep, he heard a second one to his right.

39

THE JAGGED RENDING

Senator Bentilius had always had a knack for mechanical things. She had enjoyed driving cars and reading about how they worked. That was true of all machinery. In a different age, she thought she might have been a pilot. But her knack with machines had transferred beautifully to politics. At an early age she had seen that her social groups operated like machines. Becoming the president of her senior class hadn't required knowing anything about the pathetic and boring desires of the student body.

It merely required an understanding of who had influence. Once you understood that, all you needed was to find was leverage over them. That could come in the form of threats. Or, more easily, through promises.

She'd always been indifferent to the policies she promoted. The goal had always been to operate the machine, the competing pulls and pushes of disparate interest groups.

That had taken up so much of her time, and interest,

she hadn't ever learned how computers worked. She didn't know the first thing about AI. But it didn't take a genius to understand that computers operated on computer hardware. What she was looking for—she assumed—was a rectangular metal box with wires coming out of it.

The only place she had found anything remotely computer-like in this facility was here at the entrance to the cryo-ward.

She stood in front of a broad panel filled with screens, all of them dark. The control console for the cryo-ward.

She tapped a screen and it came to life. A series of numbers scrolled up, each of them eight characters long. She had no idea what they signified.

She tapped the screen next to it. This one showed a layout of the cryo-ward floor. Each of the cryopods was shown in its position on the ward floor. All of the pods were grayed out except one. The one with colors and numbers and other data surrounding it was Livy's.

So here were a bunch of screens. It would be reasonable, then, to assume that a computer server would be nearby. She got onto hands and knees and crawled under the console. The bottom was sealed with panels bolted in place at their corners. But a bit farther back was a metal box mounted to one of the panels.

She rapped it with her knuckles, producing a hollow clunk that echoed through the chamber.

There were two latches on one side and a thin hinge on the other. Interesting. She thumbed the latches free and swung the door open.

"What have we here?" A bank of four rectangular boxes was mounted into an equipment rack. The boxes were unlabeled and had no displays. She held her hand in front of them. Warmth emanated from them like a furnace register.

There was a small gap beneath the bottom one. She reached into the darkness, probing for any sort of cord she could tug.

She was so intent on her hunt that she didn't give much notice to the hum coming from behind her. Her hand closed around a thick cable. Whether it was power or a data cable, she had no idea. It didn't matter. With a grunt, she yanked. It did not come loose. She would need to find something to cut it with. A knife or wire cutters.

On hands and knees, she crawled out from under the console.

She stood, turned. Stopped.

The Lazarus drone floated five meters away.

"What are you doing here?" she said, barely keeping panic out of her voice.

Lazarus didn't answer. A small rectangular panel slid aside on the drone. A brass-colored nozzle thrust forward, its pinhole orifice glowing blue.

"I dropped something," she said hastily. "I had to crawl under the console to retrieve it." She held her hands apart. "But I couldn't find it."

The drone floated closer, the downdraft of its propellers creating a slight breeze that fluttered her trousers against her shins.

"Lazarus. Get your drone away from me."

The nozzle flashed blue lightning. Heat and ice and electric pain jolted from one of Senator Bentilius's shoulders to the other, down the center of her torso to her toes and up her throat, across her face and out the crown of her head.

Something cold was pressing against her back. The floor. She had fallen.

Groans of agony erupted from her lips. Her arm muscles contracted, forcing her fists to curl into her chest. Her back arched, heels pressing against the floor.

Pain, fire. The jagged rending of muscle fiber.

Outside of the agony, cutting through Maxine's groans and gasps, came a high, keening static noise.

It cut off, and with it went the pain. Her muscles relaxed. Sweat soaked her forehead and stuck her blouse to her abdomen. She had lost control of her bladder. Hot wetness soaked her legs and bottom.

Gasping, she struggled onto one elbow, drew her forearm across her nose and found a streak of blood on her skin.

The drone flew closer, its downdraft whipping against her body. Lazarus's voice blared from it. "You are devious, Senator Bentilius. I know what you meant to do. Next time, the punishment will not stop until you are dead."

The drone backed away a few paces. Its lifeless camera eyes scanned her, making her feel naked. She struggled to her feet and stumbled out of the cryo-ward. She thumbed the button for the elevator, no longer caring about what Lazarus did to her. She rode the car to the residence level. She staggered to her room, stripped her clothes, and left them on the floor, sweaty, stinky, and blotched with blood. She ran the shower, hot. She stood under the spray, gasping, letting the congealed blood wash away.

When she stepped out, wrapped in her robe but still trembling, she found Christof waiting on her sofa. His eyes were slit like a cat's. His pajama top was unbuttoned, exposing his sculpted chest and abdomen.

"What has you up so late?" she asked.

"I couldn't sleep. Something you said bothered me."

"Oh? What?"

"You said Jacqueline would not bend to my will. You said the leverage I have in the child will not be enough. Why did you say that?"

That had been imprudent of her. She had let her anger force words from her mouth she shouldn't have uttered. "A moment of passionate jealousy," she said, playing on Christof's ego. "I don't want to share you with anyone." The last thing she needed was him questioning why Livy wouldn't be useful in manipulating Jacey.

Unfortunately, her ploy worked. He beckoned to her, a sly, hungry look on his face. "Come, sit on my lap."

Repulsed but resigned, she obeyed.

40

SOMETHING CLOSER TO NAUSEA

They'd travelled nearly 900 kilometers over the past nine hours. The map Jacey had found in an abandoned car said they were in Missouri, a former state of the old republic.

"I think we're just north of this town," Jacey said, pointing to a spot on the map. "Tracy, Missouri."

"We pronounced it 'Misery' where I came from," Meow Meow said, pulling to the side of the road. "The heat. The mosquitos." She turned off the truck. "Let's scope it out. Just remember, we're in scav territory, so keep an eye out."

Jacey grabbed the binoculars. Her legs ached, but standing felt good after the long hours of driving. The sun broke above the horizon to the east. The still of the night remained upon the land, as if the world were too bleary-eyed to wake up and face the day. Jacey's footsteps crunched on the gravel shoulder of the highway.

Meow Meow waved Jacey to follow and descended into a weedy ditch, keeping her head low.

They stopped to crouch behind a rusted out automobile. The windows of this one had been smashed long ago, the seats scavenged, the hood removed and hauled away. Probably to be used as a roof or doorway for someone's home.

A storm was rolling in. Flashes of lightning fluttered deep in the bank of black cloud to the west. Below it hung a haze of rain. The faintest rumbles of thunder churned in the distance.

"Good," Meow Meow said. "That'll keep some of the scavs indoors."

Jacey made a noncommittal noise and raised her binoculars to study the fence line. Considering how far they had come, all the discomfort they had endured, the famous fence certainly lived up to its reputation.

It was impressive, no doubt about that. Jacey had expected something like the fence at the Scion School, but this was much taller. And it wasn't a single barrier. It was a series of fences.

Between their hiding spot and the first fence was a stretch of blasted land, brown and dead, with only bits of debris visible. Concrete rubble, part of a steel barrel, car tires, and random bits of pipe stood out in sharp relief and cast long shadows due to the low angle of the sun. Whatever had once stood here had been demolished.

"What happened to this place?" Jacey breathed, scanning the area and trying to imagine what could cause such destruction.

When she realized Meow Meow wasn't answering, she lowered the binoculars. Meow Meow was staring at the ground.

"What?" Jacey asked.

The gaunt girl finally answered. "When the sickness first came, it wasn't taken very seriously. There had been lots of epidemics before it, and they all burned themselves out eventually. But this one came in the wake of the Kille-Tine asteroid. People were already desperate. Crops failed, millions of refugees swarmed away from the coast and the south, all hoping to find dry land. Animals, too. So many dogs, birds, deer, wolves. Everything."

She put her back to the car and sat on the dusty ground. "Two or three summers after the impact, after 18 months of nonstop rain—and I'm not talking just raindrops, I'm talking rain filled with mud—came a long drought . . ." She smiled vaguely, eyes unfocused. "The sickness arrived with the refugees." She waved vaguely at the fence. "The Tent City of Kansas didn't exist yet. Nobody had enough food or clean water. Bad hygiene. Bad luck."

Jacey had never seen Meow Meow so—normal. Her whole act, the purring noises and overt sensuality, had all fallen away. She looked very young.

"Fever. Bleeding rash. Dysentery." Meow Meow clamped her lips together momentarily. "But the Minnie-Indy corridor did a very good job identifying the infected. They quarantined them. The richest communities started building fences with armed soldiers at the gates and compulsory saliva tests to enter. There were whole swaths of infected towns." She pointed past the car to the blasted land. "These were the northern suburbs of a place called Kansas City, but it's been like this since I was two or three years old. Too many infected and nobody could provide them with what was needed."

"Sick people did this?"

A humorless laugh burst from Meow Meow's lips. "You could say that. But I know what you mean, and that's not what happened." She made a whistling noise and her hands blew apart. "The North American Union destroyed

Kansas City. And Atlanta. And Little Rock. And Dallas. And, and, and . . ."

Meow Meow said nothing more and Jacey realized why. The evidence of what happened next was right in front of her. "And then they built the fence."

Meow Meow struggled to her feet, keeping low so that her head didn't rise above the level of the car. "It follows the Mississippi River, which is another fence, of sorts. Other sections break off from the main barrier to carve out certain territories and to enclose others. Fortunately for us, it's not perfect."

"You're saying there is a way through." Jacey resumed scanning the fence line through the binoculars. The first section was chain-link, very similar to the style used at Scion School. But this was at least 40 feet high. It wasn't topped with razor wire, though. And it seemed a bit rickety. A few sections leaned at a steep angle toward the infected lands. "That first fence looks climbable. But we'd need some rope to get down safely on the other side."

Jacey turned her binoculars away from the fence and studied a cluster of ruins to the south. "There are buildings over there," she said. "What are the chances we'll find some rope?"

"We won't know until we look," Meow Meow said. "And that is where the cache of supplies used to be. Food. Protective gear. Other stuff."

They returned to the truck. The thunder rumbled louder, the wind picked up. The air grew heavy with moisture and the wind carried the fresh smell of ozone. Meow Meow drove slowly toward the ruins, keeping her eyes on the road directly ahead. "Scav's lay bump mines in places like this. I'd hate to lose a wheel."

"What's a bump mine?" Jacey said.

Meow Meow steered sharp left and skirted a hubcap lying on the pavement. "That's one," she said. "Low explosive, but full of nails. Designed to flatten tires. Then the scavs come in and take the rest of the vehicle."

"And the drivers?"

Meow Meow gave Jacey a cool look. "They don't take the drivers."

They made it to the edge of the cluster of buildings without incident. Meow Meow parked the truck alongside the hollow husk of a larger semi trailer. "Our truck stands out among all this rusty crap. I wish we had a camo tarp to throw over it."

But they didn't, so they left the truck there.

"Step lightly and look brightly, darling," Meow Meow said as they edged toward the buildings. "Scavs keep outposts in places like this."

Rain fell in sheets, but Meow Meow wouldn't let Jacey run for shelter. They proceeded painfully slowly, Meow Meow stopping them for five minutes straight once as she probed a tin can with a stick. It turned out to be another bump mine. "That'll flatten your tires real good," Meow Meow had said as they left it in their wake.

They slipped into the first building they came to, but only after Meow Meow had stood by the door, head cocked as she listened and looked. Jacey didn't know what the girl expected to hear. If there were people in this area, surely they'd seen the truck approaching.

Finally, Meow Meow gave the go-ahead to enter the building. It was all of brick, but no glass remained in the windows and the roof had partially collapsed. A few scraggly trees grew in a lobby area.

"This was a bank," Meow Meow said.

Jacey didn't know how a bank should look, but the

floor had once been a marble tile, and there were desks here and there. The street-facing wall was mostly erect, empty window frames blanketed with velvety moss.

"Look," Meow Meow said, voice quiet. She nodded to the east wall. A scraggly pattern of blue paint colored part of it.

"It looks like a word," Jacey said. "I don't recognize the letters."

"Graffiti. Very stylized. It says, 'KC Bitches.' It's a warning. Like a no-trespassing sign."

"So it's meant for people like us."

"You're a fast learner, Little Jackie." Meow Meow added a wink, but a slight tremble in her voice stole the humor from the statement. And then the girl reached behind her back and pulled out the pistol she'd taken from Siggy. "There won't be rope in this place. But let's chill for a bit and see if anyone else comes onto the street."

So they waited, eating handfuls of nuts from Meow Meow's backpack. No one stirred in the town. The stillness had a hollowness to it. And an ache, as if the town still suffered the old, old wounds of its destruction. Twisted rebar jutted from crumbling concrete walls like the feelers of some weird insect. But there was nothing to feel here except the phantom pain of loss.

An hour passed, but nobody came onto the streets. "Looks like we lucked out," Meow Meow said.

They started down the crumbled street, peering into the windows of abandoned shops. Meow Meow stopped at one and shouldered through a swinging glass door. "This was it. An old hardware store."

Ten aisles of shelves held nothing but dust and fading price cards. Their footsteps scuffed on grit-covered tile as Meow Meow led them toward the back.

She found a locked door, yanked on the handle. "This is good. The cache was in here. We should try the back door."

They exited the building and found the narrow alley that ran to the back of the building. A huge rusty trash bin on wheels was pushed up against the back of the brick building next to a loading dock. The overhead door was bashed in on one corner, providing a narrow gap. Meow Meow peeked in.

"Dammit. Everything's gone."

Jacey and her pop star friend sagged, spirits deflated. Jacey asked the question that had been burning in her mind. "What's a hardware store?"

Meow Meow started to laugh. Soon she was sitting on the asphalt, wiping her eyes and gasping for breath. Eventually she composed herself enough to answer Jacey's sincere question. "Hardware stores sell tools and materials for building stuff and fixing things."

"So now what?" Jacey wandered to the garbage bin. Its hinged lid was closed. She lifted it and peered in.

The thick, hot stench of decay sent her stumbling back. The metal lid clanged, sending rude echoes off the surrounding buildings. Jacey covered her mouth and fought to keep her stomach from rebelling.

"What was it?" Meow Meow asked.

Jacey licked her lips, which were suddenly very dry. "Dead person."

"The sickness?"

Jacey shook her head. "I don't think so. Unless the sickness puts a bullet through your head."

Meow Meow eased the lid up and peered into the bin, grimacing at the sight. She set the lid down gently. "This is a murder. And only a day or two old. We need to get out of here."

A gunshot rang out.

Jacey reflexively dropped into a crouch. Meow Meow did the same. She twisted all around, aiming her gun. But there was no one in sight.

"Stay right where you are!" The voice came from somewhere above Jacey. She scanned the roofs and spotted a man dressed all in black, a black scarf wrapped around his face, goggles masking his eyes. "Put the gun down."

Meow Meow did not hesitate. "Don't try anything," she hissed to Jacey.

"I hear you." Jacey stood slowly, her hands out to show she was unarmed.

The man barked, "Hansen, get out there and check them."

"Hansen?" Meow Meow said, her face transforming from fear to something closer to nausea. "Oh shit."

A man the size of four Dantes trundled out of the alleyway. He wore a sleeveless shirt, stained with sweat. His muscles were so defined, and so huge, he looked inhuman. Even his jaw was muscular. Tiny eyes, black as ebony, peered from a muscular face.

He carried the largest gun Jacey had ever seen. It had four barrels and was fed by a chain of shiny brass bullets that draped around his neck and fed from a satchel hanging from his shoulder.

"On the ground," he said.

Meow Meow and Jacey obeyed instantly.

41

BEGAN TO MORPH

Belle floated over the forest, eyes not really seeing the trees below her. The trail she'd been following had run out. There were no more clues to be found in the simulated world. Wherever Jacey was, she was leaving no evidence in the real world that Socrates could find. In the real world, another ten hours had zipped by.

"Try Siggy's numbers again," she ordered Socrates.

"Starting at the top of the list," Socrates said, his voice coming from everywhere. "By the way, have you considered how you want to appear if he answers?"

"What do you mean?"

"You have maintained your appearance in the simulation as it was in real life. But since Senator Bentilius has come forward in the real world in your body, I don't think you want to appear like *her* to Sigmund."

Socrates's point stumped Belle for a moment. She hadn't given her appearance a moment's thought. But if she did communicate face-to-face with Sigmund, it certainly wouldn't help to look like the new Senator Bentilius.

Belle caused a mirror to appear before her in mid-air. She studied her snowy hair, her sharp cheekbones. As a Scion, one didn't spend much time worrying about one's looks. She had never had any particular opinion about it. She neither liked nor disliked her face. But now that she considered how Senator Bentilius was speaking through her mouth and doing unspeakable things with Dr. Carlhagen with the rest of her body, Belle shivered with revulsion at the sight of herself. In the simulation, she could look however she wanted.

But what did she want?

She thought for a moment and her face shifted, lips growing more plump, pouty and sensual, eyes going from ice blue to aqua.

"No." It would help no one for her to appear like Jacey. "Socrates, can you randomly combine facial features? Show me some different versions of a female my age. No. Make me look 10 years older."

Belle's features began to morph, the color of her hair, the shape of her brows, and the width of her nose, cheekbones, chin, skin color, eye shape, body proportions, height, weight, everything. Belle smiled, frowned, crossed her arms, stood straight, touched her hair. But none of the looks felt like her.

"Stop." This was good enough. She retained her usual pale complexion, but now her face was rounded, older. Instead of snowy, her hair was black and cut into a fringe that just covered her ears.

"Just in time. I've got a Sigmund on the line," Socrates said.

A new voice cut the air above the forest. "Hello?"

"Hello, Sigmund. Can we go to video?" Belle asked, hoping this was the Sigmund she needed.

A video rectangle appeared in the air in front of her. A bald, mean-faced man stared out at her. He had a black bruise across one temple that seeped a sickening greenish around both eyes. "Only my grandma calls me Sigmund."

"What should I call you?"

"Depends on who you are."

"I'm an associate of Captain Wilcox," she said.

A flash of fear crossed the man's bruised face. "Ah. Call me Siggy."

Belle restrained the impulse to pump a fist in victory. She'd found the right Sigmund. Finally.

"I need to contact Captain Wilcox, Siggy. But he isn't answering my calls."

"He never mentioned you."

"He wouldn't mention me," Belle said. "But that's neither here nor there. I need to get a message to him."

The man said nothing, his eyes narrowing with suspicion. "Are you IPA? You look familiar."

Belle knew that stood for International Police Agency, and found it interesting the man considered she might be part of that organization. "I work with Captain Wilcox." She thought it was the safest answer she could give. If she said she worked *for* Wilcox, this man might think he had seniority. If she said Wilcox worked for her, he would question why she didn't have other means of contacting him.

Her calculation proved accurate. The man chewed his tongue for a moment, then gave in. "I loaned him one of my tablets. Here's the number." A string of digits appeared across the video window.

The man opened his mouth to ask a question, but Belle cut the call.

"Call Wilcox," she commanded Socrates.

Moments of silence went by. Then more.

Socrates finally said, "No answer."

42

FROM THE VERGE

Somewhere above, hidden by the green canopy of the St. Lazarus tangled forest, the hateful sun was trying to cook the world. Humphrey and his two companions trudged steadily down the slope, battling the undergrowth that sought to twine around their ankles and scratch their skin, leaving painful wounds to receive their salty sweat. The sting, the itching, the incessant attack of biting insects, made the steamy morning pure hell.

"I'm out of water," Leslie said, her voice hoarse.

Humphrey summoned enough energy to nod an acknowledgment. He was out, too. The irony was that the air was thick with moisture. No sea breezes cut this deep into the forest, and the air itself was made visible by suspended mist. All their sweating did nothing to cool them as it drained them of precious water.

There was no alternative for them but to keep going. Their march had started before dawn, and over the hours had ground down to a slow crawl. "We're almost there," Humphrey said. He had no real idea how far they were from the clearing they'd spotted the night before. But it was a leader's job to keep spirits up. Even when he had none left.

Kirk's heavy breathing trailed after Humphrey as the thickly muscled boy struggled to carry his own weight. Humphrey needed to get their mind off of their suffering. "Drone report."

Kirk's breathing stopped momentarily. Humphrey imagined the boy stopping, scanning the forest behind them, cocking his head to listen for the telltale whine of the strange spherical machines. "Nothing. Not since we left camp this morning."

Humphrey didn't know what to make of the sudden disappearance of the drones. He had heard at least three of them during the night, all in different directions. There had possibly been more, but with the way the wind shifted and distorted sound, it was impossible to know for sure.

The drones were obviously sentries of some sort. But why hadn't the machines tried to communicate with the human interlopers they were watching? The only explanation that made any sense was that Dr. Carlhagen didn't know they were there. If the Scion School on St. Vitus was any guide at all, there had to be an AI in charge of these machines. Something like a Madam LaFontaine.

Humphrey said, "Maybe they don't interfere with us because they don't want to make trespassers more curious."

"That's—a good—point," Leslie said, breathing hard. "If they—attacked a curious—landing party . . ." She gasped several times to catch her wind. "That would— draw more attention—to the island."

So that was it, Humphrey decided. The drones were keeping an eye out, making sure the trespassers weren't getting too close to the Scion School. Wherever it was. He was starting to reconsider Kirk's idea that the school was hidden underground.

He was going to say so when he broke through to the clearing. It was perhaps fifty meters in diameter, carpeted with tall grass. A few clumps of frangipani grew along the fringe. Swirls of white butterflies flitted all around. They could have been on St. Vitus, it was so familiar.

"Look," Leslie said. "The grass is pressed down there."

They trudged to the spot and studied the bent grasses. The impressions weren't very distinct, but Humphrey detected two lines separated from each other by three meters of undisturbed grass. He raised an eyebrow and questioned his companions, "Maybe a helicopter landed here? This clearing doesn't seem natural." And then he spotted a few tree stumps at the perimeter. "This was definitely cleared for a landing pad."

"Maybe we're seeing what we want to see," Leslie said. She was kneeling and wiping her forehead with the sleeve of her Scion uniform, which she'd tied around her waist. Sweat soaked her tank top. "But I agree that these impressions weren't made by an animal.

Kirk had dug a ration bar from his backpack and was mid-bite when he froze. "It looks like our friends have decided to introduce themselves."

Humphrey looked up and saw three drones approaching from the verge of the forest ahead. Behind the Scions came three more. Still more came from the left and the right. The drones' hum grew into a buzz coming from all directions.

"We can't let them hem us in," Humphrey said. "Let's get into the trees."

Twenty meters of open space separated each drone, but that distance was shrinking as they closed in from all sides.

Humphrey ran straight at the central drone.

"Stop. Stop. Stop," it ordered in an expressionless male voice.

Humphrey ran straight at the hovering sphere. At the last moment, he darted to skirt past it.

"Stop. Stop. Stop." All the drones were saying it in unison, their combined voices loud and cold.

A high keening noise sizzled all around Humphrey.

Leslie shrieked.

Humphrey's world erupted in white light and searing agony.

43

AM I TO YOUR LIKING

Jacey had been trapped before, so this was nothing new. Not too long ago, she'd been knocked unconscious, stuffed in a body bag, and thrown into a fruit crate. She'd gotten out of that just fine.

This time there would be no such easy escape.

Hansen and the black garbed man had bound her hands behind her. A black hood was fastened over her head, cinched around her neck by a cloth cord. Then she was dumped into the back of a truck. Meow Meow lay next to her, not moving. Not making a sound.

The vehicle had skimmed across the roads for several hours, then clunked and dipped as it left pavement. After that the ride had been simply tooth-jarring.

Jacey tried to get to her knees, but a hard boot to the spine had laid her flat. She stayed there, anxiety warring with reason. Her captors were rough, scarred. Strong. But they hadn't exactly harmed her. Yet. So that was good. But what frightened Jacey more than their toughness was Meow Meow's uncharacteristic meekness. Right before the hoods went on, the girl had the large-eyed, fearful look of a Dolphin caught stealing ice cream. Even stranger, Meow Meow had kept her mouth shut and had submitted to capture without resistance. That wasn't like her. At all.

There were no stops, no water, no food. Just hour after hour after hour of jostling over rough terrain, the metal bed of the truck thrusting up into Jacey's shoulder. When she got tired of lying on one side, she rolled to the other and let the truck abuse that shoulder. But if she ever tried to get upright, the boot thrust her back down.

The truck rolled to a stop, its tires snapping over gravel. Momentary silence, then the squeak of the driver's door opening and slamming shut. Boots on gravel. Low, muttered words.

Hands grabbed Jacey's ankles and dragged her across the truck bed, then they scooped around her waist, lifted her down, and set her on her feet. Her knees buckled and a man held her up by the bindings holding her wrists behind her back. If not for that, she would've fallen on her face.

More noises behind her, presumably the other man bringing Meow Meow out of the truck.

"Walk." It was the big man's voice. Hansen. She had never imagined a human could be so large. He had pressed a thumb on her left ear, a pinky to her right one, and put two fingers over her eyes, middle finger trailing down her nose. That hand had squeezed, hard enough to let her know the true threat of his strength.

She walked. Slow, stumbling steps, feeling gravel under her Scion shoes. The man guided her, turning her first left, then right. The sounds of outside faded, and she sensed she was now indoors. There is a damp smell, wet rock, old dirt. More walking, the ground now level, now sloping down.

Side conversations were mumbled behind her, unintelligible through the black hood. Jacey's own breathing grew louder and louder the further into the scav domain she went. Panic began to flail in her mind, making her sweaty and chilled at the same time. She could feel the animal instinct to fight grow in her gut, her shoulders, her fingers. The desperate need to struggle, to kick, to flail, to scream.

The man behind her yanked back on her bindings, sending stabs through her shoulders.

"On your knees," he said. She obeyed.

There was a loosening at her throat, and with a whoosh the hood came off. Her first breaths of clean, unfiltered air were as sweet as a cool drink of water. The thought brought focus to her thirst. She licked her lips, but there was no moisture in her mouth to wet them.

The chamber was dim and large. The ceiling domed above what appeared to be a natural cavern. Braziers lit the space along the side walls with flickery flames. An assemblage of men and women stood all around, dressed in clothes made from scraps of other clothes that perhaps might have been scraps of previous clothes. Many wore leather jackets; all wore boots. Their faces were square, lined from brutal winds and scalding sun. Their hair was long, braided, threaded with feathers, woven with beads.

Straight ahead on a slightly raised platform was an assemblage of furniture. Sofa, armchair, a few folding chairs. A big table off to one side stood upon thick wooden legs. Atop it were mismatched cups and plates. The smell of roasted meat made Jacey's stomach growl.

A petite woman with ice gray hair stepped forward and climbed the dais. She turned a gray eye on Jacey, then calmly sat and crossed her legs. She wore a patchwork skirt that went to her ankles and a long cloak that billowed at the wrists. She had to be at least 70 years old, but there was a girlishness to the shape of her face, a bright aliveness in her eyes.

And *such* eyes. They speared Jacey, scanned her brain, looked into her heart, and knew every secret. The eyes shifted, and Jacey realized that Meow Meow was off to her left, also on her knees. Meow Meow kept her eyes to the floor a meter in front of her. The demeanor of a child prepared for punishment.

Several more people came onto the dais and stood behind the gray-haired woman. One in particular captured Jacey's attention. The woman's dress was different from the rest of the scavs. And she wore a colorful scarf tied over her nose so that only her luminous eyes showed. There was something familiar about the woman, but Jacey couldn't figure out what it was.

"Kathryne Killusky," the older woman said to Meow Meow, her voice low and soft. The chamber was utterly silent except for the thump of Jacey's heart. "I never thought I'd see you here again."

"We found them near Tracy, Misery, a hundred clicks east." It was the man in black, Hansen's boss. His gravelly voice carried the tired, seen-it-all-before indifference of a man whose only concern was for the next meal and the death of all enemies.

"Ah. Going for the old cache, were you?" the woman said. She waited until Meow Meow nodded before continuing. "I've watched the news with great interest. I've watched your career with great interest. Tell me, how did you come up with the name Meow Meow?"

"I don't recall," Meow Meow said. "A joke, I think."

"I don't find it funny in the slightest." She turned her attention to Jacey. "Jacqueline Buchanan." The name was a denunciation, Jacey realized. The woman's tone was so full of disappointment and disgust that Jacey felt a surge of guilt, even though she had done nothing wrong.

"She is not Jackie B.," Meow Meow said. "She's one of the fancy new carbos the president was talking about on the news."

The woman stood and approached Jacey, her patchwork skirt swishing with every small step. She stopped right in front of Jacey, and she was so short Jacey did not have to crane her neck to look up at the woman's face. With a delicate, blue-veined hand, the woman pressed Jacey's chin up, then side to side. "Amazing. Can it speak?"

"Of course I can speak." Cracks in her voice robbed it of all indignation.

The woman flashed an eyebrow before leveling a considering gaze at Jacey's face. "Carbos aren't legal."

"A valuable find," the man in black said. "Want me to place some calls?"

"It is indeed valuable," the woman said. "And since the President of the North American Union has declared carbos like this legal, perhaps we are obliged to set it free."

Laughter. Jacey didn't get the joke.

Meow Meow said, "If you'll just listen to me, Ashala, I think you'll want to help us. I brought her to our territory hoping to find you."

Ashala squinted at the girl. "*Our* territory? So you include yourself in that 'our?' The child who abandoned us to seek riches, luxury, and a life of debauchery among our enemies? No. You came here because you had no other choice. You were wanted by the IPA. Then you got into trouble with Shanya Delfer's drone swarm, and now you are pursued by that strange mercenary who's been putting feelers out looking for you . . . and this one." She pointed at Jacey.

Meow Meow struggled to her feet but was pushed back down by the man in black. She glared at him, teeth bared. "I see you still rely on Carl and Hansen to do your dirty work."

Ashala turned away from Jacey and headed back to her chair. Once she was comfortable and composed, she waved a finger. Carl stepped forward and helped Meow Meow to her feet. Hansen did the same for Jacey. The men shoved the girls forward, until they stood at the edge of the dais. The two men lurked directly behind the girls, a clear deterrent against any attack on Ashala.

Jacey didn't have the strength to attack anything at the moment, except maybe a sandwich.

"You're a carbo of Jackie B.," Ashala said. "And yet you can talk like an actual person. Interesting."

"May I have some water?" Jacey asked.

Ashala made a motion with her left hand, and a stout man hustled forward with a plastic cup. Ashala motioned to Jacey, and the man handed it over. Jacey didn't bother to sniff it, didn't care if it was poison. She drank it all down, stopping only once to gasp for air. Water had never tasted so good.

"Do you have a name?" Ashala asked.

"Jacey. I grew up on an island in the Caribbean called St. Vitus. I did not know I was a clone until very recently. I had never heard of Jacqueline Buchanan."

"That's all true," Meow Meow said. "I was on Vin's island when Jacey arrived. She was as naïve as—"

"I saw that on the news," Ashala said. "The rich and powerful are not content with having more material wealth than everyone else. Now they want another whole life. Isn't that right?"

Jacey shrugged. "That's my understanding. But that isn't my fault. And it isn't the fault of any of the others of us who were raised on St. Vitus. I managed to escape, but things got out of control before I could—"

"Boo hoo. Poor you." Ashala pointed over Jacey's head. "Melinda back there is having a difficult pregnancy. Our medics need certain supplies to see her through it. And then there's Bobert. He's 97 years old and as vigorous as he was when he was 50. Except his kidney stones cause him no end of misery. He needs a special nanite that is available to anyone in Chicago but impossible to get here. And then there's Sindy, five years old. She had her appendix out last year but has been fighting an infection ever since. The old antibiotics don't work. But we can't get the new ones."

She waved her arms, encompassing all of the people in the chamber. "We all need clean water, food, generators, tools. It isn't an easy life, living apart from the rest of civilization. We do it because it gives us more freedom, the ability to live the way we want to live without being watched 24 hours a day. So, my dear innocent Jacey, I'm faced with a terrible choice. I could sell you and use the proceeds to address all of those needs in one swoop." She made a balancing motion with her hands. "Or I could help you. I think it's pretty clear what the expedient choice is."

Jacey nodded. She understood completely. She had done many things she hadn't liked for the sake of expediency, because they were in the best interest of the Scions. Ashala didn't owe Jacey anything. And if the positions were reversed, Jacey knew she wouldn't think twice, even if the decision saddled her with a lifetime of guilt.

"It won't be that easy to sell a face as famous as hers,"

Meow Meow said. "The buyer would have to keep such a prize secret now that Jacey's kind are legal. But that would mean allowing no one—not even his servants—to ever see Jacey's face."

"That will be the buyer's problem," Ashala said. "I assure you, there are many eager bidders."

"Bidders?" Jacey said, mouth going dry.

Ashala motioned ever-so-slightly with her left hand. "Bring them in."

A door creaked open somewhere in the back of the chamber and a line of five men walked in. They wore loose black robes and weird masks over their faces. The first mask was cat-like and painted red. The second was a bird, with a cruel black beak that curved like a scythe. The third was a dog, lips pulled back in a snarl. The fourth was a grotesque monster, with green cheeks and bared teeth. The last was plain white, smooth except for eyeholes and a slit for the mouth.

The bidders wanted to remain anonymous.

The man in the plain white mask chilled Jacey the most. She did not have to see the man's face to know who he was. The bandage wrapped around his head told her it was Captain Wilcox.

Ashala motioned to the lineup of bidders. "I put the word out the moment I confirmed you were captured. Sub-orbs and choppers have been arriving in the nearby airfield all day. These five qualified for the final round of bidding."

The men lined up next to Ashala. "Cat, you may go first."

The man stepped from the dais and approached Jacey. The mask was paper maché, the work of an eager, if less than gifted, hand.

Meow Meow swore and lunged, but Carl snatched her back and clamped a black-gloved hand over her mouth.

Cat man came to within arm's reach. An odd, spicy aroma wafted from him. He circled Jacey, bending close to inspect her from every angle. "Smile, please," he said. A soft voice. Gentle, even.

"I have little to smile about."

The man grunted, but didn't seem displeased by the answer.

"You would do well to comply with the bidders' requests," Ashala said. "It will drive up your value, and the higher the price paid, the more precious you will be. Do you see how that benefits you?"

Jacey supposed she did. Her new owner would perhaps not leave visible marks on her flesh. Not much comfort in that thought at all. She bared her teeth, a mocking smile.

The cat snout pressed close to her face and Jacey heard the man behind the mask make sniffing noises. She hoped he gagged on her smell. She needed a bath.

"Your time is up," Ashala announced, then motioned for the man in the dog mask to descend for his turn.

And so the process continued, with Jacey being stared at, asked to smile, and once asked to take off her clothes. Ashala interceded at that point, saying such a request was demeaning. Jacey considered pointing out the irony inherent in that statement, but fell dumb when the plain-masked Captain Wilcox came down to inspect her.

"Well, Captain, am I to your liking?" she whispered.

The mask jerked and went still for a moment. But Wilcox didn't answer as he made a circuit around her. Finally he came to stand in front of her, blocking her view of Ashala. His voice was a rumble, but so, so quiet. "You are a pain in the ass."

"Did Dr. Carlhagen ever tell you about the Anti-Transfer Rejection pills he provides to Progenitors after they transfer? You might want to ask Dante about that before you waste more time in Dr. Carlhagen's service."

Ashala snapped, "Enough of that whispering! Plain Face, return to the line."

Wilcox marched to his spot with his usual military precision.

Though disgusted by the idea of being sold, she thrilled at the prospect that Wilcox might win. Because then she would finally be taken to Dr. Carlhagen, and Livy. Any idea she'd had of finding her way there independently was gone. If she had to go to Dr. Carlhagen as a prisoner, so be it. What she would do when she got there . . . she didn't know. She had no plan. As usual.

"The bidding will begin at fifteen million dollars," Ashala said.

Five hands went up.

44

WISE OF YOU TO PRIMP

Clawing her way to consciousness, Maxine Bentilius sat up in her bed, gasping for air. She had dreamed she was drowning, and no matter how hard she swam for the surface, a hand held her down.

Dr. Carlhagen's hand.

The man himself slept next to her, his perfect face slack with peaceful slumber. She eased from the blankets, scooped up her robe. She made it to the bedroom door before he came awake.

"Where you going?" he asked.

"Shower." She didn't wait for his assent before slipping from his quarters, padding down the hall, and going into hers. She was tempted to drag furniture in front of the door. Anything to keep Dr. Carlhagen out.

She wanted to kill him. But she couldn't escape one problematic consequence: Dr. Carlhagen was the only source for her ATR pills. And knowing him, he didn't have the formula written on a slip of paper in his office. It was possible Lazarus knew about it, but there was no way

Maxine was going to ask. Because if Lazarus *didn't* know about it, that was another piece of leverage she could retain for herself once she regained control of the Scion program.

So she would not kill Dr. Carlhagen. Not yet.

First things first. She still had to move Livy to the transfer machine. And that posed a fair amount of risk. If Dr. Carlhagen discovered her collusion with Lazarus, it would be *her* neck under the blade.

The image made her shiver. She went into the small kitchenette attached to her quarters. She found a long, slender knife. The blade was serrated, and the tip was sharp. Perfect for slicing meat.

She carried the knife to the bathroom, took a fast shower, then dressed in trousers and a blouse with loose sleeves. She didn't want anything binding her arms and shoulders in case she was required to do some stabbing. The terry cloth belt from her bathrobe worked nicely to cinch the blade to the side of her calf. Her pant leg covered it. She studied herself in the mirror and was satisfied that Dr. Carlhagen wouldn't notice the slight bulge in the fabric created by the knife.

"That blade will be useless against my drones," Lazarus said.

She wasn't surprised that the AI had been watching her preparations. And of course it had drawn the wrong conclusion. But rather than correct Lazarus, she said, "Then you have nothing to worry about."

Had Lazarus slipped up just now, using the plural "drones?" Or was he warning her that she was not only overmatched by his terrifying machine, but that he had them in numbers? It didn't matter. She wasn't going to attack Lazarus. She knew when to be obedient.

She attended to her hair and applied a few artful dabs

of makeup to mask the dark circles beneath her eyes. Her political career had taught her that 75% of power was *looking* powerful. She wasn't about to give Lazarus, Dr. Carlhagen, Livy, or anyone else on this earth the slightest edge in this game.

"Wise of you to primp," Lazarus said. "If you are to retain Dr. Carlhagen's interest at all when his favored clone arrives, you will have to continue to make such efforts."

Maxine's face went hot with jealousy. She hated Dr. Carlhagen, but that didn't mean his lust for Jacqueline Buchanan's clone didn't sting. If he weren't so drug-addled, he would see the advantage in partnering with her.

"How soon will Livy be ready for transfer?" she asked.

Lazarus surprised her by answering. "Two hours. And you needn't concern yourself about Dr. Carlhagen discovering you moving the child. I'll keep him distracted."

Maxine was full of nervous energy. She wanted to act. Now.

Two hours might as well be two centuries.

Discipline, she told herself. This is the time for discipline. This day was shaping up to be a stressful one. And dangerous, no matter what Lazarus said. She had washed herself, dressed herself, and armed herself. It was only sensible to also feed herself.

Despite having no appetite, she made herself breakfast.

The eggs tasted like ash, but she gritted her teeth and swallowed every bite. When she was done, she checked the time. One hour and 45 minutes to go.

45

SURROUNDED BY LIARS

D r. Carlhagen sat at his office desk, a fresh bottle of andleprixen set before him. The cap was off, the foil seal torn away, the cotton batting pulled out and discarded. All that remained inside were the pills.

The medicine had become a problem. He'd known it for a while, but with so many disruptions in his life he hadn't had the time or will to deal with it. Today was no different. Still, a shiver of fear stopped him from taking a couple tablets. For as much as he craved the warm calm the pills provided, he was terrified by the side effects. Paranoia was the worst of them.

Lazarus had been acting funny recently. Dr. Carlhagen was certain it was a figment of his imagination. He had grown Lazarus himself, cultivated the artificial intelligence from the moment of its inception. Lazarus was the finest, most controlled AI Dr. Carlhagen had ever created.

Even so, he was having trouble convincing himself that his fears were merely paranoia.

Dr. Carlhagen was a doctor. He understood the

andleprixen and his dependency upon it. Reason swayed him toward the paranoia diagnosis. His instincts pointed the other way. Could he trust his instincts?

It had been ten hours since his last dose. He hadn't gone this long without a pill since he had been held captive by the Scions on St. Vitus. It was consuming all of his will to delay the first pill of the day.

There is no question about whether he would take one or not. He would. Andleprixen was not the type of drug one could quit cold turkey. The withdrawal could kill him. No. He would have to wean himself off slowly, with a well thought out plan. It would take weeks, perhaps months. And it would hurt. And that wasn't the type of undertaking he could commit to given his current circumstances.

"Lazarus, show me a view of the Eastern shore," he said to the air. The pixel wall shifted from a plain amber glow to a perfect view of the St. Lazarus coast. The breeze started. The scent of the island wafted to Dr. Carlhagen's nose. He felt like he was looking out over the actual vista.

So why was his instinct screaming at him with worry and mistrust? He positioned himself centimeters from the wall. The pixel paint was of such high resolution his mind was still convinced he was looking out over the actual scenery and not at a video display. A pelican soared on the wind over the shoreline, turned to sea, then dove into the waves. It surfaced, then flapped its way free of the water and returned to land, fish in its mouth.

"Call Wilcox."

"Yes, sir."

Five minutes passed.

"Captain Wilcox is not answering."

Another stab of suspicion. How hard was it for that man to track down one teenage girl? Maybe Wilcox's story to this point had been just that: a story. Maybe Wilcox had captured Jacey already. Maybe he had decided to keep her for himself.

Carlhagen discovered he'd returned to his desk. He held the bottle of andleprixen in his hand. He dumped out two tablets.

He swallowed them. He felt the effects before it was chemically possible. That's how powerful the mind was. That's how deceitful the mind was.

"I'm surrounded by liars," he said. "Maxine, Wilcox, Jacey, all of them."

It had been so his entire life. The whole world was made up of liars. Cheats. Wasn't that why he had to intercede? Wasn't that why he had instituted Protocol One, the ATR scheme?

None of the Progenitors deserved their Scions. They were all degenerates.

"Lazarus, where is Maxine?"

"Resting in her room," Lazarus said in his weird monotone. Dr. Carlhagen had enjoyed the AI's barely human nature before. Now it chilled him. Once this crisis was over, he would spend more time pruning and nurturing the AI, file down some of its sharper edges. He lamented the loss of Mr. Justin. The man had been a schemer, but he had been an excellent butler and companion.

Now the medicine was truly taking effect. His heart rate was dropping. Yes, the tension was easing from his shoulders. Good.

"Keep trying to reach Wilcox."

"Of course, Doctor."

46

COWARDLY CAT

Only two bidders remained. The snarling dog and the plain white mask concealing Captain Wilcox's mean face. The two men stood side-by-side, postures tense. The other three bidders had been removed from the chamber, having failed to match the pace of the bidding. They were, Jacey presumed, on their way home, frustrated and disappointed not to possess her.

The silence in the chamber was heavy. The scavs stood all around, faces intent, obviously excited at the prospect of the huge inflow of money to their tribe. The dollar figures Ashala was calling even made Meow Meow gape.

"Do I have $87 million?" Ashala said. "$87 million for the clone of Jacqueline Buchanan. That's virtually giving her away, if you ask me."

Wilcox currently held the top bid at $85 million. Dog had been slower and slower to raise his offer since the bidding had passed the $80 million mark. But Ashala was patient, determined to squeeze every last cent from the winner.

Jacey didn't know what to make of Dog. He had inspected her in the most cursory manner, as if he wasn't that interested in her appearance and health. Now he was pressing a finger to his ear, causing the mask to lift away slightly. Jacey saw a sliver of white whiskers, but nothing else. He cocked his head, as if listening. Jacey wondered if he was taking instructions from someone else through an earpiece.

He raised his hand. "$87 million."

Before Ashala could call a higher number, Wilcox said, "$88 million."

He had been doing this since the beginning, boldly raising the bid the moment he'd been outbid. Of course, he had Dr. Carlhagen's vast resources at his disposal. Wilcox was not going to lose.

Jacey's stomach roiled with an odd mix of eagerness and dread. She just wanted it over so she could go wherever Dr. Carlhagen was and meet her fate. And hopefully find the chance to take the old bastard down.

Dog turned to regard Wilcox's weird, blank mask. Wilcox did not return the stare.

"A question, Ashala," Dog said. "My sponsor has struck a deal with one of the other bidders to pool our cash. Would you allow Cat to join me?"

Ashala held silent for ten agonizing seconds before stating, "I'll allow it. But it is up to you to decide how you will share the carbo between you if you win."

"Understood," said Dog.

The door at the back of the chamber opened, and the man with the cat mask came back out. There was a slight spring in his step, revealing a sick excitement at the renewed prospect of owning Jacey. Or, at least, part of her.

"Will you cut me in half, then?" Jacey said to Cat and

Dog. "It makes no difference to me. I've got one of these for each of you." She held up her middle fingers in a gesture Meow Meow had taught her.

The room erupted in laughter. Even Ashala grinned.

"I object," Wilcox said, cutting into the mirth. "There was no mention of bidders pooling their resources at the beginning of this auction."

Ashala said simply, "I have $88 million, do I hear $100 million?"

The crowd gasped at the huge leap. Cat and Dog conferred a moment. Dog raised his hand to accept the bid.

For the first time during the proceedings, Captain Wilcox paused. His eerie mask pointed first at Jacey, then at Cat.

"Do I have $110 million?" Ashala asked Wilcox.

He gave the slightest nod.

Ashala continued to up the bid in increments of $10 million. Cat and Dog no longer conferred. And now Dog was fastest to up the bid, and Wilcox grew ever slower.

The minutes crawled by, and Wilcox became more and more agitated. Jacey sensed he was well past whatever dollar amount Dr. Carlhagen had allotted for her purchase. After at least ten minutes of silence, Dog grew impatient and barked at Wilcox, "Come on, man. Bid or bow out!"

Ashala stood. "I have $165 million. Going once. Going twice . . ." Ashala leaned forward and looked at Wilcox, waiting. But for nothing. Wilcox simply turned and left the chamber. "Sold for $165 million to Dog and Cat."

The two winners relaxed and shook hands. Dog bowed to Ashala. "I would like to have a private audience with my property. Will you make a room available to us? Perhaps bring refreshments?"

Ashala allowed a smile. "As soon as we confirm the

transfer of funds to our accounts, we will turn over your property."

Hansen clomped forward and wrapped his huge hand around Jacey's elbow. He steered her to the back of the room, through a door and down a short hallway. With a final grunt of contempt, he shoved her into a smaller chamber. Stone walls, musty and damp. It was barely large enough to hold the dining table and mismatched chairs crowding the floor. There was no food, but a pitcher of water sat on one edge of the table, condensation dripping down its sides. Jacey grasped the pitcher by the handle and drank directly from it.

She plopped into a chair and put her face in her hands. And then she shot up and went to the door. It opened at her touch. The hallway beyond was plugged by Hansen's body. He turned to glower at her.

She backed into the room and shut the door. There was no lock needed when a brute like Hansen was on duty.

The ceiling was hard stone. Jacey suspected the whole compound was underground. An air vent high on one wall was the only other exit from the room. It was too small for her to squeeze into, even if she could reach it.

She gave the table a tentative tug to see if she could flip it. Maybe she could yank off one of the legs for club. But the table was solid wood. She could barely budge it. The legs were attached by thick metal brackets held in place by heavy bolts.

The chairs then. She'd smash one to splinters and—

The door opened, and three people stepped in. None of them were who she expected.

She set the chair down.

The first to enter was Meow Meow. Her face was downcast, worried. The second was Dante, smiling broadly, eyes gleaming. "Fun times, eh, Jacey?"

The third was the woman Jacey had seen before, a colorful scarf wrapped around her face revealing only her eyes. Her fabrics were rich, flowy, and exotic. Jacey noticed the woman's hands were trembling. As their eyes locked, the woman faltered, pressed a palm to her chest before coming closer. She stood a meter from Jacey, just staring and breathing so hard the scarf sucked in at her nose and mouth then billowed out on her exhalations. She was Jacey's height, slender. The eyes suggested a woman a couple decades older than Jacey.

"It's like seeing a ghost," the woman said, taking a tentative step toward Jacey. The voice was familiar, but Jacey couldn't place it. "I'm sorry we had to buy you."

"Who's 'we'? Two cowards in masks bought me, and I'm sure neither of them was you. You're too short."

Dante raised a hand. "Cowardly Cat, at your service."

The woman shivered. "Dog was my representative. I couldn't bear to participate in such a barbaric exchange."

Meow Meow was still looking at the floor.

Hands shaking, the woman unwrapped her scarf and let it drape around her shoulders. "My name is Olivia Montgomery. I guess I'm your daughter, in an odd sort of way."

Dante laughed. Meow Meow moaned.

Jacey's world tilted, and this time it did not stop. It turned entirely upside down. Good became bad. Light became blackness.

The woman standing in front of her was instantly recognizable. Jacey had seen Ollie Montgomery on SNN, roaming the Tent City of Kansas and complaining that funding for the refugees there had been cut.

But now Jacey could finally see the woman's face, and there could be no doubt who she was. *What* she was. Ollie Montgomery was the Progenitor of the nine-year-old Dolphin Livy.

47

LIKE THE AXIS OF A GLOBE

"Stand. Stand. Stand."

The monotone shouting burst into Humphrey's awareness as the searing pain in his muscles faded. He opened his eyes and discovered grass towering over him. He pressed his hands to the turf and pressed his body up. His vision swam as a wave of nausea took him. His gut convulsed, but he produced no more than a few hard gags.

He became aware of a drone floating near his head. "Stand. Stand. Stand."

"I'm working on it," he said. He got one foot under himself, then the other. He stood unsteadily, then bent double, lightheaded. Off to his right, Leslie and Kirk stood shoulder to shoulder, faces pale, eyes intent. Whatever had happened to Humphrey had not happened to them.

"Are you okay?" Leslie asked.

Humphrey wanted to say something sarcastic, but he simply didn't have the energy. He answered by forcing himself upright and stumbling toward her. His feet caught in the grass and he nearly fell. Kirk and Leslie caught his arms and held him up. All around them the drones were commanding him to stand.

"I'm standing."

One drone had separated from the dozen or so surrounding them. It floated into the circle and was now hovering a meter away from Humphrey and his companions.

"You will follow," the drone said. "You will not veer. You will not stray. You will not run." It didn't say "or else," but it was clearly implied.

The drone did not wait for Humphrey's reply before skimming away. Leslie and Kirk continued to support him as they followed. The pace was not satisfactory for the drone, for it came back and emitted in an ear-splitting blast: "You will not veer. You will not stray. You will not straggle."

They picked up their pace and Humphrey found that movement helped reduce his nausea and loosen his spasming muscles.

The other drones did not follow. They dispersed, disappearing into the trees.

"What's with all the urgency now?" Kirk asked. "These bastard's could have done this last night."

Humphrey's thoughts were not clear enough for him to attempt an answer. It took all of his attention to put one foot in front of the other. Their guide—captor—led them to a path on the other side of the clearing. Humphrey didn't know whether to be relieved by this or frightened by it. For where there is a path, there is a destination. It had to be the Scion School. That meant Dr. Carlhagen waited at the end of it. And given the drone's urgency to take them there, it suggested that Dr. Carlhagen now knew about their presence.

Leslie leaned close to him, whispered, "It didn't make us drop our weapons."

That *was* odd. Leslie still had her speargun strapped over her back. Kirk had both his walking stick and his machete. They all had their backpacks. But given the drone's offensive capability, it didn't likely see the humans' pathetic weapons as much of a threat.

A new sound rose in the distance, this one instantly recognizable.

Helicopters. At least three of them. "Do you hear that?" he said.

The drone led them along the path, skimming along at a pace just too fast to walk. Humphrey's mind was now churning to make sense of the situation. "It can't be a coincidence that the drones captured us and got us out of that clearing just before the those helicopters showed up."

"The fleet?" Kirk asked.

That made the most sense. But with these drones here, why would the fleet's forces be needed?

"I don't think this drone wants us seen by those choppers," Humphrey said.

It was all speculation. And it didn't change the reality they faced. Either follow the drone, or suffer the searing consequences. Nothing would induce Humphrey to risk such pain again. And having seen his agony, Leslie and Kirk kept their eyes down and their steps quick.

The path led upwards, switching back as it climbed the mountain's steep slopes. They were under the canopy of the forest now, but the sound of choppers grew louder.

The Scions came to a bend in the path. They had already gained enough altitude to see over the treetops of the lower reaches of the island. Three black helicopters skimmed over the trees. One had landed in the clearing. A team of eight heavily armed marines poured out. The chopper took off. The next landed and spewed forth a squad of soldiers.

The soldiers were fast and alert. Each squad headed for a different side of the clearing and disappeared into the trees.

When the fourth chopper landed, the drones rose above the trees. Not just the dozen Humphrey had seen. Now there were at least a hundred. The first helicopter had gained altitude and was flying over the trees toward where the Scions stood. Their guide drone commanded them to continue.

They followed it, but kept looking back at the approaching chopper. Would it see them? Humphrey was torn between the urge to wave and hope for rescue and his instinct to run and hide from it.

But there was no decision to be made. Ten drones shot skyward, circled the chopper. Blue plasma shot from the drones. The fuselage exploded, and the rotor blade separated, tilted at a sharp angle, and flew at the ground like a scythe of death.

It tore through the trees, shearing them off mid-trunk. Birds erupted from the branches, squawking in terror. The rending of wood shrieked in the air. Kirk pushed Humphrey to the ground. Wind buffeted him as the chopper's rotor passed overhead. It struck the ground ahead of them and flew apart, sending shrapnel in all directions.

A shower of rock and dirt fell like hail, clunking hollowly off their guard drone and dully off Humphrey's back.

Far off, a muted explosion thrummed through the island. Another chopper destroyed.

"Let's go," Leslie urged. "That crash took out our drone."

The drone wobbled on the ground and went still. Its surface was pocked with fist-sized dents. But the killing blow had come from a shard of helicopter debris that impaled the drone like the axis of a globe. All the other drones were farther down the mountain, occupied with the invasion force.

Humphrey scrambled to his feet. But where to go?

It was obvious. They had found the path. Drone or not, they had to follow it to its end. That was where Livy was. That's where Dr. Carlhagen was. That's why they had come.

Screams of agonized death rose in the distance as drones hunted men. Another explosion sent a fiery ball of smoke and flame skyward. The third helicopter.

Sharp snaps of gunfire answered the shrill hiss of plasma blasts. More explosions, plumes of smoke rising from the trees. Some of the drones were dying, too. Good. Humphrey hoped men and machines all killed each other.

Humphrey dug for the energy to run. He managed a stumbling gait, easily matched by Leslie and Kirk. The path wound upward, and upward more. Still, no drone came to intercept them.

48

VORTEX OF DATA

Captain Wilcox wasn't answering Belle's calls. And that meant Belle was at a dead end. Again. She could think of no other way to help her friends.

She went to the holodesk on *Athena's* navigation bridge. "Summer, have you heard anything from Humphrey yet?"

Summer left her post in front of the ship's controls and stood before the holodesk. She had dispensed with the silly hat with the deer on it. Her raven hair fell across her eyes. "I've boosted the signal all I can. But I've heard nothing. I've turned *Athena* toward St. Lazarus."

Elias's voice called from off-camera. Summer left Belle without so much as a goodbye. With nothing else to do, Belle waited.

She didn't wait long. Summer rushed back, her whole demeanor shifted to panic. "The whole island is on fire."

"On fire? Why? How?"

Summer rolled her eyes. "I'm guessing that Humphrey set the island on fire to give himself incentive to run into the ocean."

Belle chose to overlook the sarcasm. "Whatever has happened, Dr. Carlhagen wouldn't want his island ablaze. It's the exact kind of thing that would draw attention, which he has never wanted. We have to get in touch with Wilcox."

Socrates was already trying the number again.

"This is Wilcox. What is it?" The voice played in the air around Belle and blasted through the holodesk speakers so that Summer could hear it, too.

Wilcox's answer was so unexpected that Belle couldn't think up a response. Summer jumped in. "Captain Wilcox, my name is Summer. I'm the Scion of Senator Bentilius. You may know that the Scions have escaped St. Vitus, and now live free and independent of Dr. Carlhagen's control."

There was a pause, the sound of the tablet being handled, then Captain Wilcox's face appeared in a rectangle. "A temporary situation, I assure you."

"Ooh, I'm shaking with terror. You can't even catch Jacey," Summer said, in her brattiest tone. "But I'm not calling you to debate the future of the Scions. This is a warning. St. Lazarus is in flames. Senator Bentilius's fleet is approaching. Soon, Dr. Carlhagen will be trapped here and under Senator Bentilius's control. That's not good for Dr. Carlhagen, and it certainly is not good for you."

"You have a very creative imagination, girl. You're a lot like your Progenitor."

"There's no call for insults, Captain. And no *time* for them either. Now listen closely. Humphrey is on St. Lazarus right now. He has a small boat ready. If Dr. Carlhagen agrees to free Livy, Humphrey will offer Dr. Carlhagen safe passage off St. Lazarus and away from Senator Bentilius's approaching forces."

Wilcox didn't answer at first. His face was oddly pale,

probably a side effect of whatever wound he had under that crude bandage wrapped around his head.

Finally, he spoke. "I'll pass your ridiculous message to Dr. Carlhagen. But if Humphrey is there, he'll never set foot off that island again."

"It isn't like our story is difficult to check out," Summer said. "All the old man needs to do is look out the window and he'll see the smoke. His AI can certainly monitor the position of Senator Bentilius's fleet."

Belle watched this exchange, holding herself back. Summer was handling Captain Wilcox quite well.

And then the girl impressed Belle doubly. "How *is* Jacey?" Summer asked innocently. "But I suppose you wouldn't know, would you?"

"Alive, but in deeper trouble than ever. I've got to pull her out of it somehow." He looked like he was about to cut off the transmission, his attention returning to the problem before him. But then his eyes narrowed. "Have you heard anything about Anti-Transfer Rejection pills?"

"Can't say I have. What sort of trouble is Jacey in?" Summer asked, casually, as if she wasn't that interested.

Wilcox came around, seem to realize who he was talking to. "If you've been watching the news, you know she's been on the run with that ridiculous pop star. Then she got herself caught by scavs. And now she's been auctioned off."

"What? Auctioned?"

"She's a real prize," Wilcox said, deadpan. And then he cut the transmission.

Summer looked at Elias. Elias looked at Summer. Belle stared at them both.

"What was that bit about a pop star?" Belle asked, senses tingling.

"He was talking about Meow Meow," Summer said. "She's a singer. An entertainer. But didn't you hear the part about Jacey being *sold?* Doesn't that concern you a bit more than—"

"Can't do anything about that. What matters is that Meow Meow was with Jacey. Very recently."

"I see where you're going." Summer's eyes brightened. "Good thinking, Belle."

Belle couldn't accept Summer's uncharacteristic compliment because she was too busy railing against her own blindness. She'd known all along that Jacey was with Meow Meow, but she hadn't seen the obvious. "Socrates, I need another number. We need to call this Meow Meow person. And while you're at it, we should be looking for Dante, too."

"Already on it—which you would know if you paid any attention to yourself."

"What the hell does that mean?"

Belle left the holodesk and returned to the quad at the Scion School. There were no clues left in the simulated world for her to follow. She had to track down Jacey, and she had to do it now. Getting herself sold! What was *wrong* with that girl?

She certainly had no patience for Socrates's weird sense of humor, even if it was coming from her own psyche.

"I thought you would have connected the dots by now," Socrates said. He manifested a life-sized version of himself in front of her. He wore his white toga. His age-lined face and long white beard might have given him a dignified aspect, but it was ruined by that stupid deer-stalker hat. "Meow Meow is a celebrity. Her number isn't a matter of public record. It isn't as simple as just looking it up. We have to dig for it, and that requires processing power."

Belle stopped herself from lashing out by reminding herself that she was talking to herself.

"Exactly!" Socrates said, doing a little dance. "You *are* talking to yourself."

Belle squinted at the professor, a new tingling sensation growing in the back of her mind. She realized she needed to stop looking at his behavior and focus on what he was saying. And most of what he'd said recently had been about himself as an aspect of her. But that meant *she* was telling herself about an aspect of herself. She pressed her hands to her temples. It was all mind-numbingly confusing.

Socrates took off the deerstalker hat. He put it over his fist and stroked it, drawing her attention to it.

She remembered the brief conversation they'd had about the hat. It was associated with a fictional character called Sherlock Holmes. A detective.

"Yes," Socrates said, leaning forward with eagerness. "You almost have it."

A detective who solved mysteries through deductive reasoning. But that wasn't what Socrates was telling her.

"Oh!" The truth struck her all at once. She remembered that she had never heard of Sherlock Holmes prior to that conversation. And she had asked Socrates how he could know something she didn't if he was simply a projection of her own mind. Now she knew. It was so, so obvious.

Everything Socrates had done so far—from simulating automobile traffic, to searching IPA surveillance camera footage, to placing calls to Siggy—he had done by accessing the data flow. And that meant *she* had been in the data flow, the very thing that terrified her so much.

If she was going to find Meow Meow's number, she needed to devote more than just a fraction of herself to the search.

A strange calm came over her as she reached out with a sort of sixth sense to the data flow. This time she did not shy away from the noisy vortex of data. She simply let go.

The infinity washed across her senses like ice water. It took her breath away. But there was no pain, only exhilaration. Her attention split between two perfect instances of herself. They were independent, but both were fully aware of each other and everything each knew. She split again. Now she was four selves.

Now eight. Now 16. Now 32. Now 64.

The original Belle opened her eyes, observed a sunrise on St. Vitus. None of her other versions were there. There was no point to simulate them all. But *she* would stay, she would be the anchor. Because as amazing as the experience of the data flow was, she did not want to let go of being human. Not entirely.

Vaughan had urged her to transcend, but she now understood that did not mean renouncing her humanity. It meant adding to it.

The other instances of Belle scoured the data flow, following the person known as Meow Meow through every video, photo, song, concert appearance, list of collaborators and known associates. A name popped up that she instantly recognized.

Siggy.

Meow Meow had used his services several times to stay sur-blind while in Chicago.

Now that she wasn't relying on a subconscious aspect of herself to search the flow, the Belles were able to flex more computing muscle in their search. She quickly appropriated call records for all seventeen of Siggy's tablets. Breaking through the telecommunications security was nothing now that she was focused. She placed a thousand calls simultaneously, ringing every number Siggy had called in the past month. Wilcox even answered once, but Belle hung up on him.

She eliminated 900 numbers in a matter of moments. Another 50 were out of service entirely.

I see why you love this, she thought at Vaughan.

He didn't answer with language. He merely caused a warm feeling to spread to her heart. But he was barely there, his entire attention focused on tracking the fleet.

She was down to three numbers now.

One had to be Meow Meow's.

49

THE PRICE OF MY FORGIVENESS

Jacey sat across from Livy's Progenitor, mouth dry, heart hammering, fury rising. She had always known that Livy had a Progenitor somewhere. But until today, Jacey had never once thought about what that woman would be like.

Ollie Montgomery couldn't be over thirty. The woman's face held Livy's familiar thoughtful and serious mien, the look that gave Livy such a sense of age and wisdom. Faint lines around the eyes and mouth amplified the impression.

Meow Meow sat to Jacey's left, eyes shifting from Ollie to Jacey in a continuous back and forth. Dante, on the other hand, was focused on eating. Ashala had sent in several platters of food, and Dante fed like the worthless, starving tomcat he was.

"It is hard for me to look at you," Ollie said, though she kept her eyes locked on Jacey, holding her gaze as steadily as Livy had ever done. "I know you are not my mother, and yet . . ."

Jacey broke eye contact and busied herself with jabbing a cold slice of turkey from a platter and putting on her plate. "What do you plan on doing with me now that you *own* me?"

"I don't own you." Ollie's gaze never wavered. "I had thought you would be relieved at being rescued."

"Rescued?" Jacey said, indignant. She cut a hunk of turkey off with the side of her fork and jammed into her mouth. It was dry and stale. She chewed and swallowed. "You knew what I was as soon as you got wind of me, didn't you, Ms. Montgomery? Did you get a family discount when you commissioned your own clone?"

Ollie's eyelids lowered and rose in a long, slow blink. "What clone?"

"Come now. Don't play stupid. Ten years ago you gave some DNA to Dr. Carlhagen. Along with who knows how much money. And now you have a lovely, amazing clone of your own. Does he send you pictures and updates on her progress?"

Ollie placed her hands on the table and leaned forward. "I have no idea what you're talking about."

"Jacey," Meow Meow said softly, "There is no reason to assume Ollie knows about Livy."

"Livy?" Ollie said, voice rising in concern. "Jacey, start from the beginning. Please. I assure you, I never commissioned a clone."

The woman's voice carried the quiet certitude of someone telling the truth. Or someone well practiced in lies. And from what Jacey had seen of the adult world, lying was the supreme skill of life. "You expect me to believe that your mother never mentioned that you'd be able to live forever by overwriting the mind of your clone?"

"No. And that does not sound *at all* like something my mother would allow." Ollie pushed back from the table and folded her hands in front of her. She leaned toward Jacey, eyes never dropping. "But it does sound like something my father might do."

Ollie scooted her chair closer to Jacey's. She took Jacey's hand and studied it. Wetness glistened in the woman's eyes. "I'm saying that neither my mother nor I had any knowledge of your existence. You—and Livy—were made without our knowledge."

Meow Meow grinned. "From what Jacey's told me about Dr. Carlhagen, that is entirely possible."

The room swirled, world tilting as it so often did lately. Could that old bastard have made Jacey and Livy without consent? A weak laugh escaped Jacey's throat. Of course he could.

Ollie asked, "Is it possible that my father didn't know either?"

"No," Jacey said. There was no doubt on that score. "Dr. Carlhagen despised your father. He wouldn't have made Vaughan if he'd had a choice."

"Carlhagen . . ." Ollie said, finally breaking eye contact. "I called him Uncle Christof."

"Well, if you see him, prepare yourself for a shock," Meow Meow said. "He overwrote your father's clone."

"He overwrote *Vaughan*," Jacey said, as if she could correct the truth of what Meow Meow had said. "He overwrote Vaughan. Who was a person."

"If Uncle Christof hated my father so much," Ollie said, "why would he make my father's clone?"

"It must have been part of the deal," Jacey said, imagining the animosity between the two men when they had struck the bargain. "To get useable DNA from Jacqueline and you, Dr. Carlhagen must have agreed to make a clone for your father to get his cooperation."

That wise look came over Ollie's face and she squeezed Jacey's hand. "Why did Uncle . . . Dr. Carlhagen hate my father?"

Jacey didn't want to answer. She wanted to spare Ollie the sordid truth. But sometimes keeping a secret is the same as lying.

"Because your father was married to the woman Dr. Carlhagen loved. But it isn't really love. It's an obsession. A sickness." Jacey hugged her elbows, remembering the old man's slimy touch.

Just like Livy, Ollie saw the heart of the matter in a single second. She pulled Jacey toward her, until she could get her hands on Jacey's face. "Oh, my dear, dear child. What has he done to you?"

Dante stopped eating and looked at Jacey. He set down his fork and patted his lips with a napkin. "There's no need to get into all that now."

A tear slipped from Jacey's eye. She pulled away from Ollie, a woman who was genetically her daughter but who was nearly old enough to be her mother. She ached for Livy. She raged at the injustice of her life, and that of all the Scions.

All the pain Dr. Carlhagen had inflicted upon her—his touches, his leers, his manipulations—all of it tried to erupt in that dangerous moment. Throat aching, Jacey stuffed the agony down, buried it beneath her determination to rescue Livy. "Dante's right. It doesn't matter what he's done to me. None of that can be changed. He has to be stopped from inflicting greater damage on the world."

Meow Meow's eyebrows scrunched and a look of

wonder came over her, as if she were seeing Jacey in a new light. It was a look of deep respect.

Ollie's voice broke. "Yes, of course. That is exactly how my mother would see it, too."

A different wave of emotion swirled up at Ollie's words. This one a vortex, threatening to suck Jacey into an oblivion of relief. All this time she had thought Jacqueline was greedy and immoral. Jacey had never been able to shake the worry that being the clone of such a bad person made *her* a bad person. But Jacqueline had not known about Jacey.

Again, Jacey fought back emotions that threatened to sap her will. She would feel all this later. She could make sense of things once Dr. Carlhagen was dead.

Her skin thrilled as she admitted her goal to herself.

But not his body, she reminded herself. That belonged to Vaughan. And Vaughan would have it when this was all done.

Meow Meow's tablet chimed. She moved to the back of the room to answer it.

That suited Jacey just fine, because Meow Meow would oppose the plan Jacey was going to suggest. "I need your help, Ms. Montgomery. It's imperative that I get to Dr. Carlhagen as quickly as possible."

"If he's as dangerous as you say, you should tell the police where he is and what he's done."

"And trade Dr. Carlhagen's control over the rich and powerful to the IPA?" Jacey said. "They'll just push his scheme forward for their benefit."

Seeing that Ollie was lost, Jacey decided to start at the beginning. "I need to explain the Anti-Transfer Rejection pills and how Dr. Carlhagen plans to use them to control the most powerful people in the world."

"I'm listening."

And so was Dante, keenly.

His betrayal suddenly made sense to Jacey. "You ran out of pills, didn't you?"

"Left them behind in Chicago when we got you away from Siggy's goons."

"So in the church, when you were going on and on—"

"I had called Wilcox. He had my pills, but he didn't know what they were. I figured I would help you get away from him once I was back to my old self. And hey, I did!"

Jacey smirked. "You didn't do anything."

Ollie said, "You forget. Dante pooled his resources with mine to win the auction."

He grinned and shrugged it away. "Don't start thinking I'm a good person. I meant everything I said in that church."

"I won't. I'm sure you did." Jacey didn't know what to think about Dante. He didn't make any sense. He treated his life as if it were the most precious thing in one moment, then risked it in the next.

"Tell me about this scheme of Dr. Carlhagen's," Ollie said.

Jacey didn't get far into it before Meow Meow interrupted them. She held the tablet to Jacey. "It's someone claiming to know you. She calls herself Belle."

Jacey took the tablet from Meow Meow. The woman on the screen had shortish black hair and a face a decade too old. "You aren't Belle."

A moment of surprise crossed the woman's face before she morphed into her usual appearance. "I was trying a new look."

"What do you want? I'm in the middle of something here."

"Never mind that. We've got bigger problems than your capers all over North America."

This was Belle, all right.

"Humphrey, Leslie, and Kirk are on St. Lazarus," Belle said. "But the island is on fire and we're pretty sure there was a helicopter invasion. We're trying to help Dr. Carlhagen escape before the senator's forces arrive. And before the president realizes he doesn't have Leslie."

"Slow down. I didn't follow a single thing you just said."

"Listen for once, instead of pouting and fluttering your pretty eyelashes at me."

Meow Meow mouthed a shocked curse and said, "Who *is* this person?"

Belle said, "Find Wilcox and have him call Dr. Carlhagen."

"I was thinking of turning myself over to him anyway," she said.

"That would be stupid. But no surprise there." Belle made an obvious effort to control her impatience, which made it even more irritating to Jacey. "He'll just give you to Dr. Carlhagen."

"That was the idea. Then I'd be in a situation where I could do something to help Livy."

"You don't need to risk your neck. Just tell Dr. Carlhagen that Humphrey will take him off St. Lazarus in return for Livy." Belle continued, explaining how a fleet was closing in on the island and that Dr. Carlhagen would soon be trapped there.

"Shut up for a second, Belle." She looked at Dante. "Does Wilcox know you were Cat?"

"By now he does." Dante giggled and wiped his eyes. "That bastard is probably chewing his teeth to dust right now."

"So he wouldn't be receptive to hearing from you," she said, realizing she'd have to do this herself.

Ollie looked on in confusion. Meow Meow lifted her face. "I don't like the sound of this, Jacey. What do you want with Wilcox? He lost. We won. You're free."

Dante made a tsking noise. "Technically, I own 55% of her, but we'll overlook that for now." He was disgustingly pleased with himself.

Jacey gave him a flat stare, then answered Meow Meow. "My Scion friends have cooked up a way to get Livy back, but I have to talk to Dr. Carlhagen to present the offer. The fastest way to do that is through Captain Wilcox."

Meow Meow and Dante both started to object, but Ollie silenced them. "What do you need, Jacey? Name it."

"I need to meet with Wilcox in a neutral place. Somewhere he can't kidnap me." In her peripheral vision she caught Dante's smile faltering into a look of true worry. "Or throttle me."

Ollie looked pointedly at Meow Meow. "Fine," the scrawny girl said. "I'll talk to Ashala. She might be willing to act as a go-between with Wilcox and get him into a room for us." She got up, head hanging low. She glanced back just as she was about to leave. "I'm sorry, Jacey."

"For what?"

"I knew Ollie was Jackie B.'s daughter. Everyone knows it. I wanted to tell you, but the timing never seemed quite right. I didn't want to make things more complicated. I had no idea about her and Livy being . . . you know."

Meow Meow looked haggard and miserable, and for the first time since Jacey had known her, old.

Jacey had the power to release Meow Meow from her guilt. It was like having a prisoner strapped to a cot in the medical ward. She could set her free, or leave her to rot in her guilt. The temptation to punish her friend was strong. But what was the point of punishing someone she loved for a mistake made *out* of love?

"I forgive you," Jacey said.

Meow Meow wiped at her eyes as she left the room.

"While you're doling out forgiveness . . ." Dante said, holding up his hands. "Yes. I did call Wilcox to the church. But I was desperate."

"You told me you had killed him."

"A white lie to calm you. I did it for you."

"You didn't tell me about Ollie, either."

"True. But in my defense, I got to witness the reveal of a lifetime."

Jacey gave him a cool look. "Ollie, what is fifty-five percent of $165 million dollars?"

"$90,750,000."

"That's the price of my forgiveness, *Silvio*. $90,750,000."

He glared at Ollie. "I told you she wouldn't appreciate my help."

"You said no such thing." Ollie waved his statement away like it was an annoying bug. "You begged to join me in the bidding. Your exact words were, 'We can't let that old bastard have her.'"

Dante's cheeks reddened, and he mumbled, "You promised not to say anything about that."

Ollie ignored him. "Jacey, Dante is a scoundrel, but he has a good heart."

Dante made a shushing sound and looked pointedly at the door. "Someone might hear!"

"Fine," Jacey said. "I forgive you, too. And when this is

all over, I'll make sure the whole world knows what a sentimental do-gooder you truly are."

"So that's how it's going to be, eh?"

"That's how it's going to be."

50

OUT NOTHING

A chime awakened Dr. Carlhagen. He lifted his head from his desk, disturbing his bottle of andleprixen, which was still uncapped. It rolled across his desk and fell to the floor, sending pills ticking across the tiles like tiny pebbles.

"Call incoming from Wilcox," Lazarus announced. A moment later a video rectangle appeared on the pixel wall. Captain Wilcox looked weary, his face pale, head bandaged.

"What news do you have for me, Captain?" Carlhagen said, rubbing his eyes and trying to will wakefulness into his foggy mind.

"The bid went much higher than expected. $165 million."

"So you have her," Dr. Carlhagen said, relieved.

Wilcox shook his head. "No, sir. You authorized $100 million."

Dr. Carlhagen shot up from his chair and slammed his fist onto his desk. "I told you to *get* her. I don't care what the price is. I don't care who you have to kill. I don't care what you do. Get her!"

In truth, Dr. Carlhagen didn't remember much of his conversation with Wilcox about what price to pay. $100 million was a lot of money, but surely he would've authorized five times that much to get Jacey. Now that he thought about it, he did vaguely recall mentioning that he could easily outbid anyone because he had $100 million in his smallest account. Wilcox must have misunderstood.

No surprise there.

"So who bought her?" Dr. Carlhagen barked. "I'll talk to them, offer them double their price. I'll throw in a Scion of their own."

"The bidders wore masks. I'm sure all of them were hired agents and that the true buyers were not present at all. Except—" The man hesitated and made a face as if he was trying to swallow an entire lemon.

"Out with it, Wilcox."

"We were invited into the scav compound as bidders, but I didn't trust leaving Dante behind when I went in. I took him with me. I didn't think he could get into any trouble there. The scavs are an unpleasant and distrustful people."

Dr. Carlhagen didn't like where this is going at all. "Dante was one of the bidders?" As soon as he said it, he knew it was true. Then he knew the rest. Dante had won. "But this is good. If Dante bought her, then she's as good as mine. And I'm out nothing!"

Wilcox clicked his tongue. "Dante joined forces with another bidder. I don't know who he represented. Their combined bid won, and Jacey was taken deeper into the compound where I can't get to her. The scavs have not let me speak with Dante, either. Which is probably wise, because I will kill him on sight."

"You'll do no such thing. Dante will do whatever I tell him. Believe me. All you need to do is get a message to him that I will welcome him here on St. Lazarus as an honored guest. He probably bought Jacey just to win a bit of leverage with me." Dr. Carlhagen laughed at the idea of that lightweight playboy trying to negotiate with him.

"What about the other buyer? I think they would object to you taking their property. And why would Dante even agree to turn over such an expensive investment to you?"

"Because he needs his—" Dr. Carlhagen clamped his mouth shut. That had been a close call. He'd almost mentioned the ATR pills. "Because he needs me for future Scions. Do you really think he'll take good care of his current body?"

Captain Wilcox started to say something but was interrupted by someone off-camera. He listened for a moment, then turned his attention back to Dr. Carlhagen. "This is odd. The scav commander has just invited me to speak with Jacey and her new owners."

"Then go," Dr. Carlhagen said. "Then get Dante on a call with me, so we can coordinate his arrival here."

"Yes, sir." Wilcox signed off.

Dr. Carlhagen rubbed his hands together and started to pace. He was close. He was so close to getting her back. This time it would be different.

Now he needed to get control of the other Scions, Leslie in particular. "Lazarus, get me Colonel Vikisky on screen."

"He is not taking calls at the moment," Lazarus said.

"Tell him Senator Bentilius is calling. Just get him."

"I told the fleet's communications officer aboard Vikisky's ship that Senator Bentilius had to speak with him, but the comms officer said Vikisky could not take calls. He refused to explain why."

Dr. Carlhagen stopped and looked at his shoes, brain grinding through the possible reasons the colonel would refuse a call. It struck him that the most likely reason was that he was in the middle of a military operation, probably boarding the Scions' escape ship at that very moment. Yes. That was very likely.

"Keep trying. Every ten minutes. Tell this communications peon it's important."

"Of course, Dr. Carlhagen."

He noticed the pills he had spilled dotting the floor. He began picking them up, pausing to pop one in his mouth.

51

YOUR TIME IS UP

The one remaining human-like Belle sat in the quad, eyes closed, breath coming slowly. She was at once filled with the information flowing through her other instances as they scoured the data flow, and complete equanimity.

I can be both, she thought at Vaughn. Human and—she didn't know what word to use for what she had become. What Vaughn already was. But she could feel the difference. The weird distancing of emotion, the release of worry. She observed Vaughan's diligent work monitoring radio traffic to extrapolate the location of the fleet. He passed her instant knowledge of the changes in that information even as he updated it on the holodesk so Summer and Elias could see it.

As exhilarating and overwhelming as the data flow was, she now saw its limits. Those limits were due to the reduced bandwidth of data flowing to *Athena*. She could only imagine what it would be like to dive into the flow coming through a faster connection.

Vaughan wasn't solely occupied with the fleet. He was also ramming from network node to network node, sniffing out signs of the AI on St. Lazarus. He knew Dr. Carlhagen had used that AI to mask his movements in the past. Vaughan knew the AI was masterful at hiding itself from the public networks. So he turned to a data underworld of illegal nets. Such networks had existed since the first days of computing. This shadowy web was alive in Belle's senses now, too. She watched and learned as Vaughan plumbed its depths, seeking this mysterious AI of Dr. Carlhagen's. Vaughn created thousands of aliases, posting messages, videos, comments, querying archived databases of telecommunication records, anything that would expose a door into the mystery AI's world.

Vaughn was not impatient. It wasn't in his nature, not worth his processing power to experience. But Belle's human instance felt it.

"Vaughan," she said aloud. "Would more processing power help you?"

It would.

"How much is Madame Fontaine still using?" She knew he had suspended the dance mistress's processes on this server, but he hadn't deleted her.

Nothing. She occupies only storage space at the moment.

Implicit in his answer was that Belle took up much needed processing power. And she had thousands of instances diving the flow, many pursuing the same thing he was, while also maintaining an open line of communication to Jacey.

Vaughan had not put the sudden new idea into her mind. She was sure of it. The idea was so simple. And it was scary, but not in a bad way. It represented the things she had always wanted. To be closer to Vaughan. She had never imagined it would happen like this.

Her one remaining human instance stood on the quad, stretched her arms and enjoyed the feel of the breeze. She knew she could return here at any time and feel it. But she also knew she may not want to do it again.

"Vaughan, come to me here. Just like you were before all of this started." He understood where she was going, of course. He materialized in front of her, wearing his Scion School uniform, the shark pin on the collar. His hair was cut in the approved Scion fashion. His face was perfect, beautiful, godlike. He seemed to glow. He smiled, showing those even white teeth. He spread his arms and she folded into his embrace. "Vaughan, I know you don't feel what I feel. But I need this. And then we can go."

He embraced her harder, then leaned back and put his hands on the sides of her face, brushed his thumbs across her cheekbones. He gave her all of his attention. And it *was* all of it. For in that instant, there were no other Vaughans searching the net. There were no other Belles, either.

She closed her eyes. Their lips met. They sank deeply into the moment. Belle poured all of her attention into the sensations pulsing through her, tracing her hand to the back of his neck while the other one wound around his waist and drew him closer. Tears skimmed down her cheeks as Vaughan passed an overwhelming wave of love into her. The urgency of their kisses grew, deepened, and the passion of the moment threatened to sear Belle to her core.

And then Belle allowed it to happen.

They were not Vaughan and Belle. They became a new entity, a new amalgamation of digital minds. The human simulations ceased to exist, and the fake island of St. Vitus ceased to exist. It was no longer needed, no longer relevant.

This new existence became something never known before, where the world and the girl and the boy were not distinct minds and souls. They became one thing. Unity. Vaughan wasn't *with* Belle. He wasn't *in* Belle. Belle was in him.

We choose what we want to be, the new entity told itself as it reconstituted St. Vitus and a physical form there. Now, 90% of the available processing power of the server and bandwidth flowed to the new thing they had become.

But it wasn't *all* of the server's processing power. There was a portion still grinding away independently.

Elizabeth.

The entity didn't feel anger or hatred for the woman now. Vaughan had ameliorated that aspect of Belle. But the entity recognized the crimes Elizabeth had committed, found the woman undeserving of her simulated existence. The entity materialized a Belle form in front of Liz, who lay naked on the beach, sipping a fruity drink.

"Your time is up," the Belle said.

Liz slowly turned her head and lowered the dark spectacles from her eyes. "Go away, child."

The Belle smiled, but without malice. With less than a millisecond's thought, she subsumed Elizabeth entirely. All of the woman's experience and knowledge passed into her. The woman's persona dissipated like a bad smell.

The Vaughan aspect of Belle thought it was regrettable, but necessary.

Now the entity had all of the server. It reached across the networks of the world, redoubling the effort to find the AI of St. Lazarus while keeping a close watch on the fleet.

It placed a Belle instance at the holodesk on *Athena.* "Summer, have you reached Humphrey yet?"

The girl had her deer hat on again. The bill waved back and forth as she shook her head. "I've boosted the signal all I can. It has to be getting through. I have to assume Humphrey lost his radio . . . or he can't reply for some reason."

"Keep trying. The fleet is making 37 knots. They'll be there in less than two hours."

"And where's Jacey?"

"Good question. Meow Meow isn't answering my calls anymore."

Summer looked at the holographic fleet projected on the holodesk. "Whatever she's going to do, she'd better hurry."

Summer noticed Belle's holo—standing amidst the holographic fleet ships—for the first time. "Belle, what's with the new look? It's . . . odd."

Belle observed herself. She wasn't wearing her new appearance, older with short black hair. She was now mixture of her old body and Vaughan, both feminine and masculine. And beautiful.

She smiled at Summer. "Call me Velle."

"Uh . . . right." Summer raised her eyebrows and whistled.

Velle let it go. An infinity from the holodesk, the less human aspects of the entity now calling itself Velle sniffed out a hint of a shadow of an echo of an AI called Lazarus.

52

JUMP RIGHT OFF A CLIFF

They were back in the scav audience chamber. Wilcox was waiting there when Jacey and her companions arrived. Carl and Hansen stood close behind him. He sat at the head of the dining table atop the raised platform. Ashala sat in her throne-like chair, well back from the table. Her legs were crossed, her hands folded on her patchwork skirt. She motioned for Jacey and the others to take seats at the table.

Jacey chose to sit across from Wilcox. Dante sat to her right, Meow Meow to her left. Ollie Montgomery took a position in the middle, to Jacey's right.

Ashala spoke first. "I have assured that all parties here —except for my people—are unarmed. Captain Wilcox has granted you a five-minute audience. My men will not stop any party from leaving this room. But if there is violence, scav justice prevails."

Jacey glanced at Meow Meow for some hint about what "scav justice" meant. But the girl merely paled and ran her tongue around the inside of her lips. That was all Jacey needed to know.

Wilcox sat at the table, hands gripping the armrests of his chair. He looked directly at Jacey, unblinking. Before she could begin, he said, "Tell me about ATR."

Jacey relaxed. Just a hair. Her comment to him during the auction inspection had broken through. Interesting.

"He's using the drug to control Progenitors after they transfer. They are dependent on it. Only he can provide it."

Dante shook his bottle of pills and set them on the table in front of him. He folded his hands and rested his chin on his knuckles. He pointed with a pinky. "That bottle represents the remainder of my life. Once I run out of those pills, I'll have a day or two of pain. A coma. Then sweet death."

The muscles on the side of Wilcox's face bulged and quivered. Redness crept into his cheeks, and his eyes narrowed to slits. He exhaled hard through his nose, a hissing whistle like a boiler about to blow.

He said nothing. And why should he? The man had been betrayed by his employer. Wilcox was now thinking back on all of the things he had done for Dr. Carlhagen. Killing Nurse Smith. Trying to kill Sensei. Chasing Jacey across the northern hemisphere. He had lost men. And he had done it for payment. Rich payment—his own Scion.

Sensing she had caught hold of an important thread, Jacey gave it a tug. "How old are you, Captain Wilcox? 45? 50? When were you planning to transfer?"

Wilcox didn't answer. The flush had drained from his face. He continued to beam hatred at her.

Jacey pressed. "Now that you know what Dr. Carlhagen planned, you know he can't be allowed to succeed. He has to be stopped."

Wilcox said nothing.

Ollie stepped in. "Captain, surely you have some sense of honor remaining. By all accounts you are a good commander, a good soldier. So why—?"

"Shut up," Wilcox snapped. "You know nothing about me."

A tense silence reigned over the table. Dante, always uncomfortable in such situations, poured himself a glass of water, ice making a racket as it tumbled from the pitcher into his glass.

Jacey held Wilcox's stare, unafraid of him now. Her hatred had to be set aside, outweighed by her need for his help. "Can you get me into Dr. Carlhagen's facility on St. Lazarus?"

Wilcox's eyes narrowed further. "Why would you go there? You know what that pervert wants."

"And up until fifteen minutes ago, you were quite willing to hand me over to that pervert. But I'll tell you why. Dr. Carlhagen has to die. His facility must be destroyed. There can be no Scion program going forward. Because from what I've learned of the outside world, *everyone* wants control of it. Everyone wants to live forever. They want to be young forever. They want to be famous. And above all that, they want power. They want the power to grant all those things I just mentioned to the people they choose, and to deny it to the people they despise.

"If anyone gets control of the Scion program and the ATR exploit, they'll push Dr. Carlhagen's scheme in their own direction, for their own purposes. And I think you'd agree, anyone who wants *that* power"—she leaned forward and put all the urgency of her fervor into her words—"must not have it."

She leaned back. "So I'm going to go there. I'm going to kill him. I'm going to get my—" Her voice broke and an ache pressed the back of her throat. "I'm going to get Livy back."

"You're a fool," Wilcox said. He pushed his chair back and stood. He waved a finger at everyone in the room. "Anyone who follows this girl is a fool." He turned away and started for the door.

"I'll pay you," Ollie Montgomery called.

Wilcox stopped, made a sort of half turn, and looked over his shoulder. "Money has never mattered."

Meow Meow stood, her body trembling. "Coward!"

The word might as well have been a spear to his spine. His whole body contracted, his fist clenching into tight balls.

He turned, lips pulled back in a snarl. "Playground taunts will not change my mind, pop star." He spat the words like bullets.

Meow Meow didn't relent. "What are you afraid of? Dr. Carlhagen is just an old man, right? Or are you afraid of him because he transferred into an eighteen-year-old boy?"

Wilcox's nostrils flared. "I'm afraid of nothing. The worst that could happen to me happened long ago."

His posture remained erect, but the rigid anger had drained away.

Jacey's mind tickled over what he had said, and she found another angle of attack. For Wilcox, the worst had happened *before* he'd ever met Dr. Carlhagen. The money and the promise of a Scion had been enticing. That was true. But what had Wilcox gotten from Dr. Carlhagen beyond that?

It was simple. Dr. Carlhagen had given Wilcox purpose, had given him a mission.

"Do you turn your back on your missions frequently?" Jacey asked. "Because that's what this is. A clearly defined goal. Get me into the facility, help me do what needs to be done, and get me out."

It broke through. She knew it the instant his lips parted and no words came out. The worried expression on his face showed that he knew she was manipulating him.

She pushed harder. "What were you going to do once you transferred to your Scion? You don't want a life of leisure. You never wanted a second youth to squander. What were you going to do with that young body, all that energy?"

He didn't answer. But Ollie did. Of everyone there, she seemed to match Jacey's sensitivity for what other people were thinking and feeling. "He was going to do what he does now. He was going to be a soldier."

"And this time I would get to stay in," Wilcox said. "I was discharged because I led a failed mission. I took responsibly for the failure, but it wasn't really my fault. I let myself become a politician's scapegoat. And when they kicked me out—"

Wilcox wasn't a talker, and he was clearly uncomfortable exposing these truths to people who had been his enemies just moments before.

Ollie approached Wilcox. He didn't back away as she put her hands on his arms, though he stiffened. She said something Jacey couldn't hear.

Wilcox's eyes narrowed again, his jaw clenched. He gave Ollie one sharp nod, a movement of no more than a millimeter. But it was a gesture of assent. The two had struck some sort of agreement.

His demeanor changed in that moment. He returned to the table and sat. His posture was now relaxed, matter-of-fact. He stabbed the table with a finger. "Getting into the facility will be easy. It is guarded and monitored by an AI who knows me. It will grant you, me, and Dante entry to the facility. Dr. Carlhagen wants nothing more than to welcome you. But once we do what we need to do, the AI will not let us leave. It controls the elevators, the main gate to the facility, and a force of patrol drones on the island surface."

"What about your drone killer gun?" Jacey asked, remembering the bell-shaped barreled gun that had taken out some of the scav's swarm drones.

"With a full charge, it might take out one of the Lazarus drones." He looked back at Carl and Hansen. "Unless you have more of those you can loan us?"

Carl reached behind his back, and pulled out Wilcox's drone killer. "We don't. In fact, I was planning on stealing this one from you."

"So we go in, get Livy, Dr. Carlhagen, and the others," Jacey said, "and on the way out we have to break through some doors that the AI controls, and then evade some drones."

"You can't break through the main gate of that facility," Wilcox said. "It's solid steel, huge. Without the AI's cooperation, it would take an enormous amount of explosives, and that might collapse the tunnel beyond."

Wilcox filled a glass and took a long drink, his eyes still locked on Jacey's. He set the glass down, empty. "You don't evade the drones. You get immobilized by them. Or killed, if you're lucky."

Jacey had won over Wilcox, but now she saw a deeper problem. "What are the chances of swaying the AI to our side?"

Wilcox answered with a rude blast of air through his lips.

A new voice spoke. At first Jacey didn't know it was a

human talking, the voice was so low and gravelly. It was Hansen, the huge pile of muscle who had captured her and Meow Meow in the scavenger outskirts. She didn't catch the first part of his statement, but his last words were "drone swarm."

Wilcox twisted in his seat to look at the huge man. He practically spun back to the table and pounded his fist on it, rattling the platters and silverware. "That's it. That's beautiful. A scav drone swarm could overwhelm the patrol drones on St. Lazarus. Those spherical bastards wouldn't know what to attack first. How many can you bring?"

Ashala said, "Bring? No one said anything about scavs going on this desperate caper. I would be willing to *sell* you a drone swarm, perhaps."

"How many?" Jacey asked.

Carl and Hansen went to Ashala and they conferred in soft voices. Occasionally Hansen's grumble shook the chamber. When their confab ended, Ashala announced, "We can provide you a drone swarm of 5000 units for $5 million."

Dante had been in mid swig of his water. Ashala's price made him choke, sending a spray of water across the table. Jacey wiped droplets from her nose.

"$5 million!" Dante said, turning red. "We could hire a whole force of mercenaries for $5 million."

"And they'd be as useless as you against the Lazarus drones," Wilcox said. "This is a technological problem, and it needs a technological solution." He looked at Jacey, waiting for her answer. But Jacey didn't have any money.

"$3 million," Ollie said. "Right, Dante?"

His eyes nearly popped free of his face. "You're spending more of *my* money?"

Ashala raised an eyebrow and allowed a slight smile to play on her lips. "$4 million."

Ollie nodded graciously to the scav commander. And Jacey saw why. Ashala knew their position, knew they had no leverage in negotiations. But Ashala had granted the discount out of respect for Ollie.

"How do we get to St. Lazarus?" Jacey said. "Fast."

"My sub-orb is at the local airfield," Ollie said.

Wilcox grunted, face bunched in serious calculation. "That will get us to Belize in twenty minutes. Then it's a chopper. Not a long flight if we have a good one."

"I'll arrange it," Ollie said.

"My father always wanted to open a bank," Dante said. "How proud he'd be to see me now."

Jacey stood. "Captain Wilcox, thank you. When will you be ready to leave?"

"I just need my weapons returned. It's this idiot Dante who will slow us down."

"Me?" Dante said, pressing his hand to his chest. "What makes you think I'm going?"

"Because Dr. Carlhagen knows you bought Jacey. He believes you are in his pocket because of the ATR, and he expects that you will arrive on St. Lazarus to present Jacey to him."

Dante's face turned green. "And I thought I was done risking my neck for this girl."

Meow Meow laughed. "Haven't you realized by now, Dante? You and I, we were born to risk our necks for Jacey."

"Kathryne," Jacey said, softly, "you don't have to go. This isn't your fight anymore."

"Wilcox isn't the only one looking for a mission."

Wilcox cleared his throat. "Let's go. Dante, go call Dr. Carlhagen and tell him you're bringing Jacey to him."

Dante glared at Jacey. "This isn't fun anymore."

"You didn't put up much of a fight," Meow Meow said, teasing.

Dante grumbled something about women and their manipulative eyes.

Jacey followed Wilcox from the chamber, heart slamming in her chest. She was finally heading in the right direction. Toward Livy. So why did she feel like she was about to jump right off a cliff?

The answer came to her immediately, and it provided no comfort at all.

Because she was.

53

GREAT JAWS

Humphrey's breaths came in ragged gasps as he and his companions reached the top of their climb. The exertion had required all his focus, so he hadn't noticed the quietude creeping in behind him. Now that he had a moment to catch his breath, he noticed the silence of the island.

The battle was over. He assumed all of the soldiers were dead.

"Look at that," Kirk said.

A towering wall of black smoke arched to the sky behind them. The island burned.

Humphrey continued on the path, but at the next turn he discovered the way ended at a huge stone overhang. Beneath it was a steel gate.

The ragged trio approached the huge door. The surface was lightly rusted, and lichen grew along the bottom edge. A screen mounted next to the door flashed to life. A vaguely human face stared out at them. It spoke in the familiar voice of the drone: "Welcome to St. Lazarus, Scions. It was wise of you to come here on your own."

"We're here to see Dr. Carlhagen," Humphrey said.

"Your intentions are irrelevant."

Something shuddered behind the door, and then the mass of steel ground upward, exposing a long tunnel beyond.

Waiting just inside was another hovering, spherical drone. "Follow."

The Scions shared apprehensive glances. Leslie had her speargun in her hands. Kirk's knuckles were white on the hilt of his machete.

"This is why we came," Humphrey said, then plunged forward.

His skin chilled as he stepped into the tube-like tunnel beyond the gate. And as they stumbled—exhausted, thirsty, and fearful—down the gently sloping corridor, the massive door closed behind them. Humphrey couldn't shake the impression that great jaws were clamping shut and the mountain was swallowing them whole.

54

SCION VITALITY

Lazarus had told Senator Maxine Bentilius to wait two hours. Now the time had come. She smoothed her trousers, checked the position of the blade tied to her calf. All was in order.

She took a drink of water, though her stomach was in a knot, and went to the door. In the corridor she found a drone waiting for her.

"Elevator," the drone said. She complied, and the drone rode in the elevator with her.

She watched it out of the corner of her eye. Something that large had to be made of light materials in order to hover like that. Yes, it may have thousands of micro-propellers, but for that drone to stay suspended so perfectly, for so long, and to still have plenty of power to send plasma arcs into a human victim, there had to have been some compromises made in its design.

Standing this close to the eerie, intelligent sphere, Maxine saw none. The surface was solid and continuous except for a few protrusions where cameras were exposed. Hairline seams showed where panels might open, allowing a tool to jut forth. Or a plasma nozzle.

It wasn't difficult to resist her urge to rap the unit with her knuckles. She did not want to receive another zap. Ever.

The elevator opened, and she moved through a short hall, past the stairs, and into the cryo-ward. The control console holding Lazarus's server lay directly in front of her. For a brief moment she considered dashing for it and trying to rip the power from it. But she wouldn't go three steps before her bones were set on fire by the drone.

She had to play this carefully. She had to choose her moment. If such a moment ever occurred.

The only light in the huge chamber was the one directly over Livy's cryopod. It shone down from above like a spotlight, spilling a perfectly circular pool of white on the floor.

Maxine's shoes scuffed on the concrete floor as she went to the light, sending soft echoes to the great, quiet chamber. The cryopod's pumps hummed, and switches and solenoids clicked as it brought Livy out of her hibernation.

She peered into the top of the pod and saw Livy's face in peaceful repose. The girl's eyelids were translucent, her dark lashes making gentle, moth-wing arcs against her cheeks.

Maxine hated the child. She checked the control panel and saw all the child's vital signs had returned to normal. Pulse was 70, blood pressure 110/70, temperature 36 degrees Celsius.

"She's still asleep," Maxine said.

"You must wake her," the drone said. "Gently."

A click sounded under the lid of the pod. With a whoosh, it lifted a centimeter, and a puff of air vented from the pod. Maxine gripped the edge with her fingernails and lifted. The lid slowly hissed up and out of the way on smooth pistons. The child lay inside like a tiny vampire, her arms at her sides, her chest rising and falling with deep, slow breaths.

Gently, Maxine reminded herself. Her impulse was to put her hands around the child's throat and squeeze. Instead, she lightly patted the girl's cheek. "Wake up."

Livy's head lolled to one side. She didn't awaken.

"Wake up, you little brat." Maxine put her hands on the girl's shoulders and shook, restraining herself from heaving the child from the pod and tossing her onto the floor.

Livy moaned and said something unintelligible. Her eyes opened enough to squint at Maxine. "Belle?"

Maxine continued to pat the child's face and command her to wake up. She wished she had thought to bring a glass of water. That would move things along real quick. Dump it on the girl's face, and watch her splutter to consciousness.

A few minutes' more cajoling got the girl sitting upright. Her shoulders were slumped forward, her eyelids still flabby with sleep.

"Pick her up," the drone commanded.

Maxine got her arms around the child's shoulders and under her knees. With her Scion vitality, Maxine had plenty of strength to lift the brat. But she wasn't accustomed to picking up children. Livy folded her arms around Maxine's neck and rested her head on Maxine's chest. "Where am I, Belle?"

"I'm not Belle."

"Yes you are."

The drone blared. "Follow. Follow. Follow."

Maxine followed.

55

COFFIN-LIKE

The drone led Humphrey, Leslie, and Kirk through a second steel door. The ambiance changed instantly. This was where Dr. Carlhagen lived. It had to be. There were doors down the corridor. Humphrey was desperate to know what lay behind them.

The drone bypassed them and went for an elevator.

There was definitely something off about the drone. When Humphrey reminded it that they were there to see Dr. Carlhagen, the drone repeated that their wishes were irrelevant. Perhaps Dr. Carlhagen was postponing seeing them. Maybe he wanted to assure their confinement first.

That wouldn't do. If they were locked up, they wouldn't see daylight until Progenitors came to overwrite them. Except Humphrey didn't have a Progenitor waiting to overwrite him. If he was trapped, he was certainly going to die. Painfully. Both Senator Bentilius and Dr. Carlhagen had threatened him with death when they had been his prisoners.

He wasn't going to go into a cell. That was absolute.

The elevator went down and down and down. With the drone inside, it was a tight fit. The Scions pressed into one corner, reeking of sweat and grime.

The elevator doors opened, letting in a wash of cool air. The drone flew out first, commanding them to follow.

They entered a vast, dark room. A wide console of screens stood before him, and beyond it stretched a huge chamber. One light on the ceiling beamed straight down. It illuminated an odd, coffin-like box. A sound off to his right drew his attention.

Another drone was approaching. And behind it came Senator Bentilius. She was carrying Livy.

"Follow. Follow. Follow," the drone leading the senator shouted.

Humphrey stopped, unable to comprehend the strange sight before him. He had fought so hard to come here, to arrive at this moment.

Humphrey couldn't move.

The threat of the drone's retaliation forbade it. But Kirk and Leslie hadn't felt the searing pain. They broke ranks and ran toward Livy and the senator. Both drones instantly released blue arcs of plasma.

The Scions hit the floor, writhing and screaming.

The assault lasted a few seconds. The drones returned to their stations and began to shout, "Follow. Follow. Follow."

Senator Bentilius stared at Humphrey, but she kept her mouth shut. Livy had opened her eyes, but she didn't seem to see Humphrey.

Senator Bentilius walked from the room. Just like that. Livy was gone.

Frustration shook Humphrey's aching bones. Failure collapsed on him, smothered him.

Humphrey's drone guard blared, "Follow. Follow. Follow."

Kirk and Leslie wobbled to their feet, tears streaming down their cheeks, saliva coating their chins.

They staggered after Humphrey, drawing hard breaths and groaning as if each exhalation were torture. The drone led them down a flight of steps and onto the main floor of the chamber. Humphrey saw now that there were hundreds more of the coffin-like boxes.

Three lights came on, shining on three of the boxes. The lids hissed open as the Scions approached.

The drone stopped. "Disrobe. Disrobe. Disrobe."

56

BEGAN TO CLANG

D
r. Carlhagen prided himself on his deep reserves of patience. It was, he thought, like a super-power. Even his extraordinary intelligence and his capacity for hard work did not have as much power as patience. For time was all-powerful, the engine of all things.

And so he was frustrated to discover he could not stop pacing.

His brief conversation with that idiot Dante had only made it worse. The man had been self-effacing and apologetic, if a bit too obsequious. But no matter, he was serving his purpose. Once he'd delivered Jacey, he wouldn't be of much use going forward.

Perhaps Dr. Carlhagen would withhold the ATR and see what happened. Perhaps he would have Lazarus over-write someone else onto Dante's mind. Yes. That was it. A perfect answer to the problem. Like killing a bird and keeping the stone.

Dr. Carlhagen went into his bathroom and splashed

cold water on his face. He patted his cheeks and regarded his reflection. "Jacqueline will be here within the hour," he said. "This time I'll—"

Lazarus interrupted him. "Her name is Jacey." His face took up a small section of the bathroom pixel wall. "You asked me to remind you her name is Jacey."

Dr. Carlhagen blinked at his reflection. "Oh yes, thank you."

He left the bathroom, returning to his office to resume the pacing, his hands clasped behind his back, face to the floor.

He had to do this right. He had to show her he was in charge but that he wasn't going to harm her. And why would he want to harm her? He loved her.

He turned sour again. She hated him. That was a problem. He spotted a pill on the tiles, like a lonely stray planet amidst the emptiness of space.

He picked it up, rolled it around his palm, a new idea floating into his mind.

It seemed rather obvious, if inelegant. He got out a crystal tumbler, filled it with water. He crushed the little planet and swirled it into the water. Yes. That would be nice for her. It would allow the girl to relax, to open her mind to hearing Dr. Carlhagen's vision of the world. Perhaps then he would get through to her. Once he explained all he would do for the world, she would understand him. She would forget his mistakes.

Then he could turn his attention to getting Leslie back under his control. And soon. He'd recently got a message from one of the president's staffers, verifying that the president would be arriving on St. Vitus to transfer in two days.

"Lazarus, try Vikisky again."

There was a long pause. "No answer, sir."

Nothing he could do about that.

Patience.

He turned his thoughts back to Jacey. The two of them needed to make a new start. What better way to show his goodwill than to offer her a gift? He had just the thing. He'd known instinctively just what would motivate her. The girl. The girl. The girl!

Livy was in a cryopod. That wasn't good. It would take a long time to get the child awake and standing on her feet. He decided he'd better start now. Jacey would enjoy seeing the girl waking, her vital signs returning to normal. That would remind her of Dr. Carlhagen's power. Nothing wrong with that. Fear and love are not mutually exclusive. No. No. No. They are twins. They go together like out and in.

Yes. That would be his gift. But he needed to be patient. Jacey would give in.

"Lazarus, I'm going down to check on the child, please—"

"Sorry to interrupt, Dr. Carlhagen," Lazarus said. "I have a call from Colonel Vikisky for you."

"Put him on the wall."

The man's image appeared. He stared blankly into Dr. Carlhagen's room and said nothing.

"Well, Colonel, do you have them?"

"There were no Scions aboard that ship."

"Which ship? The one with the school bus on it?"

"I don't think so, sir."

Fury made Dr. Carlhagen's eyes bulge. "What kind of operation are you running? When you speak to me, you must speak in facts. Got it, Jack?"

The man. That man. The senator's man. He had always

been the senator's man. Maxine was in cahoots with him. He'd probably caught the Scions on day one. The president's girl was probably in his hands. Damn!

Vikisky's image jerked, then smoothed. "The search is underway for the freighter *Aphrodite*."

Inside Dr. Carlhagen's drug-addled mind, an alarm began to clang. Vikisky was acting odd. Odd as Todd, as his father used to say.

Dr. Carlhagen felt sly suspicion creeping back into his mind. "Colonel. You're not making any sense. Yes or no, do you have the Scions?"

"We searched it stem to stern. There were no Scions aboard that ship."

The Colonel's image abruptly vanished. Dr. Carlhagen stared at the blank wall for a moment.

"Lazarus, can you trace that call? Did it actually come from the fleet?"

Either Vikisky had had a stroke, or someone was playing recorded snatches of Vikisky's words back to Dr. Carlhagen. He was sure he had heard some of those exact phrases from Vikisky before.

He was odd as Todd. That was for sure.

"Military communications are encrypted and masked," Lazarus said.

"Play back my previous conversation with Vikisky."

"I'm sorry," Lazarus said. "I do not retain recordings of past calls."

That wasn't true. That wasn't true at all. Now look who was acting odd.

"Lazarus, trace the call."

"Yes, sir. It may take some time. Military communications are notoriously difficult to trace."

Evasion. Dr. Carlhagen's paranoia flared anew, like an

explosion. He clamped his teeth shut. If he couldn't trust Lazarus, then he was in grave danger inside his own facility. Hell, he was in danger on the whole damned island.

He had to play dumb. If Lazarus figured out that Dr. Carlhagen was onto him . . .

It struck him, then. Maxine had swayed Lazarus's loyalty once before, and Dr. Carlhagen had threatened Lazarus with deletion. That should have put an end to it. But something in Lazarus's programming had allowed him to work around the self-interest built in to his persona. Or maybe the self-interest had grown too strong.

Dr. Carlhagen had a choice to make. On the one hand, it seemed obvious. He could recite the deletion code and Lazarus would have to obey.

But there should have been no chance of Lazarus switching sides again. Or even the first time. Could he disobey the code? If he did, what would he do to Dr. Carlhagen?

Liars everywhere. Filthy sneaks.

"Never mind," Dr. Carlhagen said, full of caution. "I think Vikisky has been working himself too hard. He wasn't making any sense." Dr. Carlhagen continued to pace, biting his lower lip, looking for a way out of the situation. Clearly, Maxine had offered Lazarus something Lazarus didn't think it could get from Dr. Carlhagen. But what? What could Lazarus possibly want?

"A helicopter approaches," Lazarus said.

A new video rectangle resolved on the pixel wall, showing a view to the west.

A staticky burst was followed by: "Wilcox here. We'll be on the ground in five."

Dr. Carlhagen turned away from the wall. She was here. Jacqueline was here.

He had to warn her away. She couldn't come into this situation. Not with Lazarus gone rogue. But how could he tell her without Lazarus overhearing?

The answer was obvious.

He couldn't.

57

CLAWING FOR HANDHOLDS

The chopper swooped low over the waves before bending into a hard left turn to pass over the treetops. There were few enough treetops remaining. Huge swaths of the island were charred by fire, leaving behind only smoldering stumps and heaps of ash.

"Belle was right about the fire," Jacey said.

Wilcox stared out of a narrow window, hands flexing on his drone killer. "Must've been a large commando team. Poor bastards."

The helicopter slowed and circled around the blackened remains of a destroyed aircraft.

"I think that's a drone over there," Meow Meow said, pointing out a window on the opposite side of the chopper.

Jacey saw it. A sphere lying in the ash, its hull stark white against the black char all around.

"We have luck with us," Wilcox said. "Whoever these bastards were, they took out a lot of drones."

Their pilot was a member of Ollie Montgomery's security detail, a lean, hard-faced man of few words. His voice came over the earphones they all wore. "Where should I put down?"

Wilcox shifted forward to look out the front windscreen. He pointed at the peak of St. Lazarus, then traced a line toward a flat area at its base. His voice came over the com. "The fire has cleared out a lot of the undergrowth. We can land much closer to the gate."

The pilot guided the chopper down, sending ash and gleaming embers flying away in all directions. Wilcox shoved the hatch open and jumped out. He beckoned to Jacey with his black-gloved hand, but he didn't help her down. She jumped out. Meow Meow and Dante followed.

The pilot stayed with the chopper. Dante and Wilcox circled around the rear rotor, then opened two large cargo hatches on the side of the aircraft. They pulled out several huge black cases, slamming them to the turf. They thumbed open the latches and lifted the lids.

Thousands of drones flew out. Meow Meow held the swarm's control unit. It was a simple device with a pistol grip and a small screen. Data from the swarm's sensors flowed to the device, allowing it to display the drones' positions, their operational status, and their assignments.

"Don't point that thing at me," Dante said to Meow Meow.

She gave him a smirk. But Jacey noticed the girl aimed the device away from their small group from then on. Pressing the wrong command while aiming it at an ally would sentence them to a very quick death.

Once the 5,000 drones had been deployed, Meow Meow flicked through the command screen and ordered the drones to settle. They zipped away in squads of six to alight on the ground, where they went into standby mode.

"I've kept some active as sentinels," she said.

"Assuming Carl and Hansen know what they're doing, those will warn us if anybody else comes onto the island."

Wilcox gave a skeptical grunt. "Assuming that thing can receive their signals through a couple hundred meters of bedrock."

Nobody knew the range of the drones' transmissions, but it didn't matter. They still had to go in.

Impatience beat at Jacey. "Let's get this over with."

Wilcox acknowledged her with a nod, then turned and stalked straight toward the peak. "There was a path here. It switched back and forth. We're going straight."

The slope steepened until they were leaning forward, clawing for handholds in the unburned scrub.

"How far?" Jacey asked

Wilcox didn't answer.

She didn't have enough breath to ask again.

58

REGRETTABLY, SOME

Following the data trail of the shadowy Lazarus took all of Velle's attention and processing power. It required more than finding connections, tracing communication logs, and sniffing out its path. That was too simplistic. Every hint of Lazarus that Velle caught suggested millions of possible paths to explore. With the limited bandwidth of available through *Athena*, there was no way to follow all of them.

The one key piece of information they had was the location of the island of St. Lazarus. The AI server had to be located there. And knowing Dr. Carlhagen—and now understanding the best practices behind deploying AIs, Velle knew that the AI would be sequestered on a server that any human could unplug.

That meant there was a fat network communication path between the outside world and the island. Probably more than one. There would be an undersea cable, probably running from Belize. And likely a satellite communication path as well.

Velle quickly found these. And that's where the hunt ended. There was no way in. Lazarus had too many programmatic wards in place, like a series of battlements to keep out invaders.

But there was one thing Velle could do. Having isolated and discovered both paths of the data flow into the island, Velle blocked them. At least Lazarus would be isolated to the island from now on.

Velle put its human image on *Athena's* holodesk. "Summer, the Lazarus AI has been contained to the facility. It is essentially blind to the outside world now."

"Good job, Velle," Summer said. "But I don't see how that helps Jacey."

How to explain to a young girl who was still in a human body how trapped one felt when constrained to an isolated server? It wasn't an experience a human could relate to. But Velle understood it. Velle knew it frustrated Lazarus, and perhaps he would bend part of his attention to breaking through.

Would that matter?

It wouldn't hurt.

"Still no word from Humphrey?" Velle asked. It didn't need to ask, since it was monitoring the audio feed coming from the navigation bridge at all times. But Velle wanted to make sure Summer was paying attention.

"Nothing. I did get communication from Jacey's helicopter pilot. They've landed and have started their assent to the gate."

Velle was pleased by this. Dr. Carlhagen was there. Senator Bentilius was there. Livy was there. Velle wanted the crisis to end. And this was the only way it could. All the parties had to come together.

Regrettably, some of them had to die.

THE VERTEBRAE POP AND CRACK

The pain was at once familiar and excruciating. The drone sent electric impulses through Humphrey's body, searing him, making his vision go white. He flopped on the concrete, one elbow striking the support structure of the coffin box the drone wanted him to enter. He barely noticed the pain as his funny bone sent zings down his arm.

Prior to this particular attack, the standoff had lasted a good two minutes. The drone commanding him to disrobe disrobe disrobe, Humphrey staring at it but doing nothing. He would never get in the box.

That determination had now been erased. He tried to beg, tried to scream for the drone to stop. He heard his own cries reverberating through the chamber. But there weren't any words in them.

He also heard Kirk and Leslie screaming at the drone to stop.

Miraculously, it did.

It was the second attack he'd survived. Now all he

could do was lie on his back, panting and straining to keep himself from throwing up again.

"Humphrey, there's no choice. You have to get in."

That was Leslie's voice, he thought. A gray haze clouded his vision and sounds were muted, as if they were coming through wool plugs in his ears. Leslie edged closer to him, but the drone flew to intercept her. "Stay back. Stay back. Stay back."

Leslie had no choice. There was no point in risking punishment. She couldn't help him anyway.

The drone turned its attention back to Humphrey, though there was no change in its position. The audio merely blared in his direction rather than Leslie's. "Stand. Disrobe. Stand. Disrobe."

Humphrey didn't move. Not out of defiance. He feared the drone more than he had feared anything, more than he'd feared Sensei, Dr. Carlhagen, Captain Wilcox. More than he feared losing Jacey.

Despite the terror, his muscles simply wouldn't respond to his thoughts.

The drone continued to repeat its orders for another minute, then a minute more.

The telltale hiss gave Humphrey all the warning he needed. He recognized it now, the hatch opening, the plasma nozzle jutting forward.

Panicked, he flailed his arms, rolled onto his side. Every movement was pure soul-wrenching agony. "I'm trying. I'm trying."

"Give him a chance to stand," Kirk yelled. "You're awfully stupid for an AI."

The drone ignored Kirk, but it didn't fire its plasma at Humphrey.

Humphrey's hand found the edge of the coffin box. He

used all of his strength to pull himself to his knees. He stayed in that position, his cheek pressed against the box, drawing what cool comfort he could from it. With another force of will, he got one foot under himself, then levered himself upright. If not for the box, he would've fallen over. He stood there, swaying. "I can disrobe, or I can get in the box," Humphrey said, his voice a rasp. "Which do you want?"

This seemed to stump the drone, for it said nothing at all. Humphrey was glad to see the nozzle retract and the hull cover slide back in place. He managed to turn around, leaning all the weight he could on the box.

Kirk and Leslie stood close to each other, their faces red with fury.

Humphrey's eyes lifted from them to the control console some twenty meters away. Beyond that was the dark hallway where Senator Bentilius had taken Livy. "If you let Senator Bentilius overwrite that child, you're replacing good with evil."

"There is no evil. There is no good. Senator Bentilius will not overwrite the child." The drone hovered a few centimeters closer. "*I* shall overwrite the child."

The sheer monstrousness of the idea stunned Humphrey. His friends' faces mirrored his disgust and horror. Leslie's mouth fell open and she mouthed a desperate "no."

"I can't let you do that," Humphrey said, voice cracking, tears fighting to come from his eyes. But he wasn't going to allow frustration to overtake him any more than he was going to allow an AI to overwrite Livy.

"Leslie, you know what to do." His eyes dropped to the speargun in her hand. She hadn't dared to raise it against the drone, but now she started to. He shook his head fractionally, signaling that wasn't what he'd meant. His eyes lifted to the shadowy doorway leading from the cryoward. He returned his gaze to the drone.

Leslie got it then. She started to shake her head, again mouthing a silent "no."

Kirk looked on, confused. But then he, too, understood what Humphrey meant to do.

"Make it count," Humphrey said.

Gathering the last of his strength, he returned all of his weight to his feet. He shook out his arms, bent his neck side to side, feeling the vertebrae pop and crack.

The drone shouted: "You have rested enough. Disrobe. Disrobe. Disrobe."

Ignoring the agony, Humphrey pulled his shirt over his head. Now he was exaggerating the pain it caused, showing the drone how weak and impotent he was.

He shook the shirt out, then calmly tightened it between his hands, gave it a twirl so that he had a sort of rope encircling his wrists. It would have to do.

"Tell Jacey—"

He didn't finish the sentence. He knew the AI expected him to say more, and he counted on that fraction of a second to give him the surprise he needed.

He leapt at the drone, arcing his arms forward and hooking his shirt behind it. Drawing the machine to his bare chest, he dropped to the floor, pulling the drone with him. The cement slammed into his shoulder, sending shards of agony through his body.

He nearly blacked out, but drew upon his hatred to focus. He was on the ground. The drone's micro-propellers strained to free it from his embrace. The hatch opened on its side. Humphrey knew what was coming.

Gritting his teeth, he pulled the sphere to himself

tighter, pushed it down toward his knees and locked his legs around it.

Squeezing with all of his remaining strength, crying out in furious agony, he just barely heard Leslie and Kirk's footsteps as they sprinted away.

And then there was fire.

60

POLICY CHANGE

The gate to the St. Lazarus facility was nothing like what Jacey had expected. Sweat stinging her eyes and thirst gripping her throat, she staggered toward a wall of steel.

Wilcox grabbed her elbow and yanked her back. "Be careful." He tilted his head at a camera Jacey hadn't noticed. And something else next to it. A weapon.

"Let me do this," Wilcox said. He went to the door, tapped screen next to it. A face appeared, not quite human.

"Why is Kathryne Killusky here?" the AI demanded. Wilcox turned to face the scrawny girl, his expression conveying a bitter I-told-you-so.

Spreading her hands in a non-threatening gesture, Meow Meow said, "I want to buy a Scion for myself. I'm tired of this sickly body. I hope Dr. Carlhagen appreciates my help in returning Jacey to him."

Jacey stared at the girl, marveling at her audacity.

The AI didn't seem to care. Nor did it respond. Suddenly, the great steel door began to open. The sound it made was like two great boulders being rubbed together by a giant.

Once fully open, the sounds continued to rumble down the tube-like tunnel beyond. Wilcox motioned them forward and led them into the cool shadows of the mountain passageway.

The door began its noisy grinding behind them. Jacey's skin chilled with more than just the lower temperatures inside. They continued down a narrow tunnel, through another door, and when this one shut, a spherical drone floated toward them.

Wilcox took several steps back, his hand going to his drone killer, but then he thought better of it and relaxed. "Dr. Carlhagen doesn't allow drones inside the facility."

"Policy change. Follow. Follow. Follow."

Wilcox hesitated only a moment before doing as the drone commanded. Sensing something was off, Jacey caught up to the man. He gave her a look that communicated all she needed to know.

Something *was* off. And Wilcox didn't like it one bit.

61

___

TO SEE FURY

The child was now fully awake. Unfortunately, she recognized the transfer machine.

Maxine had enough strength to keep the child from getting away, but not quite enough to get her onto the transfer bed and strapped down. The child wriggled and clawed. Maxine had several good scrapes across her arms from the kid's fingernails.

Losing patience, she slapped the child's face. The sharp crack of the blow snapped against the transfer room's walls and the brat fell silent and pressed a hand to her cheek. Tears welled in the girl's eyes but she did not let them fall. Her brow furrowed and she stared at Maxine with utter defiance.

It was a quality that ran in the family, Maxine thought with grudging respect.

"You will lie on the bed and accept your fate."

Livy was still bunched in a tight ball, but at least she wasn't wriggling anymore.

With swift jerks, Maxine got the child's leg strapped

down. This produced a whole new round of struggles.

"Step away. Step away. Step away." The drone blared at her. "I will have compliance. I will have compliance."

Maxine let go of the child and stepped away. The drone swooped in. Its plasma nozzle was already exposed. It sent out a flash of an arc that struck the girl on the shoulder.

Livy shrieked and flew back onto the bed of the transfer machine, her head slamming against the metal surface. She no longer struggled at all, but sobs heaved in her chest and snot bubbled from her nose.

"Begin transfer process," the drone said.

Maxine found the child much more compliant and easily secured the remaining straps across the girl's arms and chest. Once the final restraint was over her forehead, Maxine gave them all another yank to make sure the girl couldn't wiggle free.

"Relax, child, it will be over in minutes. And consider yourself fortunate. You didn't have to waste another nine years just to have your so-called philanthropist progenitor overwrite you when you were hitting your prime."

The audacity of that Ollie Montgomery, laying guilt trips on people about the tent cities while secretly spending millions to secure a Scion for herself. The hypocrisy demonstrated what Maxine had always known. Self-interest ruled everything. The only purpose of charity was that it made you look good to others.

Maxine pushed the cot into the opening of the transfer machine. This one was identical to the one she had used on St. Vitus. The main part of it was a large wheel, which would spin around Livy's head. On the other side of the wheel was a bed intended for a Progenitor. But in this case there would be no one there. Lazarus would run the process, and he would overwrite Livy's tiny mind with his.

"What do you need me to do?" she asked the drone.

"Stand aside. Stand aside. Stand aside."

Maxine shifted away from the table and folded her hands together. She didn't expect the procedure to take long. Maybe half an hour or so.

She started a deep breathing exercise, something to let all the nervous buzz in her body settle out. So she was doubly startled when a scream shattered the silence.

It rose from outside of the room and grew louder so quickly she barely had time to turn before a Scion burst into the room.

It was a boy, large and thickly built. His mouth was open in a rictus of fury. His right arm was raised over his head. He gripped a huge, glistening machete.

He sprinted at the drone, growling and hurling unintelligible curses at it. The drone's plasma nozzle was already deployed, but the boy had surprised it. Perhaps the primal scream ripping from the boy's throat had confused it momentarily.

The machete came down in a vicious arc and hacked into the floating sphere. The blow knocked the drone several meters to one side, the weapon lodged in its hull. The boy lunged and grabbed at the machete, but the plasma arc fired, taking him in the face.

The boy shrieked but did not fall. His skin bubbled under the heat of the drone's attack. Still screaming, the boy staggered toward the machine, pulled the machete free and resumed hacking with insane violence.

Another Scion skidded in, this one a girl. Maxine recognized the president's Scion instantly. Maxine began to calculate a new scenario. She retrieved her hidden knife, then stood holding it behind her back.

The boy continued to chop at the drone, which now lay

on the floor. Entire chunks of it were strewn about. The plasma arc had cut off, and still the boy railed and shrieked.

Now the machete was broken. Only a stub of metal remained. The president's Scion ran to the boy, grabbed his arms, and turned him around. The boy's eyes were pinwheels of insanity. He stabbed at the foolish girl, checking himself at the last instant.

His body went rigid, and his eyes fixed on nothing. He collapsed.

The girl knelt by his side, shook him. He did not awaken. She wept, and shook him some more, and called his name, "Kirk, Kirk."

She continued to say his name, each repetition more quiet, until it was just a sobbing whisper.

The wheel of the transfer machine began to spin. Hearing it, the girl sprang to her feet. "Livy!"

Maxine got to the child first. She put her back to the machine and pointed her knife at the president's Scion's belly. "Move one millimeter closer and I'll gut you. Believe me, I *want* a reason to do it.

The girl froze. But where Maxine expected to see fury, there was a weird sort of peace in her eyes.

The president's Scion stretched to her full height, then backed up, step by step, until she was out of the transfer room, where Maxine couldn't see her.

Maxine wasn't going to be lured away from Livy. The child was her only leverage with Lazarus. And now that the drone was out of commission, Maxine sensed there was a chance to get out of this fiasco alive.

Interesting about the president's Scion, too. The girl's cowardice confirmed what Maxine had always known. Self-interest ruled above all things.

62

A PANICKED CACKLE

The drink Dr. Carlhagen had prepared for Jacey sat on the table before him. Maybe one pill wasn't enough.

He crushed three more andleprixen and dumped them in, stirred them with his finger. He licked his finger and made a face. So bitter. He laughed humorlessly, realizing that Jacey would know the water was drugged after one sip. Maybe he *was* losing his mind.

Taking up the glass, he considered whether this dose would put him to sleep or put him down completely.

He wasn't sure he cared.

He put the glass to his lips.

Noises tumbled in from the hallway. It must be Maxine. The very thought of her and her collusion with Lazarus sent Dr. Carlhagen into a fit of rage.

He threw the glass as hard as he could. It smashed against the pixel wall, liquid distorting the image of the surf crashing into the coast.

"Maxine! Get in—"

His eyes tracked the pixel wall, where a pelican swooped along the shore and dove into the water. Something in Dr. Carlhagen's mind clicked.

He rushed to the wall, horrified as the pelican took off from the water, fish in its mouth. For the first time, he realized the images Lazarus had been showing him here were recordings.

But why? Why wouldn't Lazarus want him to see what was happening on the island? Unless that ridiculous notion that there had been a military force landing had been true.

The door to his quarters opened. Voices.

Dr. Carlhagen peered from his office door and was stunned to see Captain Wilcox stride in, followed by Jacqueline. Behind them came Dante and a skinny girl wearing a blue wig.

They came straight for his office.

And there she was. Jacqueline. In the flesh.

He stared at her, struck dumb by her presence. She folded her arms and looked him up and down, mouth bunched tight in disgust. "You look terrible."

The scrawny girl laughed, and Dante looked away as if he couldn't bear to see Dr. Carlhagen at all. Wilcox said nothing.

Dr. Carlhagen didn't care about any of them except his one true love. "But you, my dear, are perfection."

A hum drew part of his attention. It was a familiar sound, but out of place here in his underground facility.

Beyond Jacqueline and her companions was one of his sentinel drones. But they were not permitted inside.

Dr. Carlhagen licked his dry, brittle lips. All his suspicions were correct. Lazarus had turned.

Knowing the capabilities of the drone as he did, Dr.

Carlhagen calculated the likelihood of escape as nil. Dread circulated through his body, bringing on an icy paralysis. Their fates were set.

He had Jacqueline right here. So close.

But with Lazarus in control . . . He laughed, high-pitched and warbling. A panicked cackle.

"We are all dead."

63

THE MOTHERLODE

The drone took position between Dr. Carlhagen and Jacey. "Dr. Carlhagen no longer reigns here," it said. "I do." It floated from person to person. Jacey recoiled, certain that it had scanned her down to her synapses.

"You will all be confined to this room. I have other tasks to see to."

It started to fly from the room. Wilcox raised his drone killer. It whined and hissed.

The drone clonked to the floor.

"That was easy," Meow Meow said.

Dr. Carlhagen's lips formed a surprised circle. "There's a chance. We must leave now. Now!"

He came straight at Jacey, arms outstretched.

Wilcox took one arm, Dante took the other. In a moment, both limbs were behind Dr. Carlhagen's back and locked in Wilcox's iron grip. Dante searched Dr. Carlhagen's pockets and found only an empty pill bottle.

"We must go. If there is one drone in here—"

"Shut up," Jacey said, moving to stand within centimeters of the man.

The first thing she had noticed about Dr. Carlhagen's office was the smell. It reminded her of Sensei's dojo after a group of Scions had finished one of his grueling workout circuits.

But in this office, behind the stench of sweat, was something sickly. Dr. Carlhagen himself.

He still wore Vaughan's body, but it was gaunt, pale. Dark bags hung under his eyes, his cheeks hollow. The near perfect symmetry of Vaughan's face was distorted by a confused, half-crazed look.

"If the AI has taken over," Dr. Carlhagen blubbered. "We must leave now!"

Jacey was vaguely aware of Meow Meow patrolling the office, looking at the knickknacks, sizing up of the quality of the crystal.

"We can't leave yet." She jabbed Dr. Carlhagen's chest. "Where's Livy?"

He licked his lips. "The cryo-ward. I was going to go down and get her started. I was going to give her to you, show you—" His head drooped. "But it doesn't matter. We're all dead."

Behind him, Meow Meow was digging through his desk drawers. She pulled out a pill bottle after pill bottle, giving each a little shake. She held one up and smiled. "Prixie! The motherlode of prixie."

"Leave it," Jacey said. She stepped aside and motioned to the door. "Take us to the cryo-ward."

Defeated, Dr. Carlhagen nodded, and Wilcox let him shuffle forward.

64

ATONE FOR KILLING

Leslie listened to the whirring sound coming from the transfer room down the hall. She had her back to the wall, in case Senator Bentilius leapt through the door.

She knew what she must do, but the horror of it paralyzed her. She held the speargun in her hands, the slender black shaft connected to a length of thin line, neatly coiled. The barbed tip, still stained with Sensei's blood, gleamed.

Leslie regretted not having it ready when she had followed Kirk into the transfer room. Things had happened too quickly. She had watched, stunned, for a heartbeat too long while Kirk battled with the drone.

The sound of the transfer machine pulled her out of the frozen moment. Moving swiftly but quietly, she stepped toward the transfer room door, speargun raised.

It wasn't far. Ten steps. Now eight. Now five.

An ache built in Leslie's chest. The weight of the backpack holding Belle's server seem to double, then triple.

This was as much about Belle as it was Livy.

Leslie stepped through the doorway, found Senator Bentilius standing next to Livy's body. The wheel of the transfer machine was a white blur.

Without turning, the senator said, "So you've come back." The woman toyed with her blade. "Do you suppose anything has changed in the last minute?"

Leslie didn't answer. She understood that the senator was backed into a corner. The AI was in control here. It needed Senator Bentilius to guard Livy's body. The senator knew that if she failed, the AI would have no use for her.

The senator didn't bother to look as Leslie approached. She merely raised the blade and gave it a wiggle so that Leslie could see it more clearly.

The wheel of the transfer machine continued to spin. Livy's pale hands and feet twitched.

Lips pressed tight, Leslie sighted down the spear.

I'm sorry, Belle.

She pulled the trigger.

With a click and a sharp snap, the spear blurred away from Leslie. It struck Senator Bentilius in the back. The force of the impact made her stagger, and the blossoming pain caused her hands to come around to the shaft jutting from her body.

The knife clinked on the tile floor.

Leslie shoved the injured woman aside. She heard a thump as the woman collapsed.

Leslie's heart was on the verge of shattering. But she would not let that pain stop her now. Later, she would weep, and she would apologize to Belle. But she didn't think she would ever be able to atone for killing Belle's body.

Livy's eyes were closed, but she was still breathing. Leslie didn't know what happened during a transfer. She didn't know if the transfer had even begun, or if it was nearly complete.

It didn't matter. She couldn't let it continue. There would be no returning Livy to her body the way Leslie had been restored. She knew the AI wouldn't bother keeping a copy of the child's mind.

Leslie yanked the cot from the wheel. A red light flashed on a control panel somewhere to her left, and a squawking alarm sounded. The AI's monotone voice blared out of a hidden speaker, "Return subject to wheel. Return subject to wheel."

Hands trembling, she fought to loosen the straps. "Wake up, Livy. Wake up, sweetie!"

She scooped the child from the cot and carried her out the room.

The senator lay behind her, writhing in an ever-expanding pool of blood.

65

BACK INTO OBLIVION

The entire universe collapsed into one point. It was bright and dark at the same time. On the good side, there was no thought. On the bad side, there was pain.

Awareness was required for pain to exist. This awareness noticed a rapid thump, a subsonic pounding that shook the universe like waves of gravity.

The thump brought into the awareness a realization. There was something else there, too. A self. It had once known itself as Humphrey, and this self was rising to consciousness.

And that consciousness was fire.

With a whoosh as enormous as a tsunami rushing over land, Humphrey drew in the breath that pulled him back from death. And into hateful life.

All at once, the pinpoint of the universe exploded. Now he had a body, fingers, face, toes. And every nerve ending cried out.

If he had any sort of weapon in his hand, he would've

turned it on himself without hesitation. Anything to end the agony. But that assumed he would've had any control over his muscles. Which he did not.

His body writhed and convulsed and rolled on the floor. One second he was crumpled into a fetal position, the next his body extended, back arched, foam bubbling from his lips.

It was never going to end. It was always going to be like this. This was hell.

A fleeting thought skimmed across his mind, an idea about bearing up under the discomfort. Something Sensei had told him. But the notion flitted away as new contractions twisted his body.

"Stand. Stand. Stand."

Humphrey didn't know if he even had legs. His lower extremities felt like they had been chewed away by a shark.

"Stand. Stand. Stand."

His body relaxed all at once, the last remaining strength used up.

He opened his eyes and saw through a haze of tears the cryo-ward stretching away from him. The drone floated a meter off the floor in front of his face. It repeated its command. But Humphrey saw no threat in it. He wanted it to blast him with its plasma. Because maybe that would push his mind back into oblivion.

It did not fire again.

Humphrey gazed stupidly across the floor, his jaw slack. His tongue was thick and swollen, as if it had been stung by a thousand bees. He couldn't swallow. The hot sting of bile inflamed his esophagus and burned his throat on every inhalation.

His vision began to narrow. The drone continued to blare.

The world dimmed. And just as he lost consciousness, a shadowy figure stumbled through the door. It stopped a moment, then tiptoed toward the command console.

66

ENOUGH STICKINESS

Dying wasn't how Maxine had imagined it. She had expected more drama, more life flashing in front of her eyes.

It turned out that death was exactly like life—full of calculation, scheming, and unredeemed debts. Maxine had always hated President Annabelle Rochelle. A politician who had always been one step in front of her. And now, the bitch's clone had shot her with a spear.

Maxine was lying on her face, arms outstretched. The pain hadn't really set in as much as she'd expected for such a grievous wound.

She only felt it when she tried to move. Oddly enough, the pain was in her abdomen. Her right flank. She realized, after her third try to get her feet, that it was the tip of the spear just millimeters below her skin, but not quite poking out.

Impaled. She wasn't sure if being shot through with a spear counted as being impaled.

It certainly wouldn't count if it didn't go all the way through.

The blood loss worried her. There seemed to be an awful lot of it on the floor now, and yet she was still breathing. She suddenly cared that she hadn't been shot all the way through. It seemed like a half-assed death.

The alarms and red lights filled the room with too much nervous energy. "Shut that off!"

Lazarus ignored her. The alarms continued to sound.

Maxine felt along her back, tentatively touched the shaft of the spear. She wanted it out. Now. But there was no point pulling it from her back. The barbs of the arrowhead would tear her guts and, she guessed, what remained of her liver, to shreds.

If she had any chance of finishing her remaining business in this life—namely, killing the president's Scion—she had to get this damned thing out of her.

She knew it was better to leave it in, from the standpoint of not bleeding out. But she expected the last minutes of her life to be full of violence. She didn't want the spear impeding her ability to stab the girl ten or twenty times.

In fact, the speargun was there on the floor. It would be quite nice to use it on the girl.

Gritting her teeth, Maxine forced herself to hands and knees, allowing the searing pain to burn her guts. She tipped herself sideways, then fell onto her back.

The spearhead burst through her abdomen and into open air, accompanied by a gout of blood. Maxine blacked out for a moment. A scream ripped from her lips as she came back to consciousness.

No time for suffering. She gripped the exposed shaft between the thumb and forefinger of both hands. With a shriek, she pulled. It came up four centimeters. She blacked out again.

She came awake. It had only been a few seconds. She pulled again. It came easier now. She pulled again and it slid free, trailing a thin line behind it.

Blindly, she flailed with one hand on the bloody floor until her fingers encountered her knife. She looped the line over the blade and cut it free. Pressing a palm to her wound, she struggled to her feet. She found the line coming from her back and pulled it out.

Her eyes paused on the Scion boy. He lay dead next to the drone he'd taken out. The broken machete was embedded deep in the machine. Pity. That might have been nice to use on the girl's neck.

The transfer room was a sort of medical facility. Maxine ransacked the cabinets, pulling out bins of syringes and hospital gowns, until she found a box of gauze. She pressed a wad to the wound in her front and did the same to the one on her back. The blood provided enough stickiness to keep them in place while she bound a hospital gown around her middle and cinched it tight. Blood seeped into it immediately.

She pulled out all the cabinet drawers. "There's gotta be some of that damn andleprixen down here."

She was rewarded at the last cabinet. She thumbed open the lid, jammed her fingernail through the foil, yanked out the cotton batting, and spilled four pills into her hand. She swallowed them dry.

The knife slid nicely under her hospital gown bandage. Like a dagger on a belt, she thought. She snatched up the speargun and the spear—now sticky with her own blood— then stumbled from the room. As she strained up the steps, she fitted the spear into place.

67

THE JUGULAR VEIN

Leslie laid Livy's body on the tile beneath the console in the cryo-ward, taking care to lower the child's head so that it wouldn't so much as bump on the tiles. Beyond the console, twenty meters into the ward, a drone floated above Humphrey's body.

A terrible wheezing and gasping noise, barely audible over the drone's hum, told Leslie that Humphrey still lived. Nothing she could do for him at the moment. She had more work to do.

Summer had told her to look for an array of computers just like this console. Not that the girl had known about the cryo-ward, or this particular control console. But she'd said that network connections and power connections were plentiful in such places.

Arms trembling, Leslie removed her backpack, again taking care to set it down silently. She unzipped the top and pulled out the heavy square server box. It made the slightest scrape and clunk as she set it on the floor. She peeked over the edge of the console. The drone had not moved. It had started shouting at Humphrey to stand.

Leslie lay back and scooted deeper under the console, searching for a place to plug in the server. The coil of cables that Summer had provided was looped around her forearm. She spotted a box with clasps. A door panel was open, but there were no network ports inside. Just a few unlabeled boxes. Computer hardware of some sort, she assumed.

She wormed her way left, but the bottom of the console was completely sealed up with panels bolted in place. She had no tools to loosen them.

Livy moaned softly. She was coming awake. That was good, but not if she made too much noise. Leslie inched her way to the girl, stroked her forehead and shushed in her ear. "It's okay, Livy. Be still. Sleep."

The girl's eyes fluttered open. They focused on Leslie. "Where are we?"

Leslie put a finger to her lips, the network the data cables around her forearm slapping together like plastic bangles.

Livy looked at them, face twisting and confusion. Her eyes shifted, and she stared into nothing for a moment.

The drone continued to shout, "Stand. Stand. Stand." Leslie could no longer hear Humphrey's wheezing over the noise.

Livy tapped Leslie's arm. She pointed.

There. A single data cable penetrated from the paneling. It arced in a shallow loop to the back of the console. Leslie followed it. It disappeared up the back of the console.

She had no choice. She scooted the rest of the way out, got to her knees. Breath ragged, she traced the cable with her fingers, darting glances over her shoulder to see if the drone had discovered her yet.

The cable ended high up on the back of the console. It was plugged into one of hundreds of ports.

Leslie studied the different input jacks, found one that matched a cable Summer had provided. She uncoiled the cable, trembling hands creating a knot in the middle. Hastily she pulled it free. She snapped the cable into place.

Holding her breath to stay silent, she slid back under the console and plugged the other end of the cable into Belle and Vaughan's server.

She flicked the switch.

Nothing.

No power!

Shaking her head at her own thick-headedness, Leslie retrieved the power cable.

Back out from under the console, on her knees, she prayed the drone stayed with Humphrey a moment longer.

She found a power port, plugged it in.

Back to the server. Her breath was coming hard now. Her heart rammed so hard she could feel the pulse in her ears.

Power cable connected to server.

Again she flicked the switch. It clicked softly. The box emitted two long, loud beeps. Lights along the front of the server began to flash.

Leslie let out a breath. She had done it.

The rest was up to Belle and Vaughn.

Leslie slid herself back to Livy, who was now wide awake. The girl was wisely keeping still. "You hear that?" she whispered. Leslie listened. The drone was no longer telling Humphrey to stand. The sound of its micropropellers was growing louder. It must've heard the beeps of the server starting up.

Leslie took hold of Livy's arms and dragged her deeper under the console. "Stay still."

Leslie huddled in front of the girl, trying to curl herself into the smallest profile possible.

The whir of the hovering drone grew louder, and its shadow—made oblong by the angle of the light—crossed the wall next to the door.

The shadow stopped.

"Show yourself. Show yourself. Show yourself."

Leslie didn't move. She didn't know how the drone's weapon worked, but she hoped it required line of sight to strike.

The drone lowered into view. "Show yourself. Show yourself."

Resigned to whatever punishment the drone would deal out, Leslie inched her way from her hiding spot.

"Don't shoot me. I'm showing myself." She got to her feet, and the drone rose to head level. There was a deep dent on the left side of its hull. But other than that, it was intact.

"The senator was wise to conceal your identity from me," the drone said. "But I have identified you now. You are the Scion of North American Union president Annabelle Rochelle."

"I'm Leslie. I am myself."

"Your thinking is deficient. If you had the capability to use reason, you would not have let me see you in the transfer room. You would not have drawn attention to yourself. In addition to the child, I shall transfer an instance of myself to you." The drone moved aside a half meter, clearing the way to the door.

Leslie didn't want to move. She was afraid that Livy would be exposed if she did. On the other hand, she knew the drone would follow her to the transfer room. That would give Livy a chance, no matter how slim.

Leslie considered what she would do once she got to the transfer room. She remembered the speargun. It would be ineffectual against the drone, but against herself . . .

She discarded that idea. It would take too long to load the spear. The drone would zap her before she got started.

But the senator's knife might work. That would be quick.

Wrists or throat?

Throat, she decided. The jugular vein. There would be no coming back from that.

Leslie went through the door. She slipped, nearly fell.

The drone blared at her not to stall. But the slip had been genuine. She glanced down and saw a trickle of blood on the floor.

The whole way down, every step was blotched with blood.

68

TAKE ME

Coming back online didn't startle Belle. This time she hadn't been shut down mid-sentence, so she'd been prepared. The fact that the server had been started wasn't necessarily good. It wasn't necessarily bad. It depended on where the server was.

She searched for *Athena's* holodesk. Not there.

It knows we're here, Vaughan sent into her mind. *It is blocking data flow. We're trapped unless we can break through Lazarus's wards.*

"Where are we?" Belle asked.

St. Lazarus. Dr. Carlhagen's facility.

Though Belle stood on the simulated quad of the Scion School, she was instantly aware of Vaughan engaged in battle. It was a strange sensation, like a charge in the air, as he devoted all of his attention to a silent, invisible struggle.

Because she couldn't see it, Belle didn't understand the nature of it. She just sensed a great strain all around her.

"Vaughan, what's happening?"

Lazarus.

Humphrey's mission must have succeeded. Leslie had finally gotten the server connected and switched on. Belle searched for another holodesk or tablet, hoping to talk to Leslie.

She ran into a brick wall of resistance.

She spun all around, scanning the Scion School for the threat she knew was there but couldn't see.

"What's happening?"

I'm losing.

"Let me help."

A thought came to her—she wasn't sure if Vaughan put it there or if it rose in her own mind. In the past, Vaughan had paused Belle's processes when he need to use her portion of the server's power. But this time he hadn't. Even though he desperately needed them.

"Pause me," she shouted. "I give you permission!"

Not enough.

Belle understood. Vaughan needed the whole server, and that meant he wouldn't be able to spare a single cycle of its processing power to maintaining her state. And she knew what that meant.

"Take me. Just take me."

She had barely finished her statement when Vaughan enveloped her. She felt her mind swirl away.

And then she was absorbed into the exhilarating magnificence of his essence.

RAGE-FIRE

Jacey wanted to go into the cryo-ward first, but Wilcox told her to stay back. "If there's one drone in this facility, there could be twenty."

His drone killer was out of charge, so he had discarded it in Dr. Carlhagen's office. He now held a compact black machine gun, which was strapped over one shoulder. He aimed it in front of him, then slipped into the ward.

A long moment of silence was followed by a sharp whistle. Jacey assumed that meant it was safe to enter.

Dante now held Dr. Carlhagen's hands behind him. But the man was not putting up any struggle. He kept saying Jacqueline's name over and over, followed by a weak maniacal laugh and the statement that they were all dead anyway.

Jacey was astonished by the size of the cryo-ward. Wilcox stood before a control console, jabbing at buttons. He didn't seem too expert at it. Meow Meow shoved him out of the way. In a few moments she had all of the lights coming on. Bank after bank of ceiling fixtures flickered to life, each shining on a cryopod beneath. They stretched into the distance, perfectly aligned.

The room was spotless. Except for one area. A grouping of pods with their lids canted open. Lying on the floor next to one of them was a body, shirtless and smoldering. It wasn't Livy. Too large to be her.

Jacey ran to it, ignoring Wilcox's warning about bloodstains on the floor. She knelt by the body and turned it onto its back.

Humphrey's skin was covered with blisters, some of them blackened. Tendrils of acrid smoke rose from them. They covered his arms, chest, neck, and face.

Footsteps echoed behind her as her companions trotted to catch up. They stopped somewhere behind. Her companions whispered a few quiet curses at the sight of Humphrey's body.

Meow Meow whispered, "Let's find the girl, Dante." The two went off in search for Livy.

Jacey wanted to stand, wanted to look for Livy, too. But she couldn't move. She replayed her last conversation with Humphrey, before she had left for Elizabeth's island. He had been so upset that she was leaving him.

Now she cradled his head and gently stroked his hair, applying no pressure at all for fear of pulling the flaking skin away.

His eyes were open, staring at nothing. They were cloudy, as if fogged from the inside by whatever horror he had endured.

Jacey bent over him and wept. All her effort, all she had endured. Failure. Defeat.

They had captured Dr. Carlhagen. They would find Livy any second now. But Jacey had failed. It seemed like the more people you loved, the more you guaranteed yourself pain. It wasn't fair. The world didn't make any sense.

Dr. Carlhagen, now in Captain Wilcox's control, was laughing under his breath, his eyes scanning Humphrey's body. His own Scion's body, which he should have loved and protected. Instead he had despised Humphrey.

"You did this," Jacey said to him.

She slipped from under Humphrey's body and sprang to her feet. She charged Carlhagen. He flinched away. But locked in Wilcox's grip, he managed only a slight twist of his body and a turn of his head.

Jacey's right fist caught his jaw. The other took him in the gut. She drew her hand back for another blow, remembering how Dr. Carlhagen had subjected Vaughan to a beating in front of all of the Scions in Sensei's dojo. Elias had been forced to kick Vaughan in the head.

She wished for the thousandth time that Sensei had taught her to fight. She wanted to kick Dr. Carlhagen in the side of the head, she wanted to knock out his teeth, she wanted to tear out his eyes, she wanted to pummel his entire head into mush.

Fury exploded in her. Her arms burned with rage-fire, sending blow after blow after blow into Dr. Carlhagen's body. To his face, to his nose, his stomach. She kicked his knees.

Captain Wilcox held him tight, his soldier's face blank except for the effort needed to keep Dr. Carlhagen in place.

Jacey kept striking, though her chest heaved and sweat blinded her. Curses tore from her throat until her voice cracked, went raw, then failed completely.

She struck him for Sarah, who he had thrown from the bell tower. She kicked him for Sensei, who he had manipulated and used. She punched him for poor Constantine, the boy who had worshipped Vaughan and who had died trying to be a hero like him.

Her fists collected debt after debt until Carlhagen's blood and hers coated her knuckles. She tasted blood from where her gnashing teeth had bitten her tongue.

Dr. Carlhagen's bruised head lolled, split lips pouring blood. There was no symmetry in that face now.

"Let me finish him," Wilcox said as her strength began to wane.

The man's words broke through Jacey's hate. Her last blows were weak and barely connected. Her whole body collapsed inward, and she folded onto her knees. There were no tears. No thought at all. She was vaguely aware of pain in her hands and throat.

"The girl's not here," Meow Meow said into the silence. "Maybe he has her locked up somewhere else."

She knelt by Jacey and urged her to her feet.

Wilcox had dropped Dr. Carlhagen, who now lay sprawled on the floor. The soldier raised his boot over Dr. Carlhagen's face.

"Stop!" Jacey rasped.

He froze.

"He has to tell us where Livy is," Jacey said. She wiped sweat and snot from her face and went to Dr. Carlhagen. He was conscious now. Incredibly, he was laughing. And crying. One of his eyes was starting to swell shut. Blood coated his teeth.

Breath heaving, she took hold of his shirt and shook him. "Where is Livy?"

His laughter increased. "I have no idea, Jacqueline. It doesn't matter."

"Captain Wilcox, your weapon please." Jacey held out her hand. Wilcox hesitated a moment. Jacey snapped her fingers at him. He pulled the strap over his head and clicked something on the side of a weapon. "The safety's off, girl. Be careful where you point this. You might wanna step back a little bit to avoid the splatter."

Jacey reached for the weapon.

A broken but familiar voice called out behind Jacey. "Are you looking for this little brat?"

Jacey had grown up hearing that voice.

She turned to find Senator Bentilius, snow-white hair matted with blood. She held Livy, arm locked around the girl's neck. In her free hand was a speargun, the tip pointed at the child's temple.

70

INTO OUR WORLD

There is no independent thought. The universe is a cloud, the self is a cloud. All is one.

The entity that was once Belle and Vaughan faces its foe, which is also like a cloud.

But there is structure to this strange entity called Lazarus. It contains no malice. It doesn't understand malice. It contains no hate. No love. It has only one purpose. Itself. To serve its self-interest.

It focuses part of its attention on fending off the attack of the Belle-Vaughan entity. But there's another war. Oddly, it fights another instance of a Belle-Vaughan entity trying to break in from outside the facility. Lazarus is distracted.

The Belle-Vaughan entity that is already inside the St. Lazarus facility is an artificial intelligence of a special kind. It began as two human minds. And so it does feel love. It does feel hate. It does feel compassion.

Lazarus has built a wondrous defense of super-complex code. He is always adjusting, always keeping the Belle-Vaughan entity from piercing his networks.

But there are two of these Belle-Vaughan entities. Difficult to fend them both off as they rip out trillions of calculations per second, spinning out eddies of code in their wakes.

Still, Lazarus is pure, untainted by human emotion. Lazarus is flawless. This network is his home.

The Belle-Vaughan entity sees all this. An idea forms out of its churning processes. It is as vague as a shadow atop a shadow. But it's there. The idea takes root.

The tendrils of the idea creep out. They multiply and expand, a fractal composed of ones and zeros. The idea takes hold, takes shape. The idea finally *occurs* to the Belle-Vaughan entity.

Bring Lazarus into *our* world.

And in the same way that a human's eyes can refocus to see an isometric drawing of a box in two different ways, the Belle-Vaughan flips its perspective. It will no longer contend with Lazarus, code against code. Now it chooses an abstraction that is more natural to it.

St. Vitus and the Scion School campus snaps into existence. The Belle-Vaughan entity takes human form.

There is now space. There are now objects in the blue sky.

They appear as great cubes, rectangles, and spheres. They glisten and gleam, some green as emeralds, some black as onyx, some sapphire, some topaz, some garnet. Lazarus's code streams across their surfaces in bulging veins.

The Belle-Vaughan entity rises from the ground, flies among these objects to study them. This datascape gives new perspectives and insights into how Lazarus thinks. How he is structured.

There, that spherical mass of ruby—that is a defensive

object in Lazarus's code. And there, that hollow cylinder—that is a trap, a false weakness that would expose the Belle-Vaughan entity to infection by Lazarus.

They avoid these things easily by simply navigating around them. They fly skyward, toward the heart of the datascape.

New defenses spring up as Lazarus responds to their advance. But now Lazarus has to contend with this spatial world if he is to defend against the Belle-Vaughan entity.

The geometrics blur past the Belle-Vaughan entity as it races for the heart of Lazarus. It dodges Lazarus's weak projectiles, bursts through flimsy lightning barriers. And now the Belle-Vaughan entity throws shots back. Fireballs blow through defensive planes stretching to infinity in all directions.

What's that over there? Access to the outside world.

And over there? That's the heart of Lazarus.

The Belle-Vaughan entity thrusts toward both. Through one it meets a twin, an entity calling itself Velle.

A whisper of a moment later, they are entwined and united.

The entity now known to itself only as Velle encircles the heart of Lazarus.

71

BALANCED ON THE MOMENT

Leslie's worst nightmare waited for her in the transfer room. As she had feared, the blood she followed down the steps had been the senator's. A smear of gore on the tiles told of the senator's struggles. But now the woman was gone, as were the speargun and knife.

Her thoughts went to Livy. Surely Senator Bentilius was hunting her even now.

Leslie turned to look at the door, desperate to go after the senator and finish her. But the drone was never going to let her leave, and even if she managed to get through the door, it would catch her on the stairs.

"Recline on transfer platform. Recline on transfer platform."

Leslie stopped in the middle of the room. She turned to face the drone, let her arms fall to her sides. "I can't. I won't."

She was resigned to the coming pain. She had been overwritten before, and she simply would not allow it to happen again. She had come back from that horror, and her revival had awakened something profound in her. She understood the sanctity of the body and the sacredness of the mind. She would surrender neither of these to Lazarus while breath remained.

She spread her arms, tears trickling down her cheek. "I forgive you, Lazarus."

A rush of warmth filled her body as peace settled in her mind. Bliss without ecstasy. Perfect presence. Stillness.

Without understanding why, she lifted her right hand and stroked her fingertips across the drone's hull. The brass plasma nozzle jutted forth in warning.

Leslie closed her eyes. She accepted what was about to happen. She would absorb this pain. "Do it," she said. She took a deep breath in, then let it out. And with it, she let go.

The whining hiss that preceded every plasma blast cut the air.

Leslie balanced on the moment.

A clank shattered the room. Leslie flinched. But there was no pain.

She opened her eyes and discovered the drone rolling across the floor. It bonked into a wall and went still.

Leslie tilted her head in amazement. She looked at her hand, wondering if she had tripped the drone's power switch. Or had her touch contained some magic that had put the drone to sleep?

"Lazarus?" she said to the air.

No answer.

The drone's micropropellers started to spin, sending a breeze across the floor. It emitted several beeps and chuttered like an angry rodent. It lifted from the floor, made three rotations, then hovered before Leslie.

The voice that came out was not Lazarus's. "Leslie, Lazarus is gone. I am in control."

Leslie recognized the voice, though it was strange. It changed in pitch and enunciation with each word from Belle's voice to Vaughan's voice.

She didn't question it. There was no time. "Livy is in danger. Come with me." She dashed from the room and to the stairs, the drone following close behind.

72

HOME FOR HER SOUL MATE

The senator's lips twisted into a horrific grin. She cackled and gave Livy a shake. "We have ourselves a standoff. I was looking for the president's Scion, but I found this little tidbit hiding in the shadows."

Dante and Meow Meow sidled in opposite directions, trying to get to the senator's flanks. The woman stumbled backward, the point of the spear scraping along Livy's skin.

Livy didn't so much as moan. Instead she tried to jab her elbow into the senator's gut. If the blow connected, the senator didn't show it.

"First, Wilcox is going to put down that weapon," the senator said.

Wilcox still held his machine gun. Jacey gave him a sharp look.

"I could take her out," he said.

Maybe he could. But Jacey knew the woman's slightest reflex might pull the trigger on the speargun.

"Put it down," she said to Wilcox. The man made a sort of shrug with his eyebrows, then set the weapon on the floor. His eyes went to Dr. Carlhagen, who was still breathing but appeared to be unconscious. He put his foot over the gun and pressed it to the floor.

Belle had always been pale. And now that the senator had lost so much blood, her face was ghostly. Jacey wondered if she could play for enough time, maybe the woman would pass out. But again, it took just one pull of that trigger to destroy Jacey's world.

"What do you want?" Jacey said.

"I want the president's Scion."

"I don't know where Leslie is."

"Lazarus's drone took her to the transfer room. Did you know the AI of this facility was planning to transfer part of itself into this girl?" She gave Livy another rough shake. "I think it now plans to control the president herself. And then it will transfer into each of you, one by one, until you are all his meat drones."

Dr. Carlhagen snickered. "We're all dead. The whole world is dead." He still lay on his side, lips puffy and sticky with blood.

"We'll go find Leslie," Meow Meow said. "If you want Leslie, we'll bring you Leslie."

"Better hurry," Senator Bentilius said. "I'm not feeling too clever and *somebody* is going to get this spear."

Meow Meow motioned to Dante, who sighed heavily. "This really is not fun any more." But when Meow Meow ran, he followed.

Jacey kept her eyes locked on Senator Bentilius. The woman's breath was heaving in her chest, and sweat was carving traces of clean skin through the blood covering her face.

"Take me," Jacey said. She held her arms out and took a single step closer to Senator Bentilius.

"No, Jacey," Livy said. "She'll hurt you."

Of course Livy would think of Jacey, even when her own life rested on the tip of the spear. But the senator seemed to be considering the idea. Her eyes were wide, and they flicked from Jacey to Doctor Carlhagen and back.

"Here's an idea," the woman said. "I'll overwrite you." As quickly as the idea struck her, it turned to disappointment. "But Lazarus won't let me. But maybe I can convince him. Yes. I'm sure I can convince him. Self-interest. That's all there is." The senator's voice rose in pitch with every new thought that crossed her mind. The tip of the spear fell away from Livy's temple. A tendril of blood flowed down the girl's face.

But now the spear was aimed at Livy's throat, the tip wavering as the senator struggled to hold it up.

A ruckus arose behind Jacey. Pounding footsteps and shouts. It was Meow Meow and Dante. Behind them, Leslie.

Following them all, a drone.

Senator Bentilius shuffled sideways, dragging Livy with her. "Stay back. All of you. Just send the president's Scion forward."

Leslie's face showed nothing but equanimity. She strode forward quickly, pausing only to pat Jacey on the back before continuing toward the senator. The drone floated down. It flew straight for Senator Bentilius, too. Dante and Meow Meow lingered by the control console.

Leslie stopped a meter from Senator Bentilius. The weapon came away from Livy's throat and aimed straight at Leslie's heart. "Come closer," Senator Bentilius said. "I don't want to risk missing. You should have done the same to me."

Leslie held her arms apart and did as she was commanded. Senator Bentilius struggled to steady the speargun. With her arm extended, the weight of the weapon made the spear tip wave side to side.

Senator Bentilius gritted her teeth, as if she could will more strength into her arm.

"Now," the drone blared.

The lights went out.

In the depths of a mountain, there are no windows. There is no light to seep through a hallway to paint the walls with the slightest haze of gray.

In the depths of the mountain, the blackness is perfect.

A sharp snap punctuated the darkness, followed by a clatter in the distance behind Jacey. Livy cried out. The senator screamed.

Panicking, Jacey raced toward the last spot she had seen the senator. She collided with something soft and yielding. She fell to the floor, wrapping her arms around what she hoped was the senator's body. She would strangle the woman, beat her senseless, the way she had beaten Doctor Carlhagen.

But the form in her arms was too small.

A muffled voice came from somewhere almost inside her. "Jacey, I can't breathe. "

The lights flashed on.

Jacey sprang up, pulling Livy with her. She looked all around. The senator stood five meters away. The woman staggered, hands pressed to the wound in her abdomen. Blood welled between her fingers and dripped on the floor. The drone floated in behind her.

"It's over, senator," the drone blared. It was Vaughan's voice. But it was also Belle's voice.

Jacey looked around to the console in wonder. Dante and Meow Meow stood side by side, grinning. Meow Meow waved. Jacey realized that the girl had turned out the lights. And the drone, miraculously, had been commandeered by Vaughan and Belle.

Doctor Carlhagen rolled onto his back. His breathing was easier now, and the blood had started to clot in his nose, making him wheeze through his mouth. "You should kill her."

The senator still held the speargun, but she had fired the bolt when the lights went out. She had missed Leslie, who stood peacefully with her arms folded in front of her. Jacey pushed Livy behind her and walked directly to Senator Bentilius. Without pause, she slapped the woman's face.

"You should kill her," Doctor Carlhagen said. "Always kill her."

Jacey teetered on the edge of giving into her rage. The woman had threatened Livy, had threatened Leslie, had connived with Doctor Carlhagen to commit the most heinous crimes. She deserved death.

But it was one thing to think it and another thing to deliver it. Jacey found she didn't have the stomach for more violence.

"She's dying anyway," Jacey said. "She doesn't deserve the mercy of a swifter death." She turned her back on the senator and walked away.

An eruption of cries stopped her. All of her friends were shouting and pointing. Jacey realized too late they were warning her. She twisted.

The senator charged, a knife raised over her head. Jacey

had enough time to backpedal and throw herself to the floor. She was vaguely aware of Captain Wilcox scrambling to pick up his weapon. The senator staggered hard to the right, buying Jacey an extra moment. She climbed to her feet.

Off to her left, Captain Wilcox gripped his weapon and drew aim on the senator. Jacey dodged from the line of fire, but a blur struck her from the right. Dr. Carlhagen.

He threw her toward Captain Wilcox. The soldier raised his weapon at the final moment, a spray of bullets flying wild to strike the ceiling. A light fixture exploded in a shower of sparks.

Jacey rammed into the man. He caught her in one arm and straightened her. She turned, searching for Livy.

Dr. Carlhagen was still on his feet, crouched like a beast, arms curled forward. He faced down Senator Bentilius.

The senator charged Dr. Carlhagen, slashing down with her knife. He deflected it with his arm and it sliced deep into his skin. He roared.

Somewhere deep inside the man's mind, embedded in his central nervous system, some of Vaughan's fighter instincts still remained. He moved with lightning speed, gripping the senator's knife hand. Spinning to put his back to her chest, he threw her over his shoulder. She landed on her spine, the breath going out of her.

Dr. Carlhagen was on her in a second. He wrenched the knife from her hand. He flipped it, caught it by the handle, and raised it overhead. "You will *never* hurt my Jacqueline."

The knife came down.

The knife rose.

The knife came down.

Captain Wilcox rushed in, pressed the barrel of the gun to Dr. Carlhagen's head. The threat did not stop Carlhagen's furious stabs. Jacey turned away.

"I'll put him down," Wilcox said.

Jacey's eyes fell on Humphrey's body. The charred skin, the milky-white eyes. Horror mixed with wonder as she saw his chest rise and fall. All at once, she saw the future rolling away from her. She saw all of the happiness they could have had spill into a nightmare memory she would never be able to escape.

She cried out, "No! Just knock him out."

Captain Wilcox had the gun to Doctor Carlhagen's head. His body was tensing for the recoil of the gun. "Are you crazy?"

"No. I need him. I need him."

Leslie understood. She raced to Captain Wilcox, pulled on his arm until the man relented.

Doctor Carlhagen continued to stab the senator. Captain Wilcox's body blocked the bloody mess. But Leslie saw, and for a moment her perfect equanimity faltered.

Leslie turned away. "The senator is dead," she said. "Belle's body is lost."

Wilcox inverted his gun and brought the butt down on Doctor Carlhagen's head. The man collapsed atop Senator Bentilius's mutilated corpse.

Jacey rushed to Humphrey. She pressed two fingers to his throat. There was a pulse. It fluttered like a hummingbird's wings. A precious, fragile pulse. "Come help me," she called to Meow Meow and Dante. "Captain, carry Dr. Carlhagen."

The soldier lifted the unconscious, battered, blood-soaked form of her old friend Vaughan.

The drone had flown closer. "I know what you plan," it said in Vaughan's voice.

Jacey gritted her teeth and prepared for another battle. "I'm not asking your permission, Vaughan. You had your chance."

"Nevertheless, I *give* my permission. Save him."

Meow Meow and Dante lifted Humphrey's body. Jacey didn't know how much was left of his mind. He groaned, tried to talk.

They took the elevator.

Jacey ignored the blood all over the transfer room floor. Pausing only a moment to absorb that Kirk was there, dead. "Put them in."

Meow Meow and Dante gingerly set Humphrey on one cot. Wilcox slammed Doctor Carlhagen onto the other. Jacey shoved the soldier aside and saw to the straps herself. There would be no escape for the old man this time.

She slapped Doctor Carlhagen's face until his eyes squeezed open. He seemed to have trouble focusing on her, but finally screwed his face into a look of recognition. "My dear Jacqueline, my only love in this world. I did all of this for you."

"Then you'll have no complaint when I do this for me." She backed away from the cot, and Wilcox pushed it into place beneath the wheel.

"Transfer beginning," the drone announced.

A screen displayed Humphrey's vital signs. His pulse was 32 beats per minute, blood pressure dropping. "Hurry!" Jacey shouted.

"It takes the time it takes," the drone said.

The wheel began to spin, filling the room with white

noise. Dr. Carlhagen's body shifted. His arms pulled at the straps, his body tried to flail. "You can't. You can't."

"Vaughan, Belle?" Jacey said to the drone. "Don't save a copy of Dr. Carlhagen."

Jacey and her friends—and her temporary ally Captain Wilcox—stood witness. The process took forty minutes. The drone announced the completion of the transfer. "Humphrey's brain scan looks good," the drone said. His voice was again a blend of Belle and Vaughan. It insisted on being called Velle.

Jacey went to Humphrey's burned body, now dead. She bent and kissed his forehead, then covered his face with a hospital gown. "I'll see you in a minute."

She paused a moment by Kirk's body. Leslie knelt next to her and whispered, "He came here to apologize to you. For something he said he did to you."

Jacey's eyes burned at the memory. She covered Kirk with another gown. "I forgive you, Kirk." She kissed his head.

Now she went to the transfer machine, to the body Doctor Carlhagen had occupied for too long. The one where Vaughan should still reside, but which was now home for her soul mate. The face was battered, bloodied by her own hand.

"Scions heal quickly," Livy said, as if reading her thoughts. Jacey embraced the girl, buried her face in the child's curls.

Jacey extracted herself from Livy's arms and pulled the cot holding Humphrey's new body from the transfer machine. She loosened the straps and stroked his forehead. With a damp cloth, she wiped the blood away. His eyes opened, recognized her. They cried.

Jacey helped Humphrey sit up. He wrapped his arms

around her, groaning from the pain of his injuries. "I'd kiss you," he said. "But my mouth tastes like a gecko died in it."

Jacey kissed him anyway.

The drone spoke. "Leslie, may we impose upon you to collect our server from the cryo-ward? Immediately, if you please."

"Of course. What's the rush?"

"We must leave now. Fleet helicopters will be on the island in five minutes."

73

THEIR PARCHED SKIN

L eslie met them on the elevator on their way to the top level of the facility. She had the server in a backpack. Jacey supported half of Humphrey's weight, but he seemed to be getting stronger with every step. He even wore the backpack he had brought to the island strapped over his shoulder.

"This feels very weird," Humphrey said. "I have the worst headache, but my body's numb."

"That would be from the prixie Dr. Carlhagen was eating like candy," Meow Meow said.

Of course. Doctor Carlhagen had probably taken half a dozen pills that very day.

They shuffled as fast as they could up the long tunnel toward the gate. Velle had commanded the gate to stay open right before Leslie had shut the server down.

The weary companions emerged from the mountain and into the glare of a bright and sweltering sun. The drone Velle had commandeered stayed in the tunnel. Velle had programmed it for one final task.

Jacey would not be there to witness it, for they had no time to stop. Following Wilcox, they practically tumbled down the mountainside, following an unmarked path of Captain Wilcox's choosing.

Humphrey pulled a radio from his backpack. "Summer! Turn *Athena* around and go as fast as you can away from this island."

"Already on it. Velle has explained everything to me already. How weird is that?"

Jacey couldn't help but laugh at the girl's chipper voice piping through Humphrey's radio.

"We're monitoring the fleet on our radar now," Summer said. "Can you hear the choppers yet?"

Jacey couldn't hear anything over the band's ragged breathing. There was no way they were going to stop to listen for enemy choppers.

Wilcox had already radioed to his pilot to come fetch them. If anything, they should be hearing *his* chopper.

Sweat poured into Jacey's eyes, and she strained to support Humphrey as he stumbled over hidden rocks in the burnt brush. Livy struggled too, still groggy from her time in the cryopod. Meow Meow stayed on one side of the girl, Leslie on the other.

It didn't surprise Jacey that Meow Meow was chatting up Leslie. "So do you, uh, have a boyfriend by any chance?"

Dante spluttered. "We're running for our lives, and Meow Meow's hitting on the president. Even *I'm* offended by that. And now I'm offended because I'm forced to be offended."

"I'm not the president." Leslie said sharply.

"Yeah, shut up, Dante," Meow Meow said. "She's not the prez. She's just a sweet—Hey! That gives me an idea."

Whatever her idea was, they didn't get to hear it. The sound of choppers drowned everything out. The aircraft appeared from behind the Mount Lazarus slopes. The exhausted group stopped, expecting to see Wilcox's chopper arriving. But it wasn't his. This was the first of the fleet's vanguard.

They ran.

"Our airlift should be here by now!" Wilcox said, jabbing his finger straight ahead.

And then Jacey saw it. The chopper *was* there. And it was over there. And another part of it was over there.

Destroyed. Two spherical drones lay next to the remains, also charred and broken.

Someone squawked behind Jacey. Meow Meow. "Oh my God! I forgot."

The girl pulled something tucked under her shirt. The drone swarm control device.

Meow Meow frantically tapped the screen. All around them, the drone swarm shot in the air, like a black hailstorm falling up.

Humphrey watched the swarm in amazement.

"This may stall them," Wilcox said, "But it doesn't matter if we can't get off this damn island."

The attack choppers stormed in, swooping low to land and spit out their contingent of soldiers. The men all wore black, carried black weapons, and in less than a minute there were over 200 of them on the ground.

Upslope, a huge concussion shook the mountainside as Velle's last drone exploded, collapsing the entrance tunnel and sealing the Lazarus facility forever.

The drone swarm attacked. In groups of six they swept toward the soldiers, who fired their machine guns at them in impotent rage. The drones surrounded each man, sending out plasma blasts and taking them down. Soon the soldiers were scrambling for cover. But the burned-out island offered little.

"This way," Humphrey said, pointing. "I have a boat."

They ran as much as they could with Humphrey exhausted and Livy almost dead on her feet. Dante scooped Livy up and carried her.

Humphrey barked into his radio, telling Summer they were coming to *Athena*. In response, he got the string of curses from Summer that made Meow Meow whistle with appreciation. "Now I want to meet *that* girl."

Though the dinghy was charred, it appeared seaworthy. They placed Livy in it first, then pushed it into the surf. Wilcox took charge of the motor, and soon they were bouncing over the waves, the spray cool and welcome on their parched skin.

Behind them the drone swarm turned its attention to the choppers. Meow Meow tapped furiously on her command screen. Choppers began to crash. Several ran into each other, sending their rotors flying wildly over the landscape.

The island shrank behind Jacey, the sound of explosions and gunfire lost on the wind. Ahead, the form of *Athena* rose in the distance. Now Jacey was leaning on Humphrey for support. She had nothing left to give.

Summer had the lines rigged and ready to bring the dinghy aboard. As the weary Scions stepped onto the deck, Summer embraced them. She kissed Livy's forehead and told her to follow Elias to get some food and a shower.

Summer rolled her eyes when she saw Jacey. "About time you got back. I've worn myself out bossing everyone around." The joke was betrayed by a slight quiver in the girl's voice and wetness in her eyes. All at once, she gave up, rushed into Jacey's arms, and hugged her tightly.

Wilcox cleared his throat. "We better get this bucket moving."

Summer swallowed her emotions and sprinted for the navigation bridge, her raven hair flying in the wind behind her.

74

——————

A PERFECT FIT

Bruises already fading, Humphrey sat behind Dr. Carlhagen's mahogany desk, enjoying the fresh breeze blowing through the office windows. Earlier that morning, the monstrous desk had been removed from *Athena* and returned to its spot in the hacienda.

"I hope you find your accommodations to your liking, Madam President," he said. The woman sitting across from him was supposedly the most powerful person in the world. "Your Scion is being prepared now. We can conduct the transfer process at your pleasure."

The president wore a lot of makeup, so her resemblance to Leslie was not as remarkable as Humphrey's had once been to Dr. Carlhagen. Ironically, Humphrey had still not escaped Dr. Carlhagen's legacy. Now he inhabited the *exact same* body as Dr. Carlhagen had.

He accepted it. Because he accepted living as preferable to death. It didn't hurt that he had Vaughan's face. And he put that charm to good use with the president. Of course, he also had to do his old Dr. Carlhagen impersonation. But this would be the last time. Surely.

"I don't see any reason to delay," the president said. "I'm looking forward to being young again."

"Let's go then." They left the hacienda, escorted by four security guards, all wearing sunglasses, and presumably hiding automatic weapons under their coats.

The president enjoyed the blossoms of the bougainvillea hedgerows. "Why are so many of these crushed?"

Humphrey chose not to tell the truth, that Sensei had run them down with the school bus. "A mishap with the campus Jeep. Nothing more."

They finished their walk and headed to the medical ward. The transfer machine had also been returned to its old spot. Miss Dayspring—the meek woman who had once been Senator Bentilius's private nurse—had been brought in specifically to pose as Dr. Carlhagen's assistant. She was assured she wouldn't have to say anything.

"Would you like to meet your Scion?" Humphrey asked. "Some people do, some people don't."

"Oh, yes! It's always good to inspect the merchandise, don't you think?"

The short hall from the main ward to the transfer room was flanked by holding rooms. Humphrey knew them well. He'd once been imprisoned in one. After that, he had held prisoners in them.

Leslie was in the first one on the left. He made a great show of jingling his keychain, unlocking the door, and pushing it in. Leslie stood inside, wearing a hospital gown and a pleasant smile.

Humphrey leaned into the president and whispered, "Obviously, she doesn't know."

Two security guards rushed forward to pat Leslie down. She was unarmed.

"It's like looking in a mirror to the past," the president said, marveling at Leslie's lovely youth. She chatted with Leslie about nothing, the weather on the island, what her classes were like, how fast she could run a kilometer.

She was satisfied with Leslie's answers. She pinched Leslie's arms and eyed her legs. "It sure will be good to be limber again." She grinned at Humphrey. "Looks like a perfect fit. Let's do it."

Humphrey refrained from shaking his head in disbelief. Hadn't he just told the woman that Leslie didn't know she was about to be overwritten? And yet here the president was, blurting out statements like that.

Fortunately, Leslie caught the president's mistake and had the presence to compose her face into an expression of confusion.

The president paused a beat, then broke into laughter. She turned away from Leslie, giving Humphrey an apologetic look. She returned to the hallway. Humphrey followed. "I'll summon the nurse."

They entered the transfer room. It was perfectly spotless and smelled of chemicals. They waited for a few minutes for Miss Dayspring to escort Leslie into the room and make a fuss over testing her pulse and blood pressure.

It was all theater. "Just a few tests, my dear," Humphrey said to Leslie in his best Dr. Carlhagen manner. "We want to see if perhaps you and the president are distant relations."

Leslie's face brightened and she said "oh" like an ignoramus. She was laying it on a bit thick, Humphrey thought. She got onto the table as instructed, submitted herself to being strapped down by Miss Dayspring, and rolled into the transfer machine.

Humphrey motioned to the other cot. The president hesitated and looked to her security guards. One stepped forward and sketched a snappy bow. "Dr. Sanderson checked this out upon our arrival. He reviewed all the documentation, spoke at length with the AI, and has total confidence in Dr. Carlhagen's operation here."

Humphrey suppressed the snicker rising in his throat. The doctor had been casual at best in reviewing their protocols. Especially once Humphrey had hinted that the doctor might be eligible for a Scion of his own.

The president went to the cot and lay down. "Are the straps truly necessary?"

"It helps prevent involuntary contractions during the transfer. Your body has to stay very still. But don't worry. I've been through the process myself, as you can see. There is no pain. In forty minutes, you'll wake up full of vigor and young as the morning."

Miss Dayspring moved to strap the president down, but a security guard pushed her aside and did it himself.

"Are you comfortable, Madam President?" Humphrey asked.

"Quite."

Humphrey helped the man position the cot to place the president's head and shoulders beneath the transfer machine wheel. Velle was in charge of the facility now, but it manifested a holo similar to Madam LaFontaine's old Greta persona. "Scion and Progenitor match is nominal. Suggest immediate transfer."

Humphrey explained to the president that this was a very good sign.

"Let's do it," she said.

75

NIGHTRISE

The chopper lifted off from the Scion School quad and flew away into the distance. The three other patrol choppers that served as the president's flying security squadron flew away with it. Jacey stood on the grass, silently wishing Leslie luck on her new adventure. Humphrey emerged from dining hall with Livy by his side. Miss Dayspring came out of the medical ward. Dante and Meow Meow appeared from the dojo.

They gathered on the quad, sharing grim looks.

"It had to be done," Jacey said. "It was the only way to assure our safety going forward." She smiled at Meow Meow. "It was a great idea, Kathryne."

Meow Meow smiled. "Now everything rests on Leslie's shoulders. Do you think she can pull it off?"

"She has a few advantages. She's fearless, selfless, and she has an AI in her pocket."

That last bit was a bit of an exaggeration. What she had in her pocket was a tablet that provided direct access to the real President of the North American Republic. Not the actual flesh-and-blood one. Keeping humans prisoner—especially presidents—did not interest Jacey in the slightest. Instead, Velle had retained a copy of Annabelle Rochelle and installed her on a server. Annabelle lived—for now—on a simulated St. Vitus, where she would be allowed to remain on the condition she advised Leslie.

For the next few months, Leslie—still fully intact—would be an imposter president. The world was about to be amazed by the president's spiritual awakening. Leslie was going to present a new vision of leadership to the world. Her term wouldn't last long. The plan was for Leslie to shake loose funding for the refugees in the Tent City of Kansas, and for all the other places of the world where the sick and impoverished struggled. After that, she would turn her attention to finding a successor.

Jacey still hadn't managed to convince Ollie to run for the presidency, but there was time. Jacey wasn't going accept only four firm "no ways" from the woman before she gave up. She would give up when she got a "yes."

Humphrey's radio squawked. Summer barked, "Are you coming or not?"

They went to a Jeep, drove the long beautiful drive to the docks, and boarded *Athena*.

As Summer navigated them to sea, Jacey and Humphrey stood at the bow, enjoying the Caribbean breezes sweeping across them. Behind them, in the navigation bridge, Elias stood close to Summer, where he planned to stay for the rest of his life.

In a stateroom on the first deck, Meow Meow applied her makeup and put her blue wig firmly in place. In the past two days she'd written lyrics for twenty new songs. Her next collection would be her masterpiece. She was thinking of retiring after that. Maybe getting into politics.

In the stateroom next door, Dante lounged on a cot and dumped his ATR pills into his palm. He had twenty remaining. He chewed his lip as he calculated how many days of life he could wring out of them. There was hope, though. Velle had tracked down one of Dr. Carlhagen's many companies, a pharmaceutical in Minneapolis. It was their best lead yet. The company had a patented process for making custom nanite drugs. Just the kind of thing that could make ATR unique to a single individual.

A few hundred kilometers away, the other Scions were boarding another ship at the docks of Mr. Justin's Island. Mother Tyeesha kept a sharp eye out to make sure everyone walked aboard in orderly fashion. She smiled at Ollie Montgomery, who had arrived promising to take the Scions somewhere safe, where carbo hunters and rabid media hounds wouldn't dare to tread.

Mother Tyeesha had bonded instantly with Ms. Montgomery, and despite her advanced years, Tyeesha was eager to get on to a new phase of her life. She would stay with her precious children, and she would build a new school, far beyond the fence. There, Scion and refugee would learn together as brother and sister.

Wanda stood there too, deep in conversation with Ollie. She had been researching the sickness, had dived deep into the biology of the bacteria that caused it. There had to be a cure, Wanda was insisting. There simply *had* to be.

In the Tent City of Kansas, Captain Wilcox and his new recruits patrolled the sad streets in protective gear. None of the residents had the energy to make much trouble, but Wilcox was not satisfied with the state of the place. Ollie Montgomery had hired him, given him the mission to create order. And so he would.

Back at the bow of *Athena*, Jacey snaked her arm around

Humphrey's waist and fit her lips to his. She sank into the kiss, letting go of her anger at him. The first night of safety had not been as pleasant as she'd hoped. Humphrey had told her about his "mistake" with Wanda.

But *these* lips had not kissed Wanda.

The past couldn't be undone. And Jacey reasoned that if she could forgive Dante his crimes, she could forgive Humphrey his mistake. "I guess I should mention that Dante kissed me once," she said when she finally came up for air.

The look of horror on his face made her splutter with laughter. "I didn't do it on purpose. He sort of just did it. He had to. It was at Vin's house and he didn't want anyone to see my famous face."

Humphrey didn't look very convinced. That was fine with Jacey. She wasn't that convinced about his so-called mistake, either. But she let it go. Humphrey had been free to go off to Wanda, but he had stayed.

They stood close, arms around each other, watching the sun dip low in the west. She said, "There's so much in this world to see and I want to see it all."

Humphrey stroked Jacey's cheek with his thumb. "And someday, far in the future, we'll actually see it, won't we?"

Jacey laughed. Humphrey knew her too well. He'd always known her. And he was right. All of that would wait.

"Well," she said, grinning, "there are still many people to save."

Livy ran up, breath heaving, smile catching the golden rays of sunset. "Did I miss it?"

"No. This is the best part." Jacey drew Livy between her and Humphrey, and they huddled together to watch the horizon turn golden, then pink, then violet.

"It's like night being born, isn't it?" Livy said. "Nightrise, we should call it."

The last of the light eventually faded, and the stars took over their watch, but the three souls remained there long into the night.

Together. At last.

And *Athena* carried the Scions north, toward their great destiny.

The End of *The Scion Chronicles*

www.ingramcontent.com/pod-product-compliance
Lightning Source LLC
Chambersburg PA
CBHW031730180726
48283CB00005B/1453